# ETHER

## WILL HOFFMAN

GUERNSEY
FAIR
PRESS

Published in the United States by Guernsey Fair Press

Cover / interior artwork by Mandy Hoffman

First Edition June 2025

ISBN: 979-8-9987968-2-1 (hardcover)
ISBN: 979-8-9987968-1-4 (paperback)
ISBN: 979-8-9987968-0-7 (eBook)

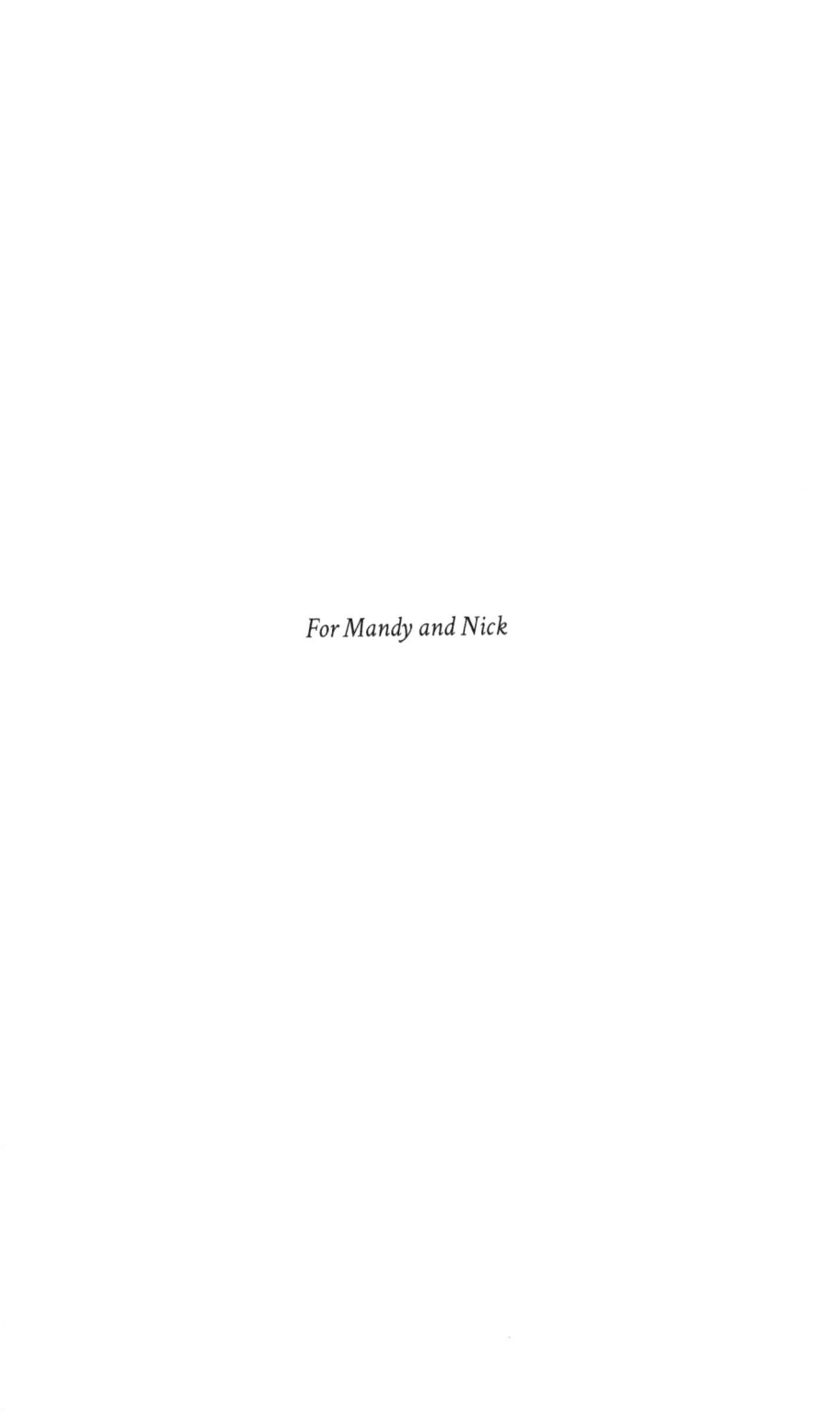

*For Mandy and Nick*

# NOTE TO READERS

This book contains mature themes and subject material that may be disturbing, including suicide and suicidal ideation, self-harm, body-shaming, miscarriage, car accidents, kidnapping, death of a child, and murder. Reader discretion is advised.

# ETHER

# THE STRANGER

REN COLE HAD no business being at the party.

Finding the crumpled-up invitation next to the overflowing kitchen trash definitely wasn't the same as being invited. She knew that. But there was something about the sketchy xeroxed flyer she couldn't let go of. *We are your people*, it said. And though she couldn't imagine having people, it made her feel like maybe hers were out there... somewhere.

So far, she'd been too afraid to find out.

She'd spent half an hour glued to a little patch of wall at one end of the warehouse, watching the strobe illuminate the strange faces that came and went, paying her no mind. That was okay. It was enough sometimes to just be. But the music was so loud she couldn't really hear it anymore, and her head was starting to hurt. And though she'd long ago forgotten what it meant to have fun, she was pretty sure this wasn't it.

As her fingers traced the rough edges of the bricks, trying to determine if the thundering beat was actually shaking the mortar loose, a kid she recognized from Elmwood caught her eye. Ren gave a nod, and he wandered over and pressed a tiny tablet into her palm. She was ninety percent sure she knew what it was, because she was eighty percent sure he was harmless. She had helped him out of a jam once; this was him returning the favor. A free dose of sensuality and connection with a sip from a red plastic cup to wash it down. He shot her a *have a nice trip* wink and disappeared onto the dance floor.

Twenty minutes later, with chemically enhanced confidence, she followed.

Her tattered thrift-store t-shirt floated up her midsection as her arms swayed above her head in a loose approximation of the rhythm. One trance track morphed into the next. She lost time. Lost her inhibition. Allowed herself to get lost in the music. And for a moment, she even dared to believe she was at home in the sea of ravers.

They were all just waves. And she was one of them.

Until she wasn't.

She didn't realize she'd overflowed into anyone's personal space until a pair of hands grabbed her shoulders and shook her like a rag doll.

*Back the hell off, you fat bitch.*

Ren didn't hear the words so much as she felt them, and she opened her eyes to find a man with greasy skin and a kitchen-table haircut glaring at her.

"I'm... sorry," she said, dazed and too quietly to be heard over the din.

His grip tightened, pinning her arms to her sides. Her heart thundered. Cold sweat rose on her neck as she struggled to comprehend—through the fog of Ecstasy—the severity of her sin and how much punishment the man intended to exact for it.

"Please let me go."

His lips curled into something between a smile and a snarl, but it was the look in his eyes that pushed her over the edge. Disgusted and vindictive, it burrowed into her heart with the unmistakable message that she was a bigger piece of shit for existing than he was for beating her up. And though Ren agreed she was a piece of shit, a different thought presented itself to her with stunning clarity:

*You don't get to do that.*

She lurched backward, wrested one arm free and swung a hard elbow up into his nose. He yelped, let her go, and cupped his face in his hands, which drew the attention of his friend. This one was tall. Muscular. Boy-band cute, with perfect hair and dead eyes. His expression never changed as he shoved her into the crowd.

In the span of a heartbeat, harmony became hostility. If there was any sort of vibe among the dancers, she was instantly out of phase with it. She bounced like a pinball, unable to regain her balance or her footing. But that wasn't the worst part. The worst part was that every face she searched—for some trace of kindness or sympathy or the simple acknowledgment that she was a fellow human being—gave her absolutely nothing in return.

Nothing.

An eternity later, the sea finally beached her aching body into a brick wall at the base of a metal staircase, then closed ranks into a roiling mass that was somehow impenetrable and hungry at the same time. She fought for every breath and concentrated on one simple task: get as far away as possible, in case the hive mind decided to un-shun her and suck her back inside.

The only way out was up.

The higher she climbed, the harder it was to breathe. The heat of the crowd was cloying, like being smothered with the microwave beanbag her mom used to warm her bed with in the winter. Ren reached the landing, prayed to any god she could think of that the door led to salvation, and threw herself against the steel crossbar handle. Harder than necessary, apparently, because the next thing she knew, she was flat on her stomach, her face mashed into a pile of weird crunchy roof gravel.

She picked herself up, dusted herself off, and walked until the knee-high parapet wall rose at the edge of the roof and she could walk no further.

If she took one more step, she'd have to fly.

As the howling late-October wind doused the adrenaline heat of her assault, the Philadelphia skyline shimmered on the horizon, and it was sublime.

*Sublime.*

That was a good word. A crossword word. Her mom would dig that word.

To calm her pounding heart, she focused on one ephemeral twinkle and tried to imagine what it was. A streetlight banishing shadows from an alley? The glare of a TV in a sleepless apartment? An emergency fixture flickering in an empty stairwell?

Ren knew she could go on speculating until she froze to death, but she'd played this game many times before and had always arrived at the same conclusion. The source of the light was irrelevant.

The real question was, what had happened to hers?

The eighteen-year-old could retrace every step she'd taken since abandoning home two years ago. Every idiot decision, painful memory, regret, broken promise and crime could be re-lived, examined, cataloged, and sequenced, but no matter which way she looked at it, there was always one piece missing: she never could figure out what set her on this path in the first place.

Why had *her* light died?

She knew it had happened, but not how or when. It had been a shadow at the edge of her consciousness for as long as she could remember. The echo of a nightmare. A floater in her eye that moved further away whenever she tried to focus on it, and eluded her still as the thumping bass vibrated through the soles of her combat boots into her goosebumpy legs.

Ren leaned over the wall.

A field of grass three stories below glowed neon green like absinthe. She distantly realized that was probably because the E still coursed through her bloodstream, rendering everything with a watery luminescence around the edges. But it looked warm. And soft. Teeming with mystery and possibility.

She leaned farther. Her necklace spilled from her collar, dangling free as she hovered over the precipice. It was no prize; only a cheap steel ball chain like a vending-machine rabbit's-foot. It held her blade and, more importantly, her mom's key. Not that she planned to use it again.

The wind swirled, vacuuming trash off the roof into tiny tornadoes. She watched as a piece of it see-sawed through the night and drifted to a gentle landing on the grass. And like a time-lapse movie, she imagined it decomposing into its constituent compounds and molecules and atoms and becoming one with the earth, as all things eventually must.

And she wondered whether every breath she drew was just delaying the inevitable.

She planted her right foot on the rim of the wall, testing its stability and her own resolve. Before her left foot could join it, a voice from behind pierced the silence and jolted her heart.

"Lauren."

Ren whirled toward the sound. A Black woman stood a cigarette-flick away. Her hair was short and natural. Her eyes were warm brown pools and her sad smile somehow made her even more beautiful. She was dressed like a boss—like, respectable—and a decade too old to be at this rave.

"Be careful," the woman said.

Ren's drug-addled brain was so fixated on how the stranger knew her name, there was no bandwidth to process her warning. Her chest locked and she whispered, "What?"

"You're awfully close to the edge."

She turned toward the deadly forty-foot drop that beckoned mere inches behind her, peered once more over the wall, and realized she was wrong.

The grass wasn't soft. It wasn't glowing. It wasn't grass.

It was concrete.

It was cracked and stained and pocked with sharp little broom marks that peel soft skin like a cheese grater. And Ren pictured her face ruined against it, blood pouring from her throat. Her shattered femur jutting through the top of her thigh where she sometimes liked to cut. A tidal wave of nausea crashed over her, and she vomited everything inside her off the edge of the building.

When the heaving subsided, she turned to apologize to the stranger for the grossness of what she'd just done.

The woman was gone.

A second tidal wave—questions, this time—hit hard. What

was in that pill? Did she jump already? Was she dead? Dreaming? Delusional? None of those possibilities felt right, but the last one definitely stung. Her dad had called her that once, after her light died.

Before he died.

Before she'd killed him.

The firestorm of unknowns was interrupted by a muffled slam in the distance. A Japanese girl emerged from the stairwell door. Light-skinned and slender, she looked a little older and a lot smarter in a dark cap and funky striped leggings that reminded Ren of Olivia the Pig. She approached tentatively, like Ren was a kitten she didn't want to scare off.

But was she real?

"I saw what happened downstairs," the girl said. Her voice was smoky and strong. "It was… pretty fucked-up. Are you okay?"

Ren looked away, then back. The girl was still there.

"Are you okay?" she asked again, but Ren's chest still pounded too hard to form words. "I'm not going to hurt you. I was just seeing—"

"Leave me alone," was all Ren could think to say.

The girl was undeterred. "Why? What are you going to do?"

In her fog of confusion and panic, Ren had no hope of answering that question, so she shot daggers from her eyes instead. The look she got back had no judgment, no malice. Only concern. It was humiliating. If there were a rock on the rooftop large enough to crawl under, Ren would have.

"My name is Katie. I promise I'm not, like, weird or anything. Will you—"

Ren clenched her fists and hissed, "Go. Away."

"Please. Let me get you out of here."

The tenderness in Katie's voice was more than Ren could stand, and she lost the battle to keep the tears in her worthless eyes. Through chattering teeth, she hurled a final "Fuck off."

Yeah, that would do it. Now she'd leave.

Katie's entire body seemed to wither with disappointment— more than disappointment, devastation—and Ren couldn't figure out why the girl gave a shit. She finally turned away, then stopped, removed her charcoal wool beret and offered it to Ren. With a wistful look, she said, *"Bonne chance à vous jeune fille."*

Ren had slept through most of sophomore French, but even she could understand that much.

Good luck, girl.

As she was about to tell *mademoiselle* where to shove her prissy little hat, the moon glinted off a beautiful, delicate pink streak in the girl's jet-black hair.

And just like that, Ren's light came back.

It hit her in three places at once:

Her eyes (like when she was hungover and dehydrated and her eyeballs were shriveled, scratchy marbles, but then the Gatorade kicked in and they turned plump and liquidy again and she could see the world had colors).

Her chest (like in the movies when a guy was getting suffocated with a plastic bag, but then the villain granted a moment's mercy, poking his finger through the mouth hole to let in one precious, life-restoring lungful of air).

Her uterus (like the static shock of touching a doorknob after sliding on carpet), except deep inside and slow and shivery and...

Muscles Ren hadn't used in forever pulled her lips into a smile. And it must have connected with Katie, because the girl smiled back.

"Thanks," Ren whispered, taking the beret and pulling it down over her numb ears.

"What's your name?" Katie asked.

"It's Ren."

"Nice to meet you, Ren. Now let's go, yeah? Nothing good's going to happen up here."

Ren could find no argument with that.

# THE RESCUER

KATIE'S VW HATCHBACK was hail-dented, its silver paint cloudy and pitted from years of road salt, but it started without a hiccup. The inside was clean and smelled faintly of lavender, a home-crafted air freshener pad dangling from the rearview mirror. The old car looked well cared for, and Ren could tell Katie was proud of it. It was a sanctuary, and Ren had no clue why the girl would have invited her raggedy ass on board at witching hour on a frigid Sunday morning.

Katie plugged her phone into an audio jack in the dash, spun a down-tempo playlist, and put the warehouse behind them. They rode in silence, though it wasn't awkward. The pulsing music, the warm scented air, and the hypnotic rhythm of lane markers ticking past were like a full-body massage. Ren stretched her limbs, then tugged her skirt back down before it could reveal the column of neat cuts on her thighs.

After a while, she shifted her focus to the girl behind the wheel. Ren had an eye for details and a talent for reading tells, taking people's emotional temperatures from the tension in their foreheads or the corners of their mouths. Katie seemed okay on the surface, but Ren sensed something swirling beneath just as Katie caught her staring.

"Where do you live?" Katie asked.

Ren hated to lose the few possessions she'd left at the Elmwood house, but it was worth it to avoid the humiliation of Katie seeing the place. She couldn't pinpoint when the girl's opinion of her had become important, but Katie made her feel safe, and she wanted to hold that feeling as long as she could.

"N.F.A.," Ren said at last. That's what always ended up on the police reports.

"What does that mean?"

"No fixed address."

"Where have you been staying?"

"Different places."

"Okay..."

Katie's dubious tone rubbed Ren the wrong way and she snapped, "Whatever. Judgey. Where do you live?"

"N.F.A.," Katie said, and her answer caught Ren off guard. At first, she thought Katie was making fun of her, but Ren sensed a wound. Her reflexive spitfire attitude vanished, kindness filling the void.

"Why? What happened?"

"My boyfriend," Katie hesitated. "It doesn't matter."

"It matters to me."

"He's the one who pushed you. Milo," she spat his name. "The asshat whose nose you busted is his friend Cody. It's my fault. It was my idea to go to that stupid party. I guess I thought they could act like grown-ups for five minutes."

"So you left him?"

Katie's silence confirmed it, and Ren was incredulous. Most of the men in her past, Alistair for one, would have gone ballistic at the insult of being ditched. And they were only landlords, not lovers.

Although they'd just met, Katie seemed to Ren like she had a zero-tolerance policy for bullshit, but the coldness in Milo's eyes made it easy to imagine he could unleash violence on this beautiful, generous girl. It sent Ren into a panic.

"No," she pleaded. "No, you have to go back. You should not have done that for me."

Ren hadn't intended the 'for me' to have a beveled edge, but Katie picked up on it just the same. "What does that mean?" she asked. "It's okay I help someone else, but not you?"

Katie let her off the hook before she could respond. "I didn't do it for you," she said. "I did it for me. He's a shit and I'm done. Should've been done a long time ago. Anyways, I should grab my things before he gets back to the house."

Ren agreed, glad to have a direction, a mission. "I'll help you. Then we'll figure out what's next."

Katie flashed a smile, then tried to erase it.

"What's funny?" Ren asked.

"Nothing." Katie gripped the wheel and leaned forward to concentrate on the road. The headlights caught little clouds of fog every so often and made the visibility spotty. After a while, she asked, "Why don't you have anywhere to stay? Have you got family?"

"My mom's around."

"I guess you guys aren't close."

"Guess not."

"What's your beef with her?" Katie asked, her penchant for

direct questions already apparent. Ren didn't enjoy being on the receiving end, but she was not above deploying the tactic herself. She'd learned long ago that someone's reaction to a pointed question could be as informative as their answer.

"We haven't spoken in a while," Ren said. "I kind of ran away." Eager to change the subject, she asked, "Do you have family?"

"No, it's just me," Katie said, but her hand drifted from the steering wheel to her stomach and the rest of the sentence echoed in Ren's mind as if the girl had said it aloud.

*And the little thing growing inside me.*

"Does Milo know about the baby?" Ren asked.

Katie's breath caught. She looked at Ren, a mix of wonder and fear shaping her expressive face. "How did you—"

A flash of movement on the road grabbed Ren's attention and she snapped, "Look out!"

Three car-lengths ahead, a pale blond girl in a loose white gown stood in the middle of the lane. Fog swirled at her feet, and Ren had the split-second impression she'd wandered away from some hospital. A thin scar traced from her left ear to the corner of her scowling mouth, but it was her eyes that chilled the back of Ren's neck. They were black and soulless and stubbornly refused to gleam in the headlights.

Katie gasped, jerked the wheel, and barely missed the girl. The worn tires broke loose from the slick pavement with the sickening sensation that gravity itself had abandoned them. The little hatchback punched through the steel guardrail with an awful shriek, and they spun sideways down a steep hill, Katie fighting desperately to keep the car from rolling on its head.

She succeeded.

Her reward was a massive half-dead oak tree that swallowed the front end of the VW with a dull thump that echoed once in the windy night.

* * *

The dream was always the same.

He sat in the rear booth of a retro 24-hour diner, the kind with checkerboard floors and little chrome jukeboxes at each table. He had on the ridiculous game-day ensemble: the turtle-neck, the number 7 jersey, the goofy green terrycloth wrist-bands. The goddamn knit hat with the fuzzy pompom.

*No self-respecting Eagles fan wears only one piece of kit,* he'd always said.

Ren's mom called him "sports dork." She'd meant it in jest when Ren was little; less so as the marriage had frayed. But he'd bought his little girl a matching outfit, so they could be dorks together. And he'd paid for it with his life.

Her dad waved to her and she hurried over. The ever-present stubble tickled her lips as she gave him a kiss on the cheek and flopped onto the opposite side of the booth. There was a half-finished BLT in front of him. She went to steal a tater tot, then stopped. The plate was crawling with termites.

She pushed it away, hard enough that it slid off the table and shattered on the floor. A busboy appeared with a black plastic dish tub to clear the mess, except it wasn't a busboy. It was Alistair.

"So, how are things?" her dad asked, as if nothing were amiss. His mouth smiled, but his eyes did not. They were cold and distant.

"Oh, you know," she said.

"This came across my desk." He slid her a yellow envelope stamped with a Philadelphia Police Department shield.

She unfastened the clasp and heard a whisper.

*Lauren.*

That wasn't normally part of the dream. She looked around the diner. All the usual suspects were there, and none appeared to have called her name.

Ren returned her attention to the envelope, reached inside and felt the glossy finish of a photograph. She knew what it showed without seeing it. "I can explain—"

*LAUREN.*

The unmistakable voice of Ren's rooftop stranger pulled her from the darkness.

The cold air hit her eyes and as the world came into focus, she found herself belted into the passenger seat of a car tilted quite unnaturally downward. Frost coated the windows and the reflection of one functioning headlamp glared off the dash.

It cost her a few moments to put the pieces together: a rave... a drive... a crash... a girl.

Katie.

Ren turned to look. Big mistake. A sharp pain torpedoed from her brain to her butt, which was strangely soggy. Her bladder must have let go during the crash. That indignity aside, nothing seemed to be broken. And there was Katie, slumped against a blown airbag, the striking pink streak of hair matted to her forehead by dried blood.

Ren's breath billowed in the frigid air. Katie's did not.

She lashed out to feel Katie's head, like her mom did when Ren used to cry fever to get out of going to school. Her body temp was no colder than Ren's. She tried to pull Katie away from the steering column, but the angle made it impossible. Her eyes leaked tears as she opened her door and fell hard onto the ground, angering her neck injury and sending another bolt of pain through her skull. She fought through it and crawled around to Katie's side to find the driver's door was bent slightly against the frame. She muscled it open and reached across Katie to unbuckle the seatbelt, but it was jammed.

"Goddamn it!" she yelled into the predawn chill, yanking at the strap like a petulant child.

No. Think.

She pressed her hand to her collarbone and felt cold steel against her skin. Her chum, her amigo, her ride-or-die. The old-school double-edged razor blade whose perfect little cuts made her feel alive when sometimes nothing else would. She unfastened it from the chain around her neck and sent it into battle against the gray polyester belt. The edge shredded her fingertips, but she ignored the pain and the blood. When the first side dulled, she flipped it over, hacking faster and faster until it broke through the last stubborn fibers.

With the restraint defeated, she pulled Katie from the ruined vehicle and laid her gently on the cold ground. Blood had pooled in the seat and soaked through the crotch of her striped leggings.

She returned the borrowed beret to Katie's head to keep her warm. A faint puff of icy breath escaped her lips and she moaned, "*Où est maman?*"

"Katie, are you okay?" Ren asked, but the girl had already passed out again.

Ren leaned into the car to search for Katie's phone. The impact had untethered its cord from the radio, and she finally found the dead, useless thing in the rear footwell. She never had much use for phones—nobody to call, nobody calling her, no funds to feed them—but at that moment she'd have given her left tit for a cheap burner if there was a chance it could save her friend.

Ren toyed with the idea of fireman-carrying the slim girl up the hill, but she couldn't kid herself for long. Though she was quite comfortable in her own skin, her armor was more pudge than muscle, and the leaf-covered slope would be far too slippery. With a pit of sick in her stomach, she left Katie behind and started toward the road.

Her legs burned and her lungs ached for every molecule of oxygen, drawing from a reserve of energy she didn't know she possessed. At the top of the hill, she crawled past the mangled guardrail and caught her breath at the shoulder.

Ren wandered the curving roadway in both directions as far as she dared, but could find no turnoffs, signs or call boxes. It wasn't dark—there were streetlights—but she couldn't shake the feeling they'd been sucked into a void where they could see out but nobody could see in.

She also could find no trace of the pale girl whose scarred visage was burned into her brain. Ren was confident they hadn't hit her, but Katie had swerved so violently, she must have seen her, too. If the girl wasn't injured or dead, then it was possible she was wandering the same desolate stretch of road, and there was absolutely no comfort in that notion.

As she was about to give up and return to check on Katie, a pair of lights rounded the bend in answer to her wheezing prayers. She hurled her arms into the air, spending her last ounce of strength to hail the white pickup truck.

The driver turned on his hazard blinkers, eased onto the shoulder, and coasted to a stop beside her.

She fell to her knees and wept.

# THE ANGEL

AFTER EIGHT HOURS of questioning, worrying and waiting, they finally transferred Katie from the emergency room to an inpatient room, where Ren was able to sneak a shower. She'd declined medical treatment despite the pain in her neck, both to keep the overwhelmed ER doctors focused on Katie, but also because she was paranoid they'd find some reason to call her mother. Like for insurance, or something. Then it occurred to her she was no longer a minor. The two birthdays she'd spent away from home sort of blurred together.

She savored the hot water—which was always in high demand and short supply at her crash-house—and watched her blood, Katie's blood, dirt, mud, urine, sweat, and makeup roll off her body in little rivulets and twirl on the tile like a macabre Rorschach ink blot. It made her think of the battery of such tests she had undergone as a child. Psychiatrists and psychologists, hypnotists and counselors, all commissioned by her parents to figure out why their sweet little girl was so profoundly sad.

Why her light had died.

As she worked her aching muscles under the heat, she indulged in a fantasy that there was something magical about this particular shower. Like it was more than just a white-tiled enclave with a striped curtain and old-man grab-bars. A holy place—a confessional, perhaps—where she could wash away more than yesterday's filth. She could sterilize her body *and* sanitize her soul.

Of course, that would be impossible. Even if the shower was enchanted, there wasn't enough soap or shampoo or scrubbing or contrition in the world to remove her father's blood from her hands, and her spirits sank as the last vestiges of her pointless daydream followed the lather down the drain.

Ren slipped into a spare hospital gown and returned to the bedside chair. Her new friend—her only friend, if she were honest—was fast asleep, hooked to machines and an IV drip. The reassuring beep of the heart monitor was the only sound in the room, leaving plenty of space for her cruel brain's incessant chatter about what a bad-luck charm she was to everyone who crossed her path.

A short Indian physician with puffy cheeks, who'd introduced himself as Dr. Prasad, had cleaned the blood from Katie's hairline and dressed it with a tidy bandage. Later, an orthopedic guy had set two of her fingers in a splint, which, for some reason, troubled Ren more than the swelling and the bruises on her lovely face. She had an odd sense the injury was disproportionately significant, as if Katie were a musician or a painter who might no longer be able to pursue her passion. They hadn't talked about it—hadn't much of a chance to talk about anything, really—but Ren's intuition told her Katie was some sort of artist.

Maybe it was the pink hair. Or the beret.

Ren was disappointed to discover the wool cap that was Katie's first gift to her had been lost somewhere along the way. The rest of the girl's bloody clothes had been cut from her body and were now moldering in a hazmat bag in the corner. In their place, Katie wore a pale-blue patterned gown, and the garment's low neckline revealed a scar: a thin straight seam that began below her throat and disappeared between her breasts. Ren was drawn to it, and though it felt weirdly intimate to do so, she came within an inch of touching it.

A red-headed nurse interrupted her exploration. She was close in age to Ren's mother, but wearier, as if her life had been exponentially more difficult. She'd visited once before, and Ren batted away a pang of guilt that she didn't yet know all the names of Katie's caregivers.

"How's our girl?" the nurse asked with a light Irish lilt.

"Okay, I guess," Ren replied, but figured it was not her job to make that call. The nurse checked Katie's vitals and made notes on a chart. Her gaze cut to Katie's face, then down to the scar. And damned if she didn't do exactly what Ren had: almost touch it before stopping herself.

"Bless her heart," she said, and looked like she was about to say something else when there was a quick double-knock on the door and a pair of uniformed cops pushed into the room.

The shorter one was stocky, with sandy hair cut high and tight. The name tag on his black winter coat said Kowalski, and he had one of those native Philly accents that made "water" sound like "wooder."

He said to the nurse, "Need a minute with these two."

She leveled a scowl at the officers but didn't interfere with their business, nor let them interfere with hers. She completed her checks and left them alone.

Kowalski pulled a cell phone from inside his jacket and aimed the camera. Ren was indifferent to the photo he snapped of her, but Katie was vulnerable in bed, and Ren roared to her defense.

"Hey, that's an invasion of privacy!"

"Tell you what, Miss Cole," he said with a mean smirk. "Why don't you come down to the station with us and file a complaint? I'll introduce you to our desk sergeant. Hell of a guy."

"Hard pass," Ren said, returning her focus to Katie.

"Yeah, that's what I thought. We have a few more questions for you and Miss Moreau about yesterday evening."

"We talked to the cops this morning already. The roads were slick. We crashed. I don't know what else to tell you."

"This ain't about your accident," he said. "We got a complaint filed by some kids at a rave that a young lady matching your description assaulted a 23-year-old male and inflicted a nasal fracture. Know anything about this?"

Like what happened last night was her fault. Like this thug would care.

"Nope."

"No, huh? Did you girls partake of any substances that might be impacting your recollection?"

Her pulse quickened. Not that Kowalski could perceive it, but her dad had been a cop and always said cops had a sixth sense about when a suspect was lying. A built-in bullshit detector. Of course, that may have been bullshit, too. Maybe a father just knew when his daughter was lying to him.

She was formulating a response when the unexpected voice of her rooftop stranger interrupted her thoughts.

*You don't have to answer.*

Ren knew it was in her head, but it didn't stop her from looking around the room anyway. Kowalski noticed. "Lose something?" he asked.

"Just leave us alone, okay?" she shot back.

"Sorry, little lady, that ain't how this works," he explained, as if to an idiot child. "We got a young man with a serious injury and there's questions need answered."

Her gut told her not to take the bait, but she couldn't help it. She sighted on his thick, smug face like a sniper. "Here's a question, Officer. Why don't you ask that human shit-stain what he did that got his nose smashed?"

If pissed-off were a cologne, Kowalski now reeked of it. No way this alpha was taking lip from a punk like her. "Because I'm asking you, you little club rat."

Nervousness flashed across the other cop's face, like what should have been a simple interview was about to get out of hand. He said, "Sean, let me take this, huh? Give us a minute?"

Kowalski snapped a glance at his partner, apparently decided he was friend rather than foe, then glared at Ren once more before stomping out of the room.

The remaining cop—his nametag said Delfino—put on a sheepish smile and said, "Sorry, Miss Cole. He's not much of a people-person." He was younger and better looking than Kowalski. Italian, maybe, or Greek. But she knew this routine and had no intention of letting him perpetrate it.

"Oh, you're the good cop," she said. She cringed at how flirty it sounded, but she was nervous. The tough-kid act was only skin-deep.

Her stranger's voice was there to reassure her.

*Smart girl. Trust your gut.*

Ren had to admit she enjoyed having the woman in her head. Unnatural as it was, she was getting used to it. Maybe even starting to rely on it.

"I'm not good or bad. Just doing my job. How's your friend?"

"She's hurt, actually. So, it'd be pretty cool if you could give us a break right now."

"Look, I know you two have been through a lot, so let me help you out here," Delfino said, like he'd been on Team Ren all along. "It'll go easier if you tell me the truth. There are cameras in the warehouse where you were partying. They're pulling footage as we speak, and we'll get an ID. It'd be better to get in front of this and tell your side."

Her stranger counseled: *He's bluffing.*

She gave Ren confidence, but Ren was also decidedly bored with the whole affair and wanted more than anything else for these cops to fuck off.

"Am I under arrest?" she asked him, point-blank.

"Not at this time, no."

She nodded toward Katie. "Is she?"

"No."

Ren locked eyes with him. "Then we're done."

Delfino looked as though he might persist, but he relented and handed her a card with his name and number. "In case you change your mind. Or anything."

This guy was no mystery. "Anything" meant one thing: him getting to see what was under her gown. She politely took the card and flicked it into the trash as the door closed behind him.

"You got some balls on you," Katie's strained voice called from the bed.

Ren grinned. "You're awake! You faker."

"I didn't feel like talking to Officer Creepowski."

Ren flopped into the chair. "How are you feeling?"

Katie shook her head. A tear escaped.

"What is it? What's wrong?" Ren asked.

"I lost the baby, didn't I?"

She had. The doctors confirmed it with an ultrasound.

Ren took her hand. "I'm so sorry. This is on me. If you hadn't—"

Katie cut her off. "No, it's… he's not a good person. It's better this way. And it's not on you. Okay?"

"What about calling someone?" Ren asked, still saddled with the guilt Katie tried to absolve her of.

"There's nobody," Katie said.

"No family?"

"I lost my mom and my baby sister in a crash when I was young. My dad went away when I was twelve. I sort of bounced around different places afterwards. Nobody I'm close to."

Each of the four sentences Katie had rattled off encapsulated its own universe of tragedy, and here she was in the aftermath of another accident that had cost her something precious. Stolen more of her joy. Ren had no words of comfort; she could only hope condolences transmitted through her fingertips.

After a minute, she said, "I'm going to let you sleep, okay?"

Ren stood up, but the girl held firm. "Stay with me. Please?" She grimaced in pain and slid over to make room for Ren in her bed. Ren didn't answer right away. Not because she didn't desperately want to stay. She wanted Katie to have a chance to change her mind.

"You don't even know me," Ren protested.

"I know you enough."

"Fine," she said. She switched off the lamp and climbed in beside Katie as gracefully as her own aching body and the narrow bed would allow. "But I don't smash on the first date."

Katie didn't miss a beat. "In your dreams, club rat."

They laughed hard, though it hurt like hell. When the giggles ran their course, their heads gravitated to the center of the lone pillow and gently touched. Ren was surprised by how natural it felt. She'd shared a few beds since leaving home. On a handful of occasions, there had been sex involved, purposeful and perfunctory, like letting off steam. But this warmth, this sense of companionship and comfort in human contact, was entirely new.

Katie yawned. "I need to ask you something before I pass out."

"Shoot."

"My memory's kind of jacked. Please tell me I didn't hit somebody. With the car?"

"Definitely not," Ren said. "But you saw her too? The girl in the road?"

"Yeah."

"I wasn't sure either, because—" Ren stopped herself from confessing the girl in the road wasn't the only apparition she'd seen last night. She knew how delusional it would sound.

"What?" Katie prodded.

"Nothing," she said. "Don't worry about it. Go to sleep, angel."

"Angel," Katie echoed, her voice warm and drowsy. "*Mon petite ange.* My mom used to call me that."

The girl was asleep a moment later, a wisp of hair fallen across her nose. Ren instinctively brushed it back into place behind her ear, which was odd because taking care of people wasn't an instinct Ren remembered having.

# THE ACCOMPLICE

BETWEEN THE NURSES checking on Katie every couple of hours and the girl moaning in the night, Ren barely slept at all. The hardest part was that she didn't think Katie's restlessness was because of her injuries. She was fairly certain the girl was having nightmares.

Katie said she'd lost her family in a crash, and Ren wondered whether their accident had stirred up that trauma. Or whether she was grieving the loss of her unborn child. Though it seemed like Katie was relieved to not be forever tied to Milo, Ren couldn't know how the girl had felt about the idea of being a mom. About having a little angel of her own.

Ren finally drifted off, but not for long. She sensed the door opening before the latch actually clicked, a hair-trigger wakefulness she'd honed over years spent sleeping in unsafe places. It was the red-headed nurse watching them from the hallway. When she met Ren's gaze, she gestured for Ren to join her.

She didn't want to leave Katie, but the night was over. Sunlight filtered through the blinds and the ginger looked like she

had something on her mind. Ren slipped from the sheets, careful not to disturb Katie, who was snoring softly, her mouth
slightly ajar. It reminded her of Jack, the old warm lump of a
Yorkie who divided his time between her bed and her mother's,
snuffling loud enough to prove he was alive, but not so loud as
to keep them awake. She hadn't thought of him in ages.

"Morning," the nurse whispered after Ren had pulled the
door closed behind her.

"You were here last night, right?" Ren asked. "What's your
name?"

"Mary Brennan. You're Ren." They traded a handshake, and
Mary asked, "How's our girl?"

Ren almost pointed her to Katie's chart, but for some reason,
the nurse wanted her opinion on the matter, so she gave it.

"I think she's okay physically. But she had a bad night," Ren
said, eliciting a frown from Mary. "Do you need to check on her?"

"No, I'm not on duty," Mary said, and until that moment,
Ren hadn't noticed she was in street clothes. All she'd latched
onto was that wild red hair.

"For real? Do you visit all your patients on your day off?"

Mary's expression said she did not. "Are you hungry?" she
asked.

"Kind of," Ren replied, but in truth, she was starving. She'd
picked the crumbs off Katie's dinner tray the night before, but
didn't want to abandon her friend simply to feed her face.

"Come on, I'll buy you breakfast."

Ren hesitated, pulling her gown tight around her. "My
clothes are totally skanky. Is there, like, something I can
borrow?"

"Of course." Mary disappeared around the corner and returned with a stack of folded blue scrubs. Ren accepted them with a relieved smile, ducked into Katie's room and suited up. In her black combat boots, nobody would mistake her for a member of hospital staff, but the nurse gave a nod of approval and said, "Let's eat."

Surveying the buffet lines and refrigerator cases of the cafeteria, Mary said, "Everything is mostly awful, but the chicken pot pie is okay. Want to give it a whirl?"

That sounded dubious. "It's like nine AM," Ren said.

"And?"

"Whatever."

Mary bought two pies and two sodas and they claimed a table by the window. Ren took a bite of the hot food, and it was a winner. After she'd scarfed hers and the last third that Mary had left unfinished, a little burp escaped her lips.

"Sorry!" she said, her face heating. She didn't bother to check if anyone had noticed.

"No worries," Mary laughed, a musical outburst that further inflamed her rosy cheeks. "So, tell me, how long have you two been friends?"

"Night before last."

Mary seemed shocked, like she'd been certain the girls were lifelong besties. Ren didn't know where to take the conversation, so she let it be. The nurse looked equally uncomfortable and said finally, "Is there anything I can do to help you?"

If Ren wasn't confused before, she was now. What had they done to deserve such fawning attention from any nurse, let alone one on her day off? Katie had a low-grade concussion and an uncomplicated miscarriage; Ren had cuts and bruises and a nagging pain in her neck. Both would recover fully in a matter of days. To a veteran like Mary, the girls had to be utterly forgettable, yet here she was, asking what *more* she could do to help. Generosity bred suspicion after any amount of time on the streets, a reflexive distrust for the kindness of strangers. Far too often, there were unpleasant strings attached.

"Why?" Ren asked.

Mary shook her head. "Honestly, I don't know. I had a feeling you two were lost. I reckon I couldn't let it be."

Ren knew there had to be more to it, but the concern in Mary's emerald eyes was genuine and the warmth in her voice suggested no unseemly motives. And there actually was something, assuming Ren could get Katie's address off her driver's license.

"Well," she said, "if you're serious... before we crashed, we were headed to Katie's to get her stuff. I'm afraid her shitbag ex is going to chuck it on the street. Maybe you could help me rescue it?"

Mary's surprise showed Ren's request was miles from what she'd expected. Maybe she thought Ren would beg fifty bucks, or a pot pie for Katie, or a place to crash after the doctors declared them fit to leave. Ren's ask was both cheaper and more dangerous, but it was for Katie's benefit, and besides, Mary had offered.

"Will he be there? Her man?"

Ren tried to downplay the danger. "I don't know. If so, we'll bolt. I thought maybe we'd get lucky, and he'd be at work or something."

The nurse seemed to assess the possible outcomes in her mind, each one less appealing than the last, but she decided faster than Ren expected. "All right. Let's do it."

\* \* \*

Ren was grateful for the sisterhood, but Mary turned out to be a shitty driver. At one point, a delivery truck almost sheared off the passenger-side mirror as the nurse weaved through traffic at high speed, leaving mere inches between bumpers. Given Ren's recent automotive experience, the ride was pretty triggering, but if Mary noticed Ren's anxiety, she didn't show it.

They finally pulled up across the street from the modest brick bungalow she assumed was Milo's; Katie was still sleeping when they left, and this was the address on her license. Ren got the impression it was a rental; it wasn't exactly falling apart, but it had a transitory look, like nobody was too invested in it. Nothing decorative adorned the place, and the paint around the window frames was flaking.

Most importantly, Katie's belongings were not among the mess of unraked leaves on the brown lawn. Ren had told Mary she was afraid Milo would discard them, but now faced with the prospect of breaking in to retrieve them, she wished her low assessment of Katie's ex had been more accurate.

Ren cased the place from the front seat of Mary's car with a practiced eye: no lights, no garage, no cars on the street, no alarm monitoring sign in the yard or stickers on the windows. No security cameras attached to the house and nobody approaching.

"Keep it running, okay?"

Mary got the implication, and her enthusiasm for their errand seemed to wane. "You don't have to do this, Ren. It's just stuff."

The nurse wasn't wrong, but Ren was sure Katie would do

it for her if the situation were reversed. "I know," she said, exiting the car.

She strolled confidently to the front door, recalling a pearl from Alistair's breaking-and-entering mentorship: *act like you belong; you're the only one who knows you don't.* She stood shivering in the thin blue scrub shirt as she tried each of the three keys on the ring she'd pilfered from Katie. The first didn't fit. The second slid in but failed to engage. Third time was the charm. Ren eased the door open and listened for sounds of danger—a barking dog, a siren, the intimidating beep of a burglar-alarm countdown. Any of those would be game over, but there was only dead silence.

She stepped over the threshold and shut the door behind her. The house was nicer inside than out, and she immediately knew they'd come to the right place. It smelled like Katie, a warm blend of laundry detergent and lavender that struck her with a sudden longing and an intense desire to get her ass out of there.

Katie's influence on the place ended with the scent. The rest was all bachelor pad. The front room had a fancy video game setup with two chairs and two headsets. Somehow, Ren knew the second seat was for Milo's buddy. Katie wasn't invited to play. Muscle-car posters papered the walls and the kitchen sink overflowed with dishes, probably because Katie hadn't been home to wash them.

Ren crept down the hall past a spare room with a weightlifting bench and a punching bag dangling from a stand in the corner. She tamped down a fresh surge of irritation at the evolving picture of Katie's ex-boyfriend and moved on to the bedroom. The bed was unmade, empty beer cans crowded the nightstand and dirty laundry was scattered everywhere. She hoped like hell Katie didn't have to clean up after this pig.

The closet had some hard-sided luggage on the floor and a couple of collapsed duffels on the top shelf. She was determined not to take anything that wasn't Katie's—not even the bag she'd need to transport it—in case Milo perceived it as another slight, a new score he'd be compelled to settle. And so she sniffed the bags, like old Jack on the trail of a squirrel he'd never catch. With the telltale scent of lavender, the blue duffel was Katie's for sure.

Ren spread it open on the bed and shoved in an armful of hanging clothes and some shoes off the closet floor. She raided the dresser and nightstands for the rest of Katie's things, then headed to the bathroom. She ignored the body spray and the deodorant spray and the five kinds of hair gel, and grabbed the girly stuff: the modest skincare products, a bottle of lavender perfume, and some half-used pink hair dye and bleach.

As she returned to toss it on the clothes pile, her toe connected with something under the bed. It was a small storage tub. She slid it out and unlatched the lid. Beneath some winter accessories—a knit hat, fleece gloves, and a tartan scarf—was a scrapbook, a few children's books, and a cute gray stuffed animal with little slits for eyes. She transferred it all to the duffel, but couldn't let go of the scrapbook so easily.

In her hands was a window into Katie's life, decorated with small purple flowers that hinted strongly at happier times. It wasn't her place to snoop inside, but she wasn't sure she'd get another chance, and the urge was too strong to fight.

The first page had a watercolor painting of a flower protected by a clear sheet of acetate. Ren didn't know what kind of flower it was, but she could almost see Katie's hand at work in the brush strokes. Turning past it, she came to a photo of a Japanese man with his arm around a European-looking woman cradling a baby. Seated between the two parents, clutching their thighs like she'd float away if she let go, was an adorable little girl, maybe seven or eight years old. Her smile lit up the world.

*Mon petite ange.*

This was the family Katie had lost.

Her mom was gorgeous. Auburn hair, green eyes and a dark-lipped mischievous grin that made Ren wish she were in on the joke. Her dad was handsome, too. She got a mental image of little Katie riding on his shoulders with a death-grip on his black, wavy mane. His eyes drew her in, a rich brown with amber flecks that seemed to sparkle off the page.

Ren must have stared too long because her vision blurred. Out of nowhere, a stomach cramp doubled her over so hard she lost her breath.

"Ugh, God," she gurgled into the empty room, and made it to the toilet in time to let go the breakfast Mary had bought her. She flushed the mess, rinsed her mouth at the sink, then checked her face in the mirror.

There was someone behind her.

# THE BRAT

THE STRANGER HAD come to Milo's house.

"Jesus tits," Ren blurted, whirling around to look at the woman. "Are you trying to give me a heart attack? Who are you?"

The woman, for her part, was unapologetic. "You need to leave. Now. He's back."

"Shit." Ren tossed the scrapbook in the bag, zipped it up, and hoisted it over her shoulder.

"This way," the woman instructed.

Ren tiptoed past the kitchen and down the hall to the laundry room, where she found a secondary door leading to the yard. She unbolted it and snuck out as a man's voice called, "Hello?" from the front of the house.

She skirted the outside of the bungalow, then hid at the corner. Mary clutched the steering wheel in a panic, fixating on the blue muscle car parked at the curb. In their haste to get the job done, they had neglected to work out any kind of signal. Rookie mistake.

Ren caught the nurse's eye and motioned for her to drive forward. She jogged away from the house, boots clomping through the leaves, and met up with Mary partway down the block. She hopped in back with the duffel and Mary gunned it as Ren looked out the rear window to see if Milo would come out or if her stranger was supervising their getaway.

The street was empty.

"Well, that was a wee adventure," Mary said, almost like she'd enjoyed the thrill.

Not Ren. For as many times as she'd paid her rent helping Alistair steal things, she never got used to the terror. As the adrenaline wore off, they returned to the hospital in silent, shared embarrassment, and Ren conjured horrible scenarios about what might have happened without her stranger's warning. Probably Milo would have beaten the shit out of her. Or worse.

Mary pulled under the patient drop-off canopy, and it was clear she was not coming back inside. The adventure, as far as the nurse was concerned, was over.

"You girls take care of each other," she said. "You've got a good one there. And she does too."

"Thanks for helping. You didn't have to do that."

"I did. Not sure why, but I did." Ren started to leave, but Mary touched her shoulder. "Hey, is that a house key hanging on your neck?"

"Yeah."

"You should use it. Whoever's behind that door needs to know you're okay. Do that for me?"

And there they were, the strings tied to the nurse's charity. She couldn't believe she'd fallen for it. She grabbed the duffel, bulldozed out of the car, and slammed the door behind her.

Then she stopped, took a breath, and realized she was being petty and stupid. It would not impact Mary's life at all if Ren went home to her mother. Still, she couldn't commit.

She turned to Mary and said, "I'll think about it."

\* \* \*

The Chinese takeout that Ren bought for dinner drained the last of her meager savings. She'd ordered the food without asking, and Katie probably would have told her not to spend the money, but it tasted way better than the mystery meat on the hospital menu. As Katie sat in bed eating noodles with chopsticks and Ren sat in the chair inhaling pork fried rice with a spoon, they plied each other with questions, probing for land mines and determining their stance on the key issues of the day.

"You can tell a lot about someone from what they like," Katie had said, but Ren wasn't always sure what she liked. It had been a while since she'd found joy in things, never mind the luxury of having a preference. But Katie eased her into it. The conversation was light and fun, and it didn't take long to develop a rhythm. A banter.

"Fruit?" Ren asked.

"Mango," Katie said.

Ren made a face. "Eww. Too slimy. Pineapple," she countered.

"Pineapple's okay. But not on pizza."

"A hundred percent on pizza," Ren said.

"Pass. Orange juice: pulp or no pulp?"

"Pulp."

"Rock on," Katie said. "Coffee or tea?"

"Coffee. Cream, no sugar."

Katie nodded; apparently that was an acceptable difference

of opinion. "Black for me. Okay, here's one," she announced, as if bringing out the big guns: "Bale, Affleck or Pattinson?"

Ren's face blanked. "Not sure what you mean."

"Batman?" Katie clarified, but Ren was still baffled. "Best actor who played Batman?"

The black hole she'd been living in admitted little in the way of pop culture, and she wished she could connect with Katie on that level. "Sorry," she said, casting her eyes into her lap. "I'm a little behind on movies and things."

Katie was reassuring. "That doesn't matter. Besides, it was a trick question. The right answer is Keaton."

Before she could stop herself, Ren blurted, "Maybe you can help me catch up?" Heat rose in her cheeks.

The corners of Katie's mouth turned up ever so slightly. "I'd like that."

"Cool." Ren said, but was unsure what to say next.

Katie ate one last bite and set aside her carton of noodles. "Thanks for the grub. And thanks for getting my things. I still can't believe you took that chance."

The girl didn't know the half of it. Ren hadn't told her Milo had gotten home mid-heist.

"I know, right? Mary drives even worse than you."

Katie cracked up. "You brat. That's not what I meant!"

"I know what you meant."

They looked at each other for a moment. With most people, Ren had one foot out the door by the time they'd showed the slightest interest in her, but she didn't want this conversation to end.

Katie broke the silence. "Do you like to read?"

Ren thought of her mom, the English professor, and her

perpetual annoyance that Ren flipped past words to find pictures whenever she was presented with a book. "I do, sometimes," she said.

Katie slid a slim, square hardback from beneath her covers: *The Gashlycrumb Tinies*, by Edward Gorey. "It was in the stuff you brought me. It's one of my favorites. Have you read it?"

"Never heard of it," Ren said, feeling out of the cultural loop once again.

She sat next to Katie on the bed and they flipped through the subtle and brilliantly morbid black-and-white A-B-C cartoons of children dying in gruesome ways. The third drawing—C is for Clara—was a dark-eyed and miserable creature who reminded Ren of herself a couple of days earlier. Clara had apparently wasted away, which Ren was in no danger of doing, but she could relate to the morose girl all the same.

Katie said, "Hey, I need to ask you something."

The hair on Ren's arms tingled. Had poor, sad Clara reminded Katie of the warehouse roof and made her wonder about Ren's intentions as she'd stood at the edge?

She remembered the isolation. The hopelessness. The overwhelming sense that the world had no use for someone like her, and yet, she hadn't really wanted to die. It was more like she'd hoped the world would just end, and whether that meant a fresh start—or eternal nothingness—was irrelevant. And while she no longer felt those things, their imprint remained on her heart, and she cringed at her own selfishness. What kind of person wished for everyone else's journeys to end just because they weren't enjoying their own?

As it turned out, the book about dead kids had reminded Katie of something else entirely.

"How did you know I was pregnant?"

The question caught Ren off guard, like a stitch had just been dropped in the delicate fabric of a friendship still being knitted. But more than anything, she was confused. "The doctors said you miscarried?"

"No, it was before. In the car. You asked me if Milo knew about the baby. I hadn't told you about that."

Ren recalled the incident, but not the source of the information. "I honestly don't know. I guess it just popped in my head. I'm sorry."

"Why are you sorry?"

Ren looked away. "I didn't mean to weird you out."

Katie squeezed Ren's hand. "Hey, you don't weird me out... that much. I just had to ask."

"Promise?"

"Promise."

Katie turned the page to put the uncomfortable topic behind them and they soon came to a drawing of a boy peeking out from behind a big dark window. N was for Neville, and he'd perished from ennui.

"*Ce mortel ennui*," Katie said distantly, and Ren wasn't sure she knew she'd done it.

"What?"

"I have this memory," she said, as if she were still immersed in it. "I'm with my dad. We're looking at pictures of my mom. Only I keep getting distracted by these little orange embers glowing inside his old stereo. Like the whole thing might catch on fire. There's a record spinning on a wooden turntable. It's kind of crackly, but the voice... the piano... it's like he's in the room with us."

"Who?" Ren asked.

"Serge Gainsbourg. My mom's favorite singer."

"*Ce mortel ennui*," Ren repeated, and attempted the translation. "This... deadly... boredom?"

Katie nodded, a deep melancholy in her eyes that Ren couldn't bear to see. She had to lighten the mood—to try, anyway—so she pretended to be insulted. "Yeah, sorry I'm not more interesting."

Katie's pained face morphed into a grin, which Ren mirrored.

"Oh my God, you're such a brat."

\* \* \*

Ren ignored the TV show Katie fell asleep to, and sat in the visitor's chair admiring her friend. She always had a thing for nerdy girls, and though Katie was the farthest thing from a nerd, she radiated kindness and warmth, and her deep, regular breathing exerted an immense gravitational pull. Katie was way out of her league, but Ren caught herself wondering whether their easy comfort left room for the possibility they could be more than friends. Regardless, she would not climb back into the girl's bed without an invitation, and since the wall clock read eight-fifteen, she knew sleep would not arrive for hours. A long, lonely evening awaited.

The girl's unflinching question about the pregnancy returned to Ren's mind, and she was surprised to realize she could think clearly about it. The pervasive white noise of guilt and worry and doubt—which had muddled her thoughts for as long as she could remember—had been silenced; undoubtedly another impact of the awakening she'd experienced on that rooftop.

Perhaps this new quiet let her attune to subtle signals all around her. Perhaps Katie's pregnancy had been a signal, a vibe she was giving off. A conundrum weighing heavy on her heart that Ren had received like a broadcast; a download she had neither sought nor particularly wanted, but had come anyway.

Was her stranger one of those signals, too?

Possibly. But the bigger question was why she was so afraid to talk to Katie about it.

Given the general weirdness of the past two days, her friend might believe her. But Ren thought it far more likely that this abnormal shit would be the last straw. Katie would regain her senses and decide this fucked-up emo chick wasn't worth the effort. And sharing a bed for the second night in a row was a bad idea.

R is for Red Flag.

She mused on it awhile, arriving at no conclusion other than the Chinese food was getting ripe. She quietly collected the remains and headed for the door.

"Lauren."

Ren stopped cold. Her stranger was in the room, standing between her and the bed. She wore a sad smile, her warm brown eyes full of love and regret.

"Go home," she said, and in a blink, she was gone.

"Wait!" Ren reached out, her mind screaming *no no no no no,* because this time was different.

This time, something was wrong.

And Ren was overwhelmed by the certainty that she would never see this beautiful spirit again.

She tried and failed to stifle a sob.

"Hey. You okay?" Katie asked, half asleep.

"Sorry," Ren croaked and swiped away tears, hoping Katie didn't find it odd that she'd been holding a bag of trash and crying into the void.

She fled the room, ditched the food in a wastebasket at the nurse's station and hurled herself around the corner. Her head pounded and the corridor spun, dizziness forcing her to the floor. She lost all grip on time and space and fought for air, as if a school bus had parked itself on her chest.

*The Lord giveth and the Lord taketh away.*

Not that she believeth that bullshit, but the words spoken by the minister at her Grammie Beth's funeral drifted into her mind and pretty much captured the sentiment.

Two nights ago, the universe had bestowed an incredible gift: an expansion of consciousness—like a sixth sense and a big sister rolled into one. And just as she was beginning to treasure it, the same cruel universe amputated it with a fucking meat cleaver. And not a drop of anesthetic or a stick to bite down on.

Probably because it had all been a mistake. She obviously never deserved it to begin with.

# THE RUNAWAY

REN DIDN'T REMEMBER going to sleep, but found herself in the bedside chair when Dr. Prasad blew into the room the next morning and woke them both. The man did nothing with subtlety—he was basically a walking jump-scare. His manner was brisk, but he always had a smile for them, and Ren knew they'd been in expert hands. The doc studied Katie's eyes with a penlight. Inspected the cut at her hairline. Felt her abdomen.

"Any pain here?" he asked.

Katie shook her head. He checked some other spots. When he was satisfied, he asked: "Headache?"

"Better."

"Vision still blurry?"

"No, it's good."

He put on his stern face. "You still need lots of rest, Miss Moreau. But do you want to get out of here?"

Katie smiled. "Yes, please."

"Let's make that happen. Give me about forty minutes."

True to form, he was gone before they could thank him. If

he'd been a cartoon, there would have been a swirling cloud of dust in his wake.

"So, that happened." Katie said.

"Yeah," Ren laughed.

Ren watched her have the same thought, but Katie voiced it first: "Now what?"

Her stranger's last words returned with a fresh surge of grief. *Go home.*

Mary had told her the same thing in a different way, but Ren hadn't been ready to hear it. Behind the forest-green door with the brass knocker would be a cup of hot chocolate and a soft bed, but it wouldn't come cheap. Pride would need to be swallowed. Conversations would have to happen, tough ones, likely involving tears and apologies. But not confessions. Her mother wasn't entitled to those. Those she would take to the grave.

In the end, it was Katie who tipped the scale. Not because of anything she said; because of what she'd done—burned every one of her own options to save Ren on that cold, dangerous night.

It was time to repay the debt.

"I'm taking you home. We're going to see my mom."

\* \* \*

As the rideshare rolled to a stop in front of the house, Ren caught the flicker of the gas porch lamps in the early afternoon sun. Her mother had never said so, but Ren knew she left them burning for her daughter, a beacon in the darkness if she were ever inclined to look for one.

"We're here?" Katie asked, as if surprised the trip hadn't taken longer.

"Yep."

Ren hauled Katie's duffel up the steps as the girl limped behind, her knee still torqued from the crash. She pulled the key on her neck chain until the steel ball clasp let go, then slid it into the lock. Faint scratching sounds, followed by a couple of tentative yelps, reverberated through the door. She smiled. It was Jack, the furry little early-warning system. Until that moment, she hadn't known he was still alive.

Katie touched Ren's arm. "Hey, don't you want to knock?"

"It's okay. Mom will be at work."

"What does she do?"

"English professor," Ren said, and pushed inside. The dog ran toward her as fast as his legs would carry him, tail wagging so hard it shook his whole body. Ren dropped the duffel and scooped him up. He squeaked and slurped her face, and Katie rubbed his ears.

"Hello, Jack. I missed you too," she said, then set the old boy down gently.

The wood floors creaked as Ren passed the bookshelf-filled study off the entry, redolent with the smell of paper and ink—rich and earthy, not musty like a basement. It was a scent she'd almost forgotten. If there had been any books in the places she'd chosen to crash, they'd long since been burned in a fireplace to keep warm when someone forgot to pay the electric bill.

She pressed on until she realized Katie wasn't following. The girl was admiring the study, though it wasn't the books that had captured her attention. She crossed the threshold and took a small brass frame from the shelf, a photo of Ren and her parents at a petting zoo. A baby lamb ate kibble from her dad's hand while Ren bashfully patted the top of its head.

Katie fixed her in a withering stare, a look she'd never expected from such kind eyes. "Why did you run away?" Her voice had a bitter edge and there was a question within the question: *Just how fucking spoiled and ungrateful are you?*

Ren understood Katie's anger instantly, and it was so justified she had to stop herself from apologizing to the girl on the spot. Katie's family was gone. Ripped from her, through no choice or fault of her own. Ren's had been here all along, not four miles from the hospital they'd just left. And she'd flushed it down the toilet.

It was unforgivable.

Ren's teeth clenched and her eyes swelled with tears. "I can barely remember," she said, which was true, but rang in her ears as hollow and flippant.

"No," Katie shook her head. "No, you need to do better than that. This place is warm. There's love here. Why did you run away?"

Something in Katie's voice pierced Ren's armor and brought clarity to the situation. If this relationship was to have a future, she had to open up, even if doing so eliminated all doubt about the ugliness inside.

She was probably screwed either way.

Jack looked up at her with bright eyes as if to say, *yeah, I'd like to hear this, too.*

"Let's go upstairs, okay? We can sit down. I'll tell you whatever you want to know," she said, which was sort of a lie, but would do for now. She wouldn't actually lie to Katie, but telling the whole truth was something else entirely. She bit her lip and waited, fully expecting Katie to call another Uber, but after a minute, the girl relented.

Ren fixed two glasses of ice water in the kitchen and led them upstairs. Katie's short, stiff bursts of breath suggested the climb was a challenge, but the girl didn't complain. Jack darted ahead, eager to lead once he knew where they were going. When they reached her bedroom, he flopped onto the carpet and inspected his nether regions.

The room was exactly how Ren had left it, mostly bare, except for the few cheerful childhood relics she never could bring herself to purge: the stuffed rhino her mom had named Renoceros, a squat pine shelf with a series of *Choose Your Own Adventures* among other vintage book-fair titles, and her dad's Eagles football pennant thumb-tacked to the wall. The sight of it sent a tremor through her heart.

They each claimed a twin bed and set their waters on the nightstand between them. Ren's mom had bought the second bed when Ren was twelve, as if having only one was why she had no friends close enough to sleep over.

"So? Talk," Katie said.

Ren's parched throat ached and the ice water beckoned, but she wouldn't allow herself relief until Katie was satisfied.

"The truth is, I threatened to run away all the time. It didn't matter what it was about. If I didn't like what mom cooked for dinner, I'd disappear up the block for a few hours just to make a point. It was ridiculous. One night we blew up over some high-school bullshit. Probably my grades, I honestly don't re-member. But I finally did it. I ran away for real. Because deep down I knew I was the problem, not her. I was doing her a favor. Giving her a well-deserved vacation from the asshole living under her roof. It was hard, but it became a matter of pride. Principle. I was doing fine all by myself, thank you. Of course I wasn't. All my pride, all my principle… after weeks—months—it turned to pain. I used whatever I could to make it go away. And after a while, the world just got blurry. That's when you found me. Lucky you."

Katie was inscrutable, her thirst for knowledge clearly not yet quenched. "What about your dad?" she asked.

"They divorced when I was ten. He died last year."

Two hundred ninety-seven days ago, to be more accurate.

"I'm sorry," Katie said. "He must have been young. How did he die?"

"He was a detective. He was killed by a suspect he was investigating." This answer was both well-rehearsed and true. And most importantly, nobody ever asked who the suspect was.

"Were you close?"

"Not really," she said, though they'd been pretty much inseparable when she was little. It was only after the divorce that they became toxic for each other.

No, that wasn't true. She stopped her own train of thought long enough to admit she'd been the toxic one. "I was sort of the reason they split."

"Oh, come on," Katie chided. "Every kid thinks their folks divorced because of them."

"It happens sometimes. It's probably impossible for you to imagine, but I was difficult."

"Yeah, not impossible. At all."

Had Katie just suppressed a smile? Maybe the ice was thawing.

"For real, though, I was a shit. And all they did was fight about how to fix me."

"What was wrong with you?"

"Depression, mostly. A couple shrinks said I had ADD. One

guy said I had ODD, but he was a dickhead. Mom was willing to try whatever—different meds, a private school. One time, she took me to a hypnotherapist."

"A what?"

"They hypnotize you and take you back through your past to see when you got screwed up."

"And? When did you get screwed up?"

"I don't know. The guy never could hypnotize me."

"Probably because you're a brat."

"I think the word you're looking for is 'headstrong.'"

"Let's settle on stubborn. So, your mom tried lots of things, what about your dad?"

"He mostly thought I should be in a padded room. You can see how their approaches were discordant."

"Nice vocab! Remind me not to play Scrabble with the professor's kid," Katie smiled and Ren's whole body unclenched. "Anyway, your ma sounds pretty cool."

Ren took a sip of water and grudgingly admitted to herself that Professor Cole could have been a lot worse.

"Does she know you're alive?" Katie asked.

"Yeah," Ren said, but didn't elaborate. During her time away, she got a message through every couple of weeks. Her determination to strike out on her own had been fierce, but she never let her mom wonder if she was dead. Ren was many things, but she was not cruel.

"She'll give you another chance," Katie said, with a confidence Ren couldn't match.

"If nothing else, she'll fix us hot chocolate before she kicks us out. She thinks it cures everything."

Katie yawned and Ren was reminded they'd been going nonstop since Dr. Prasad's whirlwind visit that morning. She stood and said, "You need to sleep."

"Ugh, I've been sleeping for days. I'm over it," Katie complained, but Ren knew her heart wasn't in it. She moved to the door and turned off the lights, but Katie stopped her. "Hey?"

"Yeah?"

"I'm sorry for what you've been through. Thank you for being honest with me."

Ren wished she could bask in the warmth of Katie's acknowledgment, but she'd never felt like more of a fraud. If she were honest about everything, Katie would run so fast her head would spin. "Need anything?" Ren asked.

Katie shook her head. "What happens when your mom comes home and finds a strange woman in your bed?"

"Wouldn't be the first time," Ren said, and twirled out the door.

# THE DANCER

TO AVOID THE potential awkwardness of her mother discovering Katie in her bed, Ren decided they should move to the kitchen around the time the professor normally got home. They sat at the table, where a book of *New York Times* crosswords inked in her mother's tidy uppercase script lay open to a half-finished puzzle, and Ren had to smile because some things never changed.

Katie eagerly worked the clues, but Ren was too distracted to be of much help. Though she hoped the reunion with her mother would be a joyful one, her anxiety had steadily increased throughout the afternoon as she braced herself for the possibility it would not.

Twenty minutes later, Jack grunted, got to his feet, and trotted to the front. A car door slammed and Ren's stomach dropped.

It occurred to her that her sudden reappearance in her mother's life—let alone Katie being there—might scare the shit out of the woman, and as the key hit the lock, she regretted not thinking more about how to stage themselves to minimize the shock factor.

The door opened, then closed. Jack's paws skittered on the hardwood.

"Hey, buddy," her mother said.

And then she swept into the kitchen with an armful of groceries in an eco-friendly cloth bag and stopped short at the sight of the girls at her table.

The gravity of the moment hung in the air like a glass knocked off a countertop.

The bag slid from her grasp, spilling a pile of reddish-gold apples onto the tile floor, and Ren knew her mother had at least recognized her.

Ren searched her face for relief, disbelief, rage… anything. All she found was love.

They walked slowly toward each other. Sarah Cole ran her fingers through her daughter's rough-chopped bottle-black hair. Ren guessed she was mourning the blond curls she used to brush and braid. Ren had always looked up into her mother's blue eyes, but they were now the same height. Sarah's thick, chestnut brows matched hers, but the age lines were deeper and the hair grayer than Ren remembered, no doubt from the worry she'd inflicted.

Ren added her mother's youth to the list of her victims as Sarah opened her arms and Ren threw herself into an embrace she'd missed more than she realized. Though she didn't want it to end, she finally released her mom, stepped back and gestured to the table.

"Mom, this is Katie."

"Hello, Katie," she said, blotting her eyes. "I'm Sarah."

Katie limped over and offered Ren's mom her uninjured hand to shake. "It's nice to meet you, Ms. Cole."

"No, please, just Sarah. What happened to you?"

The question was for Katie, but Ren intercepted it. "Long story."

"Believe me, I have time. You guys want hot chocolate?"

Ren shot Katie an *I told you so* glance. "Could we maybe eat dinner first?" she asked. "We're kinda starving."

Her mom handed the fallen grocery bag to Ren and said, "Put these in the fridge, will you?"

Ren did so as Katie gathered the renegade apples and set them in a wood bowl on the counter.

"Cheesesteaks?" her mom asked.

Jack's tail swished back and forth on the tile, keenly interested in the decision. Her mom's dog recognized a surprising number of food words, and that was one.

*Her mom's dog.*

Ren wondered if she'd ever think of him again as *her* dog. Or this place as *her* house. She couldn't allow herself the luxury of such a hope, but the possibility didn't seem as unlikely as it had a week ago.

Maybe—just maybe—this was going to be okay.

* * *

Ren ordered her steak sandwich with cheese sauce and no onions—whiz wit'out, per the local lingo—and Katie threw shade. In her opinion, provolone and onions was the only way to fly, and Ren's mom was no help as a tie-breaker. Ren had forgotten Sarah preferred chicken with bell peppers and no cheese. At least they all agreed on fries, in that drowning them in ketchup was disgusting. You had to keep it on the side and dip. Like a civilized person.

They ate heartily, but food took a backseat to the surprisingly easy conversation. Mostly, Sarah just wanted to know how the girls had met and how Katie had gotten hurt, so Ren gave her mother the sanitized, meet-cute version: Katie saw she was cold and had graciously offered her a hat. They'd hit it off, but had a wreck on the slick roads after leaving the party.

When they got home, her mom again offered hot chocolate. Katie politely refused, saying the Coles probably had lots of catching up to do, but Ren surprised her mom by declining as well.

"If it's okay, I'm pretty wiped," she said. "Tomorrow, maybe?"

Sarah studied her face and seemed to agree that rest would be more restorative and less risky than further dialog. "Of course, honey," she said, and Ren gave her a hug.

The girls readied themselves for an early bedtime in the hallway bathroom, scrubbing their faces and brushing their teeth at the side-by-side vanities. Ren was horrified to realize she looked like a goth hobbit in the flannel nightdress she'd borrowed from her mother, but Katie interrupted her thoughts.

"What are you singing?" she asked, smiling around her toothbrush.

Ren's eyes went wide. "I was singing?"

"Nerd." Katie spat her toothpaste and swallowed a couple of pain pills with a handful of water from the tap. She nestled into one of the twin beds and pulled the quilt to her chin as Ren turned off the light and crawled into the other. Jack parked himself at Katie's feet and snuffled. He was an excellent judge of character.

"That was impressive tonight," Katie said into the darkness.

Her voice felt far away and Ren stifled the urge to shove their beds together.

"What do you mean?"

"The two of you dancing around each other. You trying not to scare her. Her trying not to piss you off. It was a sight."

"Thanks for being a buffer. She was on her best behavior with you there."

"I think you underestimate your mom," Katie said. "But also I think you were amazing. I'm proud of you."

Ren's throat closed up, her voice froggy. "You can stay as long as you need to, okay? No matter what happens with me and my mom. If I, like, screw it up, or whatever. She won't take it out on you. She's not that kind of person."

"Thanks. But you won't screw it up."

"My track record suggests otherwise. Anyway, let's talk about something else."

"Like what?" Katie asked.

"Tell me something about you."

"Like what?" she said again, but this time it seemed like a guard had gone up.

"I don't know, do you have a job or anything?"

"Honestly, I'm not sure. I operate a forklift at a warehouse, but I can't work the controls with a sprained hand."

"Seriously?" Katie's answer could not have been further from what Ren expected. She was still convinced the girl was an artist.

"Seriously."

"Do they know you're, like, a terrible driver?"

Katie laughed and chucked her spare pillow at Ren. "*Espèce de petite morveuse.*"

The soft language rendered in Katie's rich voice was both endearing and incredibly sexy, but an image entered Ren's mind that stabbed at her heart. It was the woman from the scrapbook photo, and Ren was suddenly sure that every time Katie slipped into French, she was channeling her mother's memory.

"Did your mom call you that?" Ren asked and felt Katie's breath catch in the darkness.

"Yeah, she did," Katie said after a moment.

"Will you tell me about her?"

"She was smart. And funny. And brave. And beautiful. She worked for some multinational company. I don't even know what she did, really, but she should have been a singer. That's how she met my dad. He was studying abroad in her hometown near Avignon and he went into a jazz club for a drink. It was open-mic night, and she'd finally worked up the courage to sing in front of a crowd. She had him from the first note."

Ren could picture it perfectly. A crowded bar, thick with cigarette smoke. Lights gleaming off a glossy black piano as a time-worn man in a silk vest coaxed a sultry tune from the keys. A handsome, wavy-haired student nursing a glass of whiskey at a small, round table near the stage. His warm smile boosting her confidence as she settled into her song.

"*Japon et Avignon*," Katie said, interrupting Ren's imaginings. "That's what they used to call me."

"*Japon et Avignon*," Ren pronounced carefully, turning the phrase over in her mind as if each heritage were stamped on opposite sides of a gold coin. Then she realized Katie was that gold coin, mistakenly deposited in a piggy bank full of dirty copper pennies. She should be studying at the Louvre, not operating heavy machinery in some shitty warehouse.

Ren thought again of the scrapbook photo and every opportunity the universe had stolen from this sweet girl. And she decided that whatever happened between them, she would not be the one to leave.

# THE LIAR

THE INTOXICATING AROMA of dark-roast led Ren downstairs to find her mom at the kitchen table finishing the puzzle the girls had played at the day before. Sarah smiled at her approach.

"There's coffee," she said, and Ren poured herself a mug, along with a splash of half-and-half from the fridge. Only the real stuff was permitted in the Cole house, not "that powdery shit," as her mom liked to call it.

Ren was relieved to have caught Sarah before work. Not that she had any agenda, but she knew rebuilding their relationship was something to be done in small bursts. Quick, pleasant interactions that didn't risk broaching serious topics.

This was going to be a challenge, because she also knew any conversation they had wouldn't be the one her mom really wanted. That version would cover every detail of Ren's time on the streets, starting thirty seconds after their final dinner-table blow-up. It would take hours and would, by necessity, include the story of Alistair and how she'd killed her dad.

So, yeah, that one wasn't happening. But Ren hoped they could remain on safe ground while they enjoyed their coffee. Her mom likely had the same instinct, because she said, "Weak. Six letters—starts with 'A.'"

There was no way Sarah didn't already know the answer, but Ren played along. "Anemic."

"Nice," Sarah said, and filled it in. Her eyes scanned the list of clues. "Disaster. Eight letters—starts with 'C.'"

"Catastrophe," Ren said, trying to keep a straight face. To Sarah, the Sunday *Times* puzzle was no laughing matter, but Ren couldn't resist teasing her.

Her mom gave her a side-eye. "Eight letters."

"Clusterfuck."

"Eight!"

"Cataclysm."

"Did you forget how to count?"

"Wouldn't that be a calamity if I had?"

Sarah groaned and wrote in the correct answer, then seemed to hesitate before offering up another clue. Ren took the opportunity to steer the conversation.

"You still seeing that chem professor?"

At that, her mom's forehead wrinkled into the expression Ren most strongly associated with her. "Haven't talked to him in a while."

"What was his name? Gary?"

"Uh-huh."

"I forget, does he have kids?"

Her mom laid the book and the pen on the table and Ren knew that despite her best effort, she'd managed to step in it.

"Jesus, Ren, you show up here with nothing but the clothes

on your back after... what, almost two years? With this girl you've just met, who's all beat up? I want to talk to you more than you can possibly imagine, but we are not going to sit here and talk about my love life. Or lack thereof."

"Right," Ren said, swiping an errant coffee ground from the rim of her mug. That was fair.

Sarah studied her for a moment. "You're different," she said, as if it were a good thing. "I can't put my finger on it, but it's like you're... *you* again. What changed?"

"I feel different," Ren said, and if she could have offered any further explanation that made sense—even if only to herself— she would have. But at the moment, her life was a bewildering blur, and words failed her. She cast her eyes down, discouraged, which only made Sarah push harder.

"Ren, what are you doing here?"

She could feel it going off the rails, and she cursed herself for not just staying in bed. How could she tell her mom that she came home because an ethereal stranger told her to? Sarah would think she was on drugs, and with only four days sober, Ren couldn't really argue otherwise. She tried one last ditch effort to evade.

"I still *technically* live here, don't I?"

Sarah wasn't having it. "Damn it, girl. You know what I'm asking. Why did you come home? Why now?" she demanded. "What happened?"

Ren's pulse pounded in her ears as she flashed back on a life-time of fights just like this, with her mom demanding she answer for something she couldn't adequately explain. And though this type of grilling would always pull her trigger and send her shooting out the door, she desperately wanted to break that pattern. Something told her it was important to, and before she realized it, she'd blurted, "She told me to come home."

"Who, Katie?"

"No... never mind, it doesn't matter."

"Yes it does! Tell me who told you, if only so I can find her and thank her."

"I don't know! I don't know who she is."

Sarah leaned back in her chair and crossed her arms, skepticism chiseled on her face. "You don't know who she is, but she's convincing enough to get you back here after two years? Now I *really* want to meet her."

"I don't think you can."

"Why not?"

"Because I think something bad happened to her."

Whatever Ren might have expected to hear in that moment, she didn't. Instead, Sarah sat in silence, giving Ren the odd sense her mom was searching for something inside herself, not inside her daughter.

Finally, Sarah said, "Tell me about her."

Ren drew and exhaled a long breath, certain that what she said next would have her mother demanding she be drug-tested immediately.

"Oh, this is going to sound so crazy," she muttered. "Okay. She's a Black woman. Older than me, younger than you. I saw her three times. And I heard her voice—in my head—a bunch of other times. And nobody else has. So either I've lost my mind, or she's some kind of ghost, or she's a real person and..."

"And what?"

Ren didn't really know where she was going with that. "And that's all I know."

Sarah frowned reflectively. "I see."

"You see? And?"

"And nothing. I was just... acknowledging what you said."

Sarah subtly flexed the tendons in her neck, dropping the corners of her mouth. It was her biggest tell, and Ren jumped on it. "No! Bullshit! You did the thing just now."

"What thing?"

"The neck thing. There's something you don't want to say." Ren waited until the silence became unbearable, then asked, "Do you believe me?"

Her mother nodded. That was unexpected.

"You don't think I'm, like, losing it?"

Sarah didn't answer right away, and the idea she was choosing her words carefully was unnerving. Finally she said, "I think maybe you've always had a connection to things outside of yourself."

"What does that mean?"

The woman looked everywhere but Ren's eyes, and when she spoke again, her voice was hoarse, barely above a whisper. "Part of being a parent is protecting your kid from danger. Obviously. Most times, it's physical, but sometimes it's psychological. When you have information, but you have no clue whether sharing it with your kid is going to help or hurt. So you have to trust your gut. And sometimes, you're going to get it wrong. You'll have all the right intentions, but you'll be wrong."

"Mom, what are you talking about?"

"The day the light died."

Ren's ears rang like a clock-tower bell. "How do you know about that?"

"Don't you think I would remember every second of the day

when my joyful little dynamo of a daughter became a dark, sullen shell of herself?"

"Please tell me, please tell me," Ren said, tears pouring out.

Sarah extended a trembling hand and clutched one of Ren's. "It was two weeks after your sixth birthday. We were at the playground with the big orange slides. You were on top of the tallest jungle gym, and I did my crossword because I had nothing to worry about. None of the other kids could climb as high as you. You were my little acrobat, and you were completely fearless. We needed to leave soon, so I gave you a five-minute warning. You gave me a thumbs-up, and I went back to my puzzle. The next thing I knew, you were running around the playground, frantic. You were chasing after every kid there, scaring them and scaring their parents. I finally grabbed you by the arms and asked you what was wrong. You couldn't get words out. You were crying and panicked and hyperventilating and so I took you home. And that's when you started to shut down."

Ren was speechless. She had no memory of this trauma, but her soul knew it was the truth.

"Do you remember when we went to see Dr. Wise?" her mom asked.

"Kind of. Nothing happened. He never could put me into a trance, right?"

Her mom stared.

"Right?" Ren repeated, her voice breaking.

"No, that's not right. Baby, there's no nice way to say this… we lied to you. We told you hypnosis didn't work. But it did work. When you were under, you told us about that day at the playground. You said there was a girl you were looking for, but couldn't find. You said she was your person. The one you were supposed to be with this time. But something went wrong because of the train. You kept saying 'because of the train.' Your dad checked reports of train incidents around that time, and he found it. A six-year-old girl fell in front of the Blue line at Eighth Street, the same day we were at the playground."

Ren tried to take it all in, but it was like drinking from a fire hose. Her mind raced to assemble a picture of that fateful day, but despite her mom's vivid recounting of the events, she could only string together a handful of hazy, choppy images. The memory remained stubbornly outside her grasp.

"We didn't know what to do, what it meant—if it even meant anything—or if it was some wild coincidence. Your dad wanted to tell you. He always believed it would help you heal. He even wanted to take you to meet the girl's mother. But I wouldn't let him. You were so young. And I was too afraid of what it would do to you. Now I think maybe I was wrong. I'm so sorry, baby," she sobbed. "I'm so sorry. Please forgive me."

Ren pressed her mom's warm hand against her wet cheek, the goat-milk scent a primal reminder of the comfort she'd so thoughtlessly forsaken. "Thank you for telling me the truth," she said after a while. "But what am I supposed to do with this?"

"Don't thank me," her mother said, drying Ren's tears with the soft sleeve of her sweatshirt before tending to her own. "I stole your chance to know your own truth twelve years ago, so the last thing you need to do is thank me. You need to find that woman. Or find out what happened to her."

"How? I don't even know her name."

Sarah brushed off her feeble excuses. "Figure it out. Follow it wherever it takes you. I'll help you however I can. I owe you that much."

Her mother was the last person in the world that owed her anything. The debt would always be on Ren's side of the balance sheet. But to be believed in that moment—to be trusted and empowered by the woman with whom she'd battled for so long—was maybe the best feeling she ever had.

If only she knew where to start looking.

# THE OFFENDER

SARAH LEFT FOR work shortly after their conversation, but not before Ren got her to confirm that Katie could stay as long as she needed to. She didn't want to assume her mom was okay with it, and was thrilled by the response. After a shower to clear her head, Ren found the girl awake and attempting some stretches in bed. Jack—who had not left her side—was cramping her mobility, and Katie was too much of a softy to shove his fuzzy butt out of the way.

"How'd you sleep?" Ren asked.

"Great," Katie replied.

"Black, right?" Ren handed her a cup.

Katie sat up and accepted the coffee with a smile. "You remembered. Thanks."

Ren scratched Jack's neck. "I was thinking about taking this little monster for a walk. Care to join?"

"For sure," Katie said, though Ren wasn't sure if the girl actually enjoyed her company or just craved exercise. She'd heard that was a thing, but had never experienced it.

Katie kneeled to dig through her duffel bag for clothes, but Ren had a better idea. She took the bag and set it on the bed.

"Let's hang them up," she said.

The two worked together to move the items into Ren's closet, which lent a permanence to Katie's presence that made the entire house warmer. The girl dressed in jeans, an orange parka and a gray baseball cap, and looked cool as hell. Ren, who'd grown taller and wider since leaving home, had to scavenge from her own closet and her mother's to assemble a passable cold-weather outfit, and she couldn't help feeling like she still looked unhoused.

With Jack sniffing and scouting ahead, Ren gave Katie the lowdown on the neighborhood: a bike crash on this corner, an incurable hoarder over there, Mrs. Donovan who always had salt-water taffy, the convenience store that burned down, then was rebuilt and burned again. It was a good neighborhood; upper-middle class, pleasant and safe. Compared to where Ren had spent the last two years, it was paradise, and she was happy to be walking its streets once again.

The dog relieved himself on a retaining wall and they moved on, turning the second corner of the large square that would eventually deposit them back at her mom's house. Katie was commenting on how the sun had finally broken through the clouds when Ren stopped short, her breath shallow and uncertain. Jack got skittish and squeaked.

The playground was across the street.

Without meaning to, Ren had chosen a route that took them directly past it, and now that she was there, the surroundings were familiar. East of the tot lot was a line of houses adorned with Greek letters. Blue-and-gold Drexel University banners hung from streetlights, and scraggly oak trees along the north edge waged an aerial turf war with power lines.

As for the playground itself, Ren wondered if it had been refurbished, because the equipment was not as her mom had described. The orange slides were still there, but there was no tall jungle gym. Everything was shorter, more plastic, less rusty than Ren had pictured. Undoubtedly safer than it used to be, but the daredevil daughter her mom recalled would have found it quite boring.

Jack tugged at his leash so hard Ren finally scooped him up and held him. The little guy was done with this place and wasn't being subtle about it. A city bus released its brakes with a pneumatic hiss and rumbled away, leaving a cloud of sooty smoke and an unsettling silence.

"Hey, everything okay?" Katie asked.

"I used to play over there."

"Lots of memories?"

Ren shook her head. "That's the thing. I talked to my mom this morning. She said I had some kind of freak-out there when I was little, but I don't remember it at all."

Katie looked confused. "Two years gone and that's what you talked about? Some tantrum you threw when you were a kid?"

"I know, I'm a brat," Ren said, anticipating the jab. Katie laughed, but Ren wasn't in a joking mood.

"What is it?" Katie asked.

In truth, she didn't know, but one thing was certain: she didn't want to carry the secret of her stranger any longer. Maintaining the filter on her thoughts and words was exhausting, and she had enough other secrets to last a lifetime. Her mom had believed her; maybe Katie would too. And if not, surely it was better to know now, before her attachment to this girl grew even stronger.

"There's something I need to tell you," Ren said. "But not here."

* * *

Ren sat Katie on the living-room couch with a wool blanket, then turned on the gas fireplace to warm her butt. The hesitation she'd felt before sharing this with her mother was gone. Ren knew she wasn't irrational, and if Katie didn't believe her, so be it.

"The night we met—before you found me—someone else was with me on that roof. She knew who I was. I saw her and then she disappeared."

Katie's unease grew as Ren described each subsequent encounter with her mysterious stranger. To this point, the girl had seemed to accept Ren was sort of troubled, but what she was hearing now blew way past troubled and landed squarely on delusional.

"Have you had hallucinations before?" Katie asked.

"It wasn't a hallucination."

"I'm sorry, I'm not saying it was." Katie kept a level tone. "I'm asking if anything like this has happened to you before."

"I don't think so," Ren said, but then she thought about the little girl and the train. Maybe it had happened before.

"You were on something, right?" Katie asked.

"It wasn't the drugs," Ren said, unable to suppress her irritation.

"I'm just saying, E can make you see things. How can you be sure?"

"Did you take anything?"

"No," Katie said, a little self-righteously, and Ren immediately wanted to throttle herself. Of course Katie hadn't taken anything. She'd been pregnant.

"Right. Sorry. But let me ask you this: do you think the girl in the road was a hallucination?"

The question surprised Katie, as if she hadn't thought about it since. "I don't know," she said at last. "She seemed real. I mean, we both saw her, right?"

"Yeah, we did. And I know you didn't see the woman on the roof, but she felt just as real to me. More, even."

"Sit with me," Katie said, taking Ren's hands after she flopped onto the couch. The gesture was comforting and surprisingly intimate, and Ren had to look away. "I believe you, okay? At least I believe it's real to you. I guess my question is, why are you telling me?"

She forced herself to meet Katie's eyes. "Because I need you to draw her for me."

The air changed, like a vacuum had sucked it from the room. Katie paled and Ren scrambled to explain, "You know, like cops do, when there's a witness. You're an artist, right?"

Katie gaped at her. "How do you..." was all she could manage, and Ren remembered the thing about Katie's pregnancy, fearing she'd again overstepped a boundary she didn't know existed.

After a minute, Katie regained her composure enough to explain she was not, in fact, an artist. Or rather, hadn't been since she was a kid. But when she was young, it was all she did, filling whole notebooks with drawings, paintings and anime. She found solace in art when her mother and sister died, and her grief lifted her work to new heights. She made something for her dad every day until his walls and drawers overflowed with paper, but she stopped being an artist the day he went away. Abandoning her passion was not a conscious choice, and until Ren brought it up, she'd forgotten it was what she used to do.

Ren could not imagine the shame of having someone peer inside her soul the way she'd just violated Katie's.

"I'm so sorry," she said. "The last thing I wanted was to upset you. I don't know where this is coming from. Please forget I asked."

"It's okay," Katie said. "I think I need to do this."

"Are you sure?"

Katie nodded.

Ren ached for her friend, but didn't want to dawdle and risk her changing her mind. This was too important. She disappeared to her mom's study, returning a minute later with a stack of white laser-printer paper and an assortment of pencils and markers.

Katie studied the sad implements, then selected a thick black pencil with a glossy triangular barrel. She rolled it on her fingertips as if judging its weight and balance. She apparently decided it would suffice, because she braced a sheet of paper on a coffee-table book in her lap and looked to Ren for direction.

Ren closed her eyes and visualized her stranger. "Her face is heart-shaped," she began. "Chin not too pointy."

When Katie finished the portrait, she gave it over. Ren held it delicately, like it would crumble to dust if mishandled. She scanned the page, absorbing every detail and nuance of the remarkable image.

And then it hit her.

She laid the drawing on the table, grabbed a fat magic

marker in her fist and scribbled violently back and forth. Katie gasped at the defacement, but Ren knew what she was doing.

She was adding locs.

Ren looked at the shocked artist and whispered, "I know who she is."

\* \* \*

It was the mask that had captured her attention.

There was something familiar about it. Not like she'd seen it before; like she'd worn it before. Dark ebony carved into a wide, flat face with a long skinny nose, a widow's-peak hairline and two cross shapes adorning the cheeks. The plaque said it originated from Nigeria, early- to mid-twentieth century.

To a nine-year-old girl, that was ancient.

And it was practically the only thing Ren had noticed the entire trip.

Her parents were still together. They tried their best to fake it, but she could always sense the tension underneath. Her dad figured a fall-break getaway might lift their spirits, as if a few nights in a hotel, some room-service chicken fingers, and a tiresome slog through the many "attractions" of the nation's capital would fix what was broken. By day three, Ren was so disconnected she didn't even know where they were; some art museum or another. As her mom and dad rehashed their tired argument a few paces ahead, the Nigerian relic in the next gallery caught her eye.

She had no clue how long she'd been staring at the mask before someone behind her loudly cleared his throat and asked, "Young lady, are you lost?"

She practically jumped out of her skin. The voice belonged

to a pasty security guard. Her parents were nowhere in sight and a retractable "This Area Closed" strap had been pulled across the gallery entrance.

"This section of the museum is closed," the guard said, like she'd gravely offended the museum gods. "You're not allowed to be here right now. I'm going to have to make a report of this. You'll need to come with me to my office."

He sounded stern but also sort of excited, like he'd caught a big fish. Clammy sausage fingers swallowed her hand. He led her to the entrance and unhooked the barrier strap, but as they passed by, he didn't reattach it.

The walk through the next gallery seemed endless. Every step ratcheted her dread of his office and whatever report he intended to write about her. She hung her head, watching her blue Mary Janes glide across the polished concrete and saying silent prayers that her parents would come find her.

His grip tightened, pinching off her pleas. She glanced up from her shoes.

Someone was approaching.

It was a beautiful young Black woman with a spray of locs, a backpack slung over one shoulder and a colorful t-shirt that said Morcheeba, whatever that was. Her eyes were warm and brown and full of love, and when they met Ren's, they flared. The woman clutched her chest like the wind had been knocked out of her, but recovered quickly.

The guard sped up, trying to avoid the interloper, but the woman had other ideas.

"Oh, sweetie, there you are," she called out. "I was so worried about you!" Then, to the guard, she said, "Thank you so much, sir. I hope she wasn't any trouble."

His voice was hoarse and trembling, which was odd because Ren was supposed to be the terrified one.

"No, she was... fine," he stammered. "I was just... you all have a nice day, now."

He dropped Ren's hand and kept walking.

The woman kneeled to her eye level and asked, "Are you okay?"

"Yeah."

"Did you get lost?"

"I found a mask," Ren said, as if that explained everything.

"I've been coming here a long time," the woman said. "And that guard has been working here a long time. And he kind of gives me the creeps."

"Yeah."

"My name is Lailah. What's your name, baby girl?"

"Lauren Ann Cole."

"Well, Miss Lauren, shall we go and find your people?"

Lailah took her hand and escorted her through the gallery. It wasn't long before Ren spotted her parents, still walking, still arguing.

"That's them," she said, pointing.

Lailah exhaled. "Okay, good. You be careful now. No more wandering off."

Ren nodded and started away, but then she changed her mind, ran back to Lailah and tapped her arm. Lailah turned and beamed a smile.

"Hello again, Lauren!"

Without a word, Ren removed the friendship bracelet she'd made from yellow and black yarn at Palomino Day Camp last summer and offered it to her rescuer.

Lailah accepted the humble gift and slid it on her left wrist as the little lost girl turned on her heel and rejoined her parents, who never knew she'd been gone.

# THE SEARCHER

REN CURLED INTO a ball and wept.

She wept for the belated realization of the hell Lailah had saved her from. For being so self-involved, she hadn't even remembered who Lailah was. For the gratitude she'd probably never have the chance to express. And perhaps most of all, for being utterly undeserving of a guardian angel.

Except—and that was the thing Ren couldn't wrap her mind around—Lailah wasn't an angel. She wasn't an apparition. Not then, anyway. She was real. The guard had seen her. Talked to her. She'd held Ren's hand. Kept her silly bracelet.

Ren trembled under the weight of her bewilderment, and Katie tried to hold her. "No," she moaned, but Katie wrapped her even tighter. She wanted to kick and squirm and fight and shove away every good and loving thing, but deep down she knew when she was beaten. Her friend refused to let her suffer alone.

Fucking Katie.

When Ren finally stopped shaking, Katie brushed a stray curl from her sweaty forehead and asked, "Who is she?"

"Her name is Lailah. I need to find her."

Katie shook her head. "*We* need to find her."

\* \* \*

Calm prevailed after a while, and it occurred to them they hadn't eaten all day. Ren's frazzled nerves sapped her hunger, but Katie was famished and wasn't supposed to take pain meds on an empty stomach. Sarah's fridge was bare, so they headed back into the neighborhood for some street-truck tacos. When Ren smelled the grilled meat, her appetite returned with a vengeance and she couldn't refuse Katie's offer to treat.

They brought their food to the study, and Ren motioned for Katie to sit at the computer desk. Ren dragged over a second chair and settled in for what she expected would be a pointless, needle-in-a-haystack waste of time.

"You want to drive, or should I?" Katie asked.

"I don't know, can you drive a Mac better than you drive a car?"

"Oh, shut up," Katie said. She wiggled the mouse and woke the screen to a browser window. The cursor blinked in the search bar and she looked to Ren for guidance.

"I don't think she's alive," Ren said.

Katie nodded somberly, cracked her knuckles and typed the words "Lailah death 2024."

It took about two seconds.

Three hits down from the top was a story from that morning's *Washington Post*: "Prominent DC Attorney Dead at 35."

Ren's heart dropped into her stomach.

Katie clicked the link and the face of Ren's stranger stared back from the monitor.

The resemblance to Katie's sketch was uncanny.

Her name was Lailah Duncan. She was a partner at a law firm called Duncan & Holland. She was a respected attorney, philanthropist, and champion of the under-represented.

And she was found dead in her office Monday evening. Of a drug overdose.

Ren immediately regretted eating. The chimichurri sauce climbed her throat like battery acid and she made a noise somewhere between a gurgle and a wail.

An overdose?

"Bullshit," she whispered. "Bullshit. Bullshit. Bullshit."

Ren lost herself in the picture, studying every detail. Lailah's eyes, her hair, her clothes, her smile. Ren's impression from the rooftop had been dead-on: she *was* a boss. And not only because her name was in the firm's name. It was how she carried herself. Her poise. Her confidence. Ren felt it every time Lailah spoke to her; she was cool, comforting and totally in charge.

Time flew by as they searched and scanned dozens of other links referencing Lailah, all of which were a variant of the same origin story: a small-time attorney rose to prominence after winning a huge judgment against environmental polluters in a class-action suit nobody else would take on.

Most of the articles were riddled with clichés: it was a "David and Goliath" case; Lailah was a "rising star" and "one to watch." Her name topped a handful of vapid "40 under 40" lists. A few stories rewarded them with extra tidbits: Lailah grew up poor in North Philly, raised by a single mom, attended Penn undergrad and Georgetown Law on scholarship, donated her time to take on and win some high-profile death-row appeals.

When subsequent links only rehashed the same tired information, they sat back from the screen to digest what they'd learned, which felt like nothing. Ren's skull was pounding, her neck and shoulder muscles tight as a drum.

"We're missing something," she said, replaying every interaction in her mind until Lailah's last words echoed once again.

*Go home.*

"Home page," Ren thought out loud. "Can you go to the website of her law firm?"

Katie navigated to Duncan & Holland's home page, then clicked the "About Us" link.

Lailah's bio appeared first, though Ren had already memorized it. From all the hype about her success, Ren assumed she was at the helm of a huge firm, but her partner, Peter Holland, was the only other lawyer listed. His blurb said he also grew up in Philly and attended the same schools a few years ahead of Lailah.

The only photo on the page was a candid snapshot of the two, obviously from when they were younger. Peter was tall and skinny, with tousled blond hair and a patchy beard. Lailah sported the cool locs Ren remembered from the museum. The picture was taken at the bottom of what Ren thought might be the steep, creepy stairs from *The Exorcist*, and the two were laughing and poking at each other, like siblings.

The image captured so much love, it practically burst from the screen. This law firm was a family, and Peter Holland had lost more than a partner.

More like a little sister.

Ren needed to know more—about Lailah, about Peter, about herself. And she needed to know now.

Somehow, Katie knew that.

Ren's mom was like the last person in America who still had a landline phone, probably in case her daughter needed to call.

Katie put it on speaker and dialed the firm's number. They held their breath. Then realized it was seven-thirty at night.

There was no answer.

* * *

Ren did not intend to exclude Katie from the investigation the next morning, but the still-healing girl was fast asleep, and Ren couldn't bear to wake her up. Her mom had already gone to work, but she'd left a pot of coffee ready to brew with a sticky note on the basket that said, "Love you, Renoceros." All she had to do was flip the switch. The hot liquid hit her throat, her brain came alive, and she returned to the study with renewed determination.

She grabbed the cordless off the charger and dialed.

With no other employees listed on the firm's website, Ren assumed she'd reach Peter directly, but a woman answered in an old and tired voice, "Duncan and Holland."

Ren vapor-locked.

"Law office," the woman said. "May I help you?"

"Peter. I need to talk to Peter," Ren said, adding a "please" as an afterthought.

"He's unavailable at the moment. May I leave a message?"

Ren hadn't thought that far ahead, so she took a chance with the truth. "My name is Ren Cole. Peter, uh, he won't know me, but Lailah was my... friend."

"Is that right?" The woman sounded a little less tired. A noise fluttered in the background, like pages flipping in a book.

"Yes, ma'am," Ren answered, which may have been the first time in her life she'd called anyone "ma'am."

"What may I say this is regarding, Lauren?"

*Lauren.*

Her mind did cartwheels. "How did you know my name?"

"I'll ask again, what is this regarding?"

The old woman was clearly not messing around, so Ren cut to the chase. "The paper said Lailah overdosed. I don't believe it. I want to know what really happened."

The silence was so acute, Ren thought the call had dropped. When the woman spoke again, her voice was razor-sharp. "Young lady, I'm going to ask you a question. Your answer will determine whether I hang up this phone and we never speak again. Do you understand me?"

Ren's chest tightened. "Yes, ma'am."

"What color was the necklace you gave Lailah?"

In an instant, she was transported back to the museum, to their first meeting. It was a trick question. A test.

"It wasn't a necklace, it was a bracelet," Ren answered. "Black and yellow stripes. Like a bumblebee. She still has that?"

"She wore it every day. Except the day she died."

"Who are you?" Ren asked.

"My name is Nina Duncan. Lailah was my daughter. Tell me, child, did she ask you to call here?"

"No, I just... saw her. A few days ago. It's hard to explain."

"There's no need. I understand perfectly," Nina said, and Ren tingled with excitement that she'd found someone to answer any of the thousand questions overwhelming her brain.

"I'm glad you do, but I don't," Ren said, her voice rising. "Why is this happening? Why did she come to me?"

"I wish I had those answers for you, child. I surely do," Nina said, dashing Ren's hopes as quickly as they'd swelled. Her soft wisdom stood in stark contrast to Ren's youthful exasperation, but their voices shared the same anguish. This mother had lost her daughter and desperately needed to know why. "Miss Lauren, can you get here tonight? On the train?"

Before Ren could respond, Katie limped in to the office and clutched her shoulder as if to stop her spinning out of control. "What's wrong?" she whispered.

Ren froze, caught between the tortured woman on the phone and the one standing before her. And she wasn't sure she'd heard Nina correctly. "Tonight?" she asked. "Are you serious? To Washington? I can't leave! I have to take care of..." she trailed off, looking at Katie, who was studying her face for some clue to what this was all about.

"Miss Lauren, although the police have concluded otherwise, I think we both know Lailah was murdered." The word echoed down the line like a gunshot. "If she chose to spend some of her last moments on this earth with you, then—like it or not—you are connected to this. And that puts you in the crosshairs too. Now if you lay eyes on Peter and me and want no part, you can turn tail and go home. But you must promise me you'll come. And until we determine what is at play here, I urge you not to speak of this to anyone. For their safety and yours. Do you understand?"

Ren understood almost nothing, except the promise Nina asked her to make meant she had to break the one she'd made to herself two days ago. She would have to leave Katie.

*Follow it wherever it takes you.*

That's what her mom had said.

"God damn it," Ren said to nobody in particular.

"Child?" Nina's voice was urgent.

Ren slumped into the chair. "Okay. Whatever. I promise."

"You'll come?"

"Yes. Where?"

"Phone me again in one hour," Nina said, and ended the call. Ren stared at the handset a moment before returning it to the cradle, wondering what the hell she'd just signed up for.

Katie pounced. "What is going on?"

Ren trusted the girl as much as anyone she'd ever known, yet Nina's demand for secrecy made her stop herself from blurting everything. It was like whiplash.

"I'm so sorry. I can't tell you."

"You can't tell me? I have been there for you every step of the way, and now you can't tell me?" Katie was aghast, equal parts hurt and angry, and Ren knew she'd cut her friend to the bone.

Then she sprinkled salt on the wound.

"I have to go away tonight."

"To Washington?" Katie had caught one side of the conversation.

"I'll be back, I swear. Or maybe you can come to me after—"

Katie retreated and raised her palms, as if erecting a wall to protect her feelings. "Hey, look, don't worry about it. We barely know each other. You don't owe me anything. I'll just—"

A savage ache rose in Ren's soul as the deepest human connection she'd ever had turned away from her, probably for the last time.

With an impulse born not of self-confidence but of sheer panic, Ren sprang from the chair and took Katie's face in her hands. A tangle of emotions and questions danced in Katie's amber-flecked eyes, but the girl did not pull away. Two heartbeats later, Ren planted a tender kiss on her lips.

At first Katie froze, and within a fraction of a second, Ren had berated herself ten different ways for the audacity and stupidity of the advance.

But then Katie melted.

Her lips softened. They breathed each other in and out, and Ren's entire body shimmered until, at last, she broke off the embrace.

"What was that for?" Katie whispered. Ren had no answer, but there was no reproach in the question, and she couldn't help but wonder if something had fallen into place for Katie as much as it had for her.

"I don't know. I'm sorry. Can you please just wait for me? I'm not done with you yet."

"I'll try," Katie said.

Ren decided that would have to be enough.

# THE SAVIOR

THE TRAIN FROM Philly to DC was called the Acela, and even with the three stops en route, it was only a two-hour ride. Ren had read somewhere that it could go 150 miles an hour, and though the landscape was whipping by impossibly fast, she couldn't have cared less.

Instead, she studied her shabby reflection in the glare of the massive window and considered how profound her mother's guilt must have been to merit the generosity she'd shown. A train ticket, a new cell phone, some cash and a credit card, a backpack full of clothes and toiletries, and no questions asked.

*I'll help you however I can.*

As awful as her mom may have felt about the decision she'd made and the information she'd withheld all those years ago, Ren bore her no ill will. It was tempting to wonder if—or how—her life might have been different had she known then what she knew now, but she believed her mom had her best interests at heart and forgiveness came easily.

For her mother, not for herself.

The shattered promise not to abandon Katie still haunted her. The girl kept a brave face when Ren left, but she was deeply hurt. And bewildered, because this aimless drifter she'd become entangled with suddenly had all kinds of important and mysterious things to do. In Washington, DC, no less, like some movie spy.

And then there was that stupid kiss. Though Ren was undoubtedly attracted to the girl, she still could not fathom the impulse that had driven her to it. She was almost never the one to initiate intimacy, fearing not only rejection, but the revulsion she might see in their eyes at the attempt.

In the end, she concluded it was a desperate, inarticulate effort to show the girl who'd rekindled her light how much she meant. That their friendship was not casual. That Ren's leaving was not undertaken lightly. And though it had been an extraordinary sensation, she would take it back if she could, because she had no idea where it left them and was afraid to find out.

Ren surveyed her surroundings in a futile attempt to distract herself. Across from her, two little kids hard-wired into iPads excitedly pointed at each other's screens. A few rows up, a mousy brown head kept nodding off and jerking awake. An old guy in a frayed cardigan sweater eased out of his seat and shuffled unsteadily up the aisle.

She took out her new phone and swiped to her text messages. Peter Holland—Lailah's law partner—was the only thread. Nina had asked him to pick her up at Union Station, so they exchanged cell numbers and selfies. Peter was paranoid someone might show up there claiming to be him, which had her even more nervous about what she was mixed up in. She would have recognized him from the website photo, though.

He was still skinny and tousled, only a little grayer—more aging hipster than hotshot lawyer.

He reminded her of her dad. A lot.

She hoped it was only a passing resemblance, and that the rest—his mannerisms, his voice, his demeanor—would be totally different. She wasn't sure how she'd handle spending time with a man who so strongly evoked David Cole's memory. But beyond that, she wondered so many things about him. How had he and Lailah partnered up? How was he handling her death? How irritated was he that this weird girl who claimed to be Lailah's friend was now his responsibility?

The growing list of uncertain expectations and unanswered questions was making her queasy. She bought a ginger ale from the dining car, but it didn't help, so she headed to the restroom until a wave of nausea forced her back to her seat.

No, not nausea, exactly.

A sharp chill climbed her spine. Her breath shuddered. Her pulse quickened. She was not prone to anxiety attacks, but she figured this was what they felt like—a looming existential dread with the disquieting sensation that her own body was running away from her.

She begged the universe for a clue to what was going on, and out of nowhere an image popped into her brain: Katie's ex-boyfriend—Milo—in his sparkle-blue muscle car, parked in front of her mom's house, of all places.

The strange juxtaposition of Katie's world and Ren's felt like a dream, except it wasn't in her mind.

She could *see* it.

His dead eyes stared at the front door of her mother's house and rage rose off him like steam.

How the hell did he find Katie?

A dark shadow moved in the back seat of his car. Someone—or something—was whispering to him in a soft accent. Russian, maybe? She leaned in.

"You have been betrayed, scorned, forgotten," it said.

Ren inched closer, and the shadow resolved into a girl.

Pale, with a scar across her face.

The one from the middle of the road who had appeared, seemingly from thin air, when they crashed.

When she *made* them crash?

Ren was certain Milo couldn't see the girl, didn't consciously know she was there. But her words fueled his fury, driving every trace of love and mercy from his heart.

"She has made you half a man. She has already found another. Together, they laugh at you."

She was literally the devil on his shoulder. And she was making him want to kill Katie.

A silent *oh fuck* exploded from Ren's soul, and the scarred girl's attention snapped to her. Hate burned in her black eyes. She bared her teeth and shrieked like a hundred banshees.

Ren clutched her chest and, with a rush like a rollercoaster dive, she was transported inside her mom's house, beside the bed where Katie slept with Jack at her feet.

She could barely believe what was happening, but she instantly knew what to do.

"Katie, wake up now!"

Jack let out a *boof* from the foot of the bed, his attention locked on Ren.

Katie opened her eyes. "I thought you left," she said with a groggy smile, and Ren guessed her pain meds were in full force.

"I did. I can't explain. Milo is here. You have to hide."

"Milo? I broke up with Milo, remember?"

The doorbell rang.

"Katie, come on!" she said, quiet but urgent. "He's here and he's going to hurt you. You have to come with me. Now pull your shit together!"

"Okay," Katie groaned, dragging herself out of bed. She followed Ren, Jack trotting behind.

The front door opened. Her mom must have answered. Ren prayed he wouldn't hurt her, but there was nothing she could do. She was not there for Sarah.

Ren pointed. "Go in my mom's room. In the closet. There's a laundry chute you can drop through to get downstairs."

"Drop through? What are you talking about?"

"Katie, fucking run!"

Fear swelled in the girl's eyes as Ren finally cut through the Vicodin haze.

"What are you going to do?" Katie asked.

"I don't know, distract him or something."

"No! He'll hurt you! Stay with me," she said, grabbing for Ren.

Her hand passed clean through Ren's arm.

Because the physical, material, flesh-and-bone part of Ren Cole wasn't there.

It was on the Acela somewhere in eastern Maryland.

Katie stared, speechless.

A struggle raged downstairs. Glass shattered. A pained cry. A body hit the floor.

"Go!" Ren urged, and Katie limped into her mom's bedroom. Ren held her ground in the middle of the upstairs hallway. Jack stood at her feet, barking in solidarity as heavy foot-falls approached and Milo finally bounded out of the stairwell.

"Leave her alone, asshole," she yelled, but he didn't even register her presence. He ran past the dog and straight through her.

Ren winced as a flash of pain ricocheted through her chest.

It was Katie's pain she was feeling.

The rollercoaster rush zapped her to Katie's side once again as the injured girl dropped through the laundry chute, hit a basket of clothes on the counter, and toppled hard onto the tile floor. Katie screamed in anguish and Milo followed the sound into Sarah's room.

Katie gaped at Ren. "What the... how did you—"

"Come on, you've got to move."

Katie reached for Ren to help her up, but they could not touch. "Oh my god, what the hell?" Her voice shook.

"Get up! Find my mom."

"Katie!" Milo growled from above and the girl struggled to her feet. He could see her from the chute but was too big to fit through. She turned and hobbled out of the laundry room.

The rest was like slow motion.

Katie staggered into the kitchen.

Sarah Cole stood with her back to the wall, nose bloodied and shirt torn. She reached for Katie and pulled her safely behind.

Milo snarled into the room and locked onto his ex-girlfriend, his intent crystal clear.

He didn't see the gun in time.

The revolver Ren's dad insisted Sarah keep in the house "just in case" exploded twice, creating two tidy holes in his crisp white t-shirt. He dropped like a sack of concrete, blood blooming on his chest as his heart pumped its last beats.

Ren had seen this kind of thing once before. At Alistair's house, the night she'd killed her dad.

Katie's hands were clamped to her ears, undoubtedly ringing from the roar of gunshots in a confined space. Ren had no such pain, and it occurred to her that her ears weren't really there to be damaged. She met Katie's eyes through a cloud of gunsmoke and shouted, "Are you okay?"

Except she didn't shout it at Katie.

She shouted it at the gray tray-table on the seat in front of her, because the part of her soul that had been in her mom's kitchen moments earlier was now safely returned to her body.

On a southbound train, sitting beside her backpack. Right where she'd left it.

Not because she wanted to be.

Because Katie was safe.

It was her last thought before an ocean of fatigue washed over her and she tumbled into the deepest sleep she'd ever known.

\* \* \*

Ren found herself walking through a field.

Soft grass tickled her shins and a warm breeze caressed her skin like early summer, as though it were always early summer in this place. Alongside her, a stone wall stretched endlessly into the night. It was smooth and ancient, cobbled from rocks of all sizes stacked so expertly that no finger or toe-hold could be found. It was taller than she was, taller even than she could jump, and though she tried to visualize what might be on the other side, her mind could not give form to it.

Vines clung to the stone with delicate tendrils, thick with

flowers that glowed like silvery-white pinwheels in the moon-light. They were in full bloom, and she greedily inhaled their sweet jasmine perfume. She was lucid and fully aware she was dreaming, though she couldn't recall ever having a dream where she could smell something.

A faint murmur drifted on the wind, creating the disquieting sense of being both alone and not alone. If she was certain of anything, it was that the murmur originated from the other side of the wall. She closed her eyes and pressed her palm and her ear to the cool stone, but it had no impact on the volume or the clarity.

"Hello?" she spoke into the night and was surprised by the strength of the sound. There was no reverberation, no decay, as if her tentative word had broadcast unimpeded into an infinite universe. The murmur drew nearer, circling in broad arcs and swirls high above.

And somehow, she knew it needed her help to find her.

"Hello," she called again, more confident. "I'm here."

*My dearest Lauren.*

Her heart warmed and broke all at once as Lailah's unforget-table voice seemed to emanate from the flowers, like the petals were vibrating to produce the sound.

Ren could sense how far away Lailah was and how much energy the communication required, as if Lailah had to scream on one side of the barrier for Ren to receive a whisper on the other. She knew this could not be a conversation. Her role was simply to listen, and so she did, with every fiber of her being.

*We are the same, you and me.*

*Survivors on the margins of a society where we've never really fit.*

*I never learned how we do what we do.*

*But over time, I understood why.*

*We are drawn to those in pain because we understand pain.*

*We feel their trauma and their peril as if it were our own.*

*I tried my best to help them.*

*You must do the same.*

*No matter how low they've fallen.*

*Or the sins of their past.*

*Or the ugliness of their exterior.*

*You will see the love inside them.*

*You must protect it from the fear that assails it.*

*It's the only fight in this universe that means anything.*

*And it will cost you.*

*You and everyone you love will be in danger.*

*You will be hurt.*

*You may be killed.*

*But do not fear.*

*Because hurt doesn't last forever.*

*And death is not the end.*

*And I promise you will never be alone.*

* * *

*Ren, wake up.*

  *Ren...*

"Ren, wake up."

It was a man's voice. He shook her gently.

"That's me," she slurred.

"We need to get you out of here. Can you walk?"

Lifting her eyelids took all the determination she could muster. She was still on the train, slumped onto the seat beside her, the armrest digging into her ribs.

He helped her sit upright, her head lolling on her shoulders until she finally found his face. His eyes were kind.

"Peter?"

"Yeah, kiddo."

"You're a lawyer, right?" She flashed a lazy half-smile.

"Yep," he said.

"My mom's gonna need a lawyer."

# THE BELIEVER

THE NEXT PART was a little murky. Ren had no idea how she got from the train to the front seat of Peter's car, but it probably looked a lot like either a good Samaritan or a predator escorting a blitzed girl home from a party. She didn't know if anyone noticed, though certainly nobody had rushed to her aid.

At some point, she asked him where they were going. At some other point—which may or may not have been after she lost and then regained consciousness—he said, "I got you a hotel room for tonight," which sounded pervy, but she was too zoned-out to bust his balls about it.

By the time they arrived at the hotel in question, the fog in her brain had cleared, but her body still felt borrowed. This wasn't like a drug or booze hangover, and she had plenty of those to compare it to. There was no maddening thirst, no dull headache. Her stomach was not awash in acid and the lights didn't hurt her eyes. She was just bone tired, like her heart had run a marathon even if her legs hadn't.

The valet, a long-haired kid with a bow tie sticking out from the collar of his parka, opened her car door, and she felt guilty. She was no VIP and didn't deserve to be treated like one. She thanked him and stepped into the crisp night air.

The Washington Monument peaked above a shaggy cluster of trees, glowing a soft gold. Government buildings, like Greek temples with massive columns and names engraved in stone, stretched down the street. Alongside those were more ornate but less imposing structures with awnings and iron masts with flags angling off their façades. The city was foreign and surreal and made her feel like a stranger in her own life.

Peter gave his keys to the valet and carried her backpack into the hotel. They passed through an elegant marble lobby on their way to the restaurant, a pretentious steakhouse that smelled of browned butter and hickory smoke. The host greeted him with a familiar "Right this way, Mr. Holland," and had enough grace not to sneer at the shady, underdressed girl dragging along behind him. He showed them to a tall leather booth in the rear, and she wondered if Peter had requested a spot as far as possible from prying eyes and eavesdropping ears.

"You need sugar," he said. "I recommend the strawberry milkshake. Best in town."

She deferred to his obvious expertise, and he ordered her a large, along with a cheeseburger and onion rings, and a black coffee for himself. She was startled awake when a heavy glass mug hit the table, accompanied by a frosty steel cup of the extra that wouldn't fit. That part always tasted the best, so she attacked it first. She chugged half of it in a series of loud gulps and felt the color return to her cheeks. A cold belch rose in her chest, which she managed to let out quietly.

"Feel better?" Peter asked.

"What happened to me?"

"You tell me."

The way he said it made Ren think he already knew. "I had this wild dream on the train that..." She couldn't finish the sentence. It was too absurd.

"That you left your body?"

She gaped at him. "How the hell did you know that?"

"You reminded me of Lailah after she ethereated. It's a pretty distinctive brand of whacked-out. Sort of looks like someone coming off anesthesia. Truthfully, I didn't know for sure, but I decided to put it out there because I think it's important we don't bullshit each other."

Bullshitting this man had never crossed her mind. He and Nina were the only threads she could pull to unravel her bizarre connection to Lailah, and she had no intention of burning either one. But information was a two-way street.

"I'm sorry, did you say *ethereated*?"

"That's what she called it. It should get easier. At least it did for her."

Ren didn't want it to get easier. She wanted it to never fucking happen again.

"Did she do that a lot?" Ren asked. "Like, ethereate for other people besides me?"

"Not too often, but yes. For some it happened only once or twice, but she also had her... 'regulars,' she called them."

Ren thought of childhood stories about heroes summoned from afar. Unlikely alliances forged to fight desperate missions against unstoppable foes.

"Am I going to meet them? Her regulars?" she asked. "Are we all coming here?"

He looked at her warmly, as though she were a gentle but clueless thing, and she saw another glimpse of her father in his face. It broke her heart.

"I don't think so," he said.

The ground collapsed beneath her as she realized he was as clueless as she. He had no answers to offer, no insight into why her world had been turned upside-down.

"Okay. Okay, well," she spluttered. "This is... I need to go. I need to go home."

"Hold on, just wait—"

"No. This is... you don't know why I'm here. I don't fucking know. I should be home. She tried to kill Katie... and my mom shot... and there's a corpse in my kitchen and I need to go home. They need me and I have to see..."

She dragged her backpack into her lap and rummaged for her phone. He laid his hand gently on her wrist.

"Ren, it's okay. I called in a favor and got your mother a lawyer like you asked, though you probably don't remember asking. Her name is Bonnie Cooper and she's fantastic. She texted me twenty minutes ago. Your mom and Katie are fine. They're at a hotel until the police are finished with her house and things get cleaned up. They're okay. I promise."

An undeclared staring contest ensued, which Ren reluctantly had to concede when the server arrived with her food. She ate ravenously and though she couldn't quite manage all the onion rings, she sucked down the last of the shake with a rattling slurp and let the straw fall back into the mug.

"That was good," she said. "Thanks."

"Stick with me, kid. Whatever else happens here, you'll eat well." He was quiet a moment, then asked, "Ren, you said 'she' tried to kill Katie. I understood from Bonnie that the attacker was a man. Her ex-boyfriend?"

"Yeah, it was. But it's like someone else put him up to it."

Ren told him of the scar-faced girl in Milo's back seat and their first run-in with her the night of the accident. Peter accepted it without question, which wasn't comforting.

"Have you seen anything like her before?" she asked.

"No. Lailah was the only magical creature I ever saw," he said, and his grief was suddenly visible, etched in every line of his face. What a shit she was, for not having considered how he'd lost someone who obviously meant the world to him.

"I'm sorry," she said, though it sounded lame and inadequate. "For your loss."

"Yours too."

"Will you tell me something about her? Something that's not on the internet?"

"I can do that," he smiled, then thought a moment. "Okay, here's one: Lailah's first job out of law school was assistant Commonwealth attorney in Virginia. Her first felony case as lead prosecutor was against this small-time scam artist named Jimmy Rivera. A real turd, but incredibly good-looking. Like Ricky Martin."

Ren didn't catch the reference. He tried again. "Bruno Mars?"

She knew that one. "He's hot."

"He's hot. Anyway, he had this racket where he'd get beautiful women to lure men to their apartments, and he'd be hiding. He'd jump out and pretend he was the boyfriend who caught her cheating and threaten to beat the shit out of the guys if they didn't pay up."

Ren thought of Alistair. It sounded like a stunt he might pull.

"He did it half a dozen times before they arrested him, but when they did, they had him. He'd been picked out of multiple lineups. The women he conspired with all testified against him. They had DNA from one victim on the gun Rivera had hit him with. It was ironclad.

"Of course the kid pled 'not guilty' because that's the kind of guy he was, totally convinced he could flash that smile and beat the rap. Lailah tried the case of her young career. She dotted the I's and crossed the T's and left no sliver of daylight where reasonable doubt could be found. She was something to see."

Peter's pride and love for Lailah made Ren's heart ache.

"The jury deliberated nine hours and came back hung. Eleven to convict versus one little old lady to acquit. Lailah was blown away, as was the judge. He let her interview the jurors, and Lailah asked the old woman, 'Mrs. Berman, what did I fail to do to convince you Mr. Rivera was guilty of these crimes?' You know what she said? 'Oh no, madam prosecutor, you did a wonderful job. Wonderful! But he's such a handsome boy! I couldn't bear to send him off to prison. I'm sure he learned his lesson.'"

Ren shook her head. "No way."

"Yep. 'He learned his lesson.' That messed Lailah up for a while. She asked me, 'What is the point of all this? What am I doing?' And I sure as hell had no answers for her. Anyway, she kept a close eye on Jimmy, waiting for him to screw up again and give her another shot at locking him up. She never got the chance. Two months later, he died rescuing four little kids from an apartment fire. No bullshit. I mean, if that jury had convicted him, those kids don't make it. And that's when she realized we are all tiny little ripples in a universe of swirling forces. The only control we have is the choices we make. And all we can do is have faith things are going to happen the way they need to happen."

Ren looked at Peter Holland and felt her father's eyes looking back. She didn't want to disappoint him like she'd disappointed her dad. She contemplated the strangeness of her new world, where up was down and shadows loomed and clouds of uncertainty obscured everything. And—if for no other reason than she was curious what it would feel like—she chose to have faith.

"So what now?"

He removed a hotel room keycard from his breast pocket and handed it to her. "Get some rest. I'll bring you to the office in the morning."

Ren's skin got cold. "The office? That's where she..."

"Yeah," he said.

"Why do we have to go there?" she asked.

"Because that's where the work is," Peter said, though he looked as sick as Ren felt.

"The work?"

"Yeah, the work. There's work. Obligations. They didn't stop because she died, and she wouldn't want them to. And I can't stop thinking her death is connected to it."

# THE INTRUDER

REN'S HOTEL ROOM was easily the nicest place she'd ever slept. Rich suede covered the wall behind a king-sized bed decked out with an embarrassing number of pillows. A TV on the opposite wall played soft ambient music, and on the glass-top desk was a small porcelain dish of individually wrapped chocolates with a card reading "Enjoy with our compliments." It was luxurious and exotic and she felt unworthy of the extravagance, but more than anything, she longed for her mom and for Katie.

She tried her mom on the phone, but Sarah didn't answer. Though it was late, Ren could not imagine she was asleep. Not after the night she'd had. Perhaps she was still talking to the cops or to her lawyer. Hopefully, she wasn't under arrest.

She texted Katie to say she was safe at the hotel and ask whether the girl was okay. Her phone told her when Katie read the message, and she waited for the telltale dots of a response being composed. They didn't appear.

The bathroom wasn't enormous, but it had a claw-foot tub

that would fit two of her. She pulled the gleaming chrome handle to start the hot water, and brushed her teeth. When it was full, Ren pulled off her clothes and slid into the bath.

As the water, just shy of scalding, soaked the soreness from her muscles and dissolved the last of the adrenaline, her thoughts drifted to the dream she'd had on the train. She could interpret it only one way: as Lailah's last chance to help Ren understand some part of why this was happening to her.

And why it had happened to Lailah.

*We are the same, you and me. Survivors on the margins of a society where we've never really fit.*

Lailah's words had resonated deeply with her, even in the moment. Though she'd been concentrating too hard on receiving the message to fully process it, Ren had indeed felt marginalized her entire life. She wasn't sunny. She wasn't funny. She wasn't skinny. She didn't like boys. And though she'd always been fine with all these things—she was "enough" for herself— it hurt that the world constantly told her she'd never be "enough" for anyone else.

Lailah seemed to suggest this pain was where her empathy came from. And that it could somehow help others. People like Katie.

*No matter how low they've fallen. Or the sins of their past.*

And that was where things stopped making sense and Ren's head started to hurt. Because Lailah couldn't have known about the sins of *her* past. Or else she'd never have thought they were the same.

\* \* \*

Peter picked her up at eight AM in an old Jeep Cherokee. She'd been too zonked last night to notice what he drove, but given the posh hotel he'd paid for, she expected something more luxe. Black and sleek and European, maybe. Not that it mattered. She'd never owned a car, didn't much care for them, and despite how much shit she gave everyone else about their driving, could barely operate one herself. But Peter's humble ride humanized him. He may have been a fancy lawyer, but he wasn't an asshole.

"Good morning, sunshine," he said with a kind smile. The weariness that had shadowed his face last night was gone. His pinstripe suit and camel raincoat were immaculate, and she was astonished by how he'd found the energy to keep going when all she wanted to do was lie in bed in sweatpants and cry.

She chucked her pack in the back seat and took shotgun. As soon as she was buckled in, he handed her a cup of coffee.

"I didn't know how you take it, so there's cream in that other cup, and sweeteners in the glove box."

"You rock," she said, and meant it. "It's cream, no sugar. You know, for future reference." She wondered how long this man—who kept finding new ways to remind her of her dad—would be in her life. It surprised her to realize she didn't dread it anymore. She actually hoped it would be a while.

"Roger that," he said.

She warmed her hands on the cup and absorbed the city as they drove. The morning was aggressively cold, and a slow sea of umbrellas floated down the sidewalks, shielding their masters from the persistent drizzle. The monstrous stone buildings were even less inviting by day than by night, but before long, the brutal architecture transitioned to row houses, parks, and cobblestone streets.

This was Georgetown, and it felt different. Warmer somehow, though they hadn't driven far enough for the climate to change. The shops looked interesting and welcoming, and they lifted her spirits, at least until the Jeep glided to a stop beside a white brick building with large storefront windows. 'Duncan & Holland' was stenciled on the glass in black and gold like a private detective's office in an old movie. Under other circumstances, it would be a charming place of business, but someone she cared for deeply had died inside those walls four days ago.

It kind of messed with the vibe.

A small brass bell jangled as the door swung open. The office was well-worn and comfortable, with high ceilings and chunky steel beams spanning the open space. There was nothing cheap about it, but nothing flashy, either. The waiting area to the right had overstuffed chairs and healthy-looking plants. To the left, a glass-walled conference room overlooked the street. A wide hallway led toward the back of the suite. The front desk was unoccupied, but the reception counter displayed a walnut block with 'Nina Duncan' etched on its brass nameplate.

Ren picked it up, the smooth wood heavy in her hand, and asked, "Where is she?"

"We'll see her tomorrow."

Peter headed down the hall to the first door on the right, which had his name stenciled on the glass. Lailah's name was on the closed door opposite.

The sight of it made her shiver.

She didn't ask permission to intrude upon the place where Lailah had drawn her last breath, nor did he stop her, though he did not follow.

Lailah's office was immaculate. Nothing appeared to be damaged or displaced. There was no evidence someone had ever lost their life there. There was no fingerprint dust or crime-scene tape. The air carried a hint of Murphy's Oil soap, as if it had recently been scrubbed down, and Ren wondered if Lailah's mother had done it herself as a last tribute to the space where her brilliant daughter had practiced her profession.

The room had no windows, but was surprisingly well-lit by lamps and strange round pipes in the ceiling that channeled daylight directly into the space. The decor was minimal; plants and sculptures filled a shelf to the right of the door. A white rolling chair, a light wood desk and two side chairs were the only other furnishings.

She could see absolutely everything, but there was nothing to see. And though she still didn't believe in them, Ren lingered a few extra moments in case Lailah's ghost was inclined to visit.

If Lailah's office was a Zen retreat, Peter's was a Victorian library. Dark furniture, wood-paneled walls full of diplomas and certificates, shelves of law books and a leather couch large enough to nap on. His camel overcoat was perched on an ornate stand in the corner by the door.

"Have a seat," he said from behind the messy desk.

Ren didn't feel like making herself comfortable. "How did she die?" she asked.

He gestured to the couch and this time she complied, though her right leg bounced up and down to spite him.

"I found her at her desk with a syringe sticking out of her arm."

Her leg stopped bouncing.

The horror of it played in her mind like a movie: the hall door gliding open, light spilling across the wood floor, enough to illuminate Lailah in her chair. What had he thought as he first saw her? That she'd ethereated? Or fallen asleep after a long day at work? And what then, as his gaze traveled across her motionless body to find the needle? Were her eyes open or closed? Did she look at peace, or did the anguish of a painful death shadow her face? Did he check her pulse? Try to give CPR? Cradle her in his arms one last time?

"Tell me everything," she said, tears drenching her cheeks.

He obliged.

Monday evening, Nina left for her cabin by the bay and Lailah stayed late to research precedents for a class action they were assisting. Peter hadn't been in at all that day; he was in Brooklyn on a deposition, then took a nine PM flight from LaGuardia to Reagan and stopped at the office on his way home.

That was when he found her.

Police checked the M Street cameras. Nobody had entered or left the office between Nina's departure at 4:50 and Peter's arrival at 10:40. The camera covering the rear door was nonfunctional—unfortunate but not uncommon—but there was no sign of forced entry or struggle, and nothing appeared to have been searched or stolen.

Crime scene technicians collected prints and trace evidence. It all belonged to the three people who worked there, who had unimpeachable alibis. Based on lividity, the medical examiner estimated the time of death as no more than three hours prior to her discovery. Preliminary reports showed heroin and fentanyl in her system, but no other toxins. There was no suicide note, but less than twenty percent of suicides leave a note, so that wasn't conclusive either way. And with no additional suspicious injuries, he concluded she had died from a self-inflicted, accidental overdose.

Case closed.

"She never used drugs, did she?" Ren asked, though she already knew the answer.

Peter shook his head. "I told them that. The detective said, 'nobody's a drug user until they are.'"

"I think she died because of me," Ren said after a while.

Peter watched her, his face inscrutable.

"Lailah ethereated to me around eight-fifteen that night. It was the last time we spoke. If it left her unconscious, she would have been completely vulnerable. Whoever killed her had total control. That's why there was no struggle."

He leaned back in his chair. After a moment he nodded, as if one of many puzzle pieces had fallen into place.

"Yes and no," he said. "I think you're right about what happened. But if someone was here to kill her, they'd have done it regardless. My guess is, she knew it was inevitable. And she decided to go out on her own terms and see you one last time."

"But why? And why would she let them make it look like an accident? Or that she'd killed herself?"

"If she thought that far ahead, she'd have known it wouldn't fool us. And guess what? It didn't. Now if you don't mind me asking, what did she say to you at the end?"

"She just told me to go home."

"Go home?" he smiled, and she assumed he didn't believe her.

"That's all, I swear," she said. "I wish it were more."

"I'm not doubting you, kiddo. But it was enough."

"What do you mean?"

"If you hadn't gone home, do you think you'd be here now?"

She didn't have to think hard about that one. "No way."

"Now you're starting to understand her."

Starting to, maybe. But still so far to go. "Peter, what am I supposed to be doing right now?"

He took out his wallet and handed her a ten-dollar bill. It didn't exactly answer the question.

"What, you want me to get donuts or something?"

"I just hired you as my intern."

"Okay?" She stared blankly at him.

"I need you to read every case file in this office and see who had a motive to murder Lailah."

# THE INVESTIGATOR

REN STARED AT the mountain of boxes in the file room and wanted to run screaming into the street.

"Every case?" she asked. "How many is that?"

"We'll start with the death-penalty cases. There are eleven."

She rolled her eyes about as hard as she ever had.

"It's not as bad as it sounds," he said. "Each one has a folder labeled 'Contacts.' There will be a few pages listing everyone associated with the case—judges, attorneys, defendants, witnesses, relatives and friends of victims, et cetera. Pull the lists and start eliminating names."

"Based on what?"

"Probability. And instinct. For instance, it's unlikely a judge would have it in for Lailah. Most defendants wouldn't, unless we failed in our appeals and they're still awaiting execution. Maybe they'd have a grudge."

"I think I understand. So a witness, maybe? Or a relative who didn't want you interfering? Or another lawyer you embarrassed?"

"Exactly. Prosecutors don't like being told they messed up. I know murder is a stretch, but we're grasping at straws, here. So cross off the ones that don't fit and we'll research whoever's left and see if anyone feels hinky."

What he said made sense, but something tickled at the back of her mind.

"I'll do what you ask," she said. "But why would these people have a beef with Lailah and not you? You guys worked all these cases together, right? Has anybody tried to kill you?"

He bit at the stubble beneath his lip and said, "No."

"Is there anything she was involved in without you?"

"I don't know. For now, let's just get through this."

Ren spent two hours poring through the attorneys' most important life work. They handled other legal matters besides death-row appeals, but their passion for this area was clear from the sheer number of cases, and that all of them were handled at no charge. She bounced between the contact lists and the reception-desk computer, looking up names, studying photos, getting a feel for the participants in each case. It was both slow going and frustrating because she knew in her gut this was a fruitless exercise. She was certain there would be nothing subtle about discovering why Lailah was killed. It would hit like a ton of bricks.

Also, she kept wondering why Lailah hadn't just said. It struck Ren that of all the things Lailah chose to share in the strange dream on the train, the identity of her killer was not one of them. Did she not know? Or was it simply less important than ensuring Ren understood her place in the universe as some sort of guardian of love? As if she were worthy of being appointed to protect the thing she'd forsaken so many times.

Her thoughts were interrupted by the ringing of the office phone.

Peter shouted from the depths, "Grab that, will you? Take a message."

Ren moved to the reception desk and lifted the handset.

"Duncan and Holland," she said tentatively, remembering how Nina had answered yesterday morning, but there was no response. A button was blinking on the base. She pressed it.

"Hello?"

On the other end was a young woman who sounded like she wanted to be on the call even less than Ren. "Good morning," she said. "This is Olivia Willett calling on behalf of Angela Marks."

The names meant nothing to her. "Okay," she said.

"First, please accept our deepest condolences on the passing of Ms. Duncan. Angela was a dear friend and she's just devastated."

"Thank you," Ren said, and was about to suggest she leave a message for Peter when the woman launched a rambling tirade.

"The reason for my call—the other reason—is the files Ms. Duncan requested. It seemed to be a time-sensitive issue, and unfortunately took us longer than expected to gather the materials. And now we have everything, but Ms. Duncan is... well, she's not... and frankly we weren't sure how to proceed."

"How to proceed?"

"Yes, how to proceed."

"I'm sorry," Ren said. "I'm not sure what you're asking. Maybe it would be better if I had Peter call you back?"

"Well, sure. I mean, he can, but we're only trying to determine if you still want us to send these boxes."

Ren mulled it over. Peter had barely empowered her to make coffee, let alone decisions with possible legal ramifications. But if the boxes weren't important, she figured he could return them or toss them. Then again, if it was something Lailah wanted before she died, maybe it was worth a look.

"Okay, yeah. Send them. Please? Thank you?" The pleasantries were obviously forced, but in the end the woman seemed relieved to have dodged the bullet of a second uncomfortable conversation.

"Of course. We'll send them to your attention via our secure courier. Your name?"

"It's Ren. Ren Cole."

"Very good, Miss Cole. You should receive them Monday morning."

That sounded reasonable, except she didn't actually know what today was. She looked at her cell phone—it was Friday. "Great," she said, thinking her seventh-grade guidance counselor would have said she'd shown "real initiative."

No sooner than she'd hung up the phone, a dull knot formed in her gut. She second-guessed her handling of the call, then decided Peter was unlikely to fire her on her first day of not being an actual employee of his law firm. The pit in her stomach persisted. Maybe it was the tedium of the case files she was dreading. Or the coffee passing through faster than expected.

No, she realized. It was Katie.

And it was about to happen again.

* * *

With the same plummeting sensation she'd experienced on the train, the tasteful law office morphed into a large space with a saggy tiled ceiling, posters on scuffed walls, and a reception desk where a sleepy-looking dumpling of a man in a light blue police uniform was pushing papers.

The posters read JOIN PHILLY PD. OUR CITY NEEDS YOU.

A stout woman in glasses entered from the hallway, followed by Ren's mom, who looked exhausted but generally okay.

Ren rushed to give her a hug, but as she passed right through, she was actually embarrassed. Not because anyone had noticed; because she was too slow-witted to realize that her physical self was—once again—not present.

After a moment, a tall, handsome detective in a tailored suit swept into the room. Ren recognized him as her dad's old partner, Marcus Grant. She hadn't seen him in forever, but she recalled thinking he was a decent guy. He approached Katie, who slumped in a threadbare chair, shock and fear radiating from her injured body like heat off a campfire.

"We're ready for you," Detective Grant told her.

Katie looked up at Grant and nodded.

Then she saw Ren and her eyes went wide. Grant followed her sightline but didn't notice Ren's presence any more than her mother had.

"It's okay. It's going to be okay," Ren said to Katie, but the tension in her face suggested Ren's ethereal presence was in no way comforting.

Sarah helped Katie to her feet. The woman in glasses—who Ren deduced was Bonnie Cooper, the attorney Peter sent—took Katie's arm and Grant led them past the sergeant's desk and down a corridor to a small interview room.

As Grant gestured for them to step inside, Bonnie frowned. "Detective, you didn't put Mrs. Cole in the hot box. I'd ask the same courtesy be extended to Ms. Moreau."

Nice. Katie needed someone in her corner.

Grant's jaw tightened, but otherwise he kept his cool. "Certainly," he said, and led them further down the hall to a conference room which wasn't much larger but at least had a window, even if most of it was consumed by an old air conditioner.

They sat at the table, Grant with his back to the door. Ren stood behind him so Katie could see her without having to look away from the cop. Grant had a notepad, a file folder and a mug of coffee, but didn't offer any, which was probably for the best. Katie didn't look like she could keep anything down.

"Thanks for coming in," he said. "Are you alright?"

Katie nodded, but Ren could see she wasn't in the same zip code as alright, and Lailah's dream words returned to her thoughts:

*We feel their trauma and their peril as if it were our own.*

The girl wasn't in peril; not physically, anyway. But she was traumatized, both by what had happened last night, and by the fact that this detective was going to call upon her to explain it. As if there were a rational explanation.

Katie's trauma and fear had summoned Ren to this police station, as surely as the danger posed by Milo and the scar-faced girl had brought Ren to Sarah's house. And Ren understood why she was here. She needed to counsel her friend—to help her through it—as Lailah had helped Ren when the other dickish cops had barged into their hospital room.

She only hoped she could calm Katie's nerves like Lailah had calmed hers.

"Good," Grant said. "Hopefully this won't take long. By all appearances, this was a justifiable homicide. I'm just trying to clarify some details and understand what led Mr. Galanis to Mrs. Cole's home yesterday evening. Does that make sense?"

Katie nodded again. The detective flipped to a fresh sheet on his notepad, clicked his ballpoint pen, and asked, "Mr. Galanis was your boyfriend, correct?"

"Ex," Katie replied.

"Right. And how long had you been dating?"

Katie shrugged. "Year-and-a-half, I guess."

"You lived together?"

"Yes."

"When did you break up?"

"Last weekend."

"I see. And what precipitated the breakup?"

Katie shifted in her chair, her hand drifting to her stomach.

The gesture triggered a flood in Ren's mind. She'd seen Katie do that before—in the car, leaving the rave, when Ren asked her if she had any family. That's when Ren had somehow understood the girl was pregnant. And now she wondered if that baby was a factor in her and Milo's breakup, before Ren had even entered the picture. Maybe she'd told him and he'd been angry. Or worse, insisted she "get it taken care of." Maybe she'd wanted to keep it. Or at least daydream about it for a while.

Ren wanted to weep for the girl, who'd barely had time to weep for herself, but she had to stay focused. There was a time and a place for that, and it was not in the middle of this interrogation.

Returning to Grant's question, Ren obviously didn't know what the cop knew, but decided it was safer to assume he knew about the rave. Otherwise, it might look like Katie was hiding something.

"Tell him about the warehouse," Ren said. "It's okay."

"He assaulted Ren," Katie said.

"Where did this assault occur?"

"A party."

"Did you confront Mr. Galanis after the assault?"

"I told him we were done. Then I found Ren and we left."

Ren had to smile. Katie's crisp summary of events reminded her how she'd sanitized the story for her mom's benefit. But also she had to admit she'd have loved to see that confrontation. Loved to watch this beautiful, brave girl stand up for herself and defend the total stranger who her boyfriend had coldly shoved into the crowd.

In that moment, as the old tube lights in the dingy interview room flickered and buzzed, Ren Cole decided she was in love with Katie Moreau.

And just as quickly, Ren wanted to kick herself because it wasn't the time or place for that, either.

Focus, for fuck's sake.

# THE IMPOSTOR

THE DETECTIVE ASKED, "Did you have any contact with him between the night of the breakup and last night?"

"No."

"How did he know where to find you?"

Ren had been asking herself the same thing. She thought the pale ghost girl probably told him, but Katie's answer surprised her.

"It's possible he tracked my phone," she said. "We shared location data. After the car crash and everything, I didn't think to turn it off."

Ren could feel Katie's guilt like a hot, wet blanket. The girl blamed herself for putting Ren's mom in danger.

"It's okay," Ren said. "It's not your fault."

Katie stared at her hands. Grant jotted notes on his pad, then tapped his chin with the ballpoint.

"Do you think he went there with the intent to harm you?"

Ren had no doubt at all about Milo's intentions, but Bonnie interjected immediately. "Katie, don't answer that." To Grant she said, "She has no basis to comment on Mr. Galanis' state of mind prior to his arrival."

"All right," the detective conceded, and Ren wanted to hug Peter for sending this woman to watch over Katie and her mom. "We'll move on. I understand you were sleeping upstairs when Mr. Galanis arrived?"

"Yes."

"In fact, you told paramedics you'd taken some pain medication before bed?"

"Yes."

"What was it that woke you up?"

Katie's eyes cut to Ren, but before she could offer any guidance, Katie answered, "I think maybe it was the doorbell." Of course, that was a lie, but Katie seemed like she now understood how they could navigate the treacherous waters of this interview together. And there was something about being united in a common purpose that felt incredibly powerful.

The detective nodded. "Can you walk me through what happened next?"

Katie described, in the sparest detail, her physical movement through the house, culminating in the last confrontation in Sarah's kitchen. Grant took notes, his face betraying nothing.

"And you had been staying at Mrs. Cole's house for how long?" he asked.

"Last night was the third night."

"You seem quite familiar with the layout of the home."

Katie looked warily at Bonnie, but the attorney didn't object.

Grant continued, "I guess I was wondering how you managed to discover a laundry chute in Mrs. Cole's closet, of all places, that let you get safely past Mr. Galanis?"

Ren sensed Katie's heart beat faster. This was obviously a question she'd been dreading.

"I showed it to you before I left for Washington," Ren said. "So you wouldn't have to carry your clothes downstairs."

Katie's heart rate instantly slowed, and Ren marveled that the strange bond they shared allowed her to feel every emotional ebb and flow, like she was hard-wired into Katie's nervous system. It was incredibly intimate. And also exhausting.

"I told Ren I'd have to do laundry while she was gone, and she showed me," Katie explained.

"Well, that's quite a stroke of luck," Grant said.

Bonnie jumped in. She must have sensed he smelled a rat. "Yes it was, detective. No doubt it saved her life. Now, is there anything else we need to address? If not, I'd like to pull both my clients at this point. They've been more than cooperative after such a horrible ordeal, along with what I'm quite certain was a sleepless night. Of course, they'll make themselves available should questions arise in the future."

Ren was thrilled that Bonnie was pulling the ripcord on Katie's behalf, but Grant didn't answer. Instead, he leveled a steely gaze at Katie and said, "I've known Sarah Cole a long time. Good woman. Used to be married to a good friend of mine. I have no doubt she's in the right, as far as this shooting goes. But what I'd like to know, Ms. Moreau, is whether she has any idea who's sleeping under her roof."

Katie blanched and Ren felt the girl's heart rocket into her throat.

Bonnie said, "We're done here," and led Katie to the door.

Grant took hold of Katie's arm as she passed. "Tell her," he said coldly. "Or I will."

Katie wrenched free from his grip and hurried down the hall until Bonnie stopped her to ask what Grant was talking about.

"Forget it," she said, and returned to the waiting area.

Katie's pallor must have spun Sarah's maternal instinct into overdrive, because she lurched out of her chair to wrap the girl in a hug.

"Are you okay?" her mom whispered.

"I'll be fine," Katie said. "Can we just get out of here, please?"

Katie left without looking back, and Ren's world blurred to black.

\* \* \*

Ren awoke on the leather sofa in Peter's office with a pillow under her head and a wool blanket draped over her. She was warm and comfortable and, for a long time, could barely open her eyes. Finally, a soft but steady clicking sound invaded her consciousness and she sat up to see that he was at his desk, typing on his keyboard as if it were perfectly normal to have a cosmically roofied girl passed out on his couch while he worked. She wondered how many times Lailah had regained consciousness in the same spot.

Her second ethereation was as traumatic as the first, but Peter had been correct: the recovery seemed a little easier. She wondered if it would get easier still. If, perhaps with practice, she could remain awake and aware of both worlds—where her spirit traveled and where her body remained. Then she thought of Lailah's last moments, not fifteen feet away. Had Lailah experienced her own murder, or had her ethereation to Ren spared her that miserable fate? It was too awful to contemplate, and regardless, the last thing she wanted was more practice.

"How long was I out?" she asked, her voice hoarse.

"A few hours," he said. "Is Katie okay?"

It was a relief that he understood what had happened to her, and why. Nice to not have to explain that part.

"No, she's not okay. A detective was interviewing her about last night. She was terrified."

"Was Bonnie there?"

"Yeah. She was great. But the cop asked Katie a question at the end—whether my mom knew who she really was."

"What does that mean?"

"I have no idea," she said, but the only thing she figured a cop would care about was if Katie had some sort of criminal record. Perhaps in this, Ren had proven to be luckier than her friend. Even with all the shit she'd pulled with Alistair, she'd never been charged with anything.

Peter frowned. "With her involvement in the shooting, they would have run a background check. Maybe something popped. Let's be honest, you've known her less than a week. It's not inconceivable she hasn't told you everything about her past."

"She's barely told me anything. But I trust her. If she's hiding something, it's not because she's trying to hurt anyone."

"We can run our own check."

Ren thought of how she'd accidentally violated Katie's boundaries, sensing the pregnancy and her artistic ability. Peter's proposal felt like a deliberate invasion, and she wasn't having it.

"No!" she said, more sharply than she intended.

"I've got an investigator on speed-dial. We can find out in thirty minutes if this is anything to worry about." His tone suggested it was no big deal, like he did it all the time.

"I said no! Any kind of dirt digging on my girlfriend is off limits." The presumptuous word tumbled from Ren's mouth by accident, but she let it lie and took a breath. "Whatever it is, she'll tell me when she's ready."

Peter didn't look convinced, but he dropped it. "Are you awake enough to get back to work?" he asked.

She was momentarily confused, then remembered the internship thing. The case files. Her brain ached and she laid back on the couch.

"Can you scare up another one of those milkshakes?"

* * *

Ren made it through three more cases before the sun set and it became a struggle to keep her eyes open. She returned to Peter's office and handed over her list. He studied it and shook his head.

"I remember all these people," he said. "We're barking up the wrong tree."

His disappointment was tangible, which extinguished any instinct she might have had to say, "I told you so. "

"We never did eat," he said. "You want to grab a bite?"

"I'm honestly not that hungry."

"Me either. Let me ask you something. Do you want to stay at the hotel again, or would you be comfortable staying at Lailah's?"

It was the easiest question she'd faced in days. To be in Lailah's world, to have an intimate look at her life and maybe know her a bit more? Ren could not miss that chance. She answered without hesitation, "Yes. Yes, I want to stay there."

Lailah's apartment was in a renovated industrial building that felt old and authentic. Brick and glass and gritty and classy. And as soon as Ren saw it, she couldn't imagine Lailah living anywhere else. Peter parked in the underground garage, then they boarded an elevator to the main lobby where he introduced her to Stanley, one of three doormen who alternated shifts. Peter called him Stosh, and he had the biggest smile Ren had ever seen. He was like a cartoon caricature of himself, and Ren instantly adored him.

"Happy to have you, Miss Cole," he said. "It's been too quiet." He gave her a business card and insisted she call him any time, day or night, if she needed anything.

They rode the elevator to the fifth floor, which was the top, and Peter handed her the key to 501. It was heavy in her hand as she paused on the threshold of crossing into Lailah's world for the second time that day. The steel door swung in, and the fluorescent glare of the vestibule gave way to soft lamplight, citrus smells, oiled hardwood floors, and a stunning view of the Potomac and the city at night.

Art and photos filled white walls, and shelves overflowed with sculptures, none of which looked like things rich people would collect for bragging rights. The photos were of smiling children in third-world countries, volunteers at disaster sites, protesters and marchers in Pride parades. The art was chalk and watercolor and ink and kids' finger paint, and said less about who made it than who displayed it: a woman deeply interested in people. In their histories, their voices, their perspectives.

A woman who loved humanity and all its potential.

Peter looked like he might break. To be there without Lailah must have been torture. Ren hugged him, and for the briefest moment, it was like Lailah was hugging them, too.

"I'll leave you to it," he said, and let himself out.

# THE EXPLORER

REN EXPLORED EVERY inch of the modestly sized apartment like an archaeologist, trying to decode Lailah's life from the relics she left behind. She didn't know quite what she was looking for, but she definitely wasn't finding it. There were no computers to mine for details, no file cabinets to inspect for clues. Hundreds of books lined built-in shelves in the bedroom, but they were by and about other people. There were envelopes full of snapshots, but Lailah didn't appear in any of them. In fact, the only picture of her in the entire apartment was the passport in her desk, stamped with colorful visas that reminded Ren she'd never been more than four hours from her own home.

It didn't take long to exhaust the search and lapse into the depressing realization that the apartment had added little to her understanding of Lailah.

But maybe she was being presumptuous. Maybe she wasn't entitled to understand *who* Lailah was. Maybe it was enough to know *what* she was. Someone who took responsibility for Ren's life and cared for it as best she could. For as long as she could.

Her protectress.

Which, apparently, was now what Ren was to Katie. And as she reached for her phone to call the girl for what would have been the third time since leaving the police station, it rang.

Ren answered, "Hi, mom."

Relief flooded across the line. "Honey, how are you?"

"I'm fine. Are you okay?"

A long silence followed, then her mom asked, "How did you know?"

Ren had no clue what Katie had told her, and any conversation with the word 'ethereation' would have to be face-to-face, so she played dumb. "Know what?"

"What happened at the house. That I needed an attorney."

She figured partial truth was better than none. "I kind of had a vision. Like you said, maybe I'm connected to things outside myself. It doesn't matter. Are you okay?" Ren asked again.

"I am," Sarah said, and Ren believed it. "I have a mean shiner, and I'm not cooking in that kitchen again without remodeling it, but I did what I had to do. I saw it in his eyes. He was going to tear that beautiful girl apart."

She'd seen Milo's eyes, too, and had drawn the same conclusion.

"How is she?" Ren asked. "I haven't been able to reach her."

"She's shaken up. She wouldn't leave my side last night, until the police separated us for questioning. She was a little better once we got to the hotel, but I don't think she slept at all. Then she was even more rattled after talking to Marcus. She had me drive her to work afterward, but I haven't heard from her since."

"To work? Wait, she's not with you?"

"No. She said she needed a distraction. I can't blame her."

Ren was speechless, sick that Katie was no longer under her mom's protection. Not that she wanted her mom in the line of fire again, but the world had become a much more dangerous place in the last week. Their chances of survival had to be stronger if they were together.

"You there?" Sarah asked.

"Yeah, sorry. I'm surprised she can work with her injuries."

"I was too, but I guess they put her on 'light duty,' so she can make calls or something and still get paid."

"Mom, I'm so sorry for what happened. When you said to follow this wherever it led, I never imagined you'd have to deal with the fallout."

"You think this psycho who attacked Katie is connected to the woman you saw?"

"Her name was Lailah, and yes, I do. But I have no idea how or why. That's what we're trying to figure out."

"Who's we?"

"Me and Peter. He was her law partner. You'd like him. He reminds me of dad, only…" She trailed off, unsure how to finish the sentence or why she'd started it. But the idea of her mom liking Peter suddenly seemed important, so she chose her words carefully. Crossword words.

"Only what?" her mom prodded, curiosity piqued.

"Less abrasive and more incisive. Anyway," Ren changed the subject, "will you be in trouble at school? I'm guessing you're the only professor in the English department who has straight-up killed someone."

"I doubt anyone will drop my class over it. Plus, I've got tenure, so, pretty much anything goes."

Ren laughed, then realized she couldn't remember the last

time she'd laughed with her mother. Was it too much to hope that, after everything, they could end up as friends?

"Mom, I need to try her again, okay?"

"Yeah, baby. Tell her I'll come get her. Anytime, anywhere."

Ren was moved almost to tears by the selfless devotion Katie had inspired in her mom. Maybe it was a matter of principle; nobody was allowed to fuck with anybody in Sarah Cole's house. But it felt like more than that. Like if someone was important to Ren, they became important to her mom.

"I will," Ren said. "I love you, and... thanks."

She hung up and dialed Katie. To her amazement, the girl answered on the first ring.

"Hi," Katie said, her tone too neutral to gauge her emotional state.

"Hi," Ren said back. Her brain fired off ninety things at once that log-jammed in her throat, and awkward silence dropped like a stage curtain.

"Are you there?" Katie asked.

"Yeah, sorry. How are you? Mom said you went to work?"

"I needed to clear my head. Plus, I gotta eat."

Ren's first impulse was to question why Katie thought her mom wouldn't feed her, but then she grasped the meaning. The girl was trying not to get fired so she could afford her next meal. And a place to live, her hospital bill, a car to replace the one she'd plowed into a tree. She was trying to pick up the pieces of her life, which was in flight long before Ren had turned it upside down. And she didn't need Ren's help to do it.

"Where are you now?" Ren asked. Katie didn't answer, so she let it go. "Are you still hurting?"

"I'll be okay."

Ren hadn't expected a "how was your day, honey" conversation, but this was worse than she could have imagined, and it was tearing her apart. The phone simply wasn't enough. Ethereation wasn't enough. She had to *see* Katie, to touch her, to smell her, to re-establish their connection and prove—to both of them—that their bond was real. And she had an idea. Maybe she could keep Katie close without breaking the vow of silence she'd made to Nina.

"Will you please come to Washington?" Ren asked.

"Why would I do that? What are you even doing there? My job is here. Your mom is here. Why don't you come home?"

"Because everything that's happened is connected to this place. To the people here."

"You are being so cryptic!"

"I'm sorry, I don't mean to be," Ren said, cursing Nina and her stupid promise. "I just need to look at you and make sure you're okay. That *we're* okay."

"I'm not sure there is a *we*."

Ren's chest tightened. "What?" she asked, though she'd heard perfectly.

"Look, a lot of stuff has happened really fast, and it's all super weird. I just need time to figure out which end is up. I'm not sure I can do that if I'm with you."

"Okay, so, how much time?" Ren asked, knowing it was the wrong question.

"I don't know."

And there it was. She'd been dumped before, and that was pretty much what it sounded like. Katie clearly wanted nothing to do with her, and if Ren was surprised, it was only that it took the girl so long to come to that conclusion.

Ren gripped her phone so hard she thought it might break. "Promise me one thing, okay?" she asked, in as steady a voice as she could manage.

"What?"

"Be careful. The ghost girl—from when we crashed—I saw her again. She was talking to Milo outside my mom's house. Whoever she is, she wants to hurt you."

"But I'd be safer if I was there? You'd protect me?" Katie retorted, as if Ren's warning was nothing more than a manipulation, a ploy to change her mind.

"I'll protect you any way I can, here or there. Just promise, okay?"

"Okay. I'll be careful. I gotta go."

Katie dropped the call and Ren dropped the phone, her thoughts scattered and half-formed like popcorn in a hot pan. She face-planted on Lailah's bed and unleashed a primal scream into the thick down comforter.

This was not Katie's fault. It was her own.

Ren had chosen to abandon Katie—a living, breathing, beautiful human connection—to pursue the vapor trail mystery of Lailah. In a life defined by foolish decisions, it had to be one of the dumbest. And what had she gained? A milkshake from a guy who reminded her of her dad and probably wished she'd fuck off every bit as much?

But Ren could punish herself only so long before regret turned to anger, the taste bitter in her mouth. Maybe she wasn't the stupid one this time, or not the only stupid one. Katie was being stupid, too, writing off the monumental, life-changing thing that happened between them. Ren's soul was literally pulled to Katie. Ren *ethereated* to help her. To save her life.

Katie Moreau was pretty goddamn hard to impress.

Ren realized the swirling pit of emotion in her stomach was also a pit of hunger, and that she'd wallowed in her misery for long enough. She dragged herself from the bed, splashed water on her face, and descended to the lobby.

Stanley was at the desk watching a basketball game. He brightened at her approach and muted the TV. "Hello, Miss Cole!"

"Hi, Stanley. Please call me Ren."

He shot her a rascally wink. "You got it, Miss Cole. What can I do for you?"

"What's good to eat around here?"

"Everything. What are you in the mood for?"

"I don't know. What was Lailah's favorite?"

He studied her closely, as if assessing whether she was grown up enough for what he was about to suggest.

"All right," he said, pressing some buttons on the desk phone and placing an 'Off Duty' sign on the counter. "Let's take a walk."

Stanley escorted her to a hole-in-the-wall New York-style pizza joint for some of the best slices she'd ever had. The charming old guy stayed with her to eat and regaled her with tales of 'Miss D,' who was clearly his favorite tenant. Ren savored his stories and, despite burning the roof of her mouth on ham and pineapple, laughed more than she had in years. When they were finished, he walked them back to the building and resumed his post. And though it was only half-past nine, Ren crawled into Lailah's bed and was asleep before her head hit the pillow.

She tossed and turned and had feverish dreams about red lights and green lights and billowing seas of fire.

Until she ethereated for the third time.

# THE LONER

REN RECOGNIZED THE place instantly.

It was Milo's bedroom.

Her first time here had been unpleasant enough, but this was horrid. Small, frenzied flies orbited the wastebasket in the corner. The bedsheets were a tangled mess. Though she couldn't smell it, she knew the laundry on the floor had gone from dirty to rancid. A bottle of lotion towered over toppled beer cans on the nightstand. Had he pleasured himself while imagining Katie's destruction? Plotted the mechanics of his vengeance while he rubbed one out? If an etherant could puke, she surely would have. She shuddered and headed toward the front.

The house was empty, save for the ghostly echoes of Milo that her imagination rendered everywhere she looked. It had become a liminal space—a desolate wasteland of objects stripped of meaning and sentimentality. There would be no rest here, no solace. And worse, she felt trapped in this toxic purgatory without understanding why.

Ren glided through the front door—she had neither the need nor the means to open it—and surveyed the lawn. Gusty winds spread the leaves like ashes, but there was no human presence. She moved around the side of the house, past the laundry-room door through which Lailah had helped her escape, and glanced into the backyard.

Katie sat on a creaky swing set, rocking and shivering in the cold that Ren couldn't feel. Her eyes were closed, tears hardened to frost on her lashes.

"Katie," Ren whispered. The girl refused to look at her.

"I wondered if you'd show up."

"What are you doing here?"

"Trying to be alone. You should go."

"I can't."

"I'm telling you to go," Katie said. Pleading, not angry.

"I'm sorry. I'm not saying I won't. I'm saying I can't."

"Why?" Katie asked.

"I don't know. I'm not in control of this. You called me here and I can't leave until you're okay."

"Look, forget it. I'm fine. You can go. False alarm. Butt-dial."

"That's not how this works. So we have two choices: I can stand here and watch you freeze to death, or you can tell me what's on your heart and we can try to make sense of it."

Katie sat in silence, as if searching for a third option, but none presented itself. Ren probed gently. "Are you upset about the interview? What that cop said?"

"It doesn't matter."

"Of course it matters. If you don't want to tell me, that's fine. But you have to get out of here. This place is... wrong. It's going to swallow you. And you and my mom need each other right now. She's trying to be brave, but she doesn't want to be alone any more than you do."

"The last thing your mother needs is me. She doesn't even know me."

"She knows you enough," Ren said, evoking Katie's invitation to share her bed their first night in the hospital. The words seemed to have an impact, as Katie finally looked at her.

"You have an aura," she said, fresh tears swelling in her eyes. "A rainbow, like an abalone shell. It's beautiful."

Ren kneeled before Katie, wishing she could hold the girl's quivering hands. "Talk to me."

"The cop found out who I am," Katie choked.

"Okay. Who are you?"

"The daughter of a convicted murderer."

As shocked as Ren was, her guess hadn't been far off. It wasn't Katie's criminal record that had troubled Grant, but her close connection to a criminal. As if her bloodline was tainted. She loathed to imagine the bullying the girl must have endured when people found out.

"Your dad went away when you were twelve," Ren said, recalling Katie's abbreviated story and the sheer elegance of it. A throwaway line that said everything and explained nothing, undoubtedly crafted over years of painful trial and error. It was truthful, and most importantly, invited no follow-up. Like Ren's own answer about how her father had died.

"You must hate me," Katie said.

"Hate you? Are you kidding? I'm in awe of you," Ren said, hoping the warmth of her smile could banish the shame from Katie's heart. "It all makes sense now. Why else would a brilliant, talented girl bury herself in a dead-end warehouse job with an asshole boyfriend and no other meaningful attachments? Everything about you screams you're in hiding."

"I'm sorry I lied," Katie said.

"You didn't lie. You got on with your life as best you could. You're amazing. I'm so sorry that happened to you, but you don't have to hide it from my mom. And you never have to hide yourself from me."

Katie wiped her eyes. "You're like a mind-reader. I don't think I could hide anything from you if I tried."

Ren sensed Katie's pain lighten, along with her own grip on the place. "Your aura's changing!" Katie gasped. "Now it's rose-colored and shimmery, like a mirage."

"I can't stay. Quit wallowing in this hellhole and have my mom come get you. I promise it'll be okay."

"How can you be sure?"

Ren would have said, "Because she loves you almost as much as I do," but she was already gone.

\* \* \*

Peter pounded on the apartment door at ten past eight to collect her for the drive to Nina's cabin. Ren's phone told her she'd missed three calls from him and two texts from Katie. She lugged her drowsy carcass to the front and let him in.

"You're not ready," he said. She blinked at him. "Shit, did it happen again?"

"Yeah. Overnight. Katie..." she trailed off, imagining a future of being whisked away from whatever she was doing every time her sweet friend was in crisis. At least this one had kicked off from the relative safety of a bed.

"She's okay?"

"Yeah."

"Three times in two days? Jesus, kiddo, you must be exhausted. I'll let you get cleaned up. Coffee's in the car."

Ren hoped in vain for a warm day, weary of the unshakable chill in her bones. She dozed intermittently as Peter drove east from the city, the sun low in the sky. Down Maryland Route 4, the landscape turned rural and the trees thickened as they left little towns in the rear-view mirror: Bristol, Owings, Woodland Hills. The oaks and hickories were past their best fall color, mostly brown but stubbornly clutching their leaves.

The closer they got to Nina's cabin, the more Ren sensed Peter's unease. His breathing was shallow and he white-knuckled the steering wheel all the way through Chesapeake Beach.

"Are you alright?" she asked him. He didn't answer, so she touched his arm.

"What?" he said, startled.

"Sorry, I asked if you were alright."

"Yeah."

"I think it's important we don't bullshit each other."

She expected a side-eye, but Peter fixed his gaze on the road.

"My dad was a shrink," he said after a minute. "He worked out of our house. There was a waiting room downstairs where he kept toys and activities for the kids. I wasn't supposed to see his patients—or talk to them—but I was a fat kid, always sneaking snacks from the kitchen, so I ended up walking past."

Ren tried to envision a chubby Peter and simply could not.

"One day when I was twelve, this sassy little six-year-old was there with her mom. She was standing at the easel in the corner, drawing a picture. It caught my eye because it was an airplane. Not like a little kid would draw, you know, a lumpy bubble with wings and a propeller. It was a realistic World War Two bomber. I complimented her on the cool plane, and she said, 'Thanks, Peter.' I asked her how she knew my name, and she just rolled her eyes, like it was so obvious. That's how it was with her. I was six years older, but she always made me feel like her little brother. Anyway, we started talking and we never stopped."

Ren hung on every word of his stories about Lailah. His pain seemed to lessen when he spoke of her, so she kept the conversation going.

"What did your dad say?"

"He was furious. Kept apologizing to Nina for the breach of etiquette. Of course, she couldn't have cared less. He saw how we got along, and finally decided we were good for each other."

Peter clenched the wheel again, and all at once, she understood. Katie had called her a mind-reader, but it wasn't his mind she was reading; it was his heart. He was terrified Nina blamed him for Lailah's death. For not keeping her safe. He may have felt like the little brother, but he wasn't, was he? It was his responsibility, and it was tearing him up.

Words of comfort arrived from deep in her subconscious, a place that hadn't existed before the light came back, or if it had, was atrophied and inaccessible. "It's not your fault, Peter," she said. "Nina would never think it was on you. If Lailah had all these incredible gifts, she was always going to be different. The world doesn't like different. If anything, you kept her grounded. And Nina knows that. And she's so thankful for you."

Peter swallowed hard but said nothing.

A series of progressively narrower streets, drives and lanes led them at last to Nina's cabin, a powder-blue farmhouse that bore no resemblance to the Lincoln-log structure Ren had been envisioning the entire journey. Peter slid the gearshift into park and they got out of the Jeep. He retrieved a black box from the floor of the back seat, set it on Nina's porch, and rang the bell.

The door swung open and Nina Duncan emerged from the cabin to embrace her surrogate son. He picked her up in a gentle bear hug, then set her down and headed inside.

Lailah's mother was exactly as Ren had pictured from the voice on the phone: small but powerful; kind, but not someone to cross. A hurricane barely contained by a colorful headscarf and a wiry frame, with decades of smiles and scowls etched deeply on her face.

"And this must be Miss Lauren," Nina said, scrutinizing her in turn. Ren's new—or rediscovered—empathic instincts failed her; she had no idea what the woman saw, beyond a tenuous link in the chain of events leading to her daughter's death.

Nina opened her arms. "Oh, child, come here."

Ren ran to Nina and, without meaning to, poured every drop of her own anguish into the tiny body of this mother who'd lost her only baby. Nina held her tight until Ren had heaved her last sob and wiped her last tear, and then the woman cleared her throat; a dignified declaration that the time for such nonsense had passed.

"Let us break our fast," she said. "We must talk and I will not abide doing so on empty stomachs."

# THE LOSER

NINA CONDUCTED A culinary symphony on her gas stove. Blackened cast-iron pans sizzled with applewood-smoked bacon, scrambled farm-fresh eggs, and thick golden slices of Lailah's favorite "eggy bread," which was her name for French toast. A glass bottle of Vermont maple syrup heated in a pot of simmering water, and a coffeemaker bubbled and coughed on the countertop.

Ren stole a glance at Peter as he set the table. His dread had evaporated, his worry all for nothing. This woman was as much a mother to him as to Lailah, and mothers would forgive anything. Not that, in this case, there was anything to forgive.

Breakfast passed in near silence, but not awkwardly. The air was heavy with Lailah's absence, and nobody seemed inclined toward small talk. It took Ren four slices of bacon, three French toasts, and a huge scoop of eggs to fill the energetic void left by last night's ethereation, and when they were all sated, they cleared the table and Peter excused himself. He had brought his laptop to keep up with the work that never seemed to end. Ren and Nina cleaned the kitchen together, the woman washing and Ren drying and putting away.

"Thank you for breakfast," Ren said.

"You're very welcome, child. Peter won't let you starve, but he won't cook for you, either. That boy is on a first-name basis with every hostess, waiter and restaurant manager in the District."

"I get it," Ren laughed. "I can barely cook a cup of coffee."

"He says you two are a good team."

Ren was unexpectedly touched. She was unaware Peter had told Nina anything about her, let alone anything complimentary. When they finished in the kitchen, Nina ushered them to a screened-in back porch, beyond which the land dropped off sharply and Chesapeake Bay stretched to the horizon. It took her breath away.

"My baby did this for me," Nina said. "Got me out of the city."

They rocked in oversized Adirondack chairs, nursing full stomachs and studying each other. An oil-filled heater ticked in the corner, its metal fins expanding as it warmed.

"You were brave to come here, child," Nina said. "Quite a leap of faith."

"I hope it's worth it," Ren said, her frustration at having learned so little about Lailah rearing its head again.

"You had better things to do?"

"What's that supposed to mean?" Ren asked, in a sharper tone than she'd intended. But Nina didn't know what Ren had risked to come here, and suddenly Ren felt very judged.

"Lailah told me you were... struggling to find your way."

Nina's words were gentle, but they only confirmed Ren's suspicion. "Oh, that's great," she said. "Even my protectress thought I was a loser."

The woman raised an eyebrow. "Protectress? I like that. An elegant way to describe the indescribable. But the other is nonsense. She knew your potential. Probably better than you."

If that was supposed to smooth Ren's feathers, it didn't. She'd lost count of how often her parents, teachers, or counselors rode her for not living up to her "potential." Now Lailah had joined the long list of doubters. Ren readied a comeback to level the playing field and salve her wounded pride, but Nina spoke first.

"Peter tells me you have the gift. You've bonded with someone. As Lailah bonded with you."

"Yeah." She conceded the fact, but not the implication that the 'gift' was any sort of blessing.

"Tell me of your charge."

"Her name is Katie Moreau," she said, and shared with Nina all that had transpired in their brief time together. She omitted nothing, not even the ill-advised kiss she could still almost feel on her lips. There was no point in glossing over details that made her look reckless or foolish. She couldn't control Nina's opinion of her, and in the end, it didn't matter, anyway.

There was too much else at stake.

Lailah's mother listened intently, her countenance darkening as the tale unfolded. Ren expected a barrage of judgments, or at least questions, but got only stoic silence.

"What is it?" Ren asked. "What's wrong?"

Nina's jaw worked back and forth, as though arguing both sides of some debate. At last, she rose from the rocking chair with a wince, which reminded Ren of her Grammie Beth when her "old joints" registered their complaint.

"Sit tight, child. There is something you need to see."

Nina left the porch for a few moments. When she returned to her chair, she carried a book.

"Lailah had seven charges over the course of her life. You, as it happened, were her fourth." Her voice was low, almost conspiratorial, and Ren wondered if anyone else—even Peter—was privy to what she was about to reveal.

"She was about your age when her gift revealed itself. When she told me about it, I encouraged her to document the episode in this book, lest it become a routine occurrence. Henceforth, she kept record of all of you. Every interaction and circumstance meticulously logged. I took it from her home after her death," she said, without a trace of guilt. "I would not allow it to fall into outside hands."

This was it.

The exact thing Ren had searched for in Lailah's apartment, without knowing why. The thing she couldn't believe *hadn't* been there: a story of Lailah's life, not merely a souvenir of it.

Nina's hands floated across the book, then curled around the edges, gripping tightly. It was an ordinary-looking journal, except it bore an illustration cut from another source and pasted neatly on the black linen cover. She couldn't discern the details of it from where she sat.

"Child, I have read every word in this volume, though I had no right to. It was the reward I gave myself for keeping it safe, seeing as how Lailah is not here to scold her mother for being nosy. It was not my intention at the time, but I see now that I rescued this for you."

Ren's breath caught in her throat. "For me?"

"For you, indeed. But do not misunderstand. I do not offer it to you for your own sake. Or so you can be better acquainted with my daughter, though I know you long for it. You must read this as a cautionary tale."

Despite Nina's admonition, Ren did not, in fact, understand why the chronicle of Lailah's adventures as a protectress should serve as a warning.

"I'm sorry. I don't know what you mean."

Nina frowned, which Ren took as frustration with her stupidity, but the woman's tone reflected no condescension.

"Lailah had a relationship with one of her charges. Not romantic," Nina clarified quickly, "but serious, nonetheless. After the bonding—after Lailah came to her aid in the ethereal way—by chance they met again in person and became friendly. They rendezvoused for coffee, then lunch, then supper. Before long, they were thick as thieves, each one all up in the other's business. School troubles, job troubles, man troubles. For years they were friends, but child, you must understand it took a terrible toll—on both, in the end. Because what is friendship when the parties aren't on equal terms? When one is bound to the other, whether she wants to be or not? When every hiccup and heartache and moment of peril of one summons the other to the rescue?"

The questions hung in the air, and their implications descended on Ren like an avalanche. She didn't need it spelled out further.

It was the kiss.

Nina had glimpsed the spark of Ren and Katie's romance, poured upon it the accelerant of Ren's dubious "gift," and watched it explode into an inferno that could destroy them both. Ren's eyes burned salty and she leaned back in her chair. All the oxygen had left her body.

The woman's stern demeanor softened in the face of Ren's

devastation. "I'm so sorry, child. I never expected to meet anyone besides Lailah who had the gift, but here we are. I'll not presume to know the right choice for you. But I implore you, for both of your sakes, take great care with that friend of yours. It's not only her life you need to protect. It's her heart."

"What happened?" Ren asked, her throat so tight it ached. "To Lailah's friend?"

Nina gave her the book. "Read for yourself. When you're ready."

She was nowhere near ready.

\* \* \*

Night had fallen by the time Ren found Peter and Nina in the kitchen, which now smelled like a bakery. An assortment of candles flickered in jelly jars on the butcher-block island top, where the two sat sipping bourbon and picking at slices of pecan pie. Peter gestured to the bottle.

"Want a taste?"

The way he said it reminded her once again of her dad, who always gave her a sip of whatever he was drinking. Not that he hit the stuff hard, but he enjoyed a scotch and soda after work sometimes, or a Rolling Rock during a game. Over time, Ren had discovered she was a vodka girl, but as that wasn't on offer, she just shook her head. "I'm good."

"Probably for the best," he said. "Lailah was drunk once when she ethereated. Came back to a body that felt like it was poisoned. She was sick for two days. Never drank another drop."

The line of conversation piqued Ren's curiosity. "What's the worst place she ever ethereated from?" she asked.

"Oh, child, there were many," Nina chuckled. "On one occasion, Lailah was called away in the shower. The downstairs neighbor phoned Mr. Stanley to investigate the water coming through his ceiling."

Peter grinned, clearly remembering the fiasco. "One time she was giving a keynote speech at a fundraiser. She had just asked everyone to get out their checkbooks when she collapsed."

Nina picked up the ball. "Scariest was when she was driving. It was a miracle nobody was hurt. Her car rolled through two intersections and bumped to a stop at the curb without a scratch on it. That was the last time she got behind the wheel. Sold it the next day."

They were enjoying this immensely, but she couldn't figure out why they thought it was so funny. She apparently had a lifetime of this shit to look forward to. She started to squirm, but it only made them double down.

Peter said, "I'm going to order you a medical alert bracelet that says 'Please! Resuscitate!'"

"And a helmet," Nina added. "No doubt we can find one to match your eclectic style."

"Great idea," he said. "Also, only sippy-cups from now on."

The two were relentless, like old Muppet men heckling from the balcony, but it was born of love, and soon she was laughing and brainstorming along with them. And while they weren't her family, they reminded Ren of how things might have been with her own mom and dad had she not screwed it all up.

After they'd run out of ways to nerf her bizarre new world, Nina caught Peter's eye and said, "I think it's time."

Ren could not imagine what else was in store for this visit, and it certainly hadn't occurred to her that Peter had been off preparing something while she and Nina conversed on the patio. She noted their joyful demeanor had turned meditative as they put on their coats, and motioned to Ren to do the same.

Peter led them out the side door into the darkness. A light breeze blew, still chilly but not as biting as it had been the past few days. They walked carefully down a crushed-gravel path edged by smooth river rocks, meandering through a copse of woods toward the bay before emerging into a clearing where three chairs had been arranged around a fire pit.

He struck a match against the stone and tossed it into the center. Within seconds, flames consumed the kindling and began engulfing the larger logs. The fire grew and crackled, and Ren smelled more than just wood smoke; a hint of incense funneled into the air along with it.

The blaze cloaked her in its warmth, and as she watched the light flicker on the faces of her companions, she could almost imagine they were a normal family having a bonfire by the Chesapeake. She half expected Nina to unveil a tray of graham crackers, chocolate and marshmallows to make smores.

But then she saw the black box Peter had brought with him sitting on a flat stone beside the pit. And the white chrysanthemums scattered around the edge of the clearing like fuzzy snowballs against the dark soil. She remembered the flowers in her dream, and she understood.

Lailah's ashes were in that box.

This was her funeral.

# THE DREAMER

REN HAD ATTENDED only two funerals in her life, for her grandmothers, who had outlived their respective husbands by many years. The family joke was that one was pretty and the other could cook. She could not recall the pretty one, Sarah's mother. Ren was a baby in Sarah's arms at that service. But she had fond memories of the cook—Grammie Beth—with her complaining joints, thick bifocals laced to a spindly chain, and a strange bottle of smelling salts always close at hand.

They buried Beth on a hot day. Ren remembered a church with scores of sweaty people dressed in black, reminiscing about their favorite dishes, which she thought was kind of sweet. Personally, she'd liked Beth's peach cobbler best.

It had been a wintry day when they buried her father with the customary pomp and ceremony reserved for police officers killed in the line. Or so she'd heard. Given that she and Alistair were the reason for it, she didn't feel it was appropriate to attend. All she knew was there was a folded flag in her mom's house that was supposed to symbolize his sacrifice.

The fire snapped and she shook off the memory, suddenly realizing that she was one of only three people to share this moment. Where was Lailah's church full of mourners? Her twenty-one gun salute? The flag-draped casket and the trumpeter blowing Taps? She whispered to Peter, bewildered. "It's just us? Where is everyone else?"

"She loved people," Peter said. "But she didn't collect them."

"They loved her, too," Nina said. "We'll hold a larger memorial when the time is right. But for now, we are enough to honor her. And, young lady, I'm certain she'd have wanted you to be part of it."

Ren felt a wave of love even warmer than the fire as Nina extended her hands.

And so it began.

Peter held one, Ren took the other, then joined hands with Peter to complete the circle. The service was surprisingly informal, yet more reverent than any rite Ren had ever witnessed. She closed her eyes and let it wash over her as Nina spoke.

"We gather today for our Lailah. Our Lailah, who has departed our world for a distant shore. Our Lailah, whose shell is abandoned; the transition of death begun. She is without her armor, without a haven and without a guardian. Her awareness of this life fades, replaced by infinite shadow.

"Together we implore you, oh compassionate ones, bestow safe haven upon our Lailah. Guard her. Be her armor and her light. Draw her back from the great abyss. Do not permit her to return to this lesser life of loneliness and separation. Instead, elevate her to a state of perfection. Of perfect unity, where love is eternal, and fear is unknowable."

Nina grew silent, and Ren opened her eyes after a moment.

Tears streamed down the woman's face, and Ren could tell she was fighting for composure. Nina's pain started Ren's eyes leaking, and when the woman spoke again, her voice faltered.

"Together we implore you. I, her mother Nina…"

"I, her brother Peter…"

His voice rang in the night, and Ren felt them squeeze her hands. They expected her to speak. She still grappled with what she and Lailah were to each other, but her panic passed as quickly as it had blossomed. She answered unselfconsciously and they accepted it without question.

"And I, her daughter Lauren."

Nina cleared her throat and her voice returned to its full strength. "Together we implore you, oh compassionate ones, embrace our Lailah. Our daughter, our sister, and our mother. Embrace her so she may find peace."

"May she find peace," Peter echoed.

Ren choked back a sob. "May she find peace."

They held each other a few moments longer, then Nina let them go and they moved together from the fire to the edge of the moss-covered cliff. Gentle waves lapped at the shallow sandy beach below. As they shared the solemn task of casting Lailah's ashes into the uneven wind, Ren offered a silent prayer of her own.

*May peace find us all.*

\* \* \*

Peter drove them back into the city on Sunday morning, and they spent the day at the office. Though she thought it a complete waste of time, Ren continued reviewing the death-penalty cases with the same result: no promising suspects or leads.

On Monday, Ren showered at Lailah's apartment and changed into her last set of clean clothes. She posed a bashful question to Peter about where she could do laundry, but he wouldn't hear of it. He had her bag it up and leave it outside Lailah's door for the "service." She didn't know that was a thing.

What she really wanted was to read Lailah's journal, but Nina had come in for the day and the grown-ups demanded their intern help them catch up on work. Despite her disappointment, their professionalism impressed her. They had clients and responsibilities and were committed to upholding them. When they arrived at work, Peter mumbled something about emails and disappeared into the back while Nina manned the reception desk and Ren camped out in the file room to go through the last of the cases.

Thirty minutes later, the office bell jangled. Thirty seconds after that, Nina summoned her to the front, where a courier stood waiting for someone to sign his clipboard.

"Pray tell, child, what have you authorized here?" Nina said, gesturing to a dolly with four sealed file boxes. The kid already seemed antsy about this stop taking too long.

"Delivery for Ren Cole from Philadelphia District Attorney," he said, checking his manifest. "Angela Marks?"

"Oh, shit," Ren said, remembering the phone call asking if they still wanted the files. She had ethereated to Katie at the police station afterward and had forgotten about it completely. "I did, yeah."

Nina frowned, but didn't berate Ren for exceeding her nonexistent authority. "Very well," she said, and inked her signature on his clipboard. "Kindly deposit them in the conference room."

After the kid left, Ren recounted the call, then followed Nina in to inspect the boxes. They were marked 'Commonwealth v. Ando,' and they felt radioactive.

"Ando," Nina echoed, as if the name triggered a recollection.

"You know what this is?" Ren asked.

"My hip plagues me," Nina said, depositing herself onto one of the conference chairs. It seemed she couldn't tolerate standing for any length of time. She either had to move or sit. Her arthritis made the middle ground untenable.

"There were many injustices my daughter railed against in this world, but none more than capital punishment. To her it was barbarism. A blight on our country. Are you aware the only nations who execute more people than the Land of the Free are China, Iran, Saudi Arabia, and Egypt?"

Ren wasn't, but the question was rhetorical.

"There are forces of progress at work, but it is a slow march. Case by case, state by state. Our native state of Pennsylvania, as it happens, put a moratorium on such executions. Before you congratulate them on their enlightened transformation, know they only sought to study the problem. You see, executions are error-prone and irredeemably biased against poor people and people of color, but their greatest shortcoming—that which makes them truly heinous—is that they are expensive. An unjustifiable burden on the taxpayer.

"Well!" she huffed. "It would seem they have, after great academic effort, arrived upon on a workable solution, for six weeks ago, the esteemed governor lifted that moratorium and resumed the countdown for every prisoner on death row. Lailah informed us she had requested the case files for one of these unlucky souls. It had slipped my mind."

"What's the case?"

"Child, I have no idea. Normally, the firm would receive a request for assistance from one of the advocacy groups, or the inmate himself, but this was something Lailah sought on her own. She wanted to conduct some preliminary investigation before having Peter and me devote time to it."

"Was that unusual?"

"Not particularly. Though she confided to me that the moonflowers had led her to the matter."

Ren's jaw tightened. "The what?" she whispered and leaned in close, but Nina did not seem inclined toward secrecy.

"When Lailah was young, she suffered night terrors. She awoke screaming from terrible dreams about a war that ended forty years before she was born. A past life, perhaps, though who is to say?"

Nina described this incredible phenomenon as if it were the most normal thing in the world. It struck Ren that—to Nina—this subject was less sensitive, less fraught with danger than the matter of the journal.

"Dr. Holland—Peter's father—helped her come to peace with it. Helped her get past the fear by examining it in the light of day. As Lailah grounded herself in this life, her dreams evolved. Still vivid, often terrifying, they hinted at a reality larger than most of us perceive. In some, she was surrounded by flowering vines and would hear voices or see images that guided her in a certain direction. She came to refer to them as her moonflower intuitions."

Ren's mind reeled. Who—or what—had spoken to Lailah in her moonflower dreams? And what would it mean to Nina to know Lailah had been a voice in hers? Without knowing why, she fought the urge to confess it. Instead, she asked, "Did she get a lot of moonflower feelings?"

"I can't say."

"Were they a secret?"

"No, you misunderstand. I mean I'm confident she would not have shared them all with me."

"When she followed these feelings, was it a good outcome?"

"I can't say. And by that, I mean how can one know what lies down the road not taken? But her instinct was to trust them. And mine was to trust her."

"Nina, is there a chance—"

"That you ask too many questions?" she interjected, the gleam in her eye betraying her sarcasm. "It's a certainty. But if I can anticipate your meaning, I agree that, if nothing else, the timing of this moonflower is portentous. And can we further agree there is but one path forward?"

"We have to look at these files."

"No, child. This task is ideally suited to the talents of an intern. *You* have to look at these files."

After Nina excused herself to the reception desk and Ren fortified herself with a fresh cup of coffee, she examined the first box, which had a sealed envelope secured to its lid. She sliced the clear tape with a utility knife and removed two letters.

The first was addressed to Ren from Angela Marks at the Philadelphia District Attorney's office. It offered condolences for Lailah, and called attention to the other, a letter to Angela from a prisoner named Naoki Ando. In it, he stated emphatically (in all capital letters) that he did not know Lailah, did not want to be represented by her or anyone else, and would not consent to be visited by anyone for any reason.

Ren set the pages aside and cut the seals on the boxes. Box one contained records of a police investigation. Box two had witness statements and discovery. Box three had court records and transcripts. And box four was devoted to the appeals process, though compared to the others, it felt practically empty.

She dug into the police records and opened the first folder, a two-inch-thick Philadelphia PD homicide file loaded with pictures. She'd heard her dad tell her mom about "murder books" before, but she'd never actually seen one, and it took her about five seconds to decide she never wanted to again. The coffee churned in her gut and she pushed the cup aside.

The photos told the tale. In the grand foyer of an elegant home, two bodies with ragged, dark holes in their foreheads lay on a white marble floor that had become an ocean of red. One was an older man, well-dressed. The other was a boy, not quite a teenager. His dull, glassy eyes were open. It was ghoulish.

The walls and furniture were blood-spattered, still red and drippy when the images were captured, with the finer droplets dried to black. Dozens of pictures documented the carnage, but Ren had seen enough. She skipped past them.

With the wider scene established, next came the detail shots. The front door of the house with sooty fingerprint dust around the handle. A handgun with an evidence tag looped through the trigger guard. Two bullet casings on the marble beside little yellow number markers. Close-ups of a man's hands.

Finally, a dual mug shot—face-forward and in profile—of the man they had arrested for the murders.

His name was Naoki Ando, and she had seen him before.

In a photo from a flowery scrapbook.

# THE KILLER

REN KNEW SHE should summon Peter and Nina immediately to reveal the discovery—the elusive, connective thread they'd been searching for since Lailah's life was cut short a week ago.

She just couldn't.

She needed to wrap her head around it first, to understand the size and the shape of the last case Lailah ever took an interest in, which happened to be the same one that tore apart Katie's life eight years ago.

The one the girl had tried to hide from so desperately that she'd abandoned his name.

Ren opened the next box of files, spread them on the conference table, and plunged into the darkness.

Katie's father, Naoki Ando, was a Ph.D. scientist and corporate executive who managed the research and development division of a pharmaceutical company called Glass BioGen. He'd worked there almost twenty years with an exemplary performance record. By all accounts, he was a skilled leader, a beloved colleague, someone who always had your back.

A man you'd trust with anything.

Right up until the day he executed his boss—the company's CEO Malcolm Glass—and Malcolm's twelve-year-old son Eric.

The bodies in the photos—with the bullet holes in their heads—now had names.

And there was a witness. A survivor. Malcolm's twenty-year-old daughter Victoria, whose statement became the official version of events, because Ando never contested it.

Ren couldn't help but visualize the crime.

It's a cool spring morning in March. A silver Volvo SUV pulls up to an elegant white house with a shallow porch and stately columns that rise two stories to meet the roof. Naoki Ando sits in the driver's seat, contemplating what he's about to do. He opens the glove compartment and removes his gun. Maybe he checks it to make sure it's loaded and ready. Or maybe he doesn't. He's a scientist, after all, not a hitman. And he's not dressed for work. A button-down shirt and dress slacks, maybe. But no tie. And no jacket.

He exits the vehicle, sliding the pistol into his waistband at the small of his back. He walks to the door. Rings the bell. Waits. Wonders who'll answer, or if he wants anyone to answer at all.

The door swings open. It's Malcolm. Tall, fit, immaculately groomed. Salt-and-pepper hair and a golf-course tan. He lets Ando into the foyer and closes the door behind him. The CEO immediately starts firing questions at his employee. Work questions. Something Ando was supposed to have done, but hadn't. Malcolm gets angry. Maybe he shoves Ando. Or maybe not. Maybe he's afraid of Ando. Malcolm is larger, but Ando's got that look. Like a guy you don't want to fuck with.

The argument continues. Eric overhears and runs to join his father in the foyer. He's handsome like his dad, but with pale, skinny limbs jutting out of his polo shirt and khaki shorts. The boy gets in the middle of it, but not to stop the men from fighting. Eric yells at Ando, too, amplifying whatever his dad was so furious about. Ando tries to make his case, but he can't out-shout the two.

So he stops trying.

Naoki Ando pulls out his gun and shoots Malcolm Glass in the head. A second later, with no hesitation, he shoots the boy.

And at that, Ren snapped herself back to the present because she simply couldn't stand it anymore.

According to Victoria's statement, she was on the living-room sofa reading a book when she heard her family get murdered. She crawled to the kitchen, hid in the butler's pantry and waited in the dark for forty-five minutes, praying the madman didn't find her, too. Because he was looking for something. He was tearing apart their house.

Victoria's ordeal ended when the police arrived.

It turned out Katie's father had called them himself, waited for them on the front lawn, and surrendered without further violence. He refused legal counsel and confessed to the homicides. Within a matter of weeks, he had entered his plea, was sentenced to death by lethal injection, and waived all appeals, which was why the last file box was basically empty.

It was a monstrous crime, and his guilt was not in question. The case was the furthest thing from a whodunit, and yet—despite a mountain of evidence, the signed confession, and that the man had sat in prison for eight years without a peep—there was something that didn't sit right with Ren.

A single sheet of paper buried in box three had the hair on her neck standing on end. It was the victim impact statement, a standard court-issued form with pre-printed questions, completed by Victoria.

**Please tell us about the emotions you felt as a result of this crime:** *My daddy and my little brother were who I loved most in the world, and they were taken from me. I miss them so much. I constantly have nightmares about that day, and I wish I could have saved them. Knowing this man broke into our home, I will probably never feel safe again. I can't imagine what we ever did to deserve this.*

Ren should have been moved by the testament of the girl who'd lost her family in a brutal and shocking act of violence. She wasn't. She couldn't put her finger on it, but it was like the emotion behind the words wasn't... real. It had all the sentiments one would expect, but they rang hollow; scripted, even.

She had no idea what to do with this intuition as she turned away from the troubling pages, swiveling in her chair to face the credenza. The toasty aroma of a carafe of coffee sitting on a hotplate tempted her to have another cup, but as she grabbed the handle, it weighed far more than it should have, as if it were filled with clay and not coffee.

Her muscles slackened and she felt faint. She couldn't move. The red power light on the base of the hotplate caught her eye. It seemed to sparkle and pulsate. It was hypnotic, and she lost herself in it, like her feet were no longer on solid ground. It was not a good feeling. She blinked, hoping the spell might break if she could reboot her vision. It didn't work.

Her heart pounded as the shimmering light reached for her, enveloping her until her entire universe was that vibrant red hue.

Seconds later, the rollercoaster rush of ethereation dropped her into the parking lot of an enormous warehouse.

* * *

The red light—as was now apparent—shined from a fixture installed above a dock door with a trailer snugged against it, one of dozens lining the exterior of the building, as far down as she could see.

In fact, most of the door lights were red, but when one of them turned green, a dirty tug truck backed up to it. The tug driver hooked some lines to the trailer, lifted its nose off the ground, and pulled it away from the building with a belch of black smoke from its exhaust.

Through the now-empty door, Ren saw orange forklifts shuttling pallets of freight across the dock, into and out of the trailers.

Forklifts.

This had to be where Katie worked.

Was she upset about something? Or was somebody trying to kill her again?

The growl of a diesel engine grabbed her attention. A massive semi-truck with a chrome grille barreled through the parking lot toward her. She instinctively flattened herself on the ground, but it didn't matter. The truck drove straight through her.

Ren stood and got her bearings. Katie was nowhere to be seen in the massive paved parking lot, so Ren ran up the loading ramp into the building. Her first impression was that she was now in a real-life video game where you had to cross a busy street without getting squished by traffic. Except in this case, the cars were forklifts.

There was still no sign of Katie, so Ren watched for a moment and tried to understand the operation. A forklift deposited its load in a trailer, then its operator backed out and shot a thumbs-up to a guy in a uniform holding a clipboard. The clipboard guy entered the trailer, checked some things, then stepped back onto the dock. He closed and latched the trailer door and flipped a switch on the adjacent wall, turning its status light green, presumably for one of the tugs outside to haul away.

Ren guessed her friend was still in no shape to operate a forklift, but maybe she was filling in as one of the clipboard guys. Or maybe she was in the office. There was no way to know, and this place was gigantic. Her anxiety mounted.

Then her ethereated heart skipped a beat. The pale ghost girl was there.

She was skulking down the dock in the shadow of a clipboard guy, whispering in his ear, undoubtedly the same brand of poison that lit Milo's fuse.

Ren's instinct took over, and she sprinted toward the apparition, shouting, "Hey, you!"

The coal-eyed girl whipped around and bared her teeth. She abandoned the clipboard guy and barreled toward Ren. The closer she got, the more intensely the hate flowed from her. The distance between them closed so fast Ren barely had time to wonder whether the wraith would tackle her or run right through her, as Milo had done in her mom's hallway.

It ended up being both—and neither.

The "impact" did not alter their momentum in any physical way, but as their ethereal selves collided, they traded energy.

In an instant, they were rendered transparent. Any pretense or front they hoped to maintain vanished as though it had never existed. In this state, it simply couldn't.

Their souls were laid bare to each other, everything they were or had ever been.

And hers was cold.

Her name was Yana, and Ren could read the scars on her soul like a roadmap of her tragic journey.

Images flashed through Ren's mind like a slide show. Yana's father slapping her mother, then slapping the child for coming to her defense. A full-fisted punch after the teenager poured a bottle of his vodka into the toilet. A triumphal grin on the man's face as he traded the girl for two cases of that same vodka.

The inside of a shipping container, along with a dozen other young women, trying not to throw up as the ocean heaved beneath them. Fighting off a deckhand who wanted his way with her, only to be slashed across the face with his fishing knife. The deafening crash of the container when the crane transferred it from the ship to the port. The blinding sunlight as the doors flung open and a new set of captors shrouded her head and threw her into a van. Imprisoned in a laboratory and held down against her will as a doctor injected her with something and…

Nothing could have prepared Ren for the utter anguish of experiencing Yana's remembered pain. The injection, whatever it was, tore the girl's soul in two. Extinguished the love and empathy she clung to despite her tortured past, turning her into an ethereal sower of fear and hate and jealousy and rage.

Ren still had no idea why she wanted to hurt Katie, but one thing was clear: she wasn't born this way.

She was made.

By people.

They disentangled and Yana whispered in her soft accent, which Ren now knew to be Ukrainian, "That was fun, Lauren. Always nice to meet another killer."

The word hit like a hammer; her greatest shame revealed to this agent of darkness who clearly thought they were the same.

"Why are you here?" Ren asked her.

The scar-faced girl laughed, a deep, malicious cackle that chilled Ren to her core. Then she vanished.

Ren shook off the humiliation and remembered why *she* was there. Yana would not have left unless whatever doom she'd planned for Katie was already in motion. Ren looked for the clipboard guy Yana had whispered to and spotted him further up the dock. He strolled past an open door and casually switched the light to green.

At that moment, Ren understood everything.

Katie was in that trailer.

An unsuspecting tug driver would see the green light, hook the trailer, and pull it away while she was still inside. Tons of unsecured freight would topple onto her still-injured body, crushing her to death in an unfortunate "industrial accident." A beautiful life reduced to a terse headline; another "oh, isn't that sad" before you'd click past to see if it was going to rain tomorrow.

Not on her watch.

Ren focused all her thought—all her energy—on Katie, and without understanding exactly how, projected herself directly into the trailer, scaring the shit out of her friend in the process.

"Ren! What the hell?"

"Katie, get back on the dock, now!"

To Katie's credit and Ren's eternal relief, she leaped from the trailer as it rolled away from the open door.

Four barrels of hazardous chemicals crashed to the pavement in front of the dock. The drum seals split open and, as the liquid hit the air, it erupted into a searing flame.

The explosion blew Katie onto her back and she curled into a ball to shield herself from the withering heat Ren could not feel. What Ren could feel was her body already pulling her home like a drawn rubber band.

Ren kneeled beside Katie. "You have to come to me. Tonight."

"Okay," Katie said, and dissolved before her eyes.

# THE GAMBLER

THE SMELL OF lavender, woodsy and medicinal, hit Ren's nostrils as she regained consciousness on Peter's sofa for the second time. Katie's signature scent momentarily fooled her into thinking the girl was near, but it turned out the essential oil soaked a bandage that wrapped her coffee-scalded right arm from wrist to elbow.

At the diner across the street, the noisy backdrop of the Monday lunch crowd helped mask the horrors Ren had to recount. She shared her newfound knowledge of Yana and described what was now the third attempt on Katie's life. They took some comfort that the scar-faced girl was human—and not a demon—but there was no other upside to the tale.

Then she told them about Katie's father.

They pelted her with every question they could think of about the case, and she could answer all but the most important one: why Lailah had sought it out.

Peter had told Ren that Nina spent decades as a court reporter in Philly, capturing every word spoken in thousands of cases. For ten minutes, she showed the vast knowledge she'd earned, matching him point-for-point as they went back and forth. Ren didn't understand the legalese, but the gist was Lailah could not have expected to represent the man without his consent.

"I can't see the angle," Peter said. "She would have no standing to appeal on Ando's behalf. There's got to be something you missed," he insisted, now restless to settle their check. He looked around for the waitress. "We've got to get back into those files."

"I didn't miss anything," Ren said.

"We just have to double down and look—"

"God damn it, I didn't miss anything!" she shouted, finally uncorking the stress and anguish of the morning's descent into darkness. The patrons briefly swiveled their heads and gawked, then returned to their own affairs.

"The answer is not in the files," she whispered through gritted teeth.

"How can you be sure, child?" Nina asked, and not argumentatively. She was crediting Ren's opinion.

"Because I know. The only way we're going to find out how this is all connected is if Ando tells us himself."

"He won't do that," Peter said. "You saw his letter. No visitations, no correspondence. Period, the end."

Nina locked eyes with Ren. An understanding passed between them, and though Ren knew it was their only path forward, she couldn't bear the thought of it.

"Maybe he'll tell Katie," Ren said.

"Yes," Peter sat up. "I'll get a visitation request submitted to the prison on her behalf."

"No, please, not yet," she said.

"Why not?"

"If we expect Katie to be part of this, she needs to hear it from me first. Face to face."

"What do you mean, 'if'? She's part of this, whether she likes it or not."

"She's been hiding from it for eight years. We need to be careful."

"She's in danger and we don't have time to—"

"Peter." Nina silenced him, her voice cold steel. "We will not sacrifice the living to the cause of the dead."

The debate was over.

Ren attempted to reassure him and herself. "If someone tries to hurt her again, I'll feel it. And I have to believe I can get there to stop it, like I did before."

He let out a deep breath. "That's a big bet you're making there, kiddo."

The way he said it made her wonder if it was the type of bet Lailah had once lost.

\* \* \*

The concourse at Union Station was stunning.

Ren had sleepwalked through it the night she arrived in Washington, but this time she could appreciate its splendor. The space was cavernous, its ceiling a vast barrel-vault adorned with hundreds of octagonal coffers leafed in gold, its floor a sweeping expanse of white marble inset with rust-colored tiles. A legion of great stone statues—Roman centurions—watched over the bright, noisy hall from above.

It looked like the entry to heaven.

Not that heaven was real. Or that she'd ever be allowed in.

Katie was easy to spot among the throng of travelers, a limping bundle of winter softness in a heather-gray vest and a fleecy cranberry cap. The girl could wear the hell out of a hat. She was dragging Sarah's faded teal carry-on bag behind her, with a bum wheel that shimmied unevenly as it rolled over the seams in the marble.

They glided to an awkward stop facing each other, as if there were some sort of force field between them. All Ren wanted was to throw her arms around Katie and never let go again, but her friend's eyes and the set of her jaw told Ren she wasn't ready. Neither seemed to know how to behave. Ren was convinced Katie thought she was a freak, and had no compelling counterpoints to challenge that assessment. Katie looked like she would rather be anywhere else, and it tore at Ren's heart.

"Hi," Ren said at last.

"Hey," Katie replied, penetrating the force field to touch Ren's shoulder. It wasn't affectionate; it was to test if she was solid.

"In the flesh," Ren said. Katie nodded but didn't smile, and Ren labored to fill the silence. "How was the trip?"

"It was okay. I'm here, right?"

"Right. So, you want to get something to eat?"

"Okay."

Peter had offered to chauffeur, but Ren thought Katie should acclimate to this new environment before other people entered the mix, so they cabbed it to the apartment to drop off Katie's bag. The ride felt longer than it took, but when they arrived, Stanley was as warm and welcoming to Katie as he had been to Ren, and the girl appeared to loosen up a little.

Ren had asked Peter to recommend a dinner spot with great

food and comfy booths for privacy. Intimate, but not romantic. Her love for Katie was undeniable, but she couldn't assume it was—or would ever be—reciprocated, and she was terrified of sending the wrong signals. He nailed it. The family-style Italian restaurant offered the perfect vibe. Nobody was likely to get gunned down there, but it was a place where that sort of business could be discussed.

They made a few attempts at chit-chat over a shared plate of bruschetta—Katie's job, Ren's mom, the swanky hotel from Ren's first night in town. But silence kept returning like an unwelcome wind, and after a few minutes watching little garlic toasts wilt in the olive oil, Ren finally couldn't stand it any longer. She had a mountain of things to tell the girl and no foothold to climb it. So she went for the direct question.

"Why are you so uncomfortable around me?"

Katie shifted in her seat and brushed an imaginary crumb off the tablecloth. Ren persisted. "You have to say it. Or ask it. Or whatever. Just put me out of my misery."

"Nothing. It's nothing," she said, which was bullshit.

"Come on, we know each other better than that," Ren said, laying her hand gently on Katie's.

The girl recoiled, which pretty much gave Ren the answer she sought. Then she flew apart.

"We know each other? I'm sorry, but I don't know you at all. You want to act like we're regular chicks knocking around and grabbing a bite, except someone keeps trying to kill me, and you seem to be the only one who knows anything about it. And you keep showing up to rescue me, but you're not really there, are you? You're like... in my head. I mean, what the hell are you, a ghost? A superhero? Does your Spidey sense tell you I'm in trouble and you just zap to me? I mean, it's cool you think this is all totally normal, but I guess I'm not there yet, okay? You kind of scare the shit out of me."

Ren's insides were in a twist, and she swallowed hard. Katie wasn't wrong, except about the "regular chicks" part, because Ren had no idea how to act like that. She asked herself how Lailah would handle this. Her protectress would be cool. Confident. Calming. Ren was none of those things, but maybe she could fake it.

She drew a long breath. "Okay," she said. "That's fair. Should we just skip to dessert, then? Peter says the tiramisu is good, but the crème brûlée is orgasmic. Well, that's my word, not his."

Katie looked like she wanted to punch Ren in the tit, but a reluctant smile slipped through her defenses, and it warmed Ren's soul. She signaled the waiter to get some on the way. When he was well out of earshot, she said, "Katie?"

"What?"

"Can I remind you of one thing?"

"What?"

"You rescued me first."

Katie's eyes blanked, as if refocusing inside herself to watch the mental movie of her and Ren's first meeting. And after reviewing the footage, she must have agreed it was true, because tears poured out and she grabbed Ren's hand for dear life.

"Rennie, I didn't mean that. I'm not scared of you. Not really. Every part of me knows I was supposed to find you, but I can't figure out what the hell is happening and nothing makes sense anymore."

The terror in Katie's eyes stung her heart, but Ren had the opening she needed, and it couldn't wait any longer.

"It gets weirder," she said. "And I'm so sorry, angel, but you're going to hate it."

The waiter delivered the crème brûlée with a pile of fresh berries and two spoons. They cracked the glossy amber sugar crust, and Ren drove the woman she loved into a full-on, cold-sweat, throat-clawing panic attack.

She watched it swell as she led Katie through every detail and connection. Watched the color drain from the girl's cheeks and the tension build in her hands. Felt her breath slacken. She despised herself for not letting up; for not inflicting the torture in smaller, more humane doses instead of waterboarding Katie with the truth. But it was too late. There were no do-overs.

Unable to bear more, Katie finally slid from the booth. She staggered from the restaurant in search of air. Ren dropped cash on the table and chased after, finally finding Katie in front of a wine shop that had closed for the night. Her forehead was pressed against the cold glass and she was gently rocking, mumbling something to herself like a mantra.

Nina's warning drifted into her thoughts.

*It's not only her life you need to protect. It's her heart.*

Ren wrapped her arms around Katie from behind and held tight. She was trembling, her pulse fast and thready. "We'll figure it out. I promise," Ren whispered.

She breathed deep and regular, willing the girl's heart to slow down and match the steadiness of her own. After a couple minutes, Katie stopped shaking. After a couple more, their hearts found a rhythm. They didn't just beat in unison; they seemed to vibrate.

For a brief, blessed moment, everything else fell away. There was no window, no street, no people, no traffic, no cold, and no wind. There were no mysteries, no dangers, and no ghosts. Just two human beings who had found each other amid a swirling sea of chaos that itself had just evaporated.

The universe did not leave them alone for long.

# THE SURVIVOR

A VOICE CALLED: "Ren? Katie?"

Ren let the girl slip from her grasp, and they turned to find its source. An attractive dark-haired woman dressed in a black parka, yoga pants and stocking cap approached on the sidewalk.

"Good evening, ladies," she said with a smile. "Peter Holland sent a car for you. It's right this way."

He hadn't mentioned that before, but maybe since Ren wouldn't let him chaperone, he thought it would be the next best thing. The brunette gestured to a dark gray SUV parked further up the road. Katie sniffed, wiped her eyes, and said, "Damn, Rennie, you hit the jackpot."

They walked to the car and the woman opened the back door. Katie started to climb in, then Ren noticed a black and yellow yarn bracelet peeking out from the sleeve of the woman's parka.

A tremor ripped through her. A split second later, her brain caught up with it.

It was the bracelet she gave Lailah at the museum when she was nine.

Nina was wrong. Lailah *had* worn it the day she died. And the only way this woman could have it was if she stole it off Lailah's dead body like a souvenir.

Ren shoved the woman hard against the vehicle, grabbed Katie's arm and yanked her away.

"Run!"

They bolted down the street, hands clamped together. Ren could have run faster, but Katie's injuries slowed them down.

A metallic *ka-chunk* echoed from behind. The pavement five steps ahead exploded in a puff of gray powder.

She was shooting at them.

The streets were not crowded, but they weren't empty, either. The two bobbed and weaved around an older couple out for a stroll, then Katie collided with a teenage boy in earbuds, sending him sprawling to the pavement.

Another metallic crack rang out. As the bullet smacked into the base of an elm tree beside Katie, Ren distantly realized the woman was trying to take out their legs.

She wanted them alive.

Ren slung Katie around a corner, keeping herself between Katie and the shooter.

Another crack.

A searing pain like a cigarette burn flared above her left hip. Shards of brick from the adjacent building splintered into the air.

Halfway down the block, a cop car drove away from them. Ren let go of Katie's hand, raised her arms above her head, waved and screamed, "Help! Stop! Police!"

Katie joined in, and they sprinted toward the vehicle.

Ren chanced a glance over her shoulder. The woman had fallen behind and now pulled up short, stashing her silenced pistol in her parka. She retreated around the corner, apparently having concluded further pursuit was too risky.

It was lucky she didn't see the cops kept right on driving.

"No!" Katie cried, but Ren sensed the immediate danger had passed.

"It's okay. She's gone," Ren said with as much conviction as her overtaxed lungs could muster, but they didn't stop running until they arrived at Lailah's building. Stanley greeted them in the lobby and looked more than a little confused as they hurried past him into the waiting elevator.

They made it inside the door to Lailah's apartment, slammed it behind them, and leaned against it, panting.

"Are you alright?" Ren said, looking Katie up and down. "Did you get hit anywhere?"

"No. You?" Katie asked, then spotted the charred hole near Ren's left pocket. "Oh shit," she said, and stripped off Ren's jacket. Her sweatshirt had a matching puncture, and Katie gently lifted it to reveal an angry-looking burn on her love handle.

"Don't worry about it. It's fine," Ren said, pulling her sweatshirt back down. It wasn't actually fine, but at the moment she was too hopped up on endorphins to feel any pain. She tried not to think how if that bullet had struck six inches to the right, she'd be paralyzed.

"No, we need to take care of this. Where's the first-aid stuff?"

Ren's search of the apartment had left no corner unin-spected. "Bathroom medicine cabinet," she said.

Katie returned moments later with supplies, ordered Ren to lie down on the couch, then kneeled beside her. She slid Ren's waistband down and applied a soapy cloth to carefully cleanse the area, her hands wonderfully warm on Ren's cold skin. The girl's focus was intense, eyes on the task at hand, never once on Ren's face as she dried the wound and coated it with antibiotic ointment, all without the least bit of squeamishness.

"How did you know about the woman?" Katie asked as she gently applied an adhesive bandage. Ren had to expend a significant amount of energy not to quiver at the intimacy of the touch, and would have given anything to know whether Katie felt the same tingle.

Ren shrugged. "Spidey sense?"

Katie's eyes cut to hers for the first time. Ren's nerves flared and she bit her lower lip.

"Okay, I think we're done," Katie said after a minute, but she didn't stand or make any move to clean up the mess.

"Thank you," Ren said, acutely aware of how close Katie was sitting and how quiet the apartment had become. Her stomach fluttered. Her heart pounded. She wanted to pull the girl even closer. To feel Katie's warm body pressed against her own. To experience again the dizzying energy of their first kiss. After so many brushes with death, Ren ached to celebrate life. Katie was life. And love. And Ren wanted to drown herself in it and never come up for air.

She could not bring herself to do it.

She had to believe Katie knew how she felt, but as she wondered whether someone so incredible could possibly love her back, another wave of fear washed over.

Nina's warning rang in her ears like a tornado siren.

Ren still hadn't read Lailah's journal, the "cautionary tale" of how dangerous a relationship between a protectress and her charge could be. Even if Katie wanted this too, would it send them over the edge of the abyss?

"Are you tired?" Ren asked, desperate for something—anything—to break the tension in the room.

"No, I'm pretty wired, actually," Katie said, and Ren could almost sense the tightness in her chest.

"Me too. Want to watch TV?" It was the last thing Ren wanted, but she had a vague sense that's what friends did when there was nothing else to do.

"Not really."

"Okay, yeah, me either—"

"Why did you kiss me?" Katie interrupted with one of her trademark direct questions, for which Ren had never been more grateful. At least it was now in the open.

What Ren wanted to say was *because I love you, dummy*, and before she realized it, she heard those very words coming out of her mouth, followed by an intense flush of heat she knew had left her face beet-red. For a second, she wished the couch would swallow her, but Katie looked like she was fighting a smile.

"You weren't just trying to shut me up because I was being a total brat?"

"No," Ren said, and didn't know what to say next, so she filled the silence with breathless babble. "You know, you called me 'Rennie' before. A pet name is, like, a real milestone."

"Yeah," Katie said. "You ready for another one?"

Before Ren could consider the universe of possibility teased by that question, Katie laid a kiss on her lips that ignited her entire body.

The girl smelled of lavender and adrenaline, and her tongue tasted like vanilla and burnt sugar.

It was the best drug Ren ever had.

* * *

It was still dark when Katie woke Ren with gentle kisses on top of her head. She was nestled in the crook of the girl's arm, the most comfortable and comforting thing in the world. Ren smiled and hugged her closer.

"Hi," she purred. When Katie didn't answer, Ren looked up and asked, "What's wrong?"

"Everything keeps replaying in my brain," she said, her words quick and her breathing shallow. "The girl with the scar. The crash. Milo. The explosion on the dock. The woman with the gun. I can't shut it off. I'm scared."

"I know, angel. Me too. Do you want to talk about it?"

Katie didn't answer, so Ren rested her head on Katie's chest and let her fingertips play across the girl's skin. She brushed the contours of her stomach, danced up her rib cage, traced her collarbone, then found the thin straight line of the scar between her breasts. It was like touching a live wire.

Katie tensed and Ren froze. "I'm sorry," she said. "Is this okay?"

"Yeah, it's okay. I'm sorry, I'm not used to... he wouldn't ever touch it. Didn't even want to look at it. I started wearing a sports bra when we had sex so I wouldn't have to see the disgust on his face."

Ren massaged up and down the line, feeling each stroke relax Katie's muscles and, hopefully, ease the fear in her mind.

"What's it from?" Ren asked.

Katie tightened again. "The crash. The first one," she said, and Ren remembered what Katie had told her in the hospital.

*I lost my mom and my baby sister in a crash when I was young.*

"You were in it, too," Ren said, her stomach twisting into a knot. She didn't know whether to pry, whether it would make Katie feel better or worse to speak of it, but finally she asked, "Will you tell me what happened?"

Katie took a deep breath and let it out slowly. Her voice was shaky, but Ren could feel her fighting through it. Wanting to open up about it, painful as it was. "The thing is... it was, um... it was all... so fast. I only know because my dad explained it to me... after. Some kid was joyriding in his dad's sports car. He drifted into our lane. Mom... she tried to avoid him, but there was a truck coming the other way. A big... big... truck. She died... instantly. Ryoko... my little sister... broke her neck. She was on life support for a few hours, but... there was nothing they could do. My heart was damaged... by the impact. The doctors called it 'blunt trauma.' I probably would have died too, except I was lucky. There was a donor heart available, and... it just... worked out that it wasn't a match for anyone else."

Ren laid her palm flat on Katie's chest and felt the beating of the heart she'd grown to love. A heart she now knew had once belonged to someone else. And she was so thankful for it, though she ached at the thought of that beautiful child having her chest cracked open to receive it.

"Did it hurt?" she asked. "The crash? The surgery?"

"I don't remember."

"Good," Ren said, swiping away tears.

"It's okay," Katie said, playing with the curls above Ren's ear. "It was a long time ago."

"I know. But with our accident and everything, it must have stirred up so much for you."

"Kind of, yeah."

"Thank you for sharing it with me. And I'm sorry I made fun of your driving. I'm such an asshole sometimes."

Katie laughed. "It's okay. You didn't know. Besides, I like that you're not afraid to give me shit."

Before Ren could ask who in Katie's life had been afraid to tease her, she started laughing again.

"What's so funny?" Ren asked.

"I just realized… I don't have any more secrets."

"What do you mean?"

"I mean… I've never been with someone like you."

"A girl?" Ren teased.

"Yeah, that too. But I meant someone who knows every bad thing about me. Every skeleton in my closet and every blemish on my body. It's kind of cool."

Cool was an understatement. Ren could only imagine the awesome liberation of being unburdened of her secrets, because her father's death would shadow her heart forever. But with this warm, soft, beautiful woman in her arms, it was the very last thing she wanted to think about.

"And how are you feeling about the other?" Ren asked.

"The fact that you're a girl?"

"Uh-huh."

"Well… it's obviously new, but I think it's also kind of cool."

"I think it's cool that you think it's cool," Ren said, then cringed at herself even though she felt Katie smile. "And… I'll stop saying 'cool' now."

"By the way," Katie said, "did you know it's our anniversary? Nine days."

Ren had known that. She also knew it felt longer. Lifetimes

longer. "How should we celebrate?" she asked, letting her fingertips wander toward Katie's stomach.

Katie tilted Ren's face toward her, and their lips found each other again.

# THE DAUGHTER

AS A GRAY dawn broke over the Potomac, Ren wished she could stop time. It was a pointless wish, and she didn't let herself entertain it for long. But she decided if she could delay the march of the universe and everything it demanded from them, she would do nothing but watch Katie sleep.

She had a nagging sense it might be the last time Katie did so soundly.

When her phone told her it was seven AM, she reluctantly left Katie in bed to call Peter from the living room. He answered on the first ring. She guessed sleep didn't come easily for him these days, either.

"Hey," he said, barely able to contain himself. "Did you talk to Katie about her dad's case? Will she help?"

"Yes, we talked about it, but something happened."

"What?" he asked.

"I know who killed Lailah." She told him about the woman with Lailah's bracelet who claimed Peter had sent her, then opened fire outside the restaurant.

He was incredulous. "Why didn't you call me? Or the police?"

"We, uh, didn't get around to it," she said, hoping he'd take the hint.

"You didn't get—" he started, then it dawned. "Okay, then I'm calling them."

"You're going to call the police?"

"Yeah."

"And tell them what, exactly?"

"That the person who killed Lailah just tried to kill you."

"And then what?"

"What do you mean?" he asked, clearly shocked they were having this conversation.

"Peter, the police don't think *anyone* killed Lailah. You think they're going to change their minds because of a piece of yarn I saw sticking out of some woman's jacket? Don't you get it? The cops are not going to solve anything. All they'll do is put Katie and my mom back under the microscope because of Milo, and I'm not letting that happen."

Ren held her breath, awaiting his reply. She did not want to argue with him any longer.

At last he said, "Okay. I hear you. I'm just… if anything happened to you…" he trailed off.

"I know," Ren said. And she kind of loved him for it.

"How about a compromise? There's a private security firm we call to guard witnesses who get skittish. It's mostly for peace of mind, but these guys are the real deal. They take shifts. They'll watch the building 24/7 and escort you anywhere you want to go. Will you let me do that?"

Bodyguards for Katie, plus no cops? Easy decision. "You can absolutely do that. Thank you."

"I'm bringing Nina to talk to Katie. Plan on ten o'clock, if that fits into your social calendar."

"I'll pencil you in," she said, unable to resist breaking his balls. "But if you get here and there's a sock on the doorknob, you'll have to come back later."

\* \* \*

Ren intended to comply with Peter's request to stay put, so getting out for breakfast wasn't an option. It turned out Lailah's kitchen was decently stocked, with only a couple of things that had expired, so she Googled a pancake recipe. She attempted to follow it quietly, but the whisk kept clanging against the mixing bowl and Katie made waking-up noises in the bedroom.

She dropped blobs of batter in a hot pan and burned the first few, then regrouped and ended up with a half-dozen cakes that were at least not embarrassing. She stacked them on a plate, doused them in syrup, and arranged a tray with coffee and a fork and a napkin. The overfilled cup sloshed and spilled on the way to the bedroom, but the liquid missed the food; no harm, no foul.

When Katie saw her, she smiled. "Breakfast in bed? So domestic!"

Ren's face got hot and she handed over the tray. Katie balanced it on her lap and sipped the coffee.

"Mmm... good," she said, with only a hint of surprise, then ate a forkful of cakes. Her eyes registered a positive first impression—probably the syrup hitting her tongue—but her chewing slowed to a laborious grind and she needed a slug of coffee to wash it down.

"Oh, god. That bad?" Ren asked.

"A little... metallic, maybe? They're cooked right, though," she said as a consolation.

"Sorry. Lailah didn't have baking powder, so I used baking soda. Not the same thing, is it?"

"I don't think so."

Katie took her hand before she could beat herself up too badly. "I appreciate you. More than you know."

Ren wondered how long that would last.

\* \* \*

Two hours later, Peter and Nina knocked on the door. Katie, normally the furthest thing from shy, shook hands with an odd timidity and... was it embarrassment? Like she felt guilty by association with her father, whose sins were somehow responsible for Lailah's death and their own current predicament. Ren wanted to spirit her away from everything that was about to happen.

They gathered in the living room. Nina sat in the chair, Ren and Katie took the couch, and Peter paced the floor like he was arguing in front of a jury.

He handed them a loose sheet from his leather folder. "I need to know if you recognize this person."

It was an ID photo—the light-blue backdrop gave it away—of a dark-haired girl, maybe a little younger than Ren. Pretty, with piercing gray eyes and a playing-it-cool smile. She looked familiar, but Ren couldn't place it.

Katie could. "That's the woman who shot at us."

"Are you certain?" Nina asked.

"It's the lips... how they flare at the bottom. It's her. No doubt."

Peter looked at Ren for confirmation. She hadn't gotten a great look at the woman in black, and the girl in the picture had to be at least ten years younger, but Ren trusted Katie. Registering the shape and proportion of human features would be second nature to her artist's eye. Ren nodded and noted Peter's lack of surprise at the outcome.

"This is Victoria Glass," he said, and though Ren hadn't placed the face, she instantly placed the name.

The girl who escaped Katie's father eight years ago had just come after his daughter.

"How did you know it was her?" Ren asked Peter.

"I've been through the case a half-dozen times, and it kept nagging at me: what happened to Victoria? There were no photos of her in the file, which is unusual because she was at the scene. Normally the police would document any injuries, the condition of her hands, her clothes, if only to exclude her as a suspect. If those photos ever existed, they've since disappeared. When you told me a woman attacked you, I asked our investigator to get a picture. He's only had a couple hours, but Victoria has no social media presence. This is the only one he could find, from her first Pennsylvania driver's license."

Ren was impressed. Peter's instinct to search the death-penalty files for suspects had turned out to be spot-on. They just hadn't received the right files yet.

"So what did happen to her?" Ren asked.

"We're trying to figure that out," he said. "She was a junior at Dartmouth at the time of the murders, but there's no record of her having transferred or graduated. She's now twenty-eight years old. No permanent address, only a private mailbox outside Philly. Her tax returns say she's an independent contractor. Her only client is a company called Consolidated Holdings, which is basically a bullshit shell corporation. The investigator is still trying to untangle who owns it, but at this point we have no idea who Victoria actually works for or what she does."

"I think I met her once," Katie said, and three heads swiveled in unison. "I was probably six or seven. Mr. Glass threw a New Year's party. He invited my parents and they brought me along. A girl gave me some markers and paper to draw with and brought me Shirley Temples and little meatballs. I think it was her."

Katie disappeared into the photo, probably wondering how that thoughtful girl had become a vicious killer. Someone who could inject poison into the veins of an unconscious woman and then take her bracelet like some kind of trophy.

Nina gently pulled her back. "Child, this must be so difficult," she said. "It pains us to ask it of you, but there is only so much we can learn from the case files and the internet. Can you tell us more about your father? The man you remember and what transpired in the days before the crimes?"

Katie laid Victoria's picture on the table and drew a long breath. "My dad was my hero," she began, with a vulnerability suggesting she had not spoken of her father—to anyone—for a long time. Maybe since the day he was arrested. "I always remember him in his lab coat, bright white and starched stiff. He was so cool. He took me to the office on bring-your-kid-to-work day and Mr. Glass would brag about him. He'd say things like 'Your daddy is the brains behind this entire operation. If anything happened to him, we'd be out of business tomorrow.'"

She told them of her father's strength in the aftermath of their car accident when she was eight. How the tragic loss of his wife and baby daughter, along with Katie's near-death and traumatic recovery, didn't break him.

"He was devastated, of course. And he was never quite the

same, but he didn't shut down. For the next four years, he invested in me and made sure every day we spent together was special. Not with, like, presents and stuff; just something fun. A game of Yahtzee, sparring at the dojo, playing mom's Serge Gainsbourg records. After a while, I noticed him pull back from his work. I asked if he'd get in trouble for spending so much time with me, but he laughed it off. 'My job is to hire smart people and get out of their way,' he said. I took him at his word."

Everything changed on an otherwise-ordinary Tuesday in March.

He almost always picked her up from school. Their rides home were some of her favorite times with him, especially when they'd get bubble teas from the kiosk at the park, sit on the bench and blow tapioca spitballs through the big fat straws.

But not that day. He no-showed, and she sat with a teacher for an extra forty-five minutes, worrying about what might have befallen him. Finally, Tia, his executive assistant, pulled up in her car, apologizing for keeping Katie waiting. Tia brought her home and stayed the rest of the evening, but offered no insight into where her dad was.

Fueled by Dr. Peppers and sheer terror, she waited up as long as she could, but the gas finally ran out sometime after three AM. A couple hours later, she awoke to the sound of drawers and cabinets slamming. From the hallway door, she watched him ransack his office and shove things into his briefcase, too frightened of his manic eyes to make her presence known or ask him why he was so upset.

Later that morning, Tia drove Katie to school and Naoki Ando murdered two people with a gun his daughter didn't know he'd owned.

From everything Katie had said, this was so far out of character for him as to be unthinkable. Ren thought of Yana whispering her poison to Milo and the dockworker, instilling in them an utter disregard for human life. Had Katie's father been similarly influenced?

"The next time I saw him was in court," Katie continued. "He didn't have his lab coat anymore. He had an orange jumpsuit and shackles. He told the judge he was guilty and before they led him off, he turned to me and said, 'I love you, Kaede-chan. If you have ever loved me, you must live now as if I am dead.' That's the last time I heard his voice."

Rage surged through Ren's chest. Katie did not deserve any of this. Not what her dad had put her through eight years ago—if, in fact, he was responsible—and not what Peter was about to ask her to do: confront the man once again.

"Will you let us contact him on your behalf and try to arrange a visit?"

Her eyes found the floor and her grip on Ren's hand verged on painful. "What did Lailah want with my father? Why are you trying to help him?"

"Katie, you're entitled to the truth more than anyone, which is this: I have no idea what Lailah wanted, and I'm not trying to help your father. We need him to help us. To protect you and bring Lailah's killer to justice. I believe—and I think Ren would agree—you are the only one who can make that happen."

Katie's eyes cut to Ren's in search of a safe harbor, but Ren could offer none. They both knew there was no other path forward. Katie gave Peter a nod.

"Thank you," he said. "I'll initiate the request. Visits have to be scheduled two days in advance, so assuming he consents, we're looking at Thursday at the earliest. Can you two stay out of trouble until then?"

"Doubtful," Ren said, hoping for a smile out of Katie. She didn't get one.

"Try," Peter said, and left the apartment.

Nina stayed behind and studied Katie for a long while. "Peter is hopeful this will lead to answers," she said, "though I wish I shared his optimism. Miss Katie, you must steel yourself to the possibility he will refuse your request. If he does, I pray you don't take it as rejection. To the contrary, his love for you is such that he would not want your last memories of him to be in that dark place."

Ren was grateful for Nina's wise counsel, but she knew Katie too well. If Ando refused to see her, the girl was going to shatter.

# THE LEARNER

NINA DEPARTED AFTER lunch, and when Peter's security team arrived, Ren and Katie met them in the lobby. Ren was expecting buzz-cuts and black suits, but found instead a couple who looked like the instructors who gave her skiing lessons when her parents took her to the Poconos that one time.

Denise was blond and freckled. Rob had piercing blue eyes and dimples for days. They explained they would be parked outside until ten PM, at which point the night guys would take over. They were professional and friendly and the four of them exchanged cellphone numbers.

Ren was inclined to heed Peter's advice: stay indoors and avoid trouble until they learned if Katie's father would let them visit. As long as food could be delivered and Katie was there, Ren had all she needed. But an hour after the guards took their post, the same restless impulse that propelled Katie back to work the day after Milo's shooting had her bouncing off the walls of Lailah's apartment. Her injuries from the crash were finally healing, and she buzzed with energy.

"Let's *do* something," she whined.

Ren shook her head. "Peter's right. It's safer if we stay here."

"Come on… the baby-sitters club will follow us wherever we go, and if someone wants to hurt me, you'll feel it, yeah? You're batting a thousand so far."

The girl made a compelling case, even if Ren didn't catch all her references. But Katie was tempting fate, and the more Ren thought about last night's attack, the less she believed her instincts as a protectress had come into play at all.

She'd told Katie it was her Spidey sense that saved them, but that wasn't true. She hadn't felt the existential anxiety that preceded the rollercoaster rush of ethereation. Not until she saw Lailah's bracelet on Victoria's wrist did Ren understand she was in the presence of a killer. Even with bullets whipping through the air, Ren didn't sense Katie was in mortal peril.

She reminded herself that she and Yana, in that explosive exchange of soul energy, had learned everything there was to know about each other. Assuming Yana and Victoria were connected—it seemed unlikely two *different* groups were after them—then Victoria almost certainly knew about Ren as well. And something about that had changed the calculus.

Ren had no idea what Victoria now intended for them, but the point was last night felt different. She kept this to herself, of course, because she didn't want Katie to worry or feel more guilty than she already did about putting Ren in danger.

In the end, there was a light in Katie's eyes warm enough to counter the freezing cold outside, and Ren was pathologically incapable of saying "no" to the girl.

"So, what should we do?" Ren asked.

"I don't know. This is your town, what's fun?"

"My town?" Ren laughed. "I've been here five days."

"Yeah, but in five days you've gotten a job and an apartment. You've made friends with the neighborhood watch, and you know all the cool places to eat. So, yeah, your town."

Brat.

"Fine. Get your coat on. We'll ask *my* doorman."

As it turned out, they didn't need their coats.

When they asked Stanley for suggestions, he escorted them right back into the elevator. They descended to the parking garage, then exited and walked down a clean, well-lit hallway with several locked doors on either side. One door was labeled 501, matching the number of Lailah's apartment.

"Some of our apartments have separate storage units," he explained. "Miss D. used hers for something else."

He slid a key into the lock, opened the door, and turned on the lights.

It was an art studio.

Lailah was an artist.

The realization hit Ren hard as she recalled Peter describing how they'd met over a drawing Lailah made of an airplane. And judging by the canvases stacked against the storage unit's walls, Ren could now tell many of the pieces upstairs were Lailah's work as well. She felt a surge of excitement that here, in this small room, was another chance to know her protectress; this time, through her art.

But as fascinating as that was, Ren was more interested in Katie's reaction.

The girl was awestruck.

Katie hesitated, as if entering the room meant fully embracing her abandoned passion, and she wasn't quite ready to do it.

She'd flirted with art for the first time in years when Ren asked her to sketch Lailah, but only as an interpreter of Ren's vision. Before her was the chance to bring her own visions to life, whatever they may be. To express herself in paint or ink or charcoal for the first time in years. Ren wondered if Katie wasn't just a little scared of what might reveal itself on the canvas.

Regardless, Stanley couldn't have done better. He shot Ren one of his now-familiar winks and left them to it.

Ren met Katie's eyes with an unspoken question: *are you okay with this?*

Katie nodded and they began to explore.

The room was twenty feet on each side, and Lailah had established different zones in the corners, with supply shelves spanning the walls between them. Drawing and painting seemed to be Lailah's primary interests, as two corners had tall, wooden easels. Ren flipped through the canvases stacked on the floor beside them, and one motif kept reappearing: moonflowers, strikingly similar to those in Ren's dream. The stone wall, the bright moon in the night sky, the silvery blooms on the vines. And yet the unknown remained unknown; Lailah had not tried to depict what was on the other side of the wall.

Ren left the canvases and examined the third corner, which had a potter's wheel and a small kiln. She admired the handful of clay pieces on the shelf. Two were coffee mugs glazed in rich tones of rust and turquoise, and Ren wondered if Lailah had been in the process of making a set for Peter or Nina or their law office. There was a sturdy bowl, unglazed, about nine inches across. And two dinner-sized plates with a gorgeous cobalt sheen.

The last corner held a stained-glass workstation. Ren wasn't familiar with the tools of that trade, but there were a dozen jewel-tone glass rectangles laid out in an art déco pattern that reminded her of a lampshade in her Grammie Beth's living room. On the adjacent shelf was a "stained glass for beginners" book, and Ren warmed at the thought of Lailah wanting to learn a new skill later in life. Then anger flared in her chest, directed at Victoria and how callously she'd robbed Lailah of her chance to master it.

As a tribute to her protectress, and because she could barely draw a straight line with a ruler, Ren decided to take on the glass. She was tempted to ask Katie for help, but the girl was already lost in the colorful assortment of paints and brushes on the shelves. So Ren picked up the book and learned—from the pictures—how to assemble the pieces into a panel.

The cut edges had already been ground smooth, so she mixed up some dish soap and water in a small bowl and cleaned and dried the pieces. The next step was to wrap the edges of each piece in thin copper foil. Apparently, it was critical to apply the foil tightly and evenly, with a consistent margin around the top and bottom so the solder joints would be uniform. She had to re-do the first few several times, but she eventually got the hang of it.

To actually assemble the pieces, she would have to apply flux paste and then solder them together. And though Lailah had all the gear to accomplish this, Ren wasn't in a hurry. She also wondered if Lailah had hesitated at the thought of holding the 375-degree hot iron in her hands, knowing she could ethereate at any moment. Maybe that's why she'd stopped where she did.

Ren stood, stretched her aching limbs, and turned to look at Katie for the first time in what must have been a couple of hours.

The girl was standing quietly behind an easel, arms crossed, studying a canvas Ren could only see the back of. Ren approached and saw the stunning image Katie had captured in exquisite black brushstrokes.

A rough triangle pointed downward, its lines thick and not quite closed at each corner. From the top two corners, wispy arms reached out to the sides before arcing down and culminating in fingers that gripped what looked like bouquets of flowers.

The triangle itself was empty, but something about the way Katie had rendered the negative space made Ren think something should have been there. That something *had* been there.

She suppressed a gasp as she realized what Katie had painted. It was a womb. A barren womb.

Ren swallowed the girl in a hug, and Katie returned it.

No words needed to be said.

\* \* \*

Ren never cared too much for seafood, so she put her digestive health in Katie's hands and they got takeout sushi from a place Stanley recommended. Seated on the floor at Lailah's coffee table, she got her first lesson. Nigiri was raw fish on a bed of steamed rice. Sashimi was a piece of fish by itself. And a "spider roll" was made from rice and deep-fried soft-shell crab and about five other ingredients Ren couldn't identify, and it was one of the best things she'd ever eaten.

The meal was rich with laughter (mostly Katie's, because Ren sucked at chopsticks) and moaning (mostly Ren's, as each bite was tastier than the last). And though darkness swirled around them, Ren was lit by a deeper sense of peace than she'd ever known.

This was love.

Lailah said Ren needed to protect it, and she finally understood what that meant. She was willing to die for it.

Not only for Katie, but for this feeling. This energy. So someone else—anyone else—in this cold, hard world could experience a moment of this joy.

Katie flopped back against the sofa and declared she couldn't eat another bite. Ren shoved every last seaweed-wrapped morsel of heaven into her face, which made Katie laugh more; this time at her food coma. After a while, Katie reached out and laid her hand on Ren's thigh. Ren tingled every time they touched.

"I appreciate what you did today," Katie said.

"Oh, stop. That breakfast was terrible!"

Katie smiled. "Not breakfast, you goofball. And not for being brave and trying raw fish. For helping me find art again."

Ren squeezed Katie's hand, the image of the girl's painting still fresh in her mind. "Are you okay? Do you... want to talk about it?"

"Honestly, I don't. But thanks for asking. I'm not the best about sharing stuff with people. I have to kind of work it out on the canvas. And I haven't been able to do that for a long time."

Ren understood. More than Katie would ever realize. And if she'd played some small part in rekindling Katie's light as Katie had rekindled her own, she was grateful. "You have a gift," she said. "It's definitely what you need to be when you grow up."

"What did you want to be when you were little?" Katie asked.

"I wanted to be a firefighter," Ren said, surprising herself with the recollection. It had been years since she'd even thought of it. "I wanted to climb ladders and get cats out of trees and spray water on things."

"Yeah, that tracks."

Memories flooded back. "My dad took me to a firehouse once. He knew the captain, so I got the full tour. I even got to slide down the pole. It was the best day. Cops and firefighters are, like, rivals, and the captain kept busting my dad's balls. He'd tell jokes, like 'What do cops and firemen have in common? They both want to be firemen!' And he'd laugh and my dad would just take the abuse."

"He must have loved you an awful lot to put up with that," Katie said.

A pang of guilt hit Ren like a baseball bat to the stomach and it was all she could do not to throw up the meal she'd just eaten.

Of course her dad had loved her.

Though she'd always been too stupid to realize it, he'd been her biggest fan. Her fiercest advocate. Her stay-up-late-and-watch-scary-movies buddy. Her fellow sports dork. Her all-you-can-eat-buffet wingman.

He never gave her shit about wanting to be a firefighter. He didn't *really* want to lock her in a padded room. He wanted to tell her about the girl who got hit by the train, even when her mom didn't. He'd fought so hard for her that it cost him his marriage.

He still cared enough to find her after she ran away. When she was caught on camera during one of her and Alistair's burglaries, and her dad recognized her because of the Eagles hat. Because he'd bought his little girl one just like his own.

He'd gone to the house where she was staying and asked Alistair where she was.

And the sick fuck pulled out a gun and shot him in the chest. Her dad loved her.

He loved her, and she'd put him in front of that bullet as sure as if she'd squeezed the trigger herself.

She was a killer.

Even Yana had said so. And Yana was a stone fucking murderer, so she'd definitely know.

Yes, Lauren Ann Cole was a killer. The guilt and the shame of it were rotting her from the inside out.

And she simply couldn't keep it bottled any longer.

"I need to tell you—" she began, then her phone started vibrating on the coffee table.

It was Peter.

Katie grabbed for it. "Hey," she said. "You're on speaker."

"Katie, I got a response from the superintendent's office at Prescott. I'm sorry. Your father has refused to let any of us visit. Didn't give a reason. We'll regroup tomorrow and talk about what's next, okay?"

The devastating news hung in the air, and a bottomless well of pain filled Katie's eyes. She could barely manage a nod, so Ren croaked, "Got it," and ended the call.

Ren swallowed her urge to confess and put her guilt back on the shelf.

There was no consoling the girl whose father had just rejected her for the second time. All Ren could do was be the big spoon and hold tight as Katie cried herself to sleep.

# THE MONSTER

REN WENT TO bed certain that the recurring, surreal dream of her father and Alistair at the diner would torment her again that night, but when she finally fell into her own restless slumber, she saw something else entirely.

In place of a bright, bustling restaurant, there was a long, dim corridor. Instead of gleaming laminate tables, there were black doors with mesh windows and white stenciled numbers. The background noises were different, too. In place of conversations, cash register drawers, and the clatter of silverware on porcelain dishes, there were other sounds: a flushing toilet, a dull electrical hum, a man snoring, another groaning. She couldn't tell whether it was in pain or pleasure, but it made her skin crawl.

The numbers on the doors—even on one side, odd on the other—cycled from one to thirty, then reset back to one, as if she were looping repeatedly through the strange hallway. With each cycle, her heart beat faster even as her momentum seemed to slow, until she finally came to rest in front of number twenty-three. No light shone through the window, but she knew beyond a shadow of a doubt somebody was behind that door.

Somebody awake. And determined.

Anxiety gripped her chest.

This was not a dream.

This was death row.

When the rollercoaster rush pulled her soul through the steel door of Naoki Ando's prison cell, Ren was not afraid.

She was devastated.

Because she'd been hoping against hope that the gut-punch she felt when she saw his picture in Katie's scrapbook didn't mean what she thought it meant. That she'd bonded with him, exactly as she'd done with his daughter on a Philadelphia warehouse roof.

That she was now his protectress, too.

This was not part of the fucking deal.

Katie's father sat on the edge of his bed, a razor-sharp plastic shiv pressed to his left wrist. He must have sensed her in his periphery, because his eyes narrowed with rage and he sprang from the mattress with lightning speed, crossing the room in one long, smooth stride to slice the shiv across her throat.

She flinched, but of course it passed right through her. Her body was safely nestled beside Katie's, a warmth and comfort she could almost perceive. She was nowhere near functional in both places, but for the first time, she sensed her physical self still existed.

His rage gave way to fear, and he uttered a single word: "*Ikiryō.*"

He retreated to the bed, sat on the thin mattress, and stabbed the shiv into his forearm.

A searing pain shot through Ren's soul as if the blade had punctured her own flesh. Her brain exploded in a desperate plea of *you can't! you can't! you can't!* and all she could think to scream was "No! Katie loves you!"

He froze, a heartbeat from dragging the blade toward his hand, shredding the artery and bleeding out. Ren panicked. The curtains had opened. She was center-stage in the spotlight, only she didn't know what play she was in and hadn't learned her lines.

What the hell could she say to this man?

In the end, she went with the truth. "My name is Ren. I'm in love with your daughter. I'm with her right now in an apartment in Washington, DC. Someone is trying to kill us. Please! You have to tell us why. You have to help me save her."

His breathing was hard, ragged. Agonized from the blade impaled in his arm. His mind seemed to race as fast as hers. She knew he'd seen someone like her before—maybe Yana, maybe others—but he had clearly never encountered an ethereant with the remotest potential to be benign.

"Put the knife down," she begged. "Just talk to me for a minute?"

He clenched the shiv. For a split second, she thought he might finish the job, but he pulled it free with a stifled cry. It fell from his hand and clattered to the concrete. Blood poured from his arm, soaking his coveralls. She would have grabbed something to staunch it, but that wasn't how this worked. He finally broke eye contact and gripped his bedsheet with both hands. He tore a strip and fashioned a tourniquet, tightening it with his teeth.

"How can I trust this?" he asked, his voice trembling in pain.

"There's no reason for me to lie. If I wanted to hurt her, I could do it anytime. We have a chance to stop whoever is behind this. If you love her as much as I know you do, it should be a simple choice."

"You are wrong, *ikiryō*," he said, shaking his head. "When I am dead, she will be safe because they can no longer threaten me with her harm."

He leaned toward the head of the bed, slipped his hand between the mattress and frame, and removed what looked like a small piece of paper. He unfolded it, stared impassively at it for a moment, then held it out for Ren to examine.

It was a photo of Katie in her hospital bed.

She balled her fists. That fucking cop. Kowalski.

If these people had police doing their dirty work, there was nobody they could trust. And here she was, about to ask his permission to bring his daughter into a building full of law enforcement. But that picture was also old news.

"Did you know they've tried to kill her three times since that was taken?"

He closed his eyes and exhaled through his nose. His expression said he didn't know, but also wasn't surprised.

"Why is this happening?" Ren asked. "You've been in prison eight years. Why are they threatening Katie now?"

"The lawyer," he said.

Lailah.

"Because she looked into your case," she said to herself as much as to him, scrambling to make sense of the chain of events the moonflowers had set into motion. "They killed her too, you know."

He was infuriatingly unmoved.

"They were quite content to let the state execute me, but her sudden interest made them nervous. Now it would seem they want to tie up all the loose ends."

"I understand threatening Katie to keep you quiet, but why kill her? She's not a loose end. She doesn't know anything!"

"She knows me. That is why I must die. Now if you truly care for her, go back from where you came and let me get on with it."

"I'm not going anywhere. What makes you think they'll let her live after you're dead? You need to help me. And she deserves to know why you killed those people. Why you burned down her life and made her an orphan."

Her words wounded him worse than the shiv, but they also weren't working.

"It makes no difference," he said. "Tell her I am evil, or unhinged, or an addict. The devil made me do it. Or the OxyContin. Whatever you think she will believe."

Ren stepped closer. "You selfish dick! I will not lie for you! Don't make her carry this pain the rest of her life. You owe her the truth. And you owe her a chance to forgive you."

There was a change in the air. Had it occurred to him such a thing was possible? She pressed forward, emboldened. "I want to bring her to you. As soon as I can. Will you allow us to visit? Also, the lawyer that—"

"No lawyers," he cut her off. That was clearly non-negotiable.

"Okay, fine," she conceded. "No lawyers, just me and Katie."

He stared her down, then relented with an almost imperceptible nod.

"Thank you," she said, and for an instant, her mind relaxed. Her soul did not.

Something was off.

If history were any guide, she would leave this place almost immediately and return to her body because the danger had passed, and her task was finished.

She wasn't leaving.

"You don't have any intention of seeing her, do you?" she challenged him. "The second I go, you're going to pull that bandage off your arm and end it."

Ando must have realized that in her ethereated state she was basically a human lie detector, so he dropped all pretense.

"Ren, is it? Unlike the others, your motives appear to be genuine, but you do not understand. If I so much as see her or speak to her, they will redouble their efforts to kill her because they will assume she now knows too much. Please tell Kaede she is—and always has been—the light of my life, and that I hope to see her on the other side. But the road ends for me tonight. Attempting to remove her from danger is the last act of fatherhood I can perform, and I will delay it no longer. If you wish to stay and watch, that is your choice."

There was zero uncertainty in his voice. Not one hint of hesitation.

She had failed.

Ren thought of Lailah and how disappointed she would be. Lailah had said she'd find people like this—people she needed to help regardless of their sins, because there was good inside them. *Love* inside them. And Ren could see it. It sparkled like a diamond beneath his bloodstained brown uniform. He loved his baby girl more than anything, but his fear for her safety was winning out. Both of their hearts were broken in a hundred places, and he was about to destroy their only chance to heal them.

Love against fear.

Lailah had said it was the epic battle of the universe, and Ren had never understood the stakes more clearly, nor had she ever needed her protectress so badly.

Lailah had also promised she would never be alone in this fight. So why did she feel like the final girl in a slasher movie?

Then a realization shook her to her core.

She wasn't the final girl.

Katie was there.

Well, not *there* in the prison cell, but if ethereal Ren could somehow connect back with herself—with her incapacitated body in the bed they shared—maybe she could wake Katie and become a conduit between father and daughter. Maybe Katie could find the elusive passkey to his heart and convince him to see her, risk be damned.

It was their only chance. And she was out of time.

"Very well," he said, retrieving the bloody shiv from the floor.

"Wait! Please! Give her a chance to ask you herself!"

His blade remained poised for the killing stroke, but he processed this new possibility.

It was now or never.

Ren concentrated on herself, from her feet to the top of her head, trying to sense the ethereal cord that surely tethered her wandering soul to her body. For an instant, she felt something tingle, like a mosquito on her scalp. She focused all her energy on that spot as if it were the entrance to a water slide, and hurled herself through it. Suddenly she was flying, twisting and turning inside a deep blue umbilicus that seemed at once miles long and dimensionless. And then it spat her out, limbs flailing, soaring breathlessly through the air before plunging into a warm pool that grounded her to the physical world.

She opened her eyes. She was in Lailah's bed, with Katie's arm draped across her.

She couldn't move. The bodily fatigue of ethereation, bordering on paralysis, was as bad as before, but at least she could see and think and feel everything in both places at once.

"Katie, wake up! Wake up! I need your help!"

Katie startled awake and sat up. "Rennie, what's wrong?"

"I'm with him. With your dad. In prison."

"What?"

"I zapped to him, like I do for you. I'm there now. Here *and* there. He's in danger. He's going to kill himself to keep you safe. I can't talk him out of it. What do I say?" Tears coursed down her face, but she couldn't swipe them away.

"Oh my God," Katie said, but as unbelievable as Ren's plea must have sounded, she responded without hesitation. "Ask him if he remembers the pictures I used to make for him."

Ren refocused on Ando in his cell. Incredibly, it was already second nature, no more difficult than looking in a mirror and seeing what was in front of and behind her at the same time.

"Do you remember the pictures she made for you?" she asked him.

His grip on the blade relaxed ever so slightly. He nodded, and she relayed a "yes" to Katie.

"Tell him I've made his portrait," Katie said carefully. "*L'Homme à tête de chou.*"

Ren shared the message, fearing her French left much to be desired. It must have been adequate, though, because Ando allowed himself a gentle smile.

"She wants to give it to you. Please let her. It's the only thing she's ever asked you for," Ren relayed Katie's words, then added a message of her own: "I promise I will keep her safe."

Ando glared at her. She could read his thoughts as clearly as if they were projected on a screen. He knew this snarky little emo girl had power. He was asking himself if she had *enough* power to keep that promise.

Ren was asking herself that, too.

He subtly withered and dropped the knife onto the floor. Her chest immediately loosened.

It was over. For real, this time.

"We'll be there as soon as we can," she told him, and in a flash, she was gone.

With the entirety of her soul now safely back in bed, Ren still couldn't move, but she met Katie's searching eyes. "You did it, angel. You did it. He'll see us."

Katie took Ren's face in her hands and showered her with kisses. Ren could return them, but was too fatigued to lift her stupid arms and embrace her love.

"I'm sorry," she said. "This thing I do steals all my energy."

Katie stopped and stared. "You can't move? At all? Oh, this is going to be fun."

Such a brat.

# THE MOURNER

IN THE MORNING, Katie decided it was her turn to make coffee, and Ren didn't protest. The girl went the extra mile, pre-warming the mugs and Ren's cream, tweaking the setting on the bean grinder from where Lailah had left it, and using the French press she'd found in the cupboard.

The result was far superior to what Ren had brewed the day before, proving once again Katie was better at everything. It was only a matter of time before she realized she was dating down.

Ren relaxed with her drink, but Katie's restless energy was bubbling again. There was something on her mind.

"You okay?" Ren asked.

Katie shrugged. "Just thinking about last night."

"Which part?" Ren remembered the girl teasing and testing the extent of her immobility and couldn't keep the smile from her voice.

"You were so defenseless," Katie said, but there was no levity in her tone. "I mean, you were safe with me, but what happens when you ethereate from somewhere else?"

Ren wished she could minimize it, but Katie was too smart. "It's dangerous," she said. "It's bad. The first time, I was on the train. Luckily, Peter found me. The time on the dock, I was at his office pouring coffee. I burned myself."

"That's what happened to your arm!" Katie said, touching the spot. It was still pink, but no longer ached. She frowned. "I gotta be honest, as superpowers go, this one's kind of shitty. You don't get to decide when it happens, and you go tits-up as soon as it does. Not ideal."

Ren laughed, then wondered what other power she would have chosen had it been up to her. Almost immediately, she realized she wouldn't change it. No other ability could put her so close to Katie's beautiful soul. She almost said as much, then decided it would be too mushy. Instead, she said, "Don't worry about it. Whatever happens, happens."

"I'm not worried about it. Because I'm going to protect you."

Ren's first instinct was to crack wise, but then she remembered Katie said she'd sparred with her dad at a dojo. Then she thought of the punching bag at Milo's house. She had assumed it was his. Maybe it wasn't.

"Do you know how to fight?" she asked.

"Yeah," Katie said, lacing her fingers through Ren's. "I do. My dad taught me."

Before Ren could inquire further, her phone rang. Peter again. She put him on speaker.

"I don't know what changed," he said, "but you guys are on for tomorrow morning with Ando."

Ren was confused. "I thought we had to wait two days?"

"Apparently he requested an expedited visit and the superintendent approved. Possibly because..." he trailed off.

"He doesn't have much time left," Katie finished for him.

"When do we leave?" Ren asked, realizing Katie had just lost most of her time to make the art she'd promised her dad.

"We'll get up early and drive," Peter said. "The security guys will follow. I don't want to have to worry about your safety at that end."

"Okay," Ren said. "We'll talk later. We've got work to do." She ended the call and looked at Katie. "Does Lailah have what you need, or are we going shopping?"

Katie spent half an hour in the storage room inventorying Lailah's supplies and deciding whether any of them would be suitable for her first communication with her father in eight years. In the end, Katie found what she wanted: vine charcoal sticks, light gray art paper, and a can of spray fixative to stop the charcoal from smudging when it was finished.

Stanley helped them move one of the large easels up to Lailah's apartment, and after Katie had arranged her implements on the kitchen table, *L'Homme à tête de chou* took shape. The girl lost herself in her work, displaying a stunning singularity of purpose. And though Ren would have been content to spend hours watching the artist ply her talents, there was something more pressing she longed to do.

It was time to read Lailah's journal.

Ever since Nina had placed it in her hands, the book had the magnetic pull of a present under a Christmas tree—the one at the top of her list for Santa; the one she wanted most of all. At the same time, it was not a gift to tear into impatiently, shredding the wrapping paper and tossing it over her shoulder with abandon. It needed to be unwrapped carefully, reverently.

Ren moved to the living room, curled up in the leather recliner beside the expansive window, and studied the black linen cover. There was a picture glued on it, and Ren could instantly see Lailah's hand at work in the watercolor and ink. It was a loose self-portrait of Lailah, eyes closed, sitting on the ground with her legs crossed as if she were meditating. A wispy trail emerged from the top of her head, coiling upward until it resolved into a floating miniature Lailah, sitting the same way. It was the perfect depiction of ethereation.

She searched inside for other pictures, but the cover turned out to be the only one. In fact, almost two-thirds of the book was blank; Lailah's minimalism apparently extended to her journaling as well. Though there were a hundred or more entries, each reflected only the barest details of the encounter. Ren hungered to learn about Lailah's other charges, but more than that, she wanted to know how Lailah had *felt* about them, about her "gift," and the implications it had for her own life.

Once again, it seemed a deeper understanding of her protectress would elude her forever.

Ren set aside her disappointment and turned to the first entries, a simple record of the awakening of a power that was as mysterious to Lailah as it was to herself.

[June 12, 2007] *I had a vision of a boy riding his bike on Allegheny Avenue and getting hit by a beer truck. I yelled to stop him. He swerved and crashed into a mailbox. A woman ran up after. His mom, maybe? She called him Trey. I wanted to check on him but blacked out. Jonas found me in back of the bakery and called paramedics. ER doctor diagnosed me with fatigue.*

Ren was struck by how similar Lailah's experience was to her own. She, too, had thought it was a vision—in her case, Milo's car at her mom's house—and only later realized she was actually there.

> [June 16, 2007] *I remembered I'd seen Trey at the bodega a couple weeks ago. The kid tried to convince the clerk to sell him cigarettes for his ma. I remembered I felt sick when I looked at him.*

There it was: the sickness. Nina had called it the bonding. That gut-punch sensation Ren felt on the roof with Katie and after seeing Katie's father in the scrapbook photo. And she remembered the museum, when Lailah had clutched her stomach after laying eyes on Ren for the first time. She fought the urge to skip ahead in the book to read about their bonding from Lailah's perspective.

> [July 4, 2007] *Trey and his friends were setting off snappers in the alley off Westmoreland. He did not recognize me.*

So ended Trey's tale, or at least Lailah's part in it, as he wasn't mentioned again. She wondered why Lailah had been called upon to shepherd him through that one perilous moment. Maybe the boy went on to do something heroic, like Jimmy Rivera saving the kids from the fire. She liked the idea that Lailah touched Trey's life so he could touch another, and so on; a cycle of love paid forward. She hated the idea that she would never know. It made her feel small.

The next entry was dated almost two years later.

[April 14, 2009] *A woman asked me to hold her place in the concession line at the Sixers game while she got cash from the ATM. I had that sick feeling again after looking into her eyes, but worse this time. I couldn't breathe for a minute. When she returned, she thanked me and said her name was Melissa.*

Ren could imagine Lailah waiting and wondering how this chance encounter would play out. Whether the distinctive sickness—like she'd felt with Trey—portended another bond, or if it was only a coincidence. Lailah didn't have to wait long to find out.

[April 18, 2009] *I was studying in the dorm commons and had a vision of Melissa getting attacked on her way home from work. I told her she'd be in danger if she took the shortcut. She was weirded out but changed direction. She stopped and asked, "do I know you from somewhere?" I was gone before I could say. Woke up on commons sofa at 4 AM.*

Three weeks later, Lailah met Melissa again by chance, or so it would seem, at a coffee shop. This had to be the relationship Nina described; the one with such dire consequences for the women. Ren's stomach clenched and only drew tighter as she followed the thread through dozens of journal entries spanning years.

Melissa was a junior at Drexel, a year older than Lailah when they met. She was pre-med, stressed about her courses, unhappy with her MCAT scores, obsessed with getting into the "right" school to pursue her dream of becoming a pediatrician. By all indications, a perfectly normal future doctor. A funny and happy and independent young woman who Lailah clearly adored. Not that she'd said so, but Ren could read between the lines.

Lailah was there for her friend ethereally and physically whenever she was needed. A panic attack during a critical biochem exam. An ice-cream binge after Melissa's drummer boyfriend broke up with her to go on the road with his band. A friendly-looking businessman spiking her drink when she was out celebrating her acceptance to UCLA Med.

And it was not a one-sided relationship. Melissa was a great and supportive friend. She drove to Lailah's dorm at three AM with her laptop when Lailah's crashed before a huge paper was due. She consoled Lailah through a number of breakups, as Lailah seemed to fall hard for older guys who turned out to be far less mature than she was. Melissa even moved in with Lailah for six weeks to nurse her through a broken leg she'd suffered while ethereating to someone else.

But as Ren continued to read, the cracks in their friendship started to show. As they progressed through their respective graduate schools and into their careers, the ethereations grew more frequent. Melissa demanded more and more of Lailah, seemingly losing the ability to make good decisions on her own, or navigate difficult situations without her protectress holding her hand. Everything was a crisis, and only Lailah could solve it.

Lailah tried to step back, gently—and then not-so-gently— encouraging her best friend to regain her lost independence. She couldn't. Yet Lailah didn't give up on her. The friendship rose and fell in waves, each peak higher than the last, each trough progressively deeper until it bottomed out in an irreversible tragedy after Lailah made the impossible decision to end it, for both their sakes.

Melissa took her own life.

And Lailah had been forced to watch, ethereated and helpless, as she had done it.

The sparse writing chronicled the circumstances and the date, but not the motivation. For that, Ren had to fill in the blanks.

She remembered how it felt when Lailah died, the gaping void left in her head and her heart when her protectress was erased from existence. And that was after only a couple of days. Melissa had depended upon Lailah for years. Losing her constant companion must have felt like a death as well—a snuffing-out of her expanded consciousness.

It had obviously been unbearable.

Ren glanced up from Lailah's neat handwriting to see Katie immersed in her project.

Her heart was overcome by dread.

Was that their future? Would Katie come to depend on her as Melissa had on Lailah? Were they strong enough to survive it?

As quickly as the fear had swelled, so too did a terrible clarity. Being Katie's protectress wasn't a choice. Being her lover was. She was responsible for Katie's protection. She would not be party to Katie's destruction.

She had to end this relationship before it was too late.

Ren turned her back, praying the girl wouldn't see her shoulders shaking as she sobbed, and it took a long time to compose herself. After a while, she debated fixing a glass of water and a peanut butter sandwich for Katie, or reminding her to take a bathroom break, but didn't trust herself not to dissolve back into tears at the sight of the girl's face. And so she returned to the journal, though she could barely recall why she'd been tempted by it in the first place. The wretched thing now felt like a movie she had to peek at through her fingers, as if that could temper the terror of its words.

If nothing else, she was still eager to read about her own first encounter with Lailah at the museum, but the next charge, who merited only two entries, sent her mind reeling once again.

[March 8, 2012] *I drove mom to the ER for abdominal pain. It turned out to be an ulcer. I bonded with a little girl named Alex in the waiting room. Sweet kid chatted me up. Said her babysitter canceled last minute, so her mother brought her to work.*

[March 17, 2012] *Ethereated to subway on 8th. Alex let go of her mom's hand and walked to the edge of the platform. I waved and called, but she couldn't see me. She stepped in front of the train. Nothing I could do. Woke up in my bedroom. Can't get it out of my head.*

Ren reread the entries a dozen times, as if the ink would rearrange itself into something that made sense. A little girl killed by a subway train twelve years ago. Exactly as Sarah had described.

Lailah was there the day the light died. She saw what happened. Tried to prevent it and failed.

Putting aside her extraordinary connection to the event for a moment, Ren lost herself imagining how it impacted her protectress to have two charges she'd been unable to save. She must have been devastated. She must have questioned everything. When Ren asked Peter why there were so few in attendance at her funeral, he'd said Lailah didn't collect people. Now Ren wondered if that was a polite way of saying she'd become reclusive. Reluctant to be out in the world and risk bonding with others, or getting emotional downloads about them, like Ren did.

She couldn't continue reading. Her tank was empty; her mental engine sputtered and stalled. And the universe had never felt so broken.

It was just as well, because moments later, Katie called her into the kitchen to present *L'Homme à tête de chou*—the man with the cabbage head.

# THE ABOMINATION

THE DRAWING WAS a masterpiece.

Katie explained it was originally a sculpture that became the cover and title of a Serge Gainsbourg album, and she used to tease her mop-haired father that it looked exactly like him.

Her charcoal image depicted the man from the chest up, with broad shoulders and a big, round cabbage head so finely textured, it made Ren want to reach in and pull off a leaf. It was dark and moody and funny all at the same time. She hugged Katie from behind and kissed her cheek. "He's going to love it."

Katie shook the can of fixative, sprayed the paper with some short bursts, and slid it into a large envelope for protection. Ten minutes later, she was asleep on Lailah's bed and Ren called her mother from the living room.

She hadn't bothered to check the time, but luckily she caught the professor between classes. They exchanged "how are yous" but that was not Ren's reason for calling.

"Mom, do you remember what I told you about the woman who appeared for me when I was in trouble?"

"Of course. Lailah, right?"

"She kept a journal of people like me, who she protected. The girl who got hit by the train was in there. Her name was Alex. Lailah was there the day she died. She saw it happen. She couldn't stop it."

"My God," her mom gasped. "How is that possible?"

"I don't know, but—what Lailah could do—I can do it, too. I've done it for Katie and," she hesitated, "I've done it for her dad."

"Her dad? In prison?"

"Yeah."

The line went silent. Ren gave her mother space to process the revelation and all of its implications. Finally, Sarah said, "That's how you knew I needed a lawyer. You were there. You're how Katie found the laundry chute and found me. Honey, that's incredible."

Ren shook off the compliment. "I'm not telling you this to impress you. I'm telling you because we're going to see him in prison tomorrow, and you need to know—it's possible to fail at protecting people. Lailah failed to protect Alex. I could fail to protect Katie or her dad. And they could get hurt or killed. And so could I."

To Ren's amazement, her mother didn't panic. She didn't plead or protest or try to talk her out of it. Instead she said, "Well, that's life, isn't it? That's kind of how it feels to be a mom."

Ren broke as the realization of what she'd put her mother through for so many years landed on her like a cartoon anvil.

"I'm so sorry. For everything."

"You don't need to apologize to me, understand? You are who you are, and I love you more than anyone ever."

"I know. I love you, too. I should go."

"Hey wait," her mom stopped her. "I've got to ask. What does it feel like? To..." she trailed off. Her vast vocabulary had finally met its match, but Ren knew what she was asking.

"To ethereate. It's like... Skyrush," she said, naming the rollercoaster they used to ride at Hersheypark. It was their thing, just the two of them. Her dad was too scared, though he'd never admit it. He'd make up a lame excuse, like a strained shoulder, and remain safely on solid ground as they hurled through the air.

"Unreal," her mom said. "Be careful. And I'm proud of you."

The professor hung up the phone, leaving Ren with those four little words spoken as a salve but cutting like a knife.

*I'm proud of you.*

Katie had said that, too, and it was every bit as difficult to hear. Their pride would never withstand the truth of what she'd done to her father.

\* \* \*

The prison was an hour outside Philly, a four-hour drive northeast from Georgetown. The visitation was scheduled for ten AM. To allow for traffic, rest stops, parking and check-in, Peter planned to collect them from Lailah's apartment at four-thirty sharp. Although neither Ren nor Katie were sleepy, the ungodly wake-up time and the emotional toll of the day's activities prompted them to turn in early.

Their heads lay upon a single pillow, touching as they had their first night in the hospital. Ren closed her eyes and prayed for sleep, but Katie had other ideas.

"Will you tell me about my father?" she asked.

Ren realized that with everything moving so fast, she'd taken no time to reflect on her experience with the man at the center of the storm. He was, by far, the most formidable personality she'd ever encountered. He projected strength, confidence, and composure. More so even than Lailah, and Ren's previous suspicion—that he'd been influenced to commit the murders—flew out the window. Naoki Ando was in complete control. He was not a monster, and he was not insane. He knew exactly what he had done and why, and Ren was shocked to admit she'd already given him the benefit of the doubt that he had a damn good reason for it.

Of course, this was all speculation, and she wasn't comfortable sharing any of it with Katie.

"What do you want to know?" Ren asked.

"Did he look okay? What was his cell like? Did you like him? Did he like you?"

"Whoa, one at a time." Ren would have laughed, but she knew Katie was terrified and desperate to calibrate her expectations for what tomorrow might bring.

Ren described his appearance as best she could, though she didn't mention the wound he'd inflicted on himself. The prison cell was a less-sensitive topic and Ren painted a detailed verbal picture, adding that it was clean and organized, matching the impression she had of the man.

Katie's other questions gave Ren pause, because their undertone of hopefulness stung her heart. The cold reality was that it made no difference if she and Katie's father liked each other. The Commonwealth of Pennsylvania was going to stick a needle in his arm in seven weeks. The man would not live to see another Christmas.

But in the end, Ren told the unvarnished truth: despite everything, she liked him a lot. And he didn't like her at all.

"What? How could he not?" Katie asked, then proceeded to answer her own question. "I mean, you're kind of an acquired taste. And you probably scared him half to death zapping into his cell in the middle of the night. And you wouldn't leave him alone until you got your way. But, like, other than that?"

Ren smiled. All of those were correct, but there was something else. "What is an *ikiryō*?" she asked.

She felt the shockwave rip through Katie's mind.

"Oh my God, Rennie. I haven't thought about that in forever. It's a ghost story. Sometimes when I was little, we'd spread sleeping bags in the living room and pretend we were camping. We'd drink tea out of Thermos bottles and toast marshmallows in the fireplace. My dad would spin these wild stories. I found out later they were old Japanese fables that he embellished. One of his favorites was the tale of Shiryō and Ikiryō."

Katie told the story exactly as Ren imagined Ando would have. Her voice even took on a hint of his gruff Japanese accent. Shiryō was a brave warrior who fought many battles and retired honorably to the countryside. One day, while visiting town for provisions, he met Ikiryō, a beautiful young widow whose husband had drowned after falling asleep in his fishing boat. They fell in love and lived together happily for many years until one day Shiryō went hunting and was mauled by a black bear. Ikiryō sensed her husband was in peril and hurried to the forest. In a sunlit clearing, she found him standing next to his own broken body.

He was confused and disoriented. "How can this be?" he asked his widow.

"You are Shiryō," she replied. "The spirit of the deceased. But how is it that I can see you?"

"You are Ikiryō, the living ghost," he said. "You have left your body behind to visit me in this place."

"I must return," she said. "And you must move on, my love."

Shiryō haunted the clearing in the woods until the new moon, after which the villagers never saw him again. Not so for Ikiryō. It was said that until her death many years later, she would appear in the forest from time to time, as if from thin air, to warn hunters and travelers away from hungry bears.

*Ikiryō.*

Ren turned the word over in her mind. The answer to Katie's final question was obvious. Her father didn't like Ren because she was a living ghost.

To him, she was an abomination.

\* \* \*

Ren could not believe how many rules the Pennsylvania State Correctional Institution at Prescott had about visiting inmates, starting with the fact that there was no waiting room. Ando had added only Ren and Katie to his approved visitation list, so Peter had to remain outside the prison grounds. She hoped he was staying warm in his old Jeep under the watchful eye of Denise and Rob.

As they waited to pass through the metal detector, a female guard waddled over to confront them. She had a mousy brown ponytail and skin that looked like it hadn't seen sunlight for months.

"What is that?" she asked, pointing to the envelope Katie had been clutching since they left Georgetown early that morning.

Ren answered on her behalf. "It's a drawing for her dad."

"I need to see it. Take it out, please."

Katie's hands trembled as she removed the paper and presented it to the guard, who looked mildly skeptical, as if the image of the shirtless leafy-headed man verged on pornography.

"No gifts allowed."

Ren's heart rocketed into her throat and her mind raced for a counter-argument that would prevent Katie's passionate labor from having been in vain.

"Okay," Katie choked. She was ashen and swooning like her legs were about to fold beneath her. The guard must have realized the impact of the prohibition, because her next words were like a life preserver for a drowning swimmer.

"You'll have to take it with you when you leave," she said. "If you want him to have it, mail it to him. They'll scan it into the logging system, and if they determine it's appropriate, they'll print out a copy and deliver it to him in his cell."

Relief washed over Ren because she felt it wash over Katie. She also sensed something else, and strongly: the guard's quiet gratitude that her job did not require her to devastate two young women today.

"Thank you," Ren said. Katie bit her lip and nodded.

Ten minutes later, they sat on chairs bolted to the concrete floor, waiting for the buzzer that would admit Naoki Ando to the room.

There were other visitation rooms on either side of theirs, visible through steel-reinforced glass. To the right, a young Hispanic prisoner sat with a pretty woman, his wife or girlfriend, Ren assumed. Every so often, they snuck a little affection, letting their fingertips touch. Ren sensed the man hadn't been in prison all that long, and was determined not to let the place break him.

The room to the left had a different vibe. The guards had not yet brought in the prisoner, but his visitor—an older white guy with a shaved head and a mustache—was wringing his hands and kept glancing over his shoulder, as if paranoid someone was watching him. Given the number of security cameras, someone obviously was. His restlessness made Ren nervous, and she forced herself to look away.

Katie was not tuned in to any of it. She emitted every emotion in the spectrum, dancing on the razor's edge of another panic attack. Ren took her hand and said, "Talk to me."

After a while, she said, "I'm lost."

"Don't be afraid."

"How can I not?"

"Because there are only two possibilities here. This will either be the best thing to happen to you in the last eight years, or the worst. There's no in-between."

"What if it's the worst?" she asked.

Ren wanted more than anything to assure her it wouldn't be, but she had no such certainty. The best she could offer was, "Then we'll get through it together."

A buzzer pierced the air and they both jumped. The door opened. Katie's father entered, then stopped and turned, allowing the guard escorting him to unlock his handcuffs. He turned to face the women and the door closed behind him, leaving the three of them alone in the room.

In his shadowy cell, Ren had focused more on his energy than his physicality. Here in the bright light of the visitation room, she took in the full picture of the man. His height was average and he was thin, but it was all sinew and muscle. He was handsome and rugged, with bronze skin, high cheekbones and sharp eyes that painted him as both predator and protector. He'd lost the wavy locks he'd worn in the scrapbook photo, but his hair was still full and now flecked with gray throughout.

She looked at Katie, the soft-focus version of him; just as gorgeous, but with the edges smoothed over and her mother's eyes and pale skin. The girl was frozen to her seat as her father approached, stone-faced and locked on to her like a heat-seeking missile. Ren watched him convince himself it wasn't a dream. Or some trick engineered by the living ghost who had scuttled his plan to ensure his daughter's safety forever.

Katie drew a shaky breath. "Hi, Daddy."

That was all it took.

She decimated his defenses, exactly as she had the other night. The smile on his face lit up the room. "*Konnichiwa, tenshi,*" he said, and she leaped into his arms.

Ren didn't speak a word of Japanese, but she was pretty sure he had just called her 'angel.'

They squeezed each other tight and a bonfire of love roared between them. Ren wished they could hold on forever, but prison had to prison. Father and daughter quickly exceeded their allotted time for physical contact, and a voice crackled from the loudspeaker, admonishing them to separate.

This fucking place.

They sat at the table, faces slick with tears. Ando finally acknowledged Ren with a crisp nod that suggested she meant as much to him as the chairs underneath them.

He returned his attention to Katie. "Have you brought me something?" he asked.

"I made your picture like I promised."

She pushed the drawing in front of him and held her breath. He appraised it impassively, then broke into peals of laughter. "My brilliant daughter," he said. "My life has been devoid of your art for too long. I did not realize how much I missed it."

Katie clasped Ren's hand. "Rennie helped me find it again."

If Ren hoped to see his demeanor toward her soften, she was sorely disappointed. If anything, calling his attention to her presence brought an abrupt end to the joy of the reunion.

"I see," he said. "Now there is much to discuss, and our time is limited." He looked squarely at Ren. "Your insistence on bringing Kaede to this place has imposed a death sentence on her as well. There is but one way to lift it: you must ensure her knowledge of the truth becomes meaningless to them."

"How?" Ren asked.

"You must do what I failed to do eight years ago. You must burn them to the ground."

# THE GHOST

REN LOOKED AT Katie and swallowed hard as Naoki Ando shared his story.

"There is a Japanese proverb: a child is a shackle for the three worlds. Nothing a parent does—past, present or future—is separable from their feelings for their child. We sit here today because Malcolm Glass loved his son Eric as any parent would… beyond all rational measure. And the boy was going to die."

Katie's father explained that the son of the pharmaceutical company CEO had epilepsy. It was both severe and drug-resistant, and had almost killed him twice when he stopped breathing in the throes of a tonic-clonic seizure.

Unsurprisingly, the condition became a primary area of research for the company. Malcolm would spare no expense in developing a next-generation treatment to save his son, so Ando assembled a team of the finest minds from mainstream and traditional medicine. Researchers, pharmacologists and chemists worked side-by-side with herbalists, homeopaths and even spiritualists to tackle the problem.

Drugs based on psilocybin—magic mushrooms—soon yielded promising results. This wasn't a discovery so much as a re-discovery. The compound had been used for centuries in mind-expanding rituals and had even been marketed as a pharmaceutical half a century earlier, before the war on drugs crippled research into what the U.S. government considered to be the most dangerous ones.

The team held a firm belief, supported by mounting evidence, that the substance could help "reboot" the brain, restoring balance to what was essentially a faulty electrical system that caused epileptic seizures. The problem was new drugs took time to develop, test and refine. Years, sometimes decades.

Eric didn't have years. Over the winter break, the boy—twelve years old, at the time—was with his sister Victoria when he experienced a massive seizure, causing an arrhythmia that stopped his heart. Her quick thinking got them to the hospital in time, but Malcolm knew his son might not be so lucky again. Two months later, the chief executive turned to his chief scientist in desperation. His last and best hope.

"I'm going to ask you for the impossible," Malcolm said to Ando. "Something that violates every moral, ethical and safety standard both of us have spent our careers upholding. I need you to give me the psilocybin protocol."

Ando's protests would have been ignored had he raised any. But he didn't. He knew the pain of losing a child and almost losing another, and he wouldn't wish it on anyone, least of all his friend, mentor and boss.

Of the moments in his life he wished he could take back, the one that haunted him most was when he handed Malcolm a sealed plastic box containing three vials of serum.

That night at his home, Malcolm used himself as a human guinea pig, testing the drug before risking it on his son.

The effect was almost instantaneous.

As Ando sat in his lab nursing a shot of whiskey and contemplating the travesty he'd allowed to occur, the living ghost of Malcolm Glass visited him for the first time.

"I recognized the *ikiryō* for what it was," Ando said, "the result of *rikonbyō*."

"What is that?" Katie asked, speaking for the first time since Ando had begun his tale.

"It is a notion spoken of in Japanese literature. Soul separation illness," he said, looking at Ren as if she, too, were sick with it.

Was that what was wrong with her? Had she contracted an illness when her light died? She sat back in her chair, her mind whirling as it tried to reframe her experience around the idea that she was somehow diseased.

Then she thought of Nina, who'd called it a "gift."

Then she thought of Lailah and decided Nina was right.

Katie was one step ahead of her. "Daddy, don't look at her like that. She's not sick. She's sacred."

Ren wanted to throw her arms around the girl, but restrained herself for Ando's sake.

"Perhaps," he said grudgingly, addressing Ren. "Matters of the soul are not my area of expertise. I cannot speculate on how yours was torn in two. As for the drug, over time I developed a hypothesis. Are you familiar with the concept of a Faraday cage?"

Ren was not. "Refresh my memory," she said.

"Simply put, it is a shield that prevents electromagnetic

energy from penetrating to reach whatever lies inside. It also prevents that same energy escaping from within it. I have come to believe the human brain functions as a sort of Faraday cage, containing the soul while also preventing other souls from invading it. The psilocybin drug may have disrupted the electrical patterns of the brain, creating a breach in the cage from which the soul could escape."

"Wait," Katie said. "You said the cage keeps other souls out. Does that mean your cage is faulty if you can see an *ikiryō?*"

"I believe so, yes."

"You can see them," Katie said to her father. "And I can see them. Why?"

Ando took a deep breath and studied his hands, and Ren could sense it was not the first time he'd thought about this.

"Grief and trauma impact the brain in ways we are only beginning to understand."

Ren was reminded of Lailah's moonflower message. Her protectress may not have grasped the science, but she understood the truth of it.

*We are drawn to those in pain because we understand pain.*

The two souls in front of her had suffered so much. No wonder they could see ghosts.

"Malcolm was drunk with power," Ando continued, clearly more at ease discussing facts than feelings.

The CEO was manic, raving about how the drug—the "discovery"—would change the face of the world and make them all rich beyond their wildest dreams. The ability to split oneself and travel elsewhere, to learn the secrets of others as the proverbial fly on the wall, would be priceless to governments and the world's elite.

Whether it had any curative effect on epilepsy—his son's or anyone else's—no longer seemed to matter to Malcolm, but Ando asked him if he had given the drug to Eric. Of course he had. Why would any father not want his child to possess such power?

An image flashed in Ren's mind of a frail boy sitting on the edge of his bed, looking at his father through wide, terrified eyes. What had Malcolm told him? That this shot would "cure" him? That his son should trust him? That everything was going to be okay? It almost brought her to tears.

Ando had then asked Malcolm about Victoria. Had he given the drug to her, too? Not yet, but only because she was on spring break with her college friends. It was his first order of business when she returned.

He begged his boss not to allow this atrocity to go further, but it was no use. Before Malcolm left, he insisted Ando plan to produce additional samples of the serum and safeguard the formula and the procedure to synthesize it. It was now the most valuable trade secret in the world and had to be protected accordingly.

Ando did the opposite. Within the hour, he'd destroyed every sample of every variant of the lab's psilocybin drugs, every raw ingredient, every reagent and even some of the key pieces of lab equipment used in the process. In the hours that followed, he deleted all the files on the project server, and—with the help of an old college roommate who was a hacker—introduced a virus that reformatted the drives and propagated itself to eradicate the data backups as well.

The only bits of information to survive the scourge were notes the other researchers may have kept in offline journals, none of which would be sufficient to reconstitute the formula or the process.

The next morning, he drove to Malcolm's home, hoping to convince him to surrender himself and Eric to research, to develop an antidote, a cure. But in his heart, he knew it was a fool's errand. Malcolm was already beyond the reach of reason. And so Ando had brought his pistol.

When the CEO learned what the scientist had done to the lab and to the data, his rage was volcanic. His *ikiryō* separated and howled at Ando alongside his body. Then Eric entered and did the same, modeling his father's behavior exactly, as if he aspired to assume the mantle of leadership someday. Their utter contempt for him—the disdain they expressed for everyone who was now a lesser being in the face of their godlike power—was beyond redemption.

"I ended them." Ando's face was haunted, eyes distant, as if he were reliving the shocking act. "And to this day, I believe my actions were righteous. But they were insufficient. I did not understand the plague had already spread. Malcolm had already given the third dose of the drug to Victoria."

The lone anomaly in the case file launched itself back into Ren's mind like a stone from a slingshot: Victoria's victim-impact statement, with all the emotional weight of wet cardboard. It rang false because it was false. Victoria could no longer feel those emotions, because the same godlike ability that robbed Malcolm and Eric's humanity now coursed through her veins.

"Victoria seized upon Malcolm's desire for wealth and power and found someone to help her pursue it. I do not know who. All I know is they have been trying to reconstruct what I destroyed. In the process, they have made monsters. Unwitting victims upon whom they have tested sample after sample. Some have been sent to visit me. To torment me."

"Yana," Ren said.

"Yes. She is one, there have been others. And now you see: this evil cannot be exposed. It cannot be prosecuted. It must be eradicated."

As the full scope of the horror Katie's father set in motion clouded Ren's heart, a jarring voice crackled over the PA system.

"Two minutes remaining."

They looked at each other in disbelief as to how quickly their hour had passed.

"Daddy, no, we need more time!"

"Indeed," he said, and the weight of their situation dawned. Unless the superintendent granted another exception, it would be two days before they could meet again. And if Ando was correct, this visit would only cause Victoria and her organization to accelerate their efforts to eliminate them. He turned to Ren. "There is more we must discuss. Can you appear to me in my cell, as you did before?"

"I don't know. It's not exactly voluntary. I was only drawn to you because—" She was going to say *you were about to kill yourself*, but he cut her off. Probably for the best.

"Find a way," he said. "For Kaede."

There was nothing Ren would not do for her. "I'll try."

The dreaded buzzer screamed once more and the guard appeared at the door at the far end of the room. Ando stood and opened his arms to receive Katie's embrace. He squeezed her tight, but addressed Ren.

"Do not fail us, *ikiryō*."

Katie pulled back and fixed him with a hard stare.

"Ren, Daddy. Her name is Ren."

He nodded in acknowledgment but not contrition, and as he turned away, Ren noticed their surroundings for the first time since she'd laid eyes on Katie's father. The young prisoner in the room to their right still sat with his girl, and Ren idly wondered why his hour was more generous than Ando's. In the visiting room to the left, the guy with the shaved head and mustache was engrossed in conversation with a burly prisoner, who was also bald but sported a bushy biker beard that she imagined smelled like a nauseating cocktail of barbecue sauce and cigarette smoke.

Then her heart skipped a beat.

"Oh, fuck," she said, and grabbed Katie's wrist.

Katie followed Ren's gaze and gasped. "Daddy!"

He turned, and together they watched Yana whisper her venom to the men in the next room.

The buzzer blared again.

The pale girl flashed a demonic smile.

And all hell broke loose.

The door to the left visiting room unlocked with a sharp snap. The bald duo sprang from their chairs and vaulted into the prisoner transport corridor. They overpowered Ando's escort, with Mustache slamming the guard's head against the cinderblock wall and Beard savagely kicking the man in the face as he dropped to the ground.

"Go!" Ando barked as he retreated from the corridor and put himself between the women and the rabid attackers.

Ren dragged Katie to the exit, but it was locked. "Open it!" she screamed at the observation camera.

Mustache and Beard closed on Ando. "You're fucking dead, Jap," Mustache growled. Beard grunted and took a wild swing at Katie's father.

Ando easily dodged, then went on the offensive. He chopped Mustache in the throat and swept Beard's legs out from under him with an impossibly fast kick. Beard hit the floor hard but recovered quickly, hurling himself at Ando and grabbing him around the waist.

As they scuffled, Mustache set his sights on Ren and Katie. With an outstretched arm, Katie blocked Ren from stepping in front of her and took a fighting stance.

Before Ren could utter a word, Katie said, "This one's mine, Rennie."

Mustache laughed. "Oh, yeah. Bring it, baby girl."

This was all wrong. Ren was supposed to protect her.

But Katie didn't need it.

She brought it.

Her fist exploded into his face. He howled in pain, clutching his gushing nose. She dropped into a crouch, firing two solid blows into his massive gut and a third into his groin.

His hands traveled instinctively from his nose to his balls, but wide-eyed rage subsumed his pain. Mustache lunged at Katie. She sidestepped, letting his momentum carry him into the wall. He was dazed, but she refused to let up, connecting with a roundhouse kick to his head.

Ren looked to Ando, who straddled Beard, raining blows on his face like the wrath of God.

She barely had time to think *they picked the wrong family to fuck with* or *why haven't the guards come to help us* before a bolt of anxiety ripped through her soul.

The young prisoner from the other visiting room quietly strolled in amid the chaos.

A blade appeared in his hand and just as quickly disappeared into Ando's neck.

A fountain of red erupted. Ando clutched at his throat, fell to his knees, then backward onto the floor.

Blood dripped from the shiv as the man who wielded it turned his attention to Katie. She hung on Mustache's back, arms locked around his neck in a sleeper hold. It looked like she was getting the upper hand, but the brute was still fighting hard.

Katie was an absolute bad-ass, but there was no possibility she could handle them both.

Ren stepped in front of the young prisoner.

"You don't want to do this," she pleaded, but his eyes were as cold as outer space and just as vacant.

"Oh yes you do, my brave man," whispered a soft accented voice behind her.

Ren whipped around.

Yana winked at her.

She turned back toward the prisoner.

A flash of silver streaked past.

Ren's face burned with blinding agony and she fell backward, cracking her head on the concrete floor. Warm salt and liquid metal filled her mouth. She gurgled and choked on the blood.

A buzzer rang hollow in the distance.

Doors smashed open.

Guards stormed into the room.

As Ren's world began to dim, Yana leaned close and purred into her ear.

"Now you are pretty like me."

# THE FAILURE

REN HAD ALWAYS thought the dream rendition of her final encounter with her father was the cruelest trick her mind could play on her. Forever presenting her with a cold, mirthless version of the man she loved, as he confronted her with evidence of the crime she wanted so badly to explain, but never could.

In the endless dark, where she could barely distinguish memory from nightmare, she realized the dream was merciful.

The truth was the ultimate cruelty. And she relived it over and over again.

It had taken about seven months after Ren left home for her to exhaust the last of her options. All available couches had been surfed. All favors called in. All welcomes long overstayed. Summer was approaching. There was a brief window where sleeping outdoors—while never safe—might not be too unpleasant, and as she debated whether it would be worse than swallowing her pride and returning to her mother's house, Alistair Brody arrived in her life.

They'd met in line at a McDonald's, of all places. She'd come up a few nickels short on her value-menu chicken sandwich, and he stepped in to save the day, her knight in blue coveralls.

Street recognized street, and they started talking. He gave her a place to stay, for free at first, but as month's end approached, he expected rent. He was candid about the fact that he preferred cash, but would also accept other forms of payment, which many of her housemates took him up on, but she couldn't bring herself to do. As she had no reliable source of income, he offered her one other choice.

She could be his accomplice.

By day, Alistair was an exterminator. He drove around in a white minivan with a disgusting termite decal on the side, placing glue traps and spraying for roaches all over town, but mostly in the rich neighborhoods. Chestnut Hill, Queen Village and the like.

With unrestricted access to his customers' homes, he could determine their layouts, inventory their valuables, learn their habits and patterns, understand their security systems, and formulate careful plans for how to rob them absolutely fucking blind.

His problem was, he couldn't do it alone. He needed a lookout. She had her license, and though he didn't trust her driving, she'd sit behind the wheel and keep watch while he was inside. If he came out walking, she'd move over and he'd take them home. If he came out running, she'd drive just until they were far enough from the scene of the crime to safely switch places. That had only happened once, but she'd done a decent job and he started thinking of her as his good-luck charm.

Idiot.

A few months later, his pest-control gig brought him to the

home of Bill and Paula Nelson, an accountant and his country-club wife. While inside, he'd seen Bill's high-dollar wristwatch collection and decided they would pay Ren's rent for the month. It was a pretty steep rack-rate for a dirty mattress in his back bedroom, but it was a seller's market and it became her job to help him acquire them.

Alistair timed the heist to coincide with the Nelson's vacation and was in their home less than six minutes before he walked out with the timepieces nestled in the belly pocket of his hoodie. It had gone perfectly, at least from his perspective, and if he had done the job a couple of days earlier, both of their lives would have taken a different course. But there was an unexpected cold snap the weekend before Christmas, and she'd neglected to dress warmly enough. As she sat shivering in the poorly insulated car, she remembered her hat was on the floor in the back, and she pulled it onto her empty head.

She slid over as he got behind the wheel, so pleased with himself that he didn't notice she'd violated one of his cardinal burglary rules: don't wear distinctive clothing; especially nothing with words or logos. Two blocks later, a traffic camera captured a stunningly clear picture of a 2004 Honda Accord with a young woman in the passenger seat wearing a vintage Eagles stocking cap.

It was this picture that led Detective David Cole to Alistair's house a couple weeks later, and though he'd held in his hand irrefutable evidence that Ren was party to a felony, she would always know in her heart that he hadn't gone there for his suspect. He'd gone there for his daughter.

The doorbell rang. Not the cheerful two-tone chime of her mom's house, rather the grinding clang of a steel bell with an exposed clapper. She peeked out from behind the smoke-saturated sheer drapery of the sitting-room window and saw his unmarked car on the street. A fine mist of falling snow coated its roof, but the hood and windshield were still warm enough to melt it.

Alistair answered the door.

Her dad's voice rang out, clear and authoritative. His cop voice. "I'm Detective Cole," he said, and though she couldn't see it, she was certain he'd presented his badge for Alistair's inspection. When she was little, she loved to snatch the shiny gold shield from his belt and make him chase her around the house to get it back. And when he caught her, as he always did, and wrapped her in a hug, she loved the scratchy feel of his cheeks and the spice of the Polo cologne that wafted from beneath his starched shirt.

"I'm looking for the girl in this picture," he said.

"Nah, man, I ain't seen her," Alistair said, and she could hear the smirk on his face. He was a horrible liar.

"Don't jerk me around, kid," her dad said. "I know—"

A gunshot rang out like a cannon. Ren literally jumped, pulling the flimsy curtain and its rod clean off the wall. Then came another two explosions, in quick succession.

She ran to the door.

Alistair lay in the entryway with two holes in his chest, a chrome pistol in his dead hand, and the stench of shit mingling with the acrid smoke that clouded the air.

Her dad had fallen backward onto the porch, a single wound oozing red next to his yellow-striped necktie. His breath billowed in irregular clouds. His eyes overflowed with love and terror.

She knelt beside him. "Daddy, what do I do?"

He took her hand and guided it to his coat pocket, where she found his cell phone. Even as shock numbed her mind, she knew enough to call 911. She dialed it on speaker. The dispatcher answered, and she held it to his lips.

"RA... to this... location. Officer... down," he said, and she could feel the struggle in every word.

He ended the call and told her to wipe her prints from the phone, which she did with her shirt, then set it down beside him. With a trembling hand, he pointed to the photo lying on the porch. "Take it. Go. You were... never here."

*You were never here.*

As he faded from consciousness, all she could think was how much better the world would have been if those words had been true.

\* \* \*

When Ren opened her eyes, her mother, Peter, and Nina were beside her bed. She had never seen three more somber faces, but her mom's was the worst. She looked like she'd been crying for days.

Had it been days?

And where was Katie?

Ren had a vicious headache and a steady, dull throb in her left cheek. She lifted her hand to her face and found a thick padded bandage plastered there. Her arm dragged an IV line with it. Whatever dripped into her veins coated her mind in a hazy film.

Peter spoke first, probably because he was the only one who wouldn't dissolve into tears.

"Ren, you're in the hospital. They pulled you out of Prescott about forty hours ago. You have a concussion and a severe facial injury, both of which mean you should talk as little as possible. But we need your help. Naoki Ando is dead. And Katie is missing."

He continued speaking, but a high-pitched whine drowned his voice as she closed her eyes and the magnitude of her failure swept over her. One of her charges had died under her useless "protection," and the other—who she treasured above everything else in the world—was gone. Crying was agony. Her severed facial muscles screamed in protest as she tried in vain to stop the tears.

Her mother's hand was cool on her feverish forehead. "Stay with us, baby," she choked. Ren opened her eyes.

"We saw the security footage," Peter said. "We saw what happened. But we need to know what Ando told you. We need to know where to look."

She didn't have the full picture, but there could be no doubt.

"Glass," she said, her tongue thick in her mouth.

"Yes," Peter said, looking discouraged. "We're still trying to learn more about Victoria."

"No," Ren moaned. "Glass… Biogen. Find out what happened to the company."

Peter's eyes flashed understanding. "On it," he said, and headed for the door.

"Wait," she whispered. He didn't hear her.

"Peter, wait," Nina called out, and he returned to her bedside.

"Bodyguards," Ren whispered.

"There still here, baby. Right outside," her mom said.

"Not for me. For you. All of you."

* * *

According to the official report, Naoki Ando had been pronounced dead by prison medical staff at 11:14 on Thursday
morning, murdered by inmate Tomás Ramirez, a forger serving
a three-year sentence for making fake IDs. Ramirez had no history of violent offenses, had never met Ando prior to that day,
and claimed to have held no grudge against him. He also
claimed he barely remembered the incident or how he'd come
into possession of the shiv.

The other two attackers, prisoner Robert "Ringo" Barnett
and his visitor Charles Corwin, insisted the attack was racially
motivated. Corwin had lost a grandfather at the Battle for Oki-
nawa and spontaneously decided payback would be extracted
from the Japanese inmate in the adjacent room. Ringo, already
serving a life sentence, simply backed his play.

Ren knew these men believed they were telling the truth,
because she knew something they did not; that a smirking, demonic waif had pulled their pins and tossed them like grenades
into Ando's visitation room. Of course, that was the unofficial
version, and none of it was on camera.

What the video did show was five guards—who could not
fully explain why they'd taken so long to respond—eventually
subduing the attackers and removing them from the room. It
showed Katie cradling Ren's head in her arms, trying to staunch
the gushing facial wound with a balled-up shirt until more
guards arrived and pulled her, kicking and screaming, from the
bloodbath. Paramedics from a private ambulance service administered first aid to Katie, then left the prison grounds with
her at 11:25, presumably headed for the same hospital where
Ren was currently being treated.

It was Sunday morning. Katie had not been seen since.

Ren's mother sat beside her and held her hand. "They found the shell of the ambulance under a freeway overpass yesterday. Totally burned up. No evidence."

Ren didn't need her to state the conclusion.

There were no leads.

A hundred unanswered questions accompanied the disappearance of Katie Moreau, but the one that troubled Ren most was why she had not ethereated to the girl.

The most obvious possibility was that Katie was dead.

Ren refused to accept it. Refused to believe in a universe that would allow such a thing to happen. There had to be another explanation. There was so much she still didn't understand about her power and its limitations. Maybe her brain injury hampered her ability to ethereate, or the drugs she was on prevented it. Maybe she was no longer Katie's protectress, their bond severed after Ren's complete failure to keep her safe.

But whatever had neutered Ren's gift, one thing was clear.

"Mom, we need help to find her. Like, real help." She gripped the guardrails of her hospital bed. "I can't do shit from here."

"What do you want to do?"

Ren couldn't believe she was about to ask what she was about to ask. Her father aside, there was nobody she liked less than cops, especially ones who'd been gaping assholes to Katie.

"How much do you trust Marcus Grant?"

# THE MANIPULATOR

THE DETECTIVE JOINED them two hours later, along with Peter and Nina, in Ren's room. He sat in a chair by the window and studied her with pained eyes, either disdain or sympathy. She was counting on the latter; it would help if he had a soft spot for his ex-partner's bratty little girl.

"Long time, no see," he said. "I thought you ran away to join the fire department."

Even if she'd felt like smiling, it would have been too painful. "I couldn't pass the physical, so I decided to be a cop instead."

He laughed. "Still a ball-breaker. You and your pop didn't always see eye-to-eye, but he loved you to pieces. Even if you were going to the dark side."

Ren's heart quivered at the mention of her father, but this wasn't the time to reminisce. She got to the point. "Are you looking for Katie?" she asked him.

"It's not my case. County detectives and Staties own it. Your mom said you wanted my help, but she won't tell me anything. Says I need to hear it from you."

She signaled to Peter, who handed Grant a copy of Victoria's old driver's license photo. The detective looked it over.

"Her name is Victoria Glass," Ren said.

"I know who she is. She's the one who escaped Ando's rampage."

Knowing Ando's motive for the killings, Ren certainly wouldn't have called it a "rampage," but she let it go. "She's behind all of this."

He leaned forward. "What makes you say that?"

"Naoki Ando murdered her family. She wants revenge."

He wrinkled his brows. "The man's been incarcerated eight years and his daughter's been walking around on the street. Victoria could have had them anytime. Why now?"

It was the identical question she'd asked Ando in his cell, but she refused to put Lailah and her moonflowers on his radar. "Why does anyone do anything?" she said, knowing it wouldn't fly.

"Yeah, I'm going to need more than that."

Her instinct told her it would be safer to let him ask the questions and then decide which ones to answer, so she held him in a steady gaze.

"Is there a connection between her and the inmates who attacked you?"

"You won't find one."

"Is there a connection between her and Katie's ex?"

It had taken him no time at all to put that together. No way she'd convince him Milo's attack was a coincidence. He was too smart.

"You won't find one," she said.

Grant shook his head. "In the Army, they call this the mushroom treatment. I'm not sure how you expect me to help if you keep me in the dark and feed me shit."

Though she flinched at the words 'mushroom treatment'—and how close they actually were to the heart of the case—he was right. He needed something tangible to go on. Enough to be useful, without revealing the existence of the evil Ando had sacrificed his own life to conceal. An evil the world would never be prepared for. She drew a breath and stepped into the minefield.

"Katie's father made a boutique drug for his boss, Glass. It wasn't approved, but the guy took it anyway. It had some unexpected side effects that he… liked. So he gave it to his kids. He gave it to Victoria. He wanted more, but Ando destroyed everything. Victoria has been trying to recreate it, and maybe she thinks Katie knows something."

He leaned back and considered the narrative. After a minute, he said, "That sounds like about ten percent of the story, but for giggles, let's say she's responsible. I'll ask again: why now? What set all this in motion?"

Perhaps it was the painkillers, or maybe she was too stupid to outwit a cop with half a brain, but Ren was at a loss to explain further without divulging facts she couldn't allow him to explore. She'd already said too much, and was cursing herself for involving him at all, when her mother spoke up.

"Marcus, Katie's father believed the side effects of this drug were so dangerous, so horrific, that he murdered two people to keep it from coming to light. He murdered a *child*. Victoria is only alive because he was unaware she was exposed to it. If we find Victoria, we'll find Katie, but we need to find her without anyone knowing why we're looking."

Grant was quiet, probably questioning how far his loyalty to his old partner's family could be pushed.

Nina touched his arm. "Detective, we are putting great faith in you. And we are asking for your faith in return."

He remained silent and contemplative. Ren tried one last time to tip the scales.

"I understand if you can't help us find Katie. But please look for Victoria. She's going to come after us. All of us. We know too much and she has too much to lose."

Ren watched the detective's mind work. And she saw the moment they had him.

"You said Victoria wants to make a drug. How would she do that?" he asked.

Thankfully, Peter jumped in, sparing Ren the agony of further speech. "Her dad was the majority shareholder of Glass Biogen. When he died, she inherited the company, but she wouldn't have the know-how. She'd need someone in the industry. About a month after the murders, the company's assets were acquired for an undisclosed sum by a Swedish pharma giant called Nyqvist AB. Over the years, Nyqvist quietly sold off the patents for Glass's mainstream medications to other pharma companies, but I think the real reason they bought Glass was because of Victoria. Because of this drug. I think she's been working with them to develop it; to reverse-engineer it from the only sample that was left—the one in her body."

"Jesus," the detective muttered. "This Nyqvist... do they have any facilities around here?"

"Not that we could determine. But this isn't the kind of thing you'd want a paper trail for."

He stood up. "All right. Let me see what I can dig up. Maybe the forensic people can do an age progression on this," he said, referring to the ten-year-old photo Peter had given him. "Do you want me to request a security detail for you?"

"No cops," Ren said, almost before Grant could finish his sentence.

"Why not?" he asked.

"Whoever's investigating the prison will find a picture in Ando's cell, of Katie in her hospital bed. It was taken by a cop and sent to her father as a threat."

"What cop?" Grant asked, laser-focused.

She'd never forget their names. "Kowalski and Delfino."

Grant looked confused. "Philly?"

"Yeah," Ren said. "They interviewed me after our car accident. Did you find their report when you looked into Milo's shooting?"

"There was no report."

"Are you serious?"

"Hold on," the detective said, then took out his phone and dialed a number. "Clark, it's Grant.... Real quick, you got a Kowalski or a Delfino in uniform in your division?... Okay, thanks.... Yeah, catch up soon."

He ended the call.

"No such people," he said gravely. "I'll check the hospital, maybe they'll pop up on a security camera. If not, can you sit with an artist and give a description?"

She nodded. There was only one artist she wanted to sit with, but this was a genuine lead and she'd do whatever it took to help.

"All right. Be careful," Grant said to Ren, then to Peter: "You're keeping your private detail in place?"

"Yeah. For as long as it takes."

"I'll be in touch," Grant said, and left the room.

* * *

Ren's mom brought chicken soup for dinner and sat with her while she tried to eat it. She managed a few spoonfuls, but her face was both numb and aching, and she ended up wearing most of the broth on her hospital gown. The pitying look on Sarah's face made her even more miserable, so she asked her mom to walk with her instead.

The first steps sent bolts of pain through her concussed skull, but she could deal with it. Her mom draped a robe around her shoulders and Ren wheeled her IV stand into the corridor.

Her babysitters gave them a smile. "How you holding up, Ren?" Denise asked.

"Never better."

Denise was perceptive enough to know Ren wasn't in a chatty mood and lagged a few paces behind her and Sarah. Rob remained stationed at the door. They walked to the end of the hallway and back; then, over her mom's protest, Ren pushed herself to do it again. The faster she could regain her strength and her mental faculties, the more use she was to Katie.

Upon their second return, she said goodnight to her mom and the guards and entered her room alone. She used the toilet, washed her hands and headed for bed.

"Jesus Christ, I thought she'd never leave," said a voice from behind. Ren turned so fast she thought her head might fly off her shoulders.

Victoria Glass sat in the visitor's chair.

She wore a cream-colored blouse and a navy mid-length skirt, and her dark hair was pulled back in a neat ponytail. With her legs casually crossed beneath her, she looked like she'd just dropped by for tea.

Ren pictured Denise and Rob bleeding out in the hallway... or not. Victoria appeared to be unarmed, but Ren's skin turned to ice at the sight of Lailah's bracelet on her wrist.

"You're getting around pretty well," Victoria said, then gestured loosely at her cheek. "Sorry about your face. Yana can be a little catty sometimes. I mean, not that you were any great beauty to begin with."

Ren ignored the slight and tried to stop shivering. "How did you get past the guards?"

"Let's not waste time, shall we? You can walk unassisted, so that's what you're going to do. Walk out of here."

"Why would I do that?"

"Because if you don't do it in the next five minutes, I'm going to take your girlfriend's hands off with an angle grinder. If you aren't moving after that, we'll do her feet. She doesn't need limbs to serve her purpose."

Her purpose?

Ren's stomach turned over and she tried to concentrate, aware that a clock was now ticking. Victoria wasn't bluffing. Ren asked herself again why, if Katie was in mortal peril, she hadn't ethereated to her.

"How do I know you haven't killed her already?"

Victoria arched her eyebrows and five seconds later, Ren's cell phone rang, a video call from an unknown number.

She answered the call, and Victoria stared back at her from the screen.

"Surprise," the Victorias said in unison, their lips twisted into identical grins.

# THE PRISONER

REN REMEMBERED ANDO describing how Malcolm and Eric Glass had raged at him in physical and ethereal form simultaneously, an ability bestowed by a drug administered to only one other person.

This was what it looked like.

Victoria was conscious and fully in control of her body at some other location while her spirit was here in the room, manipulating the situation to devastating effect.

A godlike power, indeed, but Ren never took such things on faith. She walked painfully over to Victoria, balled her hand into a fist, and punched it through the woman's ethereal face.

*Ikiryō.*

Ghost-Victoria laughed. "Welcome to the party, honey. Look at your phone."

Phone-Victoria panned the camera to show a bank of black-and-white security monitors, and zoomed in on one that showed a medical exam room. Katie was cuffed to a table. "Say hi, doll," she commanded.

"Rennie," Katie shouted, her voice tinny through the security camera's microphone. "Don't you come for me. Don't you do it. I'm—"

The call cut off; the connection snatched away like candy from Ren's lips.

"You get the idea," said Ghost-Victoria. "Now get moving."

Ren ignored Katie's admonition. There was no universe in which she would not try to rescue the girl, even at the cost of her own life. She disconnected the IV from the port on the back of her hand, then found the bag of clothes she'd worn into the hospital and put them on, bloodstains and all.

"Drop your phone in the toilet," Victoria said, and Ren complied. "Down the hall, elevator to the lobby. Out the front entrance. There's a white van waiting."

"What do I tell the guard?" Ren asked, expecting to be confronted by one of her babysitters. She assumed they were still posted outside her door.

"They've been distracted. Just go. I'll be watching. Say a word to anyone and they're dead. I will find them and I will kill them."

Ren exited the room and found it unguarded, as Victoria had promised. She walked to the elevator and pushed the down button. It arrived a moment later, thankfully empty.

She reached the ground floor and noted the directional sign pointing to the entrance. Beyond the sliding glass doors, an unmarked van idled under the portico. Ren moved toward it and no sooner than she'd exited the building, her mother's voice called from behind.

"Ren! What are you doing?"

Ren was certain Victoria would keep her promise to kill anyone she spoke to, so she kept walking. The door of the panel van slid open. A stocky guy with a brown buzz-cut waited inside and she realized with a start that she'd seen him before, in Katie's hospital room.

The cop. Kowalski.

Except he wasn't a cop, was he? And that probably wasn't his real name.

"Get in. Now," he said, looking past her toward the hospital. Ren didn't turn, but felt her mother following. She stepped into the van and he slammed the door behind her. The driver—the other asshole "cop" Delfino—hit the gas, and the vehicle lurched forward, throwing her painfully to her knees.

The next part happened so fast, she barely had time to process it. A rough cloth bag dropped over her head, catching on her bandage and sending a screaming pain through her cheek.

Before she could lift her hands to pressure the reopened wound, her arms were pinned behind her and a zip-tie encircled her wrists.

And something very sharp stabbed into her thigh.

* * *

"Ren, I'm Dr. Kimber."

The old man sitting at the foot of her bed had a comb-over and thick glasses. The pocket of his white lab coat had an ID badge clipped to it that read NYQVIST in blue block letters. His paisley tie had a crusty stain that might have been mustard.

Her headache hurt less than before, but her cheek was on fire. She tried to concentrate on his mouth. His teeth were straight but smoke-browned. His lips wore a coarse mustache like a Russian fur hat and moved more than seemed necessary to form the words he spoke.

"I'm afraid your laceration was aggravated during your journey here, but we've attended to it and it's healing nicely."

He paused, as if waiting for her to express gratitude for this kindness, but she just stared at him, so he resumed. "Of course there will be quite a scar. Regretful, but unavoidable. What we need now is for that concussion to fully resolve so we can get started. So, young lady, lots of sleep, no strenuous activity, and for heaven's sake, try not to think too much!"

He chuckled, delighted by his own wit, and though Ren had listened to his words, she hadn't really heard them. The doctor's face was cartoonish and unsettling, so she willed her eyes to land somewhere else. The room was clean and bright. It had the cold, hard sterility of Ando's prison cell, its walls blank and windowless. There was no furniture aside from the bed she was lying on, and no separate bathroom, though there was a sink and toilet.

"Where's Katie?" Her words came out dry and thick.

"All in good time, dear." His chipper bedside manner and bizarre animatronic mouth gave her chills. He'd said something about not thinking too hard, but her brain was not inclined to cooperate.

"You said 'get started,'" she croaked. "Get started with what?"

"The tests, of course."

"What tests?"

"All in good time," he repeated, like the Wicked Witch of the West. "Must rest!"

"Go fuck yourself," she said, a mild lisp blunting the impact of the missive. "I want to see Katie, now!"

Ren tried to sit up, but pain shot through her head and forced it back onto the pillow. Kimber eased his mass from the edge of the bed, stood and looked at her like she was mentally deficient. His brown suit pants were a size too big.

"My dear, please remain calm. We have important work! We need to unravel the mystery of that brain of yours. How you do that wonderful thing you do. We've been at this for quite some time, and you are, without a doubt, our most valuable asset. Our index case, if you will. So please don't worry. We're going to take excellent care of you. You have my word."

Which was evidently the last word on the subject, because he turned on his heel and headed to the door. He scanned his badge on a card reader and typed numbers on the adjoining keypad. The lock emitted a sharp buzz, then he pulled open the door and closed it behind him. The overhead lights dimmed to a soft glow, which made Ren's head hurt less.

It was the only thing she had to be thankful for as she accepted her new reality.

She was a lab rat.

And this room was her cage.

\* \* \*

Ren did not see Kimber again for a while. Instead, she had the misfortune of daily visits from a doctor named Markle, who was tall, gaunt and balding, and was either on the spectrum or had zero confidence in his own authority. His eyes were always downcast; they never met Ren's or anyone else's.

While waiting for her brain to heal, Markle and his team checked everything else: temperature, blood pressure, a heart scan. Techs drew blood, collected urine, and swabbed her cheek for DNA. An excruciating lumbar puncture to extract spinal fluid, after which she had a splitting headache for hours.

The procedures grew more invasive as the days passed: an ultrasound, a mammogram, a pelvic exam with Pap smear, as if her ability to ethereate originated from an as-yet-undetected anomaly in her lady parts. Doubtful. They probably just got off on it.

At every turn, Ren tried to be as uncooperative as possible, but they threatened to hurt Katie and her nerve faltered. They also wouldn't let her see Katie at all. She had to take it on faith that the girl was alive and unharmed.

Eventually, Kimber returned to reassess her brain injury and, with unbridled joy, declared her concussion healed. This pronouncement was followed immediately by an EEG, which was basically a shower cap with a hundred wires snaking off it like Medusa. All she had to do was sit and let it eavesdrop on her brainwaves.

In the morning—she assumed it was morning; windows and clocks were non-existent—came the first MRI. Two orderlies led her down a short stretch of hallway to a room labeled [127—IMAGING] where one scanned his badge and entered a code on the keypad. Not that she could remember all the numbers, but she'd started paying attention to them. It seemed like each door had its own code that changed daily. Today's was 4721.

The MRI suite comprised three separate spaces; the anteroom off the hallway, a control room with a bank of monitors, and the MRI machine room, behind a closed door ominously tagged with a red stop-sign symbol that read [NO METAL OBJECTS ALLOWED].

The younger of the two orderlies picked up a metal-detector paddle and swept it across her body, as if she'd made it this far with some kind of weapon concealed on her person.

"Seriously?" she asked, unable to stomach the absurdity.

"I'm sorry," he said. He sounded like he actually meant it, and Ren wondered what had brought him into this sick situation. Money? Scientific curiosity? Victoria's threats?

"Rules are rules. Also, shut your mouth," the other orderly snarled. She sensed the command was intended for his colleague as much as for her.

They walked her into the machine room, which itself had two zones. The MRI was plopped on the right like a giant marshmallow with a hole through it and a table attached to the front. Compared to what was on the other side of the room, it was not an intimidating piece of equipment. To the left was something much more alarming: a sort of dentist's chair, except fabricated from a transparent material like acrylic and fitted with thick straps with plastic buckles. Ren did not want to find out what it was used for.

The men positioned her on the MRI table, secured her wrists, ankles and head with velcro straps, and left the room. A couple minutes later, Markle entered with a sleepy-eyed technician who explained the proceedings—to him, not her.

"This will be our baseline scan. Pre-travel. It's important she remain still so we get optimum imagery."

"Fuck your imagery. And fuck you," she said to the tech. "And fuck you," she told Markle, to be thorough.

"Charming," Markle replied, staring at the floor. "So you know, we can do this with or without sedation. It's your choice. Some people feel a nasty hangover from the sedation."

As if any of this were her choice. "Eat me," she said.

Without looking at him, Markle directed the technician, "Prepare one-fifteen of propofol."

"One-fifteen? Wow, she is a little chunker, isn't she?"

The tech left the room and returned with a syringe and an alcohol pad. He swabbed her arm and injected the sedative. As it dulled her senses, she absently hoped she could thwart the machine's accuracy by thinking random thoughts, but it probably didn't work that way.

She wasn't unconscious by the time the marshmallow sucked her inside and began thumping and humming, but she was too far gone to move. The "baseline scan" proceeded without incident, and the sedative hangover was indeed nasty.

When they brought Ren into the room the following day, someone was strapped to the clear plastic chair.

# THE TORTURER

IT TOOK REN a moment to recognize her.

The girl wore the same sort of shitty clothes they'd issued to Ren: a men's white t-shirt and boxers, gray sweatpants and socks, no bra or shoes. Her mouth was sealed shut with a thick strip of surgical tape and she looked absolutely exhausted.

Then Ren noticed the beloved pink streak in her hair, and it took both orderlies to hold her back as she kicked and clawed and tried to reach the chair.

Kimber addressed himself to Ren. "There, there," he said, more amused than annoyed. "I'm sure it's delightful to see each other. As I told you, all in good time." He gestured to the MRI table and the men wrestled her onto it and strapped her down.

"We understand you two have a unique connection; a bond, if you will. We're going to test that bond to determine if we can induce you to travel. I'm afraid this will be unpleasant for her, but the methodology is sound."

"Don't touch her, you sick fuck," Ren screamed.

"I won't, young lady. That's his job."

Kimber referred to a fourth man, dressed in surgical attire and a face shield. He carried a plastic box like a kindergarten pencil case and removed from it what appeared to be a plastic or bone letter opener. He wiped the blade with an alcohol swab and looked to Kimber for the go-ahead. The doctor nodded and he stabbed Katie's left arm, above her wrist.

Katie's pain echoed in Ren's soul and the rollercoaster rush transported it on the shortest journey yet; twelve feet away to Katie's side.

"Holy shit," one man uttered. They were oblivious to Ren's *ikiryō*, but fascinated by how abruptly her body had gone limp on the table.

"Ms. Glass?" Kimber asked, and only then did Ren see Victoria watching through the window.

"Bingo," she said, smirking at ethereal Ren.

"Initiate scan," Kimber called to the MRI technician in the control room, and the machine whirred to life. The table retracted to pull her inside, and the rhythmic banging filled the room as they mapped her ethereated brain. The man who stabbed Katie tended to the wound, which Ren knew was painful but superficial.

Victoria sidled up to the girl strapped to the chair and brushed the pink streak of hair off her forehead. Katie flinched at the touch, and the fear on her face seemed to energize Victoria.

"You remember me, don't you?" she asked.

Katie nodded.

"You were our little party crasher. I got stuck watching you because dad was too chicken-shit to tell the brilliant Dr. Ando that he'd fucked up and should have gotten a babysitter."

Ren recalled Katie's story of how they'd met before, but she couldn't tell if Victoria actually held this petty grudge or just found it amusing to torment Katie. Regardless, the remorse on the girl's face was genuine.

Victoria's lips puffed into a phony pout. "It's okay, little one. I forgive you. Even at the end, my dad couldn't stand up to your dad. It is what it is; every relationship has an alpha. But you get to make it up to me now. You're going to help us crack the code on this one," she said, jerking her thumb at Ren.

There was nothing Ren could do about any of it, except to tell Katie, "I'm sorry."

* * *

For three more days, they repeated the sick routine of fastening Katie to the chair, inflicting her with an injury, then scanning Ren's brain. Ren couldn't believe there was anything left to learn from this madness, but on day four, it stopped working.

The blade punctured Katie's thigh and she howled. Ren did not ethereate. The man in the face shield stabbed her arm. She writhed in pain, eyes swollen with tears, but Ren remained conscious. And so he pierced Katie's skin yet again, in the delicate web between the fingers of her left hand. Ren's soul remained stubbornly anchored to her body.

"Stop it! Just stop!" she screamed.

The tormentor looked up at Kimber, who waved him off. The doctor's lips wrinkled as he pondered. It didn't take him long to posit a theory.

"She's calling our bluff," he said.

He was right. On some level, Ren's soul had learned that Katie, while in extreme pain, was not in mortal danger. As such, ethereating was an unproductive waste of energy.

"This is a problem," Markle said. "We still need contrast."

"Indeed. Come with me."

The doctors departed, and Ren was struck by the overwhelming feeling she'd made a terrible mistake. After the second day, Victoria had not returned to confirm the separation of her *ikiryō*. Ren assumed this was because the men now knew what to look for and Victoria had gotten bored. How much pain could she have saved Katie if she'd thought a little faster, faking ethereation by playing possum on the MRI table and letting them proceed with the scan?

Kimber and Markle returned a few minutes later. "Prep for contrast," Kimber ordered the tech, who swabbed Ren's arm with an alcohol pad and shot a clear liquid into her vein. An icy sensation spread from the injection site.

Markle carried a small styrofoam cooler labeled with a red [HAZARDOUS DRUG] sticker. He removed the lid and extracted a serum vial and a syringe, which he offered to Kimber.

"You sure?" he asked. "We only get to do this once."

In answer, Kimber removed the safety cap from the syringe and filled it from the vial. He held it up to the light, flicked the stray air bubbles to the top, and juiced the plunger enough to send a stream of blue liquid into the air.

He approached Katie with the syringe.

"What are you doing?" Ren screamed, fighting the table restraints like a wildcat. If she hadn't been so tightly secured, she would have beaten herself into another concussion, or worse, to delay for even a moment what was about to happen.

"It seems our little pinpricks are no longer sufficient to trigger your separation response. We've decided to administer the psilocybin protocol."

Katie struggled harder, the surgical tape gag trapping the screams in her throat. She knew what it was, as did Ren.

The drug in the syringe was the bastardized derivative of Ando's original formula, which Kimber and Victoria had been trying unsuccessfully to reverse-engineer for the last eight years.

It was the drug that created Yana.

The drug that made monsters.

Kimber grabbed Katie's arm. He didn't bother with an alcohol swab. As he aimed the needle, Ren lost all hope that this was another bluff. Her soul knew better. It left her body to be by Katie's side once more.

"Initiate scan," Kimber ordered, upon seeing Ren go limp.

Katie's eyes abandoned the syringe and found Ren's. Their unspoken plea shattered her heart.

"Wait!" a voice called from behind.

For a fleeting instant, Ren allowed herself to believe Katie had received a last-minute stay of execution. That their captors had reconsidered the plan and deemed it too barbaric.

No such luck.

Ren followed Katie's line of sight to the door.

"I want to watch," Victoria said.

"Of course, dear," said Kimber.

"I wasn't talking to you."

The woman was talking to Ren, her eyes icy hot with anticipation, and even as Ren began to beg for mercy, she knew there was none in the woman's heart.

"Victoria, please! Please don't do this. Katie would never hurt anyone. Don't make her pay for her father's mistakes."

"Mistakes," Victoria said, reflectively. "Mistakes were made, is that it?"

Her hand lashed out and pinched Katie's nose, surprising the men every bit as much as the women. Katie's eyes widened, her air supply cut off as Victoria shook with rage.

"What were his *mistakes*, exactly? Failing to treat my brother's condition, despite almost unlimited resources? Giving my idiot father a half-baked drug that had never even been tested on an animal? Destroying the lab and any hope of producing more of it, or an antidote to it? Or blowing my family's fucking brains out all over the foyer?"

Katie convulsed in the throes of slow suffocation. Ren had never felt more useless, as her ethereal state allowed her to do nothing but watch.

"Ms. Glass?" Kimber prompted, his voice betraying a genuine fear that his unhinged boss was about to irreparably damage a valuable asset. "If she dies, it could be a significant setback."

She ignored him. "No, his mistake was leaving me alive. And he prayed it wouldn't come back to bite him. Today it does."

Victoria released her grip. Katie drew a desperate, ragged breath through her red nose.

"Please! You're getting what you need," Ren said, pointing to her own body lying prone in the MRI. "They're scanning me like you wanted. You can figure out why I'm like this without hurting Katie. You have nothing to gain!"

"You're partly right," Victoria said. "I don't have *much* to gain. Mostly it's just fun. But then again, Yana's getting tired. Harder to control. More resistant to her assignments. We need a replacement, and Little Orphan Katie will be perfect."

Before Ren could fully process the horror, Victoria commanded Kimber, "Do it."

He stabbed the needle and pushed the plunger, slow and steady, emptying the drug into Katie's arm.

Time stood still.

Ren studied the faces in the room for insight into what was to come. Kimber assessed Katie with clinical detachment. Having injected Yana and countless others, he'd undoubtedly seen this many times before. Markle's head swiveled between Katie and the MRI machine, whose steady thump had become white noise in the background. His preoccupation seemed to be the successful completion of the scan, as if his livelihood—or his life—depended on it. Victoria watched with an expression Ren could only describe as gleeful.

The girl groaned softly. She squirmed on the table, her eyes rolling back in her head. Her muscles locked, contorting her body into a ghastly and unnatural form constrained only by the straps holding her down.

A distant and tiny ember of pain in Ren's soul blossomed into a wildfire of anguish as Katie's soul—to which she was forever bonded—tore itself apart.

A moment later, it was done.

Katie's living ghost sat up from within her unconscious body.

Her ethereal face was slack with shock and fear as she gazed upon her material face, peacefully slumbering on the chair. Confusion finally morphed into understanding, and she turned her attention to Ren. Her amber eyes darkened with hate, her beautiful lips twisted into a snarl.

"How could you?" Katie hissed. "How could you let them do this to me?"

Ren had no words for the creature before her, the vengeful and terrified thing that was and wasn't Katie Moreau.

Victoria answered on her behalf. "Because she's weak and stupid and useless. Katie, you really were slumming, you know?"

As Ren's soul returned to her body, she had to admit she couldn't have said it better herself.

# THE SISTER

THE DESCENT INTO crushing depression was swift and un-relenting, like slipping on a patch of ice and freezing solid to the ground upon impact.

Ren curled in a fetal position on her bed for what might have been days, too devastated to weep, too exhausted to sleep. Her brain danced in circles, trying to envision a world in which she had not failed in every way there was to fail. She was dead weight, something Alistair had called her once, disparaging her physique and her usefulness with a single, cruel remark. The moniker seemed to fit as well as it ever had.

If they'd wanted a real protectress to study, they should have taken Lailah. They must not have known. Then again, how could Lailah have believed someone like Ren could even be a protectress?

It was like asking a monster to babysit your children.

Ren had the sudden urge to see herself for the monster she was, and sat up too quickly. The room spun and she plunged her head back to the pillow to keep from throwing up. Not that she'd eaten anything; the trays of food her captors provided three times a day were removed hours later, barely touched.

On her second try, she was able to right herself and plant her feet on the floor without the vertigo. She shuffled unsteadily to the utility sink and stared into the shatterproof mirror above it. Dark circles shadowed her sunken eyes. Her skin was blotchy, her lips dry and cracked. Her hair was a greasy mess, blond roots showing as the inky black grew out.

At some point, they had downsized the thick bandage on her left cheek, but she had yet to see what lay beneath. She worked a dirty, chipped fingernail under the edge of the tape at her cheekbone and dragged it, stretching the tender flesh and the still-healing muscles. It was agony, and she deserved every ounce of it.

When the last of the bandage peeled free, she dropped it in the sink and took a hard look. Kimber and crew had done an adequate job restoring the functionality of her face and avoiding infection, but they had done nothing to address the aesthetics. The wound was nasty; red, raised, scabby and sort of rigid, with a texture like a dried-out rubber band.

Seeing it made her think of an injury she'd sustained on her favorite jungle gym, before the light died. Leaping from rung to rung, she'd missed a handhold and popped the tip of her chin on a steel cross-member. She registered no pain, but soon noticed a steady drip-drip-drip of blood falling to the gravel below. She calmly descended and found her dad, whose turn it had been to watch her that day. He took one look at her, scooped her in his arms, and drove her directly to a plastic surgeon's office, where she received a shot of lidocaine and five delicate sutures that perfectly restored her little face.

She jutted her chin toward the mirror but could see no trace of that wound.

The new one would mark her forever, and though some part of her thought she should be more upset about her appearance, self-loathing left no room for self-pity. At least now everyone could accurately judge the book by its cover.

As she tested the range of motion of her aching cheek, a silky Slavic voice whispered beside her.

"Hello, beautiful."

She didn't have to look to know who it was, but she looked anyway. She expected Yana's gloating smirk, but found instead the girl wore a neutral expression; mildly welcoming, even, as if she were pleased to see Ren. As if her dark heart had room for pleasure.

"What do you want?"

"They say you are here, so I see for myself," Yana said. "Sometimes they talk when they think I do not listen."

"Well, now you've seen," Ren said, doing a little curtsy. "So fuck off."

Yana feigned offense. "Ooh, so touchy."

Ren turned away. She had neither the energy nor the desire to engage with the creature who'd helped destroy the person she loved most in the world. And that was how she'd come to think of Katie: destroyed. A beautiful and tender light snuffed out—or worse, forever imprisoned in a world of pain and darkness. She hung her head over the sink and dry-heaved, clutching the sides of the basin to keep from passing out.

When the nausea abated, she leaned back against the adjacent wall, slid to the floor, closed her eyes, and tried to find the will to draw breath.

"You are no fun," Yana said after a minute, and though Ren refused to look at her, she knew the girl was pouting. And though she wanted more than anything to be left alone, something nagged at the back of her mind: a faint notion that Yana might know something that could help Katie.

If Katie could be helped at all.

Ren opened her eyes and the world came back into focus. Yana was still there studying her, standing so close it made her skin cold. She had no idea how to begin.

"So, like, where are you?" Ren asked. "I mean, where's your... body?"

Yana immediately brightened, despite Ren's pitiful attempt at conversation. The girl sat beside her, and Ren wondered when was the last time Yana had spoken with someone who wasn't her captor.

"In this building. Same as you!"

This seemed to be important to Yana, as if it put them on a level playing field.

"Don't you have some, like, accidents to cause, or people to brainwash?"

"Yes, I have mission," she said, as if spreading terror and hate gave the girl some twisted sense of purpose.

"Why do you keep helping them?" Ren asked. "What do you get out of it?"

"The more I help, the more they let me help," Yana explained, like it was the most obvious transaction in the world. "On mission, there is no pain. In my body there is only pain. They give drugs to dull it, but it never stop. Even in sleep, is there. Your friend now knows this pain. Is all she will ever know."

Though none of this was new information, Ren's heart shattered all over again for how thoroughly she had failed Katie. She felt her mind detaching, drifting back into the now-familiar black melancholic haze. She fought it, pressing her palms flat against the tile to stay grounded. She had to keep the girl talking. Despite all Ren had learned about Yana during their exchange of ethereal energy, she still didn't understand how Kimber and Victoria exploited her ability.

"Can you go on missions whenever you want to?"

"No, only when they let me out."

"How do they let you out?"

"They take me to different room. Blue room," Yana said, then frowned. "In white room, I cannot help."

If Ren grasped her meaning, Yana was saying there were places where she could ethereate and places where it wasn't possible. It reminded Ren of Ando's explanation of the Faraday cage. Had Kimber designed rooms that functioned the same way, letting spirit energy through only when it served their evil interests? Maybe that was why Ren couldn't ethereate to Katie after the prison attack. And if her theory was correct, Yana being here now meant that Ren's cell was not shielded.

Good to know.

"Can you tell me about the white room?" Ren asked.

"White room is bare and soft. Nothing to hurt me."

Ren understood Yana was describing a padded cell, but her implication was unmistakable. "Bare" and "soft" were not virtues. What she meant was that in the white room, there was nothing she could use to hurt herself. To end her endless pain. And she desperately wanted to.

In that moment, the full extent of the girl's misery finally dawned on Ren. Yana was as much a victim as Katie, and had been suffering for years. Though Yana had been her shadowy nemesis since the night of the rave, every drop of anger and hatred she harbored for the girl simply vanished, replaced by an avalanche of pity.

"How did you stand the pain for so long?" Ren asked, tears swelling in her eyes.

"Pain is all I have ever known. From time I was little girl. The masters changed, the rooms changed, the pain changed, but always fear was the same: death, the great unknown. But now," she said, weariness overtaking her voice, "pain has worn down fear. I do not want to help anymore. I want game to be over. They know this. This is why they take your friend, to replace me."

Ren tried to picture Katie in Yana's role, spreading fear, hatred and poison. It made her physically ill. She wanted to believe Katie could fight the pain, refuse to help, suffer in silence and stubbornly deny them the satisfaction. But Ren knew better. Katie was strong, but nobody was that strong. A fresh surge of resolve flowed through her.

"I won't let that happen," she said.

"It has already happened. All you can do is end her pain quickly."

Ren wasn't shocked by Yana's suggestion. It spoke clearly to how far their situation had deteriorated, and Ren knew it was born of mercy. If there was no way to rescue Katie from this hellish fate, then surely putting the girl out of her misery was the next best thing. But Ren was not going down that road without a fight.

"I refuse to believe there's no way to save her. Or you."

Yana just stared, as if Ren had suddenly switched to a language she didn't understand. Then a profound sadness washed over her pale face, and Ren had the overwhelming urge to hug her. That wasn't possible, so she tried the next best thing. She extended an open hand. Yana responded by feathering her ethereal fingertips through Ren's solid skin and bone.

"You are naive child," the girl said. "I cannot be saved. Even if I could live with pain, I could not live with what I have done to avoid it."

Ren knew that kind of guilt all too well. "I understand."

"No, *sestrychka*. You do not understand. When our energy touch, I said we are both killers—"

"We are," Ren interrupted, but Yana raised her fingers to Ren's lips in an ethereal shush.

"No. This was lie. You are not killer. If you knew what that man Alistair was capable of, you would never choose to help him. You are good girl, Lauren. Maybe best I have ever known. I said it only to hurt you. I see your weakness and I exploit it. This is what I do."

Yana's words rang in Ren's ears, and as her mind processed them, a feeling swelled inside her like nothing she had ever experienced. The cold guilt that had coursed through her bloodstream since the night of her father's murder seemed to withdraw from her extremities, leaving her fingers, toes, arms and legs warm in its wake. The icy shame gathered in her heart, offered one last dying plea, then exploded from her body in a series of heaving sobs that left her lying in a heap on the tile.

Her absolution had just come from the most unlikely source she could have imagined. And all this time, she'd been wrong.

She was not a monster.

She was a protectress.

And it was time to go to work.

Ren scrubbed the tears from her eyes and pushed her fingers through her dirty hair. "How can I save her, Yana? They'll never let me see her again."

"This is true. But never is not as long as you fear."

"What do you mean?"

"You think they will keep you forever? Feed and clothe and care for you the rest of your miserable life? When your body has given all its secrets, they will make you disappear."

Of course, Yana was right. There was only so much blood they could draw from her veins before they ran out of chemicals and genetic markers to screen for. There were only so many MRIs, CAT scans, PET scans and other tests they could subject her to before they decided enough was enough. Especially since she had no other charges; no further opportunities to ethereate while they studied her unconscious brain. Hell, they might decide to shoot her up with the psilocybin drug for shits and giggles, just to see what happened. Regardless, Ren was now certain her days were numbered. She just didn't know how much time was left on the clock.

"Will you help me?" she asked at last.

"How do I help you? We are caged animals."

"When they let you out to help them, could you find Katie?"

"Who knows? Perhaps if we are in blue room at same time. Why?"

"When our spirits touched, we learned each other's secrets, right?"

"Yes."

"If you touched Katie's spirit, maybe you could see something that could save her. And you can tell me."

"If, and if, and if," Yana mocked. "If we had borscht, we could have borscht and bread, if we had bread. You do not hear yourself. Is impossible."

"It can't be impossible," she protested, though the enormity of the task almost strangled her nascent hope in its crib. Yana shook her head, as if Ren were simply ignorant.

"Listen to me! This is not Russian prison. Is medical lab inside office building. With brains and luck *you* can escape. You, not us. We sleep. Deep like coma, because of drugs. You are not strong enough to carry Katie. You are not strong enough to carry me. So now I see your wheel spin. You think you go and get police and we are rescued? No. We burn in furnace before you reach end of street. You understand now? You must make choice. Save yourself or do nothing. You cannot save us."

Everything Yana said made sense.

Ren flat-out rejected it.

"Maybe you're right," she said. "But if I'm right, I promise to set you free. And you can do whatever you need to do. Will you help me?"

Yana rolled her eyes as if it were all too exhausting to contemplate. "Whatever."

Ren couldn't help but smile. "Now you're starting to sound like me."

For the first time, Yana smiled back from a place of joy rather than malice. It transformed her face completely. Ren saw past the scar, the anguish, the cynicism and the guilt, to the beautiful young woman Yana would have been.

In another life, where the universe held her in higher regard and was not so mercilessly cruel.

In another life, where they were sisters.

# THE SEEKER

AFTER THE GLIMMER of hope kindled by Yana's visit, Ren grew more and more frustrated by her confinement, both the powerlessness and the isolation. All she could do was wait and wonder whether Yana might return with more info that could help, because the only times Ren could leave her cell and learn more about her prison were for the medical procedures and for shower day. And shower day was not something to look forward to.

It had taken them a couple of weeks to establish the routine, a dehumanizing ordeal under the lustful gaze of a guard who seemed to enjoy the assignment a lot more than anyone should. At the appointed hour on every third day, after she undressed, they buzzed the electronic lock to let her out. A guard with a cattle prod aimed at her naked back escorted her fifty feet down the hall and through a door marked [117—LOCKER ROOM], except there were no lockers inside. The room had been stripped of everything but the shower enclave and a wood bench bolted to the floor with pipe fittings.

When she stepped beneath the shower head, the water would flow and she could wash up with an unscented bar of soap left on the floor. Apparently, a tube of toothpaste was too dangerous, so they issued her a travel-size plastic bottle of mouthwash for her oral hygiene. As for shaving, she wasn't big on it to begin with, but she could sure as hell forget about it now. They would never permit her a blade.

After cleaning up, she dried off with a towel she had to leave in the locker room, then made the cold, humiliating trudge back to her cell, where she would find they had exchanged her dirty clothes for a clean set, still creased from their packages and carrying the faint chemical odor of big-box store apparel.

Every time she pulled the stiff, itchy cotton-blend garments onto her body, she thought of Katie's lavender scent and longed to breathe it again. Longed to fall asleep once more beside the girl in the safe, warm bed in Lailah's apartment, with sheets that smelled like grapefruit. Or in one of the twin beds at home, with sheets that smelled like fresh rain.

Home.

The word brought with it a memory of her and Katie's last night in the hospital, and Lailah's final words imploring her to go there. It seemed like a lifetime ago. She remembered Katie sleeping peacefully; the TV playing some program where a handsome athlete had to decide which of a dozen fawning women to keep around for another week. Ren hadn't paid it too much attention, just enough to notice he'd kissed an awful lot of them. Sampling the merchandise, she supposed.

It was a lovely memory, and she wished she could start again with a fresh slate in that calm before the storm.

The calm.

It hit her like a thunderclap.

Ren had not been in danger at that moment. Yet Lailah had come to her anyway.

Every other time, it had been Ren's peril that summoned her protectress: at the edge of the roof, freezing to death in the car, tiptoeing around the loaded questions of two sleazy "cops." But that last time, it was Lailah who had been in peril, not Ren.

Which meant Lailah *chose* to come to her.

And if Lailah had that power, surely Ren did, too.

This possibility had to be explored, and she could barely contain her excitement. She assumed ethereation, whether voluntary or involuntary, would cause the same fatigue as always, so she hopped into bed and got comfortable. Whatever happened, she didn't want to appear as though she had zapped to Katie, and collapsing to the floor in a heap would be a big tip-off. Better to let them think she was napping, at least for now. There might come a time, however, when it would be advantageous for them to know she was ethereating. If they had a reason to pop her back inside an MRI, it might buy her a few more days of life.

Ren closed her eyes, emptied her thoughts and searched for rhythm; first her breathing, then her pulse. She systematically relaxed every inch of her body from her limbs to her core and retrieved an image of Katie from her mental library. It was not her favorite, but one that touched her deeply: the moment in the prison visitation room when Katie threw herself into her father's arms and eight years of anguish instantly left her heart.

Ren focused on the image—on that energy—with all of her being. She sought it out, reached for it, willed herself to it.

Her skin began to tingle, a low-frequency resonance like her blood sugar was dropping. It grew stronger and deeper until it seemed she might turn herself inside-out.

And then... nothing.

The sensation ended more abruptly than it had begun, and she was left relaxed but intact, still anchored to her body.

It didn't work.

Or—and there was that faint glimmer of hope again—it *might have* worked.

The part she couldn't be sure of was whether Katie was in a blue room or a white room. To protect her sanity, Ren had to assume the latter: that Katie was, at the moment, like a cell-phone with no bars.

And Ren only needed to wait until she had reception.

*  *  *

The energy expenditure of reaching out for Katie wasn't as steep as ethereation, but each successive attempt left Ren more drained, and she could manage only two or three per day.

Outside those few hopeful minutes, there remained little to do. They had obviously not designed this facility to accommodate captives who were awake all day long. It was one thing to keep soul-rended victims like Yana and Katie under heavy sedation in a padded room until they were needed; it was quite another to leave someone alone 24/7 with no mental stimulation. Even prisons had libraries. And yards.

During Kimber's next routine check-in, she threatened to inflict another concussion on herself unless he gave her a way to pass the time. And with nothing *but* time on her hands, she'd figured out how she would do it. The door to the hallway was solid steel. She would pretend it was a Dallas Cowboys wide receiver and take it out with a good head-forward running start, like Brian Dawkins on defense for the Eagles.

Her dad would be proud of her. "Boom! Didja see that hit?" he'd say.

Ren set aside her football fantasy and addressed the vile doctor. "Give me a music player," she demanded.

"No, I'm afraid that won't be possible," Kimber said with his weird overly expressive lips.

"What, am I gonna swallow it? Hang myself with the earbuds? Just a little speaker for shit's sake. I'm going out of my mind here."

The doctor flatly denied her anything electronic, but she did finally convince him to get her something to read. A couple hours later, an orderly delivered some magazines. Though she got a twinge of satisfaction that Kimber had tasked some minion with fetching them for her, she couldn't have cared less about reading them.

She needed every excuse she could manufacture to watch them enter her door code.

If there was any prayer of escaping this hellhole, she had to understand the security system, and though she was close, it was agonizingly out of reach. Her room number was 114. Today's code was 3411. The last three digits were the same every day, and the reverse of the room number, which held true for the two other rooms she'd visited. The locker room code always ended in 711, the MRI room code in 721.

But the first digit remained a mystery.

Initially, she thought it might be the day of the week, like Tuesday equals three, but it could differ between rooms, even on the same day. Also, she had completely lost track of days, which made testing the theory difficult.

It was also not possible to try every digit in rotation. The keypad locked out after three unsuccessful attempts, and the guard station had to override. This had happened once when Ren tried being recalcitrant and struggled so hard that her escort kept fat-fingering the code. For now, the answer evaded her. She would have to keep hammering at it.

Two days later, after she'd read each of her pointless magazines half a dozen times, she was finally bored enough to try exercise. It was shower day, so she figured it wouldn't be the worst thing to sweat a little. She started with sit-ups, but the abdominal strain telegraphed up her torso and made her lacerated face ache, so she tried push-ups instead. She was on number five and already winded when a voice rang out beside her.

"Lauren!"

She flopped onto her side to see Yana, wide-eyed and bursting with news. "Katie is—" she began, but was gone before she could finish the thought.

Ren groaned in frustration. Katie was what? Dead? Alive? Savable?

Or maybe Yana had seen her in the blue room.

She had no way of knowing, but it was the only possibility she could act on. She hoisted herself into bed. As before, she found her rhythm and her calm, but chose a different memory to focus on this time: their first night together in Lailah's apartment. The passion and the tenderness. The excitement of shared discovery and the feeling that, in that moment, nothing in the world could hurt them. It was easy for Ren to tune into that frequency, and the familiar tingle came even faster this time.

A heartbeat later, Ren's ethereated spirit was standing over Katie in a room painted a deep midnight blue.

Katie sat on the floor, her back against the wall. She was trembling. Ren kneeled beside her, agonized that she couldn't grab and shake and hold the girl.

"Katie?" she said, but her friend barely registered her presence. "If you can hear me, please nod. Or blink. Or anything!"

Ren searched her face for some sign of comprehension. At last, one came. Katie blinked twice in rapid succession. Though Ren swelled with renewed hope, she instinctively knew time was short. She spoke as quickly as she could.

"I know you hurt so bad right now, and they brought you here and told you to do something. But *I* need you to do something, okay? I need you to ethereate to me. I need to touch your spirit so I can learn how to save you. Do you understand?"

Ren imagined her words were warriors, slashing and kicking through the opioid haze shrouding Katie's consciousness, but the girl's blank stare meant they weren't fighting hard enough. She dispatched another battalion.

"Katie! You need to focus on me, okay? Try to feel my energy and let yourself be drawn to it."

A tear slid down Katie's cheek, but Ren didn't know what it meant. Was she trying and couldn't do it? Or was the tear just a silent testament to her unbearable pain?

Voices echoed outside the door, then grew louder. Ren screamed in desperation. "You need to focus! Don't be such a brat! Come to me, now!"

Katie looked up at Ren for the first time. Her sparkling, vivacious, amber-flecked eyes had disappeared. In their place were pools of sadness that did little more than reflect Ren's own failure back at her. Her hope dimmed like a candle burning the last of its wax.

The door opened. Two men entered, dressed in scrubs as if they fancied themselves medical professionals—men of science—and not simply jailers; abusers of defenseless women. One pushed an empty wheelchair. The other, apparently higher-ranking, said, "Lock the wheels. I'll get her legs."

Together they hoisted Katie into the chair. Ren desperately hoped she would kick and scream and struggle against the men, but the girl had no fight in her.

Boss man leaned into Katie's face and spoke loud and slow, as if the Japanese girl didn't understand English. "Time's up. You did not complete your task. You get no medicine tonight. I hope that will motivate you to try harder tomorrow." He stood up and shot a chin-nod to the other guy, who released the wheel locks and backed the chair out of the room.

Try harder tomorrow. Motherfuckers.

A bitter surge of guilt washed over her. If she had distracted Katie from her "task," she was now responsible for the night of anguish the girl would have to endure. But at least there might be a tomorrow; a chance to try again, unless Kimber got wise to Ren's game and moved her to a white room, too.

Katie was in the hall and the door was closing, its narrowing gap mimicking Ren's remaining hope.

There was only one thing left to say.

"*Je t'aime, mon petite ange.*"

I love you, my little angel.

Katie slumped in the chair.

"Whoa, she just passed out," one man said. Ren couldn't tell which, and didn't care.

Because Katie's soul was in the room with her.

Ren wasted no time with words.

She stepped into the energy field and lived seventy-two hours of the girl's life in a millisecond, through the eyes of the precocious eight-year-old who still thought of herself as Kaede.

# THE CHILD

THE DASHBOARD GAUGES cast a soft orange glow on her mother's gorgeous features, but it was the silhouette of her auburn locks that always struck Kaede. It was controlled chaos, like a photo captured in a windstorm. Sophie's hair was one of Kaede's favorite things to draw, and though she had the talent, it was as if the pencil or marker or paintbrush had not yet been invented that could fully render its tension—the raw energy of a firework primed to explode.

The girl so wished she'd inherited that hair. Even her dad's wavy mop would have been better; anything but the thin, straight, flat black blah she saw in the mirror every morning. She'd already decided that when she was old enough, she would try to dye it in the hope it would look half as cool as her mother's.

One thing Kaede did inherit, thankfully, was Sophie's smoky, pitch-perfect voice. And there was no sound in the world she adored more.

"Sing it again, maman! Please?"

Sophie's face was pained. "Kaede, I spent the entire day on the phone with Brussels. The connection was so bad, I almost had to shout. My voice is broken glass."

"But Ryoko loves to hear you!" Her baby sister was fast asleep in her car seat, but Kaede wanted Sophie to sing anyway. "Pleeeease," she cooed one last time, knowing her mother would cave.

"Oh, all right. If you insist."

"I insist!"

Her mother took a deep breath, then began.

"Sur le Pont d'Avignon, l'on y danse, l'on y danse. Sur le Pont d'Avignon—"

The car lurched, dropping speed as Sophie focused on something in the road.

"Qu'est-ce qu'il fout?" she said, more to herself than to Kaede, who thought little of it.

"Sur le Pont..." Kaede prompted, as if her mother had forgotten the words.

Sophie tightened her grip on the wheel, then resumed. "Sur le Pont d'Avignon, l'on y danse tous en rond. Les beaux messieurs font comme ça, et puis encore comme ça."

She never got the chance to sing the next verse.

She slammed the brakes and jerked the car hard to the left. Headlights erased the night like a sunrise, and the blare of a horn drowned every thought in Kaede's mind.

* * *

Kaede felt her father holding her hand before her eyes found him at her bedside. There were days when he spent sixteen hours or more at work, focused on some deadline, but she had never seen him so tired. He hadn't shaved and his face was puffy, like he'd been stung by a bee.

"Hi, daddy," she said, but couldn't understand why the words sounded distant or why her head was swimming and a dull ache throbbed in her chest.

"Kaede-chan." He smiled at her. "I'm very happy to see you."

The lights were low, and it took her a moment to realize this was not her bed. It was a hospital. She had been in one before, when Ryoko was born, and though this room was much smaller, it had the same look and smell and feel.

"What happened?" she asked him. She had no memory of arriving here or the last thing she'd done.

Naoki lifted her small hand to his lips and kissed it sweetly. "My angel, you and your mother and your sister were in an accident."

A faint melody drifted into her mind. Her mother's soothing voice.

"Where's maman? Ryoko?"

Her father didn't need to speak the words. The tears streaming down his face gave Kaede her answer.

The man did not cry. He *never* cried.

* * *

When Kaede woke again, she knew something was wrong. Her lungs struggled for air, but she didn't actually get scared until she rubbed her tickling nose and found a plastic tube in her nostrils.

She forced her drowsy eyes open. Her room had a large interior window, the space beyond bright and bustling with activity. Her dad was speaking to a doctor. At least she assumed that's what the woman was; her white coat was like the one he wore at work. He turned to look at Kaede, then nodded and shook the woman's hand.

\* \* \*

A man in a surgical mask and paper hat leaned over her. His brown eyes were creased at the corners and looked friendly.

"All right, Katie-girl, you're gonna do great," he said. "We're going to put this on, and let you breathe as deep as you can. Count backwards from one hundred, okay?"

The man's gloved hand descended and a clear, pillowy mask closed over her mouth and nose.

"It's Kaede," she said, correcting his pronunciation.

She never got the first number out.

\* \* \*

The heart that was transplanted into Kaede's chest must have brought with it an imprint of its former owner's soul, because it had its own story to tell.

Ren found it oddly familiar.

Her name was Alex, and she fell in front of a train when she was six years old.

\* \* \*

Trains were alive.

They had to be. Alex just knew it.

She sensed each one had a unique personality, like Thomas, Percy, and the rest of the gang, and she could not wait for her mechanical friends to whoosh into the station and blow her fine dark hair out of her eyes.

Riding the subway was a special treat, like ice cream on the way home from school or opening one present on Christmas Eve, and it made her every bit as giddy. When they went to grandma's apartment or the playground nearby, they took the train. She'd always thought grandma was sort of weird, but the playground was awesome, with cool orange slides and a super-tall structure to climb. Also, it was on Melville Street, marked by a sign which read 'Melville,' but with a small 'S' centered above it, for South. The first time she saw it, she'd misread it as "Smellville," and now sometimes she and her mom made up funny songs about it.

*We ride up the hill to Smellville*
*Where everything smells okay*
*Oh, what will we smell in Smellville?*
*What will we smell today?*

Something else drew her to that playground, but she never quite knew what it was. Maybe a feeling she might make a friend there. She didn't make friends too easily. Her mom made her play with other kids, and she didn't throw a fit about it, but she never had much fun. Her mind was always swimming with questions, and kids never seemed to have answers.

Like last month, she watched an episode where the boss made Thomas pick up a load of stinky cheese from the dairy. It was mind-blowing. She thought the powdery stuff in the blue Kraft box was cheese, but it turned out there were lots of kinds. Her mom let her try some. Most were gross, but it didn't matter. She wanted to catalog them all, and the other kids were no help.

Alex held her hand as they descended into Eighth Street station. It was a cool spring day, so she had a sweater tied around her waist, just in case. And of course, she wore the blue and red

Thomas backpack, which held her adventure kit: a walkie-talkie, a bottled water, a pair of binoculars that always left smudges on her thick glasses, a bundle of clothesline (in case she had to swing across a chasm, like when Luke rescued Leia), an Eagles hat, and some peanut-butter crackers.

She swiped her fare card and clicked through the turnstile, but when her mom swiped her card, it buzzed and she slammed hard into the steel bar.

"Oof. Shite," she exclaimed.

"Quarter for the swear jar," Alex taunted.

"Hang tight, Lexie, my card's out of money."

A minute later, her mom rejoined her and they trudged down a second set of stairs. When they got to the eastbound platform, which Alex always thought looked like a big waffle, she tried to count the floor tiles, but it quickly became overwhelming.

She looked to her mom for help. "How many?" she asked.

Ren recognized nurse Mary Brennan's flame-red hair before ever seeing her face, but when she did, it looked far younger than expected. The last twelve years had not been kind to the woman.

How could they have been? She had to bury a child.

"Four hundred and thirty-seven," Mary said.

It was a different number every trip, but Alex trusted her mom's count more than her own. "You're probably right," she said.

They meandered through the Saturday-morning crowd to their usual waiting spot. In her excitement to get to the playground, Alex the wiggle-butt—as her babysitter Tara liked to call her—slipped out of her mom's grip and stared at the gaping mouth of the tunnel until a bright light drew her gaze across the tracks to the opposite platform.

It was a woman. And she sparkled.

Alex could not tell how old she was; anyone over fourteen was a grown-up to her. But the woman was like nobody she'd ever seen, somehow old and young at the same time. And that hair. Beyond blond—silvery—though even that didn't do justice to the soft glow of its aura.

The same shimmer emanated from the colorless dress that shrouded the woman's body, and she exuded a welcoming warmth and a smile Alex could feel in her chest. In her mind, Alex smiled back, though anyone looking wouldn't have seen it.

If she could have articulated what she felt from—and for—this woman, she could only have called it love, though it was not like the habitual 'I love you's' she exchanged with her mom at bedtime, nor the heartfelt adoration she had for her sweet and patient babysitter.

This was the love of coming home; of a part reunited with the whole.

The irresistible allure the flame has for the moth.

Alex did not *decide* to go to the woman.

She simply had to.

* * *

As if to spare her the pain and indignity of such a death, Alex's soul left her body a heartbeat before the blue-line train thundered into the station. For a fleeting moment, she floated above the aftermath: the screams of the crowd, the horror on her mother's face, her Thomas backpack on the ground, grinning up at the ceiling.

But when Alex looked again for the shimmering woman, she was gone.

In her place stood a young Black woman with long, ropey hair, still waving frantically to stop a little girl from stepping off the platform.

\* \* \*

Ren never felt Katie's energy disentangle.

Her perception returned to the blue room in time to see the men wheel Katie's chair around the corner. Though she didn't have the chance to say goodbye or plant a seed of hope, she had to believe Katie understood it from their brief spiritual union.

Ren's soul was pulled back to her body and the weariness claimed her as it always did.

Except now she had a plan.

# THE DECEIVER

YANA VISITED TWICE the following week.

The first meeting lasted less than five minutes. They agreed Ren's escape attempt needed to happen at night, when the lab ran with a skeleton crew of two guards and an in-case-of-emergency orderly.

Yana also confirmed Ren's assumption that they were still in Philly. She explained the building where they were held captive was one of several identical ones in a large complex near a big industrial wasteland. Ren thought she must be describing the Philadelphia Gas Works.

On the second visit, Ren brought up her only remaining hurdle. "Do you know how the door codes work? I cannot figure out the first digit."

Yana didn't seem too troubled by it. "I do not know logic, but must be simple for these idiots to remember. You are smart. Pay attention. You will figure out."

Ren appreciated the encouragement, but hoped Yana's faith wasn't misplaced. Because when the time came to put her plan into action, she was on her own. At night, there was no chance Yana would be in the blue room for a real-time assist. She wondered if the girl could do anything beforehand to lay the groundwork. A subliminal nudge for an unsuspecting guard. A gentle whisper to facilitate her escape.

"Could you influence anyone to help?" Ren asked tentatively, unsure if Yana would be offended by the suggestion.

"No influence." And by her tone, no debate either.

"Okay," Ren said. "I'm sorry I asked. I'll do it on my own."

"Is not that. I *want* to influence. I cannot influence. When subject in blue room, facility on high alert. All personnel have panic alarm. If anyone sense influence, they press button. Subject immediately brought back to white room, no question asked. And they are punished," Yana said, almost certainly with firsthand knowledge of what that entailed.

"Jesus, they thought of everything, didn't they?" Ren muttered, her optimism waning with each passing moment.

"Not always. Nacho was one of first girls. From blue room, she whisper to guard to kill himself. He put gun in mouth. This is why panic alarms. And no more guns, only batons. And no more Nacho," she added grimly.

"Her name was really Nacho?"

"She was Consuelo. Victoria give subjects new name, like pets. It help guards not see us as human."

"What's yours?" Ren asked.

"Scarface," she said, looking away. And though they'd never spoken of it, Ren finally understood the girl had only wanted to see her maimed so they would have something in common. It was a perverse way of bonding, like getting matching tattoos. The surprising part was Ren didn't mind so much anymore.

"What's mine?" she asked.

"Is Butterball," Yana said, "but I do not understand."

Ren chuckled despite herself. She'd been called worse. "It's a turkey," she explained, gesturing with her hands. "Like, plump."

"Plump," Yana echoed, then smiled, as if enjoying the way the word felt on her lips. "Plump and perfect."

Ren warmed at the compliment, even if the latter part was untrue. "What do they call Katie?" she asked.

"Orphan."

Yeah, Ren had heard that gem before, and was curious why Victoria—who was every bit as much an orphan—hurled it at Katie like an insult.

Yana suddenly became anxious and said, "I stay too long."

"One last thing?" Ren pleaded. Yana frowned, but remained. "Tell me how to get to you."

Yana surveyed the space and her eyes landed on Ren's tired stack of magazines. "Open one of your papers and show to me."

"Which one?" Ren asked.

"Any!"

She picked up the *Cosmo* and opened it at random to a two-page spread advertising a luxury watch. Yana pointed to each location. "You middle. We bottom right. Front door and guard office, bottom left. Kimber office top left. Back door—like warehouse—top right. Understand?"

Ren understood.

"You try soon, yes?" Yana asked, then vanished before Ren could answer.

As the words echoed in her mind, their meaning became clear. Yana wasn't asking if Ren was going to try soon. Yana was telling her to try. Soon.

Time was running out for both of them.

Ren was as ready as she'd ever be, though she still hadn't figured out the door codes. She'd have to trust that one to fate. But as the hour of decision drew near, another question haunted her.

Was she prepared to kill to escape this place?

She'd spent the last year punishing herself for the death of her father, for whom she hadn't even pulled the trigger. Could she deliberately end a life to save Katie's? Or Yana's? Or her own?

In truth, she might not need to do it herself. Ren could simply unleash Yana and let the girl's vengeance sweep through the facility like the Black Death. But it felt disingenuous to absolve her own responsibility by leaving the killing to somebody else, like a politician sending other people's kids to war from behind the safety of a podium. The blood would be on her hands, too.

So what was the karmic calculus on murdering someone to protect love? And how did forgiveness come into play?

If Ren could forgive herself for her father, if she could forgive Yana for the violence she'd wrought, could she forgive Victoria?

How big a sin was too big to forgive?

Yana was a victim; purchased like a piece of property and injected against her will. But wasn't Victoria the original victim? Her father—the man who was supposed to protect her from every bad thing in the world—had given her a dangerous drug in the name of sharing his twisted power. Had she consented? And even if she had, did she understand what she was consenting to?

The drug made her insane, but wasn't insanity a defense? And had she followed in her father's footsteps because she had no other choice? Because another drug company run by men like Malcolm Glass saw her not as a human being who needed help, but instead as their golden ticket?

And what about Kimber? An amoral sadist, to be sure, but was he a victim, too? And who had victimized his victimizer in the vicious cycle of cruelty that spanned the course of humanity? Who was Ren to say where it should stop, and what gave her the right to stop it?

Then she remembered something from the night all of this began: the rare moment of contentment and connection she'd felt on the dance floor before Milo's friend decided to punish her for having the audacity to exist. She remembered her reaction as she fought him off. It was pure instinct.

*You don't get to do that.*

In a flash, the nuance of the argument was swept away.

There was no answer. There was only a choice. And the consequences would have to be sorted out between Ren and her god, if she decided she believed in one.

She would do whatever she had to do to get Katie out of there.

Because they don't get to do this anymore.

\* \* \*

The lights in Ren's cell were extinguished that night as they were every night. She pretended to sleep, listening for faint sounds of activity until she was confident the last of the day-shift employees had left their posts. She slipped out of bed, stumbled across the room to the toilet, dropped her pants, and peed.

Not that she had to go that badly, but she assumed if anyone was watching, they'd be particularly attentive to that show. It improved the odds of them noticing what came next.

After she finished her business, she washed and dried her hands, then leaned against the sink. In the dim light, the small mirror reflected the whites of her eyes and the surgical tape strips straddling the scar on her cheek.

Katie's voice echoed in her thoughts.

*Bonne chance à vous jeune fille.*

Midway back to her bed, Ren stopped, feigned a swoon, closed her eyes, and let her body go limp. She dropped hard to the tile floor. But would they buy it? And would they care?

Seconds turned to minutes. She lost count.

The overhead lights flared to full brightness. The door latch buzzed. Two sets of footsteps entered, one heavier than the other. Boots versus shoes. A boot nudged her in the ribs. She didn't flinch; she'd expected that.

"Your call," said a husky voice that Ren decided was the guard. He sounded a bit like Delfino, but she couldn't be certain.

"His call," a thinner voice replied. Ren pegged him for the af-ter-hours orderly Yana had told her about. He spoke again sec-onds later, on one side of a phone call.

"Dr. Kimber, it's Morgan... Yes... Sorry to disturb you at this hour. Butterball collapsed. It's possible she's traveling. We can get her into the scanner if you want... Yes... No... You want me to what?... Poker face."

Surely she'd misheard.

The guard said, "For real?"

"Yes. Press on her cheek. We'll find out pretty quick if she's bullshitting."

Oh, sweet Jesus, she hadn't expected this. And what the hell else hadn't she thought of that was liable to get her and Katie killed tonight?

She barely had time to consider before two gloved fingers touched her scar, gently at first but with increasing pressure. From a deep well of memory, she recalled her dentist telling her to aim her eyeballs away from the pain when he was probing her swollen gums. Behind closed lids, she looked up and to the right and tried to ignore the agony. She managed not to scream, but couldn't keep her jaw from clenching to suppress it. Hopefully, they didn't notice.

"Okay," said the orderly. "Get a chair."

The hand pulled back and relief flooded her senses so fast she almost laughed. The boots clomped away and returned soon after. Two sets of arms muscled her into a wheelchair and she snuck a peek at the code—5411—as she exited her cell for what she prayed would be the last time. They turned left out of the door, then another quick left down the corridor to the MRI room. The badge scanner beeped, 5721 was keyed in, the lock buzzed, and they were inside the anteroom.

Apparently today's show was brought to her by the number five.

"We carry her from here," the orderly said. "No metal in the room."

"Jesus," the guard complained, then grabbed her arm.

"Stop. No metal," the orderly said. "Badge, belt, baton, everything. Take it off and leave it on the table by the window."

The rustle of movement and the clatter of objects told Ren the guard had complied. Supporting her from both sides, the men lifted her from the chair, her feet dragging on the floor. They opened the door to the main MRI room—which did not require a badge or code entry—and moved her to the patient table that cantilevered off the front of the machine.

They sat her against the platform and hoisted her legs to lay her flat on it.

Ren took a deep breath, opened her eyes and registered the guard was not, in fact, Delfino, as she lashed out at his acne-scarred face with as hard a kick as she could muster. It connected with his orbital socket and he yelped in pain as it cracked under her heel. The startled orderly leaped backward and she made a break for the door. From the other side, she shoved the wheelchair back through. The orderly instinctively moved to block the metal appliance from entering the room, which was exactly what she was counting on.

In an instant, the magnetic field of the MRI inhaled the chair like a vacuum cleaner. Or it would have, were it not for the screaming man in light-blue scrubs now pinned between it and the gaping maw of the machine.

Ren had no time to enjoy the sight. The guard was regaining his wits, clutching his face with both hands. She grabbed the baton, hung the badge lanyards around her neck, and scanned one on the reader. She keyed 5721 into the number pad and waited for the green light to confirm she'd cracked their system.

The red light flashed.

She tried it again.

Red light.

# THE FUGITIVE

ALL THE WIND left her sails as she realized she was now trapped in this room. A hand grabbed her roughly and spun her around. The guard glared at her through squinted eyes and slapped her face so hard her ears rang and her cheek felt like it had split open once again. He grabbed the two lanyards and pulled them opposite each other, tightening them across her throat like a garrote.

Then she remembered she was holding a baton. She jabbed the sharp, electrified tip into the center of his chest. It hissed and crackled as she pushed his convulsing body away from her and toward the open door of the MRI control room. He fell to the floor, dazed and twitching, but not unconscious.

She glanced around frantically, looking for any way out of the catastrophe. Her eyes landed on a wall phone, then on a digital clock on the far side of the control room. It read Thursday 12-5-2024, 1:30 AM.

It was Thursday—day five. It was the fifth of the month. Five had to work. It had worked on the way into the goddamn room. Had she mistyped it twice? She had one more try, if her fingers would stop shaking long enough to get it right.

She scanned the badge, hovered over the five, then paused. It felt wrong. She blew a defeated breath, hung her head and looked at the badges dangling against her belly.

Two badges.

Fuck.

Maybe the first digit was tied to the badge, not the day. Maybe the badge she'd scanned to leave wasn't the one used to enter. It was the orderly who had typed the codes, but the badges had no names or pictures, so she couldn't tell which was his.

But both of them had a three-digit number. One ended with a five, the other with a two.

There was only one way to find out. She scanned the number-five badge and entered 5721 on the keypad.

The light turned green and the lock emitted its sharp buzz.

She hurled the door open and was about to bolt from the room, then remembered the phone, ripped it from the wall and tossed it into the MRI before stepping into the corridor. As one final precaution, she stabbed the baton tip as hard as she could into the smooth plastic surface of the badge reader. It sparked as an acrid puff of smoke seeped out from its edge.

The facility was quiet and the lights were low; only every third fixture was lit. There was nobody in sight, but she did not know where the patrolling guard was or when Kimber would get there. She had to assume he was on his way to assess the results of the MRI she was supposed to be having. All she could do was keep moving.

She turned right, then left down the long corridor toward where the subjects were housed, at least according to Yana's bare-bones description. As she passed each door, she peered through its narrow window. First came another room similar to Ren's cell. Then an office. Then a large lab with glossy black tables full of equipment and test tubes. Next were two other offices before the hallway cornered to the left. Panic bubbled in her stomach. This had to be the correct section, but the only door on this stretch of hall was marked [122—STORAGE] and didn't have a window.

Ren scanned in and opened the door, which was at least twice as heavy as the one to the MRI suite. She expected a closet but was confronted by another hallway; dark, with a faint glow at the far end. She proceeded slowly, holding the baton out ahead and wishing it had a longer reach.

The air smelled faintly of ozone, and a low electrical hum grew louder the further she walked. As she inched toward the opening, a stocky silhouette crossed in front of it, then disappeared. Her heart skipped a beat. It was the other guard making his rounds. She waited a few seconds before peeking beyond the end of the hall into a cavernous space, as long and wide as her high-school gymnasium and at least ten feet taller. In the center was a huge metallic mesh cube supported by a metal scaffolding.

The Faraday cage.

This was it. Katie and Yana had to be inside.

Beyond the cage—but connected to it by a mesh-covered walkway—was a smaller room built from two-by-fours that remained exposed on its outside walls. All she could see of its interior was a soft blue glow.

The guard ambled into sight from the far side of the blue room and continued walking the right-hand perimeter toward the corridor where Ren hid. She made the split-second decision to sprint to the left of the cage and circle behind him, hoping the electrical hum would drown out her footsteps and the pounding in her chest.

She waited by the far corner for what felt like an hour before he disappeared down the corridor and she heard the door slam in the distance.

There was no way into the cage from the blue room, so she hurried to the opposite end. Set into the center of the front face was a metal-framed mesh door secured by a lever, with no badge or keypad hardware at all. Maybe the signal-rejecting cage prevented such devices from functioning.

She pulled the lever, and the door swung open on a spring-loaded hinge to reveal another structure, which looked like two long shipping containers butted together to form a large rectangular block. There were no openings on the side she could see.

Her instinct was to charge in, but something stopped her. She couldn't afford stupid mistakes, and this seemed too easy. Upon examining the door hardware, the issue was immediately clear: there was no lever on the inside. If it closed behind her, she would be trapped. Game over.

Aside from the stolen baton she carried, there was nothing available to prop it open, and even that was going to be dicey. The gray metal cylinder was an inch-and-a-half in diameter and the gap at the bottom of the door was taller. If she pinched the baton between the door and the frame, it might fall under its own weight. Her only option was to wedge it into the hinge at the top of the door and pray it held.

Holding the door ajar with one hand, she arched up on tiptoes and slid the baton between the two metal bars that scissored together to form the closer mechanism. When the bars pinched the baton, she eased back, keeping her hand on the edge of the door latch in case it failed to hold.

She held her breath and waited.

And waited.

And right as she decided it was going to work, the spring let go of the baton, slamming the door on her hand.

Her scream echoed in the chamber along with the harsh clatter of the weapon on the concrete, and she shoved the door open to release her hand. She didn't think it was broken, but the sharp metal had punctured the thin skin on the back and it was already beginning to bleed. As she considered tearing a piece off her shirt to wrap her wound, the solution came to her.

She slipped out of her sweatpants, removed her boxer shorts, folded them into a bundle, and shoved them between the latch and the frame to keep it from engaging.

She pulled her pants back on and retrieved the baton, noting the impact had snapped off the tip. With a sinking feeling, she realized it could still bludgeon but not shock.

Ren backed away, walking to the left around the container structure until she came to a door with a window and a lever-lock similar to the cage door. She peered through the window into the blackness.

A face launched itself at the glass.

The eyes were red and swollen. Blond hair dangled in wispy strands. The mouth was a grimace of anguish, teeth clenched behind bloodless lips.

The perfect line of a thin scar across a pale cheek.

Ren instantly realized Yana had stopped taking her sedatives—maybe for days—to be awake for this moment; for when

Ren finally worked up the nerve to attempt her escape. She marveled at the faith it must have required to endure the pain, and
it was a coin flip whether the girl would hug her or strangle her.

She didn't care.

Because although Yana's cell was Pandora's box, there was
no way Ren wasn't opening the door.

In the end, Yana didn't embrace her or choke her. She simply
frowned and said, "You are noisy like circus."

Ren grinned and said, "Let's get out of here."

"Your orphan," Yana said, jerking her thumb at the room to
their left.

They moved down the hall and opened the door. The space
was slightly smaller than Ren's prison cell, its walls light-colored
and padded. On the floor to the right was a mattress made up
with white bedding.

And there was Katie.

Ren's heart swelled. She dropped to the girl's side, kissed her
forehead, and gently shook her shoulder. "Katie, can you wake
up? Katie?"

It was like shaking a corpse. Katie was beyond mere sleep,
and Ren now understood why Yana thought rescuing either of
them by herself would have been impossible. She wouldn't have
been able to hold the cell door open to reach Katie, let alone
haul her from the room.

"Can you help me?" she asked Yana.

"Come," Yana said, and led her around the perimeter of the
container structure. They passed the walkway to the blue room
on their left, then turned the corner to find yet another latching
door. Yana pulled it open and a light came on inside. This space
was twice as large as the cells, with a doctor's exam table in the

center and a row of cabinets along one wall. Against the opposite wall was a wheelchair, the same one they'd used to transport Katie to the blue room.

"Take it," Yana said. Ren fetched the chair, then held the door while Yana rifled through cabinets and drawers, shoving things into her pockets. A minute later, they were back in Katie's room, working together to position the chair in the doorway, lock its wheels, and hoist Katie into it.

They exited the cage, crossed the open floor, and hurried down the dark hallway to the access-controlled door. Ren scanned the badge and entered the code.

Nothing happened.

No red light, no green light. Nothing but a dull chirp from the reader. She tried again, then tried the other badge, with the same result. Ren looked up at the clear glass dome of a security camera on the ceiling and cursed her galactic stupidity.

The badges were dead.

The electrical fields of the cage must have nuked them. No wonder they'd only installed manual latches inside it.

"I'm so sorry," Ren said, fighting back tears. "I've killed us."

# THE DESTROYER

REN BRACED FOR the banshee shriek and for Yana's hands to find her throat, but the girl just smiled, as if Ren's worry was all for nothing.

"Is okay," she said. "I can help, but you must decide."

"Decide what?"

"We are free from cage. I can influence guard to open door, but when I play…"

"You'll be unconscious," Ren finished the thought.

Which meant she would to have to deal with the guard by herself. As she wondered exactly what that might entail, Yana removed a scalpel and a capped syringe from her pocket and held them out. It reminded Ren of when she'd stood in her mom's living room and offered Katie a selection of pens and pencils to sketch her protectress, and she wished the stakes were still that low.

"Are those the only choices?" she asked.

"What, you like switchblade better?"

"No, I mean… can't you just influence him to let us go?"

"No, little one," Yana sighed, sadness darkening her eyes. "I cannot overcome devil inside. I can only feed its hunger. There is no *good* influence."

Ren figured as much, and would have felt stupid for asking, but mostly she just ached for Yana. What a toll that kind of negativity must have taken on the girl's soul.

She took the scalpel and flicked her wrist back and forth, imagining slashing someone as she had been slashed, an effortless motion with devastating consequences. She wasn't sure she could do it, but slid the blade into her pocket, anyway. Then she took the syringe, which was filled with clear liquid, and asked, "What is this?"

"Sedative," Yana replied, gently stroking Katie's unconscious head. "What they give for sleep."

That was more Ren's speed. "Okay. What now?"

Their strategy session came to an abrupt end as Yana sat on the floor, leaned against the wall, and passed out. An instant later, her *ikiryō* appeared beside Ren. "You will know what to do," she said, and disappeared through the heavy steel door before Ren could protest.

Minutes crept by—more than Ren would have thought necessary for Yana to steer the guard to their location—and she started to worry something had gone wrong. She pressed her ear to the cold metal to listen for the approach of boots, but all she could hear was the hum of electricity from the cage.

From behind came a whisper, and she jumped.

"He is coming."

Ten seconds later, the lock buzzed and the door swung open. She recognized the bulky silhouette immediately.

Kowalski twirled a baton as he assessed the situation: Yana

unconscious on the floor, Ren slowly backing away, and Katie slumped in the chair further down the corridor.

"Looks like our turkey broke out of her pen," he said with an appraising look and a calculating smile. He was already enjoying this, and a sheen of cold sweat bloomed on Ren's body. She'd never be able to overpower him. Her only chance, she knew, was to push his buttons. To test his alpha-ness until he lost control and made a mistake, as he almost had in the hospital.

"Don't come any closer." She made a show of taking the scalpel from her pocket and brandishing it at him, while subtly moving her other hand beside her hip to uncap the syringe.

Kowalski chuckled. "You gonna cut me?" Clearly he wasn't convinced she had it in her to do so. She wasn't convinced, either. "How the fuck did you get out?" he asked, with maybe a hint of admiration in his voice.

"Your mom let me out," she said.

"Is that right?"

"Yeah. She needs help around the house, and all her pedo son likes to do is take pictures of little girls in their beds."

The smile remained on his lips but departed from his eyes. "Oh, I like to do more than that," he said.

"Like what? Jerk off to them in your sad bathroom down the hall from mommy? If you can even get it up, that is."

The smile vanished altogether, and he shook the baton at her to punctuate his words. "Keep it up, Butterball. See what happens to turkeys when they cook."

A distant memory of her dad preparing Thanksgiving dinner flashed through her mind. "Let me guess," she taunted. "They get basted. Covered in all those hot juices."

He licked his lips and she could almost see his sick imagination at play. "Drop the knife," he said. "Put your hands on your head and turn around."

"Fuck. You."

His jaw tightened, but his voice remained level. "Look, kid. They still want you alive. I'm not going to kill you. But I swear to God, the more you fuck with me, the more I'm gonna make you pay."

As if to illustrate his point, he leaned down and jabbed the baton's electrified spike into Yana's chest. Her body spasmed and her head cracked against the wall. Her bladder let go, a dark stain spreading on her sweatpants.

"What were you saying about hot juices?" Kowalski laughed and shocked Yana again.

Unmitigated hatred surged through Ren's gut. "Leave her alone, you fucking psycho," she said, her voice flinty and cold.

"Is okay," ethereal Yana said from behind, then stepped toward him. The pale devil whispered her poison in his ear, and Ren could see it working on his mind.

Without warning, he lunged at her, and Ren unleashed the loudest, shrillest scream she'd ever uttered.

It wasn't what he was expecting.

He hesitated for an instant, long enough for her to feint with the scalpel, then jab the syringe into his outstretched arm and push the plunger.

It didn't stop his momentum. The baton speared her breastbone and delivered a wallop of an electrical shock, locking her limbs and dropping her to the concrete floor. Her muscles cramped, tendrils of pain shot through her body, and the corridor spun like the bottle in the kissing game. Shadows beckoning sleep danced across her vision like puppets.

"Playtime's over," he said through gritted teeth.

Kowalski plucked the spent needle from his bicep and tossed the baton aside. He gave her a savage kick in the stomach that snapped her back to consciousness and left her gasping for air. He grabbed her wrists in his massive hands and flipped her onto her back as easily as if he were fluffing a down pillow, then wrapped his fingers around her throat.

He'd said they wanted her alive, but his face—a twisted mask of lust and fury—told her he no longer gave a shit. Her body was as limp and useless as when she ethereated. All she could do was brace herself for the pain.

It never came.

He hovered above her, still as a statue, for about ten seconds before his eyes went wide and his jaw dropped, like he was desperate to draw breath but couldn't.

He leaned back and clutched his own throat, from which a low growl began to emerge, and he started to shake; first his beefy arms, then his entire body. Just as she thought he might shake himself to pieces, he hugged his barrel chest and collapsed to the ground, a bloody froth dribbling from the corner of his mouth.

Yana sat beside her. "Good girl," she said, beaming with pride, but Ren felt none for what she'd just done. She focused on his dying eyes as she willed her limbs to relax and her pulse to find its rhythm until at last she could sit up.

"That wasn't a sedative," she said, stating the obvious, but also wondering if deep down she'd known Yana was lying about that.

"Oops."

"Did you tell him to attack me?" Ren asked. Yana shook her head. "But you knew he'd try."

"They always do."

"What did you say to him?"

"I say he must hurry before his boss get here."

Kimber. She'd forgotten he was en route to check on his most valuable asset. She forced herself to stand on aching and wobbly legs, then snatched Kowalski's badge from his corpse.

"We need to go," Ren said. "How long before you wake up?"

"Too long," Yana said.

Ren hurried to Yana's prone body. She hooked her arms around the girl's bony chest and dragged her toward the chair. It would be heavy, but she could ride on Katie's lap long enough for them to get away.

"Lauren."

"What?" she asked, looking at her ethereal ally.

Yana said nothing, but her eyes said everything, and in that moment, Ren knew the girl had no intention of leaving this facility alive. She never did.

"No, no, no, I'm not letting you stay here," Ren cried, but even as she spoke the words, she knew it was a pipe dream. Her plan to save Katie was half-baked at best, and she had no plan whatsoever to heal Yana. And it broke her heart.

"Take your orphan. Van parked on loading dock. Key inside. I will try to delay doctor."

"Please, no," Ren begged, but Yana's mind was made up.

"One last favor," Yana said, her voice fragile and childlike. "Don't leave me in dark?"

Ren scanned Kowalski's badge—which carried the number eight—and keyed in the code. She pulled the girl gently through the door and left her propped against the corridor wall, then returned for Katie.

"Do I need this badge to get out?" Ren asked.

"No."

Ren kneeled beside Yana's slumbering body and looped the lanyard over her neck as she spoke to the ethereant. "The door code is eight, plus the room number in reverse. Got it?"

"Got it."

With tears streaming down her face, she kissed Yana's forehead. "I owe you. Everything."

Ren stood, turned, and wheeled Katie until they reached a sign marked [LOADING], with an arrow pointing down a hall to the right. About twenty feet ahead was a large, open space with the rear doors of a white van jutting into view.

Every instinct told her not to glance back, that if she saw Yana lying helpless at the end of the corridor, she could never leave her behind.

She looked anyway. Yana was gone.

Ren's first thought was to give chase, but she pinched it off. She knew better. The girl was up to something and wanted Ren to have no part of it. So be it. She focused on the van and jogged Katie toward the dock.

Whatever slammed into her chest as she crossed the threshold may as well have been a train. It lifted her off the ground so fast Katie's wheelchair was still rolling forward when she landed on her back hard enough to knock the wind from her lungs.

Dr. Kimber peered at her over his bristly mustache and pursed lips.

"We have a problem," he said into the cellphone pressed against his ear.

Victoria zapped into the room, looked down at Ren and said, "You've got to be fucking kidding me."

Kimber pocketed his phone and addressed the ethereal woman directly. "You need to get over here. Walz is dead. Morgan and Willis are trapped in the MRI room. And Scarface is wandering around somewhere."

As if on cue, a chirping siren pierced the air, synced to white strobes on the ceiling. A fire alarm.

"Fuck me," Victoria said, then zapped away. Ten seconds later, she was back. "She's in the lab, dumping chemicals and setting fires. Secure Butterball and go find her."

Before Ren could comprehend Victoria's instruction, Kimber was dragging her roughly across the floor to a row of bolted-down metal shelving racks that lined the wall opposite the large garage door. The racks were full of blue metal barrels, each labeled with a chemical name—benzene, acetone, methanol—and various diamond-shaped hazard symbols, mostly red flames. He zip-tied her wrist to a shelf and moved to do the same for Katie, but Victoria waved him off.

"Forget her, she's baked. Run, you idiot."

She vanished again—Ren assumed to keep track of Yana's movements—and Kimber hustled down the corridor from which she and Katie had entered. Based on his speed and how hard he'd hit her, he was in better shape than she would have guessed from his droopy appearance.

Alone for the moment, Ren called out, "Katie!" knowing it was useless. The girl was still too far gone to help. Ren twisted and struggled against the heavy plastic strap, but couldn't get leverage on it and gave up before she dislocated her wrist. She sat in frustrated agony, marveling once again at the effect of Ando's drug, compared to the version Kimber had synthesized and her own natural ability.

Where Ren, Katie and Yana were rendered defenseless by ethereation, Victoria was strengthened by it. She could literally double herself to become her own lookout, her own spy, her own decoy. It also seemed she could choose when and to whom her *ikiryō* would be visible, functioning as either a shadowy influencer or a holographic projection.

With that power, if there was a more dangerous human on the planet than Victoria Glass, Ren never wanted to meet them.

Her thoughts were interrupted by an explosion that rocked the building.

At the far end of the corridor, an orange glow flared and smoke billowed, and she wondered how long before the inevitable flames reached the stockpile of flammable shit she was handcuffed to. She didn't have to dwell on it for long.

Yana emerged from the cloud at a full sprint, carrying a long-handled fire ax and heading directly for Ren.

Victoria materialized an instant later, howling, "You ungrateful little bitch! I made you a god, and this is how you repay me?"

Yana ignored Victoria and carefully cut Ren's zip-tie with the ax blade. She gifted Ren a final sad smile and whispered, "*Sestrychka...* go now."

Ren struggled to her feet and watched as the pale girl transformed into a whirlwind, dancing and spinning, swinging the ax with abandon to tear ragged gaping holes in the barrels stacked on the metal racks. Their clear contents spilled and splashed onto the floor, noxious fumes shimmering in the air, searing Ren's eyes, throat and lungs.

Ren rolled the chair alongside the van and opened the sliding door. She muscled Katie inside, pulled the door closed, and clambered behind the steering wheel. And as she found the key in the center console and cranked the ignition, Victoria ethereated into the passenger seat.

"This is so far from over," she hissed. "There is nowhere you can hide from me. Sweet dreams." Victoria zapped away, and Ren heard her voice echo from across the dock. "Stop her!"

Through the side window, Ren saw Kimber burst from the corridor, a wall of black smoke behind him. He ran toward Yana, who stopped destroying barrels and raised her ax as if to defend herself.

But that was not her intent.

Victoria screamed, "Don't you fucking do it!"

As Ren punched the accelerator and the van tore through the garage door in a cacophony of shredded sheet metal and exploding rivets, Yana turned and smashed the blade down onto the sharp edge of one of the metal shelves.

The steel-on-steel spark ignited the cloud of chemical vapor, and a massive, hellish fireball billowed forth into the night. In her side-view mirrors, Ren watched it consume the building and it occurred to her that Yana had done exactly what Katie's father had asked.

She'd burned them to the ground.

# THE SOULMATE

FIFTEEN MINUTES LATER, with Katie moaning in the passenger seat, Ren screeched to a stop under the emergency room portico, clipping a trash receptacle and sending it flying into the building. She swore if she survived the night, she'd never make fun of anyone's driving again.

The commotion brought two paramedics to investigate as she exited into the frigid early-morning air, circled to Katie's side, and opened the door. Katie, who'd been slumped against it, almost rolled onto the pavement, but Ren caught her in time.

One of the medics, a short, dark-skinned guy with a goatee, said, "Lady, are you okay?"

She couldn't imagine how haggard she must look for someone to call her "lady," but her appearance was the last thing she cared about. "Help me!" she screamed.

"Calm down, miss," said the other, a middle-aged woman with a messy blond bun. "Tell us what's going on."

"We need a wheelchair. She can't walk. And we need Mary Brennan. She's a nurse. Do you know her?"

"No," the blond said, and Ren's heart sank.

"I do," the man spoke up. "But this isn't your doctor's office, it's the ER. Your friend will be seen by whoever's available."

"Listen to me," Ren said. She tried for a level tone but knew her adrenaline-fueled hyperactivity was throwing up major red flags. "There's a woman coming to kill us. Please call the police and tell them to look out for Victoria Glass. *Glass*," she repeated. "She's your height," Ren said to the female medic. "Pretty. Dark hair. Fucking psychotic. Now take us to Mary Brennan. Please!"

The medics looked blankly at Ren, then at each other. And shrugged. "Get security to watch these two," the man said. "I'll page Brennan."

The woman nodded and set off. The man stepped away for a minute and returned pushing a wheelchair with EMERG DEPT stenciled in white on the dark blue vinyl backrest. Ren eased Katie onto the seat and the medic wheeled her inside. In the wee morning hour, the waiting area wasn't as crowded as it had been on their first visit, which was a slight comfort given the danger that was surely following close on their heels.

Ren's head was on a swivel, marking every way into and out of the space from which Victoria might enter or to which she and Katie could flee. Three long minutes later, Mary strolled into the room and Ren's gratitude almost brought her to tears. The nurse's gaze swept from the girls to the medic to the two security guards monitoring the developing situation.

"Jesus, look at the state of you," Mary said to Ren, shaking her head.

Ren threw her arms around the redhead and whispered, "Can we go somewhere private? As far from the entrance as possible?"

Mary thought for a moment, then dismissed the medic and the guards. "Go on now, guys. We're grand."

She took command of Katie's chair and led them to an elevator, where they joined two doctors and a disheveled old man headed up from below. Mary pushed the button for the sixth floor, and they rode in anxious silence until the other passengers disembarked on four, then five.

The doors closed and they were alone.

Mary asked, "Does she need a doctor?"

"No doctor can help her. She needs us."

"You'll have to be more specific, Ren."

They exited onto six and Mary walked them most of the way down the hall, stopping at the first room that didn't have a patient name on the door. They pushed inside.

"Can we get her in bed?" Ren asked, and Mary helped her do so. Katie whimpered, her painkillers clearly wearing off, as Ren dragged furniture—side tables, chairs, even the wastebasket—in front of the door, which did nothing to diminish the nurse's unease.

Ren picked up the bedside phone and dialed her mother, thanking the universe that Sarah had kept the old landline, whose number she'd committed to memory all those years ago.

"Hello?" her mom answered, her voice alert despite the early hour.

"Mom, it's me. We got away. We're at Mercy Hospital, room 614. She's coming after us. You have to tell Marcus. You have to get him here to stop her. Do you understand?"

"Yes, but—"

"Mom, I've got to go. Mercy. 614. I love you."

She hung up the phone.

"Start talking," Mary said.

In the back of her mind, Ren had tried to plan this conversation alongside the plan to rescue Katie. Predictably, she hadn't come up with anything brilliant. She took a deep breath and tugged Katie's shirt collar down to reveal the transplant scar.

"Mary, I don't know how else to say this. Your daughter's heart is in here."

The nurse stared blankly for a moment, then her jaw clenched, her cheeks reddened, and tears rolled down her face. She rested her palm flat on Katie's chest.

"I know," she said at last. "I could feel it when you two were here. Only I wasn't sure what I was feeling."

Ren squeezed the nurse's hand. "I need to show you something. Because I don't have time to explain, and you need to understand what's possible. Do you trust me?"

Mary nodded. Ren laid on the floor and closed her eyes. She focused on Katie's energy until the telltale tingle zoomed from her extremities to her core and her soul separated once again.

The nurse stepped back, speechless, as ethereal Ren turned to address her.

"You were on your way to a playground when Alex died. I was there with my mom. I was going to meet your little girl for the first time that day. I was going to meet my soulmate. When she died, my soul was torn. And so was yours. I don't know how to fix that. But we can fix Katie's."

"What's wrong with her? What's happened?" Mary asked, her voice trembling.

"It's complicated, but it comes down to this: some very bad people put her in a dark and terrible place. We need to show her the way home."

"How?" the nurse asked.

"Love."

"Aww, that's so sweet," came a familiar voice.

Ren and Mary snapped their attention to the door, where Victoria stood with her arms crossed, gloating. Ren knew it was the ethereal one, as their makeshift barricade remained intact, but Mary was terrified nonetheless.

"Ignore her," Ren said. "She can't hurt us."

Victoria laughed, a cruel and brittle sound Ren fought to tune out. "I can't hurt you? All I've done is hurt you. I broke your little doll. And I'm going to hurt you more. I'm going to put a bullet in her brain and it'll be the last thing you see before I put you back in your cage. Tick-tock, Butterball."

She vanished, presumably deploying her *ikiryō* elsewhere to help her get past security and gain entry to the hospital. Ren could not believe that even after the research facility and its lead scientist had been destroyed, the woman was still intent on making Ren her captive.

Their time was growing short.

"What do we do?" Mary asked.

"Keep your hand on her heart," Ren said, bidding the nurse do what she desperately wished she could. She moved to the opposite side of the bed. "I'm going to whisper for her. Tell her I love her. Ask her to come out of the darkness. You do the same for Alex."

"But Alex is... gone," Mary said, a question as much as a statement.

"Yes... and no. Her heart remembers her soul. I..." Ren faltered. She wanted so badly to seem like an authority on the subject, as if she had all sorts of experience mending souls. For this to work, Alex's mother needed to believe, but the same uncertainty that weakened Ren's voice clouded Mary's eyes. "I honestly don't know what will happen," she admitted at last. "But there's nothing else I can think of to try."

Mary nodded, faintly at first, but with increasing conviction. "I'll do it," she said.

Ren moved her lips to Katie's left ear. The nurse followed suit, leaning to whisper into the right. Ren couldn't make out Mary's words, but she could feel the love they carried.

"Katie," Ren began. "If you can hear me, I need you to come out. I know how scary it is. I know what it means to let go of your body. You have to do it one more time. You have to get free of the pain and receive our love. Our friend Mary is here. She's calling for her daughter. Together we can save you."

Katie gave no sign any of it was getting through. Ren tried the tactic that had worked before, in the blue room.

"Focus on my energy, okay? *Je t'aime, mon petite ange. Je t'aime.* Listen to me and let go. I need you. I love you."

Nothing.

She wanted to wail, but was terrified of distracting Mary— or worse, planting a seed of doubt that this was the wrong course of action. It took every bit of strength to keep her voice in check. "Please, Katie! I'll never ask you for anything else. Just come to me now."

Nothing.

Ren searched her heart for something different to say, anything more to try.

And she came up empty.

She closed her eyes as her last and greatest failure washed over her like a tide of sewage.

She couldn't speak. She couldn't think. She couldn't feel.

But she could hear.

A small, joyful voice called out, "Hi, mommy!"

Ren snapped her head up to find a freckle-faced little girl standing at the foot of the bed beaming a smile. She had fine, dark hair and thick glasses that magnified emerald eyes just like her mother's, and for a moment, Ren thought her chest would burst.

"Hello, Lexie!" Mary's eyes brimmed with tears, but she matched her daughter's smile. "I'm delighted to see you again."

"You too!" Alex Brennan said. "Are you having fun at work?"

"I am," Mary said. "We're taking care of Miss Katie. She's got your heart."

"I know. She's cool. She can draw and stuff."

Ren finally found her voice. "That's right, Alex. She's sick, though. We're trying to make her better."

"Yeah." The girl seemed to understand the situation perfectly.

"Do you think maybe you could help?" Ren asked.

"Yeah."

Ren was about to thank her when Victoria zapped into the room once again.

"Say your goodbyes. I'm almost there," her tone was cheerful, practically sing-song. Then she noticed the little girl. "Who the fuck are you?" she asked Alex.

"Quarter for the swear jar," Alex replied.

Victoria didn't respond. She just looked confused and disappeared. A few seconds later, Ren heard a muffled series of cracks, perhaps gunshots, but not nearby.

Not yet.

"She's not very nice," Alex said. "But don't be scared, mommy. She won't hurt you."

"All right. If you say so."

"I. Say. So!" she giggled. "Okay, love you, mommy."

"I love you too, my girlie. Always."

"I know." Alex approached Katie, then stopped, pushed up the glasses that had slid down her little button nose, and said, "Hey, Rennie? Sorry I couldn't come to the playground."

"It's okay. It wasn't your fault." She smiled at Alex and Alex smiled back. Her beauty stole Ren's breath.

"Yeah. See you next time," Alex said.

And then she vanished.

In an instant, Ren felt every trace of Katie's fear, anguish and bitterness evaporate, as if a blazing sun had risen above her bed and burned it away, shining for her and her alone. Katie opened her eyes and sucked in a desperate gasp of air, like a baby drawing its first breath outside the womb.

The girl had done it.

The girl whose heart healed Katie's body twelve years ago had just healed her soul.

With her mission completed, Ren returned to her own body, awake but immobile.

She had no time to savor the joy.

Gunshots echoed in the corridor. A woman screamed. Shadows darted back and forth across the door's narrow window.

Katie slid off the bed and laid on top of Ren, a human shield. "I've got you, baby," Katie whispered in her ear.

Another gunshot. Another scream.

The door lever rattled and it opened against the barricade.

"No, no!" Mary cried and threw her weight against it. It held for a moment, then exploded open, sending the nurse sprawling to the floor.

Victoria swept into the room, clad head-to-toe in black, a gun in each gloved hand. She circled the perimeter so she could watch the entry door, keeping one weapon trained on Mary and the other on Katie and Ren.

"Shut the door," she told Mary. The nurse had no choice but to comply, and as the latch clicked, Ren knew nobody was coming to save them. Marcus Grant could helicopter in with the entire Philly SWAT team, and it wouldn't be enough. Victoria would paint the room scarlet with their blood before the cops could fire a shot.

The woman leaned down and pressed the hot muzzle of one gun against Katie's cheek. The girl's eyes squinched, but she remained silent and fearless.

"Hello again," Victoria said, her cool authority infinitely more menacing than her usual manic taunts. "I'm here to keep my promise."

She stood, wedged the toe of her boot between them, and rolled Katie off of Ren and onto the floor. The action was brutish, but it communicated something critical: Victoria assumed Katie was still drugged and damaged.

She didn't know Katie had been saved.

She waved a gun at Ren and said, "Get up."

"I can't," Ren said, and watched Victoria realize she was in the throes of post-ethereal paralysis and telling the truth.

"Ugh, you useless twat." She slid her weapons into the waistband of her jeans and dragged Ren toward the wheelchair.

It was the only time Ren had ever been grateful for the cosmic roofie.

Katie seized the moment, reaching up from the floor to snatch one of Victoria's pistols while the woman's hands were full. The assassin dropped Ren, spun into a crouch, and had her remaining pistol in hand and jammed between Ren's eyes faster than seemed humanly possible.

Katie was on her back with her gun pointed at Victoria's head in a two-handed grip, the room dead silent as the orphans stared each other down.

Emotions paraded across Victoria's face and radiated from her body: disbelief, jealousy, sadness.

"She fixed you," Victoria said to Katie.

"Yeah, she did," the girl replied.

Victoria looked into Ren's eyes and pressed the gun harder against her forehead. "Could you fix me, too?" she asked.

It was the first thing the woman had ever said that approached sincerity, and an empathic download flooded Ren's mind like a dam breaking.

Victoria had never allowed for the possibility she could be healed. If she had, she never would've perpetuated her father's plans. She wouldn't have dedicated her life to exploiting the helpless so that others might amass power and privilege. She had, without a moment's hesitation, become a willing agent of the system that created her. And she hated herself for it.

In the end, Ren had no idea what Victoria hoped to hear, so she could only speak the truth. Even if it sealed her fate.

"No. I can't fix you."

Victoria exhaled the breath she'd been holding, clenched her teeth and tightened her grip on the pistol. "Then fuck you."

A small voice called out, "Quarter for the swear jar."

As Victoria stared, bewildered, at the bespectacled girl standing beside Katie, she loosened her grip. The gun drifted away from Ren's face.

"What the f—" she started to say, but her head exploded into a fine red mist and she toppled over backward.

The smoke was still curling from the barrel of Katie's gun when Mary scrambled across the floor to scoop them into a hug, one under each arm.

Katie's eyes met Ren's.

*I told you I'd protect you*, they said.

Thirty seconds later, Marcus Grant burst into the room.

## Killings Linked to Deadly Office Fire

by Devin Peretti

Published December 9, 2024

PHILADELPHIA — Following the discovery of human remains in the Southwind Industrial Park office building that burned to the ground in the early morning hours of Thursday, December 5, police now say that a string of homicides throughout the city—which began as the blaze was underway—may be related.

Twelve people are confirmed dead across several area neighborhoods in what police are calling a "bizarre murder-suicide pact."

No names have been released, but investigators say a security guard who worked inside the burned facility—and is believed to have perished in the fire—emailed a list of employee names and home addresses to a colleague on the outside who subsequently shot and killed all eleven individuals on the list before turning the gun on himself.

Police so far have refused to comment on multiple eyewitness reports that the gunman appeared to be wearing a Philadelphia Police Dept. uniform, but they have emphatically stated that no PPD officers were involved in the incident.

Officials also declined to comment on the activities of the business whose employees lost their lives in last Thursday's tragic events, but a representative of the property owner confirmed the burned building was leased to a corporation called Consolidated Holdings.

We will continue to report on this story as it develops.

# THE STUDENT

IT TOOK KATIE six days to detox from the drugs she'd been given in captivity.

Her opioid withdrawal symptoms—nausea, shaking, sweating—began the day after they'd escaped, and Ren recognized them at once. She'd spent many sleepless nights dabbing cool rags on the foreheads of housemates, covering them in blankets, and cleaning up their vomit. And not just because Alistair had put her on DT duty to earn her keep between burglaries; she did it hoping to bank some good karma in the event someone had to do that for her one day.

At the first sign, she'd whisked Katie back to DC to stay at Lailah's. The apartment felt safe, and though a controlled and medically supervised environment would have been safer, Katie didn't want methadone, and they were both beyond done with hospitals, clinics, or anything that resembled them.

It was not a decision taken lightly. There would be consequences for Ren as well. The doctors who treated them in the aftermath of Victoria's shooting had recommended she undergo immediate reconstructive surgery to help minimize the scarring on her face. And though it devastated her mom, Ren had refused.

She decided she'd live with it for two reasons. First as a reminder of Yana, of Lailah, of Ando and everyone else who hadn't been so lucky. Not that she'd ever forget them, but it seemed selfish to waste time and effort reversing the cosmetic damage for the sake of her vanity. Selfish and vain didn't seem like words that should describe a protectress.

The other reason was that Ren had to be certain Katie was on the road to healing before she shattered the girl's heart one last time.

The specter of Lailah and Melissa's tragedy—and its implications for Katie's safety—had haunted her ever since Nina issued the dire warning, and the shadow in her mind had only darkened as she'd read the journal. Throughout their imprisonment, Ren had repressed the thought of ending their relationship, ironically clinging to the idea that if one or both of them were killed by Victoria, at least she wouldn't have to go through with it.

But by some miracle, they'd survived. And their borrowed time was running out.

It hadn't run out yet, though. So Ren savored every moment, especially after Katie made it through the worst of her recovery. The girl's restless energy returned, along with her appetites. They shared bubble teas and great food. They watched Batman movies and shopped for clothes. Katie cajoled Ren into working out together in the building's small fitness room. They found joy and comfort and pleasure in each other, drifting off to sleep every night entwined so thoroughly they could no longer determine where one body began and the other ended.

They spent time in Lailah's studio, sculpting and glazing and painting and drawing and laughing and crying. Ren watched Katie process her trauma through her art, bringing beautiful and terrifying images of soul separation to life on the canvas. Ren hoped it would be enough to heal her, though she knew at some point Katie might need to seek therapy. Either way, Ren gained confidence that the girl would—eventually—be okay.

Peter and Nina checked on them regularly, and after a week, he asked Ren to come into the office for a little while. She'd assumed her "internship" was over now that they'd solved Lailah's murder, but she agreed without complaint. He collected her in the Jeep the next morning, with a hot coffee for her trouble.

When they arrived, she found the Ando case files had been boxed up and returned to the file room, and she was grateful not to have to lay eyes on them again. Nina sat at the conference table, on which a couple of folders with printed documents had been laid out.

"Good morning, child," the woman said with a smile. "You're looking well."

"Thanks, you too," Ren said, and gave her a hug.

"Katie is getting stronger?" Nina asked, and though Ren may have only been projecting, she heard an implied question: *Is she strong enough for you to do what must be done?*

"She's amazing," Ren said, and that was all Nina was going to get right now.

Ren took a seat. Peter entered a moment later and sat beside her. She looked at him expectantly; the ball was in his court. She had no idea why she was here, but Nina clearly did. The woman watched her with warmth and anticipation.

"There's something we need to discuss," he began.

Her mind immediately churned with possibilities, though it wasn't the first time she'd thought about what the future held. She remembered Peter had said something about focusing only on death-penalty cases from now on. And Nina was going to delay her retirement to help him. Were they going to ask her to stay, too? She had a sudden vision of 'Duncan, Holland and Cole' stenciled on the front-office window glass and just as quickly dismissed it. She hadn't even finished high school. Surely she wasn't smart enough for law school. Or was she?

Peter must have seen she was spinning out, as he gently reeled her back with a comforting hand on her forearm.

"Ren," he said. "Lailah changed her will before she died."

\* \* \*

Three days later, Peter accompanied Ren and Katie on the Acela back to Philly. He'd been cagey about his reason for making the trip, but Ren got her answer when her mom picked them up from 30th Street Station and took them to a quaint cafe in University City for lunch.

He and Sarah shared one side of the booth and seemed completely comfortable with the arrangement. Ren glanced at Katie to see if she noticed, and got confirmation back: yeah, there was something there. Ren couldn't have been happier. The two suited each other, and they deserved every chance at love in their lives.

Hoping to avoid questions her mom would undoubtedly have about her plans for the future, Ren drove the conversation.

"Are you prepping for spring term?" she asked. Her mom was always diligent about ensuring the next semester's courses were fully mapped out before she settled into her vacations.

"Actually, I'm not teaching next semester."

Ren's eyebrows shot up. She couldn't remember her mom ever taking a break, but apparently that was exactly her intention.

"I'm taking a sabbatical to do research and evaluate my long-term teaching priorities," she said in a prim and proper tone. "At least, that's what I told the dean. Mostly I want to clear my head and do some traveling."

Katie kicked Ren under the table, and she suppressed a smile. "Peter's an excellent tour guide, if your travel plans include DC."

"Noted," Sarah said, and he shifted uncomfortably in his seat. "And you guys?" she asked.

"Taking it a day at a time," Ren said, hoping her mother would let it lie and that Katie wouldn't bristle at the response.

And omitting the fact that Ren intended this to be their last day.

After lunch, Ren's mother dropped off the girls at a cemetery nestled alongside the Schuylkill River. A December breeze blew northeast off the water as they searched for a section of grave markers arranged in four concentric rings. Mary Brennan had highlighted her daughter's final resting place on the map she'd given Ren. It wasn't difficult to find, and they had not encountered another soul along the cemetery's curving paths.

Katie laid a bouquet of purple pansies beside the flat stone slab engraved with Alexandra Maeve Brennan's name, then kneeled beside it and dusted the debris from its crevices. Ren took from her backpack the heaviest item it contained, a pint-sized mason jar with a few dozen quarters. The loose change didn't come close to settling her swearing tab, but she supposed restitution had to start somewhere. She set the jar next to the stone and stepped back.

"We should place a marker for Yana," Katie said.

Ren had been thinking the same. No evidence of the woman's existence remained outside the memories of the two she'd saved. And though she had both suffered and inflicted more than her share of pain and violence in her twenty-four miserable years, Yana Grigorivna Silchenko deserved better.

"We will," Ren agreed. "And one for your dad?" It had not escaped Ren that today would have been the day of his execution.

Katie shook her head. "When my mom and sister died, we spread their ashes at her childhood home near Avignon. That's where he'll want to be." She paused, then added, "I can't wait for you to see it."

Amazingly, Ren could already see it, as sharp as a photograph. Trekking through a vineyard on a humid summer day to reunite Katie's father with the family he'd lost twelve years ago. But in her vision, they weren't alone.

"Wait," she said. "Do you have family in France?"

"Yes. My grandfather and two aunts."

Ren was stunned. Victoria had called Katie "orphan," which was how Ren had always thought of her as well. As someone alone in the world, adrift without a place to call home. She assumed she'd learned all there was to know about Katie during their exchange of soul energy, yet this had remained hidden. Perhaps it had been locked too deeply in her heart.

"Why didn't you live with them after your dad went away?" Ren asked.

"They weren't able to come here to take care of me. And I knew if I left to stay with them, I would never make it back."

"Make it back for what?"

"For him."

Ren had thought it impossible to love or understand this woman more, but she was wrong yet again. For eight years, Katie had held onto the singular hope of reconnecting with her father. It was the gravitational pull that kept her in his orbit, never straying further than ten miles from his prison cell. It was why she never went to college, never took shelter with her mother's family. Why she'd been so reluctant to join Ren in Washington, even when she was in mortal danger.

His death had finally set her free.

Now Ren had to do the same.

She led Katie to a wooden bench marking the entrance to a family plot of graves. They sat on the aged gray planks and Ren opened her pack once more to extract a large envelope. Katie undid the clasp and slid from it a familiar charcoal drawing. Save for a few dark flecks of dried blood, *L'Homme à tête de chou* remained nearly intact.

"Thank you," Katie said, her fingers gliding over the stains.

"I thought you should have it for your portfolio."

Confusion shadowed Katie's face. Ren explained, "When you apply to art school, you need to submit a portfolio. This would make a pretty strong first impression."

Katie scoffed. "Art school? I can't afford art school! I'm broke, unemployed and homeless." The sentiments were bleak, yet there was optimism in her voice, as though none of those obstacles were insurmountable.

"You're not broke," Ren said.

"Uh, yes I am. My bills have bills."

"A lot happened last week. Peter told me Lailah made a new will. Literally the day she died. She left me her apartment. And most of her savings. I'm sending you to art school."

She watched Katie absorb the news and wasn't surprised that the girl's first thought wasn't about the money.

"Did Lailah know?" Katie asked. "That she was going to die?"

Ren nodded. "I think she did."

As Katie had endured the fitful sleep of drug withdrawal, Ren had finally worked up the nerve to return to Lailah's journal and read the remaining entries, including the three about herself.

[October 9, 2015] *Spent the morning at Smithsonian to clear my head. A little girl was being escorted by that creeper guard. She was terrified. She looked up and we bonded. It hit so hard, worst ever. I pretended she was with me and took her from him. Her name was Lauren Ann Cole. We found her parents and she gave me a friendship bracelet. She was so sweet and so sad. It broke my heart.*

[October 27, 2024] *Ethereated to Lauren at a rave in the middle of the night. A guy got in her face. She fought him off, but another man assaulted her and she ran. I transported to the roof, and she was at the edge. I called out, but she didn't recognize me. I'd always hoped that little girl from the museum would someday find her joy, but she was... empty. I held her there until this Japanese girl found her. She introduced herself as Katie. And then I saw something I've never seen before. Lauren bonded with Katie. I'm certain of it. Lauren is like me. Dear God, she's like me.*

*I was called to Lauren again that morning. She and Katie were in an accident. And once again that evening, as two cops questioned her about the rave. There was something off about them. There's a darkness surrounding these girls, and I sense it surrounding me as well. I need to discuss with mom and Peter tomorrow. I only hope there's time.*

That had been the last entry in the journal. Lailah never had the chance to note how she'd rescued Ren at Milo's house. And their final meeting that same evening immediately preceded her murder. But based on those words, Ren had to believe that Lailah, smart and intuitive as she was, somehow knew her time on this earth had grown short. And Ren knew how such a thing could galvanize you into action. Into making quick, tough decisions, like risking it all to escape from kidnappers. Or changing your will to provide financial security for someone who you thought might carry on your work.

Katie gaped. "That's incredible, but... I can't take money from you."

"It's already done," Ren said. "My lawyer drew up a trust with half a million dollars. You can spend what you need for tuition and supplies and living expenses, and you get the rest when you graduate."

"Your lawyer?" she laughed. "You mean Peter?"

"Yeah. It sounded more official the other way."

"I get the rest when I graduate?" Katie repeated, her smile fading. "Wait a sec. Why is this starting to sound like goodbye?"

Ren blew a cloud of steam into the frigid air and fidgeted with the bumblebee bracelet Marcus Grant had returned to her. She summoned the courage to look Katie in the eye.

"Because it is."

Katie looked shocked but didn't crack. "Why?"

"Lailah left me something else," Ren said, and as she removed the journal from her backpack and gave it over, she distantly realized she was about to permanently break the promise she'd made at her mother's house. The promise that no matter what happened, she would not be the one to leave Katie. That the universe had taken enough from her and Ren would take no more.

"What is this?" Katie asked.

"It's a diary of all her ethereations... all the people she protected. I want you to read it. And when you do, you'll understand, because you're brilliant. There was someone she got close to. Very close. It didn't end well."

"What are you saying?"

"I'm saying that what we have is too dangerous. Because of what I am. It's too close. Too intense. It destroyed Lailah's friend and almost destroyed Lailah, too. I can't let that happen to you."

Katie turned the book over in her hands and glared at it. "So this is it? This is the gospel? Nobody can go against the word of God, or Lailah, or whoever? Thou shalt not love Katie henceforth, lest ye be stricken down?"

The façade of strength Ren had been projecting finally broke. And she wept.

"I will love you until the day I die. Nothing can change that. And I'll miss you more than you'll ever know. And I will be there to protect you if you ever need it again, but I will not put you in danger. I won't do it. Just read it, okay? It will all make sense."

Katie exploded from the bench and stormed around the clearing. "No! No, I won't read it. You're not the boss! You don't get to decide what I'll risk."

"You don't understand—" Ren tried to interject, but Katie would not be silenced.

"No, *you* don't understand. This is not our story," she shouted, brandishing the book at Ren. "*We* get to write our story, and *we* get to decide how it ends. You don't get to decide for both of us just because you're *scared*."

The word hit like a brick, and Lauren Ann Cole was utterly appalled with herself.

Had she learned nothing?

She had almost sacrificed the love of her life on the altar of her greatest fear—losing that love. She had almost traded immeasurable joy for the cold certainty that no misfortune would befall them. Like a military general, she'd strategized how to do it with minimal collateral damage, while surrendering the eternal battle so subtle she forgot she was fighting it.

And the whole time, she'd thought it was Lailah's counsel she was following, but it wasn't.

It was Nina's.

Lailah hadn't given Ren the journal. Nina had.

Maybe Lailah would never have wanted her to see it at all, for this very reason. In learning about Lailah and Melissa's tragedy, Ren had internalized Nina's fear of what a relationship like that could mean. The fear of a mother who'd almost lost her daughter over it. But nowhere in that journal—or in any other message Lailah had gotten through to her—had her protectress expressed a moment of regret.

It wasn't a "cautionary tale" to Lailah.

It was just life.

With all its risks and rewards. All its joys and heartbreaks.

Thankfully, Katie could see that, even when Ren couldn't. But then again, the girl was still better at everything, and Ren would never understand how she'd gotten so lucky.

"You're right," she said at last, wiping the endless tears from her eyes. "You're right. I can't even… I'm so sorry, angel. I made a mistake. I'm just so scared for us."

Katie sat beside her and cupped her face between soft knit gloves, mindful of the wound still mending on her cheek.

"I'm scared, too, but…" she trailed off.

"But what?"

"But… fuck it. It's go time."

Ren grinned. "Quarter for the swear jar."

Katie's kiss swept away the fear and the cold and the past and the future, leaving only love.

Here.

Now.

# THE ARTIST

## TWO MONTHS LATER

NEAR THE WESTERN border of Le Thor commune outside Avignon, shielded from the road by a tangle of cedars, stood a humble one-story maison at the edge of a vineyard. By the light of day, its walls were sand-colored stucco, stained dark in spots by wind-blown soil, with white trim and a sun-baked terracotta tile roof.

Katie arrived after dark, passing through a wrought-iron gate left open for her. The tarmac transitioned to a gravel drive, which made a satisfying crunch beneath the wheels of the tiny rented Peugeot.

She eased to a stop and killed the ignition. Before she had time to gather her things, the maison door flew open and a slender woman in a thick wool sweater sailed out to meet her. The auburn hair, dark-lipped smile and dimpled chin stole Katie's breath and filled her heart at the same time. The woman was the living picture of Katie's mother, but of course, it wasn't Sophie.

It was Sophie's younger sister, Camille.

Katie exited the car and her aunt wrapped her in a hug.

"Bienvenue, mon ange."

"Merci, Tante Camille," Katie said, already weeping with joy.

She retrieved her purse from the front seat and her suitcase from the trunk, which Camille insisted on carrying for her.

"Entrez," her aunt said, and they went inside.

The home was lamp-lit and warm, with plaster walls, stone floors blanketed by well-loved rugs, and a jazzy piano record playing from deep within. It smelled of garlic and fresh-baked bread, but another scent lingered beneath: subtle, metallic and unpleasant; a smell of sickness.

Camille frowned as Katie noticed. "Élodie is resting," her aunt said. "Come, see your grandfather."

Katie's aunt led her through to a back door that opened onto a patio, where the distinctive pot-bellied silhouette of Jean Moreau smoked in the corner. Papy Jean had kept his thick gray hair, but seemed shorter than the last time she'd seen him. In fact, he was barely taller than his youngest daughter.

"Bonsoir, Papy."

The retired physician turned to see her, and a smile lit his craggy face. He stubbed out his cigarette in a planter and opened his arms. Katie hugged him close and the smell of tobacco and amaretto uncorked a flood of memories.

"Bonsoir, Kaede-chan," he said, and she realized her grandfather had never known her as Katie. He had always insisted on using her birth name and her father's Japanese term of endearment as a show of respect for his son-in-law, an affirmation that Naoki's culture was welcome in their family. She wondered if it was time to reclaim that name, to own it once more, along with everything it represented.

The old man stood back to admire her, running his fingers along the colored streak in her hair, now an electric blue. "So beautiful," he said, then looked past her. "And where is your chéri? Lauren, is it?"

She would have answered if she knew, but she just shook her head and said, "Something came up. She wanted me to tell you how sorry she was that she couldn't make it."

Although Ren had been breathlessly excited to join Katie on this trip—it would have been her first time outside the US— she had bowed out at the last minute with an odd excuse. A week earlier, she'd had what she called a "moonflower dream," which she explained was how she'd gotten a message from Lailah after her murder, and how Lailah had similarly been in- spired to research Naoki's case.

Katie was very interested and mildly nervous about all of this, but Ren had promised full disclosure once she understood more. Total transparency was a ground rule they'd established when they first committed to pursue their relationship, and so far, they'd both been true to their word.

"A pity," Jean said. He didn't pry, which she appreciated. He held up an empty wineglass. "It is cold, and I need a refill. We go inside."

Camille joined them, and Jean poured stout glasses of a fruity rosé while a housekeeper Katie hadn't noticed on the way inside prepared dinner in the kitchen. They lost themselves in conversation beside the hearth, but while her family knew of Naoki's death, Katie opted not to share the events before and since.

She told them instead about the medieval village in Lacoste that would be her home for a semester next year while she pursued her art degree. The site was affiliated with Savannah College of Art and Design, where Katie had been admitted based on the strength of her portfolio and a glowing recommendation from a certain English professor.

Jean and Camille were quite familiar with the village, which was only twenty miles from where they sat. His bushy eyebrows arched mischievously. "An interesting place," he said. "Did you know the Marquis de Sade lived there for a time?"

"No, I didn't," Katie said.

"Oh, yes! They say his ghost roams the halls and offers to pose nude for the students."

"Tais-toi, papa," Camille said, jabbing her father in the ribs.

"Oof," he groaned, then laughed, a hearty roar interrupted by the housekeeper's announcement that dinner was served. They moved to an ancient wood table in the center of the kitchen. One of the four chairs was empty.

"Tante Élodie?" Katie asked.

Camille shook her head. Metastatic breast cancer was ruthlessly snuffing the life from the Moreau clan's middle daughter, and she would not be joining them for dinner. Papy Jean had made over her childhood bedroom for hospice care, where he, Camille, and a day nurse kept the patient as comfortable as possible. Élodie was asleep for the night, but Katie vowed to see her in the morning, if only for one last chance to hold her hand and say goodbye.

After an incredible meal bookended by a creamy carrot soup and a sweet, crisp apple tart, Papy Jean kissed Katie on both cheeks, enjoyed one more smoke, and headed to bed.

"He sleeps later and later," Camille said. "But he will wake early with you here. He will not want to miss a moment."

Katie smiled, grateful beyond measure to bask in the love of a family once again. They returned to the living room and Camille threw a small log on the dwindling fire before joining Katie on the sofa.

"You have brought your father's remains?" Camille asked.

"Yes."

"You should wait until the spring. Your papa hated the cold."

This was true, but raised a dilemma almost too terrible to voice. "Will Élodie..." she trailed off.

"Do not trouble over this. She will join them soon enough."

"What can I do to help?" Katie asked.

"Very little, I am afraid. Élodie is here and gone, here and gone. So much pain. Sleep is the only relief, and even then..."

Katie knew the feeling all too well. Though less frequently now than in the early days, she still suffered nightmares of Kimber and his injection. The blinding explosion in her mind, the ear-piercing headache, the soul-shearing anguish from which sleep brought no respite. The drugs they'd fed her day and night blunted the sharpest edges, but were withheld when they sent her to the blue room to hone her ethereation ability and perform like a trained seal. Only then did the pain abate, but her *ikiryō* leaving her body was its own special brand of hell.

Ren and Alex had healed the rift, but her soul would never forget the agony.

"Is there anything that would make her happy?" Katie asked.

"Only to see you, her little artiste," Camille said. "She loved your drawings. She kept every one you made for her. Her heart is happy that you pursue your talent. As is mine."

"Then I will paint her a picture," Katie declared.

Camille squeezed Katie's hand. "Ce sera bien. Ce sera parfait."

* * *

Sunday was the nurse's day off, so Katie watched from the door as Camille tended to her older sister, changing the shawl covering her bald scalp, massaging her frail hands with lavender cream, and giving her a sip of ice water from a straw. She threw open the drapes, letting the winter sun spill across the stone floor, and beckoned Katie to enter.

"Élodie," she said, "look who is here."

The patient squinted past her caregiver, then her eyes widened in recognition.

"I can't believe it!" Élodie said, in a surprisingly rich voice that brought Katie another swell of memories. Wandering through the vineyard eating tart, marble-sized Roussanne grapes off the vine and spitting out their seeds while listening to her mother and her aunt bring old Édith Piaf standards to life in their breathtaking contraltos.

"Bonjour, Tante Élodie." Katie approached the bed, kissed her aunt's cool cheek and held her trembling hand. "I know it hurts to speak. I'm here to paint for you. Give me a few minutes to set up my things, okay?"

Élodie could only smile and nod, tears streaming down her face.

Katie had found an old wooden easel in the foyer displaying a small impressionist piece. She set the canvas aside and carried the easel to the sunny patch of the hospice room. Camille dragged a side table and stool from the corner and positioned them beside it. Katie filled a heavy-bottomed glass with water from the kitchen and retrieved from her suitcase a travel box of forty-eight watercolor paints, a white plastic palette, several brushes, and a pad of paper, which she arranged thoughtfully on the table.

Camille excused herself and left the artist to work. Katie tore a sheet from the pad and taped it to the easel, then dipped, wetted, blended, brushed and daubed the translucent watercolors as Élodie faded in and out of sleep and Papy Jean stuck his head in the door every few minutes to beam with pride at his only grandchild.

And while nothing about her labors appeared to be out of the ordinary, what none of Katie's relatives could know—and she would never be able to explain—was that something had been stirring inside her.

She had begun to think of it as a seed.

Perhaps it had always been there. Or perhaps it had accompanied the tender heart of little Alex Brennan. Or perhaps it had been planted when her soul-rending ordeal granted her temporary access to the ether.

Perhaps it had been nourished by the energetic and emotional overload of the last weeks—by the anxiety of Rennie's departure; by the love and grief she felt for Élodie; by the anticipation of reuniting her father with his wife and baby girl; by the promise of a new adventure at a new school.

By all of it.

She gripped her paintbrush like she was just along for the ride as the seed seemed to blossom and take on a life of its own. It captured her frenetic energy in soft, luminous watercolor, creating an illustration that gave shape to peace and joy and courage and all the blessings she hoped the universe would confer upon herself and everyone she loved.

But it wasn't the brush that was enchanted.

It was Katie.

The result was a whirl of peach and baby blue and a dozen other hues in an abstract burst that seemed to move on the page, denying her eyes a place to land, frustrating their ability to understand the image she'd just rendered.

Lost in her work, Katie failed to notice Camille had returned to check on her, and was startled when her aunt grabbed her wrist.

"Mon Dieu!" Camille whispered, her jaw dropping, eyes wandering about the page as Katie's had. "Papa!" she called out, and Élodie awoke at the sound.

Jean hurried to join them, undoubtedly mistaking Camille's urgency for alarm. His reaction mirrored his daughter's, but he had no words to offer. Instead, with Katie's blessing, he gently lifted the paper from the easel and brought it to Élodie. He sat in the bedside chair, turned on the lamp, and showed her the painting.

Élodie craned her neck forward to focus on the page, and though the expression on her face never changed, everything else about it did.

The color returned to her cheeks and her lips. The lines of tension left her forehead. Her eyes sharpened, no longer clouded by the drugs coursing through her veins.

It was as if, for one fleeting moment, the excruciating cancer had released its grip on her body.

As if the painting itself had taken away her pain.

She looked at Katie, love and relief softening her angular features.

"Merci, ma belle," she said.

As her father, sister and niece held their collective breath, Élodie Michelle Moreau exhaled her last.

Her eyes closed. Her head slumped to the pillow.

The woman was dead.

Katie's hand flew to her mouth in shock and horror.

She fled the room, leaving Jean and Camille in stunned silence. Her mind was a blur, scrambling to explain what they had all just witnessed.

That could not have just happened. Could it? What had she done?

Amid the chaos, a moment of clarity dawned.

There was only one person who could possibly understand.

Ignoring the mid-morning chill, Katie stepped onto the patio and dialed her cell phone.

"Good morning!" Ren answered.

"Rennie, I..." Katie's voice cracked and she faltered, still trying to catch her breath. "Something just happened to me."

Her girlfriend's next words shocked her to the core, yet somehow didn't surprise her at all.

"I know, angel. I dreamed this. We need to talk."

## STAY CONNECTED

Thank you for reading ETHER. If you enjoyed this book, please consider leaving a review.

To connect with the author online or sign up to receive future story updates, visit **willhoffmanbooks.com** or scan the QR code below.

# ACKNOWLEDGMENTS

Writing my first novel was a monumental task, and I could never have accomplished it alone. This book was the product of not only my labor, but everyone who gave their time and insight to help make it better.

To my writing group partners—Inga Jones, Jenn Crowe and Jennifer Brannon—thank you for your friendship, your feedback, and your constant encouragement throughout the process. I am so grateful to have found you.

To my sensitivity readers—Victoria from Inquillery Editing Services and Lizzy Sparks—your guidance was transformative. You made this a better book, and you made me a better writer.

To my family and friends—Mom, Dad, Nick and Ashley—thank you for being my beta readers and my sounding boards.

To my sister Lindsay, thank you for inspiring me to try my hand at this writing stuff. I kinda like it.

Finally, to my wife Mandy, my first and best editor and friend, thank you for your endless patience, your tireless support, and for inspiring this story. As an empath, you touch the lives of strangers every day in ways you'll never fully understand. And it truly is a superpower.